On My Honor

On My Honor

Barbara D'Amato

Five Star • Waterville, Maine

First Edition
First Printing: March 2004

Published in 2004 in conjunction with Tekno Books and Ed Gorman.

Set in 11 pt. Plantin by Christina S. Huff.

Printed in the United States on permanent paper.

Library of Congress Cataloging-in-Publication Data

D'Amato, Barbara.
  On my honor / Barbara D'Amato.—1st ed.
    p. cm.
   ISBN 1-59414-183-5 (hc : alk. paper)
    1. Mothers and sons—Fiction. 2. Single mothers—Fiction.
 3. Police chiefs—Fiction. 4. Boy Scouts—Fiction. I. Title.
 PS3554.A4674O5 2004
 813'.54—dc22   2004041151

On My Honor

Table of Contents

On My Honor

One

The barracuda shot out of a rough gap in the coral reef. A blue angelfish saw it coming and swerved sharply, but too late. The barracuda sank its teeth into the flat belly of the fish, twisted its head from side to side to loosen the mouthful, and jerked away, leaving a half-moon-shaped space. Silvery flecks of the angelfish exploded in slow motion into the surrounding water. Listing to the left, the angelfish swam on.

Over this destruction, the voice of Rod Serling spoke grimly. Rod Serling, Samantha thought, always talked as if his teeth were clenched. The undersea world, he implied, was damned serious business.

The barracuda stalked the angelfish. Like a snake lazily uncoiling, it stretched forward and bit down on silver flesh, silently tearing away another mouthful. Samantha stood behind the sofa and watched. The angelfish was being nibbled away. Its belly was entirely gone now. It swam in uncontrolled spasms. Slowly, the barracuda reduced it to a head, a ragged backbone, and a tail that still twitched.

Ricky sat on the sofa, enthralled. Samantha was uneasy. It was not the methodical destruction of the angelfish that appalled her. She realized that barracudas had to eat to live. The horror was in its silence. All that agony took place under the still surface of the water in complete silence. She wanted the angelfish to be able to shout, at least to voice one last shriek of rage against fate before it died. There should be screams.

Then there was a scream. It blended with the action on

11

television, but after a moment of dislocation, Samantha realized it was the teakettle. She left Ricky to watch the barracuda as it munched the shreds of flesh along the fish's spine.

In the kitchen, Samantha nudged the shrieking kettle off the burner with one hand and with the other automatically reached for the jar of instant coffee she kept near the stove. Damn! From the weight she guessed it was empty. She shook it. It was.

Annoyed that she had left the empty jar around to fool herself, she checked the pantry. Great! Sometime last week she must have bought a new jar. One black mark and one credit so far this morning.

The top unscrewed with a dry hiss. It was a different brand from her usual. Inside the lid, the glued-on paper "safety seal" was printed all over with the words "rich, fresh-brewed flavor and aroma." She blinked at it. Surely if the flavor was really rich, it would be self-evident from the taste. This label was designed to precondition her mind, and convince her that the flavor was good, no matter what the stuff actually tasted like.

There were days when all the world seemed to her to be engaging in con games. Pale carrots were sold in red-striped plastic bags so that they looked bright orange. Toilet paper packages boasted that they had twice as many sheets and neglected to add that they were one-ply, not two-ply. Students came in to tell her how hard they'd worked on the term paper, and handed in a creation that had come off the top of the head between dinner and the 9:00 break for pizza and beer.

And husbands—

Shit.

She poured water into the rich-fresh-brewed-flavor-and-aroma instant coffee and sipped it carefully, to avoid being burned. It tasted like instant coffee. She was definitely going to have to go back to the real thing—just as soon as she got her life in order.

Odd.

She had heard something that sounded like another scream.

She glanced at the kettle, but the burner was turned off and the kettle sat silent on the chopping block. And the scream had come from much farther away.

Tad must have fallen out of his tree house!

Samantha ran to the back window of the breakfast room. She could see Tad's legs up in the tree, or at least roughly two thirds of a pair of Levi's. As she watched, a piece of clothesline that snaked down the side of the tree grew taut. A chunk of extremely dirty lumber lurched up from the ground on the end of the clothesline, turned half around in midair, and levitated, to disappear into the leaves.

Samantha's heart slowed to normal. She glanced back at the playroom, but Ricky was still watching television, and she could just barely hear Rod Serling gritting through his teeth, "Falco lowers the shark cage over the side—"

Really, it was no wonder people found mothers dull. There were other people in the world besides her children, and somebody might be hurt.

Ricky's friend Garvey Fiske appeared, jogging around the side of the house. Maybe Garvey had been calling to Tad; maybe that was the sound she'd heard. He ran over to the sliding glass door of the playroom and knocked. Ricky clicked off the television set and got up to let him in.

Distantly, Samantha heard choking.

She rushed to the front door, threw it open, and hurried out onto the lawn. The street was entirely empty.

When she heard a groan, it sounded so close that she looked first into the bushes that surrounded her front door. Then she saw—and it was so obvious that it seemed a magic

13

trick that she had missed it up to now, but her eyes had focused too near.

In the driveway of the house next door lay a man. He was sprawled loosely, surrounded by a splatter of viscous black paint, and looked like a huge asterisk. He twitched once, flinging one arm out, printing a black line on the concrete.

She ran across the lawn.

"Jim!"

Against the side of the house leaned a ladder. A bucket of paint lay next to the body. Samantha wanted to make him speak, to find out whether he was conscious. Trying to sound calm, she knelt and asked, "What happened?"

His eyes were closed but the lashes were trembling. She could not be sure he knew she was there.

"Jim, this is Samantha. I'm going to go get help."

His eyes snapped open. Before she could get away, they fixed on her. And they widened in terror.

"Why—"

"Lie still, Jim. I'm going to call the ambulance."

"No!"

"What do you mean? You're hurt. You have to have a doctor. Is Maggie home?"

She looked at their garage. Maggie's car was gone. The only car in the garage was Jim's red Ford.

"Listen, Jim. Maggie must be at the store. Is that right?"

He was looking at her with a terror she didn't understand. She felt confused, as if she had done something wrong. There was blood leaking from his left ear, running in a narrow stream that blended with the black paint on the side of his face. A spray of paint spots freckled his nose and forehead. She thought he was bleeding from the nose also, but she couldn't be sure because of the paint.

"Jim," she said in an even tone, "I'm going to my house to

14

call the paramedics and get a blanket. Just lie still. Don't try
to move."

But he tried to raise himself up. "No! You get away from
me!"

He was delirious. Probably he didn't even recognize her.
Samantha got up to run for the telephone and saw Ricky and
Garvey standing on the lawn between the two houses, staring
with open mouths.

"Ricky! Go dial nine-one-one. Tell them a man fell and
may have hurt his head. And then get a blanket from the hall
closet and come back quickly!" Ricky stared.

"*Move*, Ricky! Mr. Dubcjek's hurt. You're a boy scout.
Now's the time to show it!"

Ricky turned and raced away. Garvey shifted from foot to
foot but did not go along to help. It didn't matter what
Garvey did, anyway. The only thing that could help now was
a paramedic team.

She turned back to Jim Dubcjek. The expression on his
face made her draw in a breath. His face was frozen in a look
of horror, his lips drawn back, his eyes staring. Staring at her.

Slowly the expression, and all expression, faded from his
face. The pupil of one eye was larger than the other.
Samantha choked. It was a bad sign for the eyes to look like
that. It meant a brain injury.

"Here, Mom."

Ricky held out the old car blanket from the hall closet. But
he held it at arm's length, leaning back away from the body.

"Did you call them?"

"Yes."

"Thanks, Ricky. You don't have to stay if you'd rather not
watch. You did your part." She let the blanket fall gently over
Jim's legs and chest.

"Um—okay."

15

"Or maybe you'd like to go to the corner and point out the house when the ambulance drives up. That would help save some time." Paint was soaking up into the blanket from the pavement. There was a thin glaze of sweat on Jim's face.

"I'd like that!" he said. As he raced away to the corner, she barely noticed that Garvey stayed and watched.

"He was conscious when you first got here? Mrs.—"

"Lawton. Yes. He was speaking. Not very—I don't think he was really coherent."

"Onset of unconsciousness about five minutes ago," the young man said into a telephone. The telephone came out of a box and the box had no wires. Samantha felt drained now that other people had taken over and she could afford to let go.

"Pupils unequal, inactive. Bleeding from the ears and nose. B.P. is—what is it?"

"One-fifteen over seventy-five."

The young man repeated it. "Respiration variable and shallow. Skin clammy—"

Samantha turned away. She could not bear to leave, but it was also too painful to watch. An older man with a roll of fat over his belt was pulling a stretcher out of the ambulance. From inside, a long arm handed him sandbags, which he piled on the stretcher, one after another. Samantha looked away from this, too, and caught sight of Ricky, standing with Garvey.

"Where's Tad?" she asked.

"Over there."

Tad was on the lawn, one foot slightly toed out, a small ten-year-old. She raised her eyebrows at him, asking silently whether he was all right, but he had two fingers in his mouth, a habit he had given up at the age of seven, and he was staring at Jim, just as everyone else was. He didn't see her.

For an instant she thought, fiercely, *Let anyone, anyone be hurt as long as it's not my children!* Then she felt guilty to have had such a thought while Jim might be dying, and immediately knew also that it would not affect him. The thoughts came all in a flash, in the time it took her to look back from Tad to the injured man.

Someone had locked a soft, padded collar around his neck. There was an IV running into his arm. The younger man—surely he was too young for this sort of responsibility—was holding up a plastic bag attached to the tubing as the others slipped Jim onto the stretcher. Then they packed him around with the sandbags.

This was what she would emphasize later, talking with the children. Not the injury, but the care these men took. Make it positive. Somehow.

Jim's face no longer had that sweaty shine. It looked dry now, as if it had been powdered. They slid the stretcher into the ambulance, the younger man backing in first with the IV. The older man followed the stretcher in and glanced up at a senior policeman who was about to close the door. Just perceptibly, he shook his head.

He thinks Jim's going to die.

The policeman slammed the door. Samantha winced for Jim at the noise, but she knew he hadn't heard it. The ambulance backed out of the driveway, then shifted into drive, accelerating, the siren coming on as they reached the corner.

All this time, only two cars had stopped in the street, and only two or three neighbors had come out to look. A very quiet suburb.

"Do we have to wait, Mom?"

"No, Ricky, you go on and do something with Garvey. I want to wait for—you know, to talk with Maggie."

She caught sight of Tad, who had moved over to one of the

thicker bushes and for some mysterious small-boy reason, had sat down far underneath it.

"Tad? Why don't you go get a peanut butter sandwich? No reason for you to stay here."

"Okay. Want me to bring you one?"

"No. It's too early yet for a peanut butter and jelly for me." The older policeman smiled at her.

"I'd like to talk with you about the accident." He had a notebook and pen. In a distracted way she resented this. It was like a postmortem, while she was trying to believe Jim would live. She didn't want Maggie and the children to come home to a police car in the driveway. She wanted them at least to drive in, stop safely, and then hear the news quietly. And there was an errant thought, something disturbing, in her mind. It stayed just beyond the reach of consciousness. Something about Garvey. Something about Garvey—

"Ma'am, I have to get some information—"

"I'm sorry. I didn't hear you."

"Nine-thirty, you think?"

"It must have been. Some of the paint was still running down the driveway when I got here—"

"Good. Had you noticed him painting up there?"

"No."

Their eyes went to the window over the ladder. The shutter on one side was a fresh black. The ladder was under the second shutter, which was black on its top third—a couple of brush strokes, and under it, she noticed with a chill, a streak.

"Must've got down after he did the first one. Moved the ladder, went back up."

"I guess."

"Kind of funny," he said.

"What is?"

18

"The ladder's still there. I mean, if the ladder fell *over*, that would make sense. But it didn't; he just fell off."

"He could have lost his balance."

"How? Placed the ladder carefully enough. Look. You put it too close to the wall, it can overbalance. Backward. But this is pretty solid."

"He was like that. He was careful."

"Oh?"

"Maybe he stepped up or stepped down and lost his footing."

He looked at the shutter, not at her. "Maybe. But it looks like he was still painting the same part of the shutter."

"Yes, but—well, how can we know? Maybe he was climbing down to get something."

"More likely something startled him. A hornet, maybe."

"I suppose." Samantha hesitated. She wished he'd leave, but she guessed he was waiting for a member of the family to show up. "Can you get the hospital on your radio? Could you find out how Jim is?"

"Lady, he wouldn't have got there yet. Give them a while. I'll call when the wife gets here."

"She's not 'the wife.' And I'm not 'lady,' " Samantha snapped. "Her name is Maggie Dubcjek. And I'm—oh, God, never mind. I'm sorry."

Suddenly he smiled. He had a large, square face, all the parts of which smiled at once. "Now, wouldn't you call me 'the cop?' "

"I'm upset."

"Small wonder. Relax. It's all right. My name is Henry Ax. People make jokes about that. I'll let you call me 'cop' if you want, Mrs. Lawton."

"I feel stupid."

"Don't. You were right."

19

He swung around to face the street. "There's a car slowing down."

"That's Maggie's car. Let me tell her."

"I wish you would."

Impulsively, she added, "Help me, if I seem to be doing it wrong."

It was worse. It was worse than she had anticipated. She had imagined Maggie's stunned face, and the littlest girl, Henny, not understanding. Asking over and over again what it meant. The child had asked, "Is Daddy dead?" and really didn't know what she was saying.

Samantha had imagined ten-year-old Britt crying and trying not to make a sound. And Maggie asking why it had happened, just as if anyone knew.

She hadn't imagined the grocery bag falling out of the car, the eggs breaking into the black paint on the concrete, yolk and white running slimily down the slope where the rivulets of paint were now dry. Or the milk carton falling on its corner and cracking open at the seam, and Britt stepping unconsciously in the milk and egg white. She hadn't anticipated the frozen pizza falling out of its cardboard box, rolling down the driveway like a Frisbee.

She had expected that Maggie would be very brave and want to drive to the hospital herself—"So I'll have the car," she said—and would turn down Samantha's offer to drive her. And Henry Ax's offer to take her in the police car. She had imagined that Maggie would want the children along with her. But she had not expected that the car door would slam on a whole bunch of celery that hung halfway out, pale green juice running down the side of the door as Maggie reversed, with terrible care, toward the street. She hadn't anticipated the car running over the pizza, squeezing cheese and bloody sauce from it, then the whole pizza spinning out from under the wheel.

Were human disasters always half farce? Always filled with such indignity of detail? Samantha remembered the day when Frederick had left for good. He had closed the back door—he was too well-controlled to slam it—but walked unseeing into the man who was emptying the garbage. Frederick had stepped painstakingly around scattered trash and driven off, and she and the garbage man had spent several minutes picking up hamburger wrappers, cardboard cylinders from toilet paper rolls, and shaving cream aerosol cans, the leavings of a life. Then the man had driven away in the garbage truck and Samantha had gone back to the kitchen to produce more garbage.

"Well—" said Henry Ax.

"Maybe I should have gone with her."

"Don't second-guess it. You offered." He took half a breath and said, "Don't look for guilt where there isn't any."

He was being too personal, she thought. Then she thought, *Hell, why not?* "Thanks," she said, smiling for the first time. "I needed that."

He smiled. "Go home. Sit down. Have a cup of coffee."

Samantha stood at the pantry window with a tub of raspberry yogurt in one hand, studying Jim and Maggie's house. No activity. She considered calling the hospital, but decided it wouldn't be much help to bother the family in the middle of a crisis. Certainly Maggie knew she could call Samantha if she needed someone to come take the children home.

"What's gonna happen?" said Tad, from behind her.

"To Mr. Dubcjek, you mean?"

"Yeah. What's gonna happen?"

"I don't know, Tadder. I've got to be honest; I don't know."

21

"I liked that ambulance."

"So did I. I also liked the way they come in a hurry if somebody's hurt. That's pretty reassuring, isn't it?"

"I guess so. But sometimes you're already dead, aren't you?"

Well, there it was. And without all the circumlocutions that adults put between themselves and the facts.

"Yes, Tad. Sometimes you're already dead."

Ricky came in carrying a badly bent peanut butter sandwich and a jacket. "I gotta go to Schultz's."

"Why Schultz's?"

"We're gonna get the swarm."

"What are you talking about?"

"Oh, Mom! I told you *last week* and I told you *yesterday*. This guy Swan was gonna let us know when they were swarming. And then Fiske and Schultz and Grey and Camelli and us all go and get it. It's today. I *told you.*"

"Oh, the *bees*. So that's why you're wearing your uniform."

"Yeah, I told you. And I gotta hurry or I'm gonna get left behind. When they swarm you gotta get them right away. Before they find a different place to live."

"Is it safe, Ricky?"

"Mom, this guy knows all about bees. He's been keeping them for a thousand years, since he was a kid. And he's got a bee suit he's loaning to Schultz for a while. And when they move it, we're supposed to stay in the truck or Camelli's station wagon."

"Sounds all right."

"Sure."

"But then how do you get it back here? Doesn't Mr. Swan live in someplace like Bolingbroke?"

"In the back of the truck. Mom, I gotta *go!*"

"All right, all right. You stay in Dan Camelli's station wagon."

"Bye."

"Take your bike. You'll go faster."

Ricky was out the door, but the screen had hardly slammed when Samantha called, "Wait! I'll drive you. C'mon, Tad."

"Sure," said Ricky. "Are you going to the store?"

"Yes." *No. Be honest.* "Well, I will, since I'm going out. But the accident this morning got me uneasy, I guess. I'm afraid some car will run into your bike. Pretty silly, huh?"

"Oh well, I can understand *that*," he said graciously. He jumped into the car.

Not so hard to understand irrationality in adults, she thought. *Don't they see it every day?* Maybe knowing you could be silly too made them love you better. She certainly hoped so.

"Look, Mom!" Tad said. "Beverly's dog is eating a pizza in Dubcjek's driveway."

Two

The swarm hung on the tree branch like a huge, heavy growth, composed of thousands of bees. The branch bent with its weight. Even from where he stood on the lawn, Ricky could hear it hum, and he thought for a moment that it pulsed. Then he realized that what he saw as pulsing was really the flicker of thousands of tiny glassy wings reflecting the sunlight.

The troop's discussions about the swarm had not conveyed anything like this. He was appalled. He had pictured a pretty little cloud of bees who would fly obediently into a little straw hive like the one on the label of the honey butter jar at home, not this seething mass humming with latent power.

Mr. Swan beamed with delight. He walked right up to it, but slowly, Ricky noticed. Swan had no bee suit on, nor any special equipment at all.

"The queen's in the very center," Swan said, gesturing a basketball shape with both hands. "They surround her to keep her safe, and they'll follow her if she flies away. Boys, you can get a little closer. Not too much. Just move slowly."

Ricky forced himself to go forward a few steps. He was one of the few who did. Peter Winterthur was standing near the car, and seemed to press farther back against it. Dan Camelli came forward and his son, Tony, stayed near him. Two of the other scoutmasters, Ira Schultz and Lee Grey, moved closer to the swarm, but Ricky saw Monty Fiske shift gingerly from

24

foot to foot as if he were walking, and yet he didn't get any closer.

Garvey Fiske walked right up to Swan, until the man said, "Not so fast, son. Hold it right there and step back a little. Then stand still. Bees are very sensible critters, but you want to know how they think. They want you to move real slow. If you don't move, it's like they don't even see you. Even if you've bothered them and then you hold still, they don't pay you any mind. But if you bother them and run, they'll chase you and sting you."

Ricky caught a scent of fear from Schultz, which was odd, because Schultz was the scoutmaster who was going to keep the swarm in his backyard. Ricky eyed the man and knew from his rigidity that he was frightened; Ricky had stiffened the same way himself a moment before. Schultz was wearing full scoutmaster kit, with tan shirt and tie, regulation boots, and today, because it was warm, regulation tan shorts with belt loops for equipment. The shorts had an enormous waist to fit his enormous waistline, and short legs with cuffs, like two tan beer kegs. Ricky thought Schultz looked ridiculous.

Scoutmaster Lee Grey was not like Schultz. Ricky thought Grey wasn't afraid of anything in this world. He strained his eyes forward as if he wanted to walk up to the living horde and challenge it.

Camelli said, "Mr. Swan, can you tell us why they swarm?"

Now, Ricky knew that Camelli knew the answer. And generally Ricky was intolerant of devious behavior by adults. In his opinion, there was a great deal too much of it. But Camelli was not really being hypocritical. Ricky thought that Camelli recognized in Mr. Swan a fellow enthusiast, and wanted him to talk because he believed the man would enjoy it. That made it an act of kindness. Swan really *was* having a wonderful time showing off his knowledge of bees. In Ricky's mind this too was okay. He didn't object, when a person really knew about something, if he got a charge out of talking about it.

"In the spring, when all the flowering trees come out, that honey really starts flowing into the hive. The queen's already laid more eggs to have more workers to harvest more honey. Real little planners, these guys. After a while, they have more workers than the hive'll hold. Then they know they're going to have to split the hive."

"If they didn't, there'd never be any new hives," Kiri Obisawa said.

"Right. So what they do is build some queen cells. And the queen lays eggs in them. Then the old queen takes a lot of the workers—leaves enough to feed the larvae and keep the old hive going, of course—and she flies off with all those workers flying after her, to find a place to build a new hive. They land on a tree or somebody's roof, or a porch railing and scare the folks to death."

"Why?" said Kiri.

"Well, they have to land somewhere to wait while the scouts go around looking for a place to build. They have to find a hollow tree or maybe a brick or stone wall with a big empty space inside. That kind of thing. And dry. And not near animals that might attack it. They do a lot of scouting. When I see one of my hives starting to swarm, I pick them up and put them in a new hive box."

"Why not this time?" Kiri asked.

"Well, you see my hives over there?" There was a row of clean, square white boxes along the border of an orchard beyond Swan's house. "I'm up to seventeen hives. I can't handle any more. Or anyway, I don't want to. I figure I've got enough bees to take care of."

Ricky could see that Swan was getting more and more enthusiastic, and he wondered what was coming. Swan clasped and unclasped his hands and sidled closer to the hive.

"I'm gonna show you boys something neat," he said, "but you got to promise me you're not going to move or jump around or anything. Okay?" They promised.

"You dads, too," he said. "Just everybody hold still." They said they would.

Swan leaned toward the swarm. It hummed steadily. He reached closer, with bare hands, with nothing to protect himself from the bees, not even a hat. His plaid shirt and denim pants looked thin and soft. The branch loaded with the bees hung down to the level of his chest. With a slow, continuous motion of both hands, he reached around the thousands of bees and scooped them up.

"Bet you boys never thought a fellow could grow a beard in three seconds, did you?"

His left hand pulled the bees toward him; his right guided and herded them into a ball. Gently, he lifted the ball to his chin, where he spread it along the jawline. The bees clung to his chin, to his whisker stubble, to the edges of his nose, to the collar of his plaid shirt. They hung down from the chin in an amber sheet. There was even a small point at the bottom, as if the beard had been carefully trimmed.

Ricky heard Peter Winterthur gag, and he looked around. Peter was pressed rigidly against the car, his skin white, his eyes closed tight.

"Boys, I don't want any of you ever to try that. *Ever!* Well, at least not until you're as old as me and you've been working with bees for years and years. But I wanted you to see that bees are gentle. In fact, they're unusually gentle when they're swarming. Maybe it's because they don't have any hive to defend. I'm going to get my bee suit on now, because we're going to drive the bees over to Mr. Schultz's and I don't know but what the car might jiggle and the bees might get mad. A swarm of bees if they're real mad can sting you to death as easy as anything."

Swan went into the house to get on his bee suit.

Lee Grey said, "Now let's go over the procedure. When Mr. Swan is ready to pick up the swarm, you guys will get inside the cars. I don't care who goes in which car, but I want everybody inside with the windows closed before he comes over to the truck with the bees."

"Aren't they going to be in a box?" Kiri asked.

"We won't be able to see!" Garvey complained.

"Yes, they'll be in a box, but people have been known to trip and spill things. And yes, you will be able to see. Just arrange yourselves at the windows in an orderly fashion and *no shoving.*"

"Anybody who pushes gets fed to the bees," Garvey said.

"Bees don't eat people," Ricky said, scornfully. "Bees don't eat meat. They're herbivores."

"Okay. Now, at that point Mr. Swan, with the box of bees, will get into the back of the pickup truck. He'll hold the box on his lap during the drive over. The truck will leave the property first, with Swan and the bees, and the station wagon will follow and stay behind the truck the whole way, so we don't have some strange car following that might run into the rear of the truck and make a god-awful mess. Is that clear?"

"Okay."

Garvey said, "That'd be great! Somebody'd get a real surprise! Running into a beehive!"

"When we get to Mr. Schultz's place," Grey said, ignoring Garvey, "Swan gets out first. Mr. Camelli will get out second, or with Mr. Schultz, and they will show Mr. Swan where to put the bees. When Mr. Swan says that everything is safe and the bees aren't riled up, you guys will be let out of the cars by Mr. Fiske and me. We do what Mr. Swan tells us. You guys got it?"

"Right."

"Yeah."

"Why do we have to stay in the cars?"

"Yeah, why? Those bees are really tame!"

Camelli said, "Those bees are *not* tame. They are wild animals and they're only prepared to be reasonable with somebody who knows how to handle them. We're going to do it this way because a scout is ever prepared and ever safety conscious and because if one of you got stung to death by a swarm of angry bees, your parents might be moderately annoyed, though I certainly don't know why. Right?"

"And that's final," said Schultz. "Here he comes."

Ricky thought Swan looked dressed for a moon landing. He picked up a wooden box and a brush. Without making any fast moves, he approached the swarm. He held the box under the bees. As if he were brushing dust off a hat, he swept bees into the box.

"What if you lose the queen?" Ricky asked.

"Oh, I won't lose the queen, the bees won't let me. They'll stay around her, for sure. If they got separated from the queen, the whole swarm'd die. She's the only one that can lay the eggs."

"What about the hive they left behind? What if the queen doesn't hatch? Will the hive die?"

"It would. But I told you they make three or four queen cells. They put ordinary eggs in them, but they feed the larvae royal jelly longer than they feed it to larvae they want to turn into workers. And so they turn into queens."

"Ordinary eggs? Not queen eggs?"

"Ordinary eggs. The queen lays only two kinds of eggs."

29

Swan shook the branch and a remaining gob of bees fell into the box. "Drone eggs, those are the males, and worker eggs, which are female. Ordinary worker eggs can be turned into queens. There's no such thing as a queen egg."

"So the hive they left will have three or four queens?"

"Nope. One queen per hive." Swan brushed off the last bees that clung to the branch.

"But you said they make three or four queen cells."

"Yup. Clever little beggars. They work it out so one queen hatches the first day, and one the second day, and so on."

"So what do the others do? Do they leave the hive with a swarm?" Kiri asked.

"No, that would divide the hive too much and weaken it."

"Then what?" Kiri and Ricky both asked.

"When the first queen emerges from her cell, she runs through the hive, searching for developing queens. They would be younger, and not quite mature. She rips the top from their cells and pulls them out."

"And what?" Ricky asked, fearfully.

"And bites them in half."

The swarm behaved as one organism. It was made of separate individuals, but they reacted as one, clustering around their queen, isolating and protecting her.

The swarm was unaware when the twenty-minute journey was over. Comfortable in the dark, it let the man walk it to a spot in the shade of a pear tree that would be its new home. The man tipped the bees directly into the brood comb. They seized the wooden frames with their legs and moved across the sheets of wax.

The man placed a final wooden lid on top of the hive and stepped back. Then he took a plug out of the door in the front of the hive and immediately replaced it with a little metal plate with a hole in it. The hole was large enough to let the worker bees out, but not large enough for the queen to pass through. Now the worker bees could leave to forage, but the queen could not, and so she could not lead the swarm away.

Deep within the remnants of the tight cluster, the queen stirred. She flicked her antennae back and forth. Over the bodies of her subjects, she made her way out of the swarm. Her handmaidens followed.

At the entrance of the hive, several of the worker bees hesitated. The first bee straightened and flew into the air. Behind her another followed less hesitantly. They circled the hive, rising in the warm air, and just above them found the limbs of the pear tree, covered with blossoms. Here was food. They hurled themselves into the hearts of the flowers, scuffling the petals aside, rolling their bodies in the pollen, wriggling with joy, stuffing the pollen baskets on their legs full of the light yellow fluff. Heavily laden, the first bee flew back to the hive. The entrance was thronged with bees. She ran inside, scattering pollen grains, and inside began to dance, dancing round and round, telling them all that there was food close by.

The other bees watched and understood. One by one they hurried to the entrance, hung poised on the lip, and then flew up into the pear tree.

The queen paused at the entrance and tasted the outside air. In all her life, she had been in the outdoor air only twice, first on her mating flight, where she mated once for all her life, and then on the swarming flight, when she and these workers had left their home. She had never visited a flower.

The queen turned her back on the entrance. Her life was twenty times as long as the lives of her daughters and sons, but she would never again leave the hive, or fly in the sunlight.

31

Handmaidens rushed up to clean her and to offer food. There was pollen and honey brought from the old hive. They clustered around her, holding the food, waiting for her to accept the offering. She tasted the honey.

A tremor of satisfaction ran through the colony. The queen had accepted the new home. She was eating. They would survive.

Three

The town of Rivercrest, Illinois, was one of many suburbs strung out north from Chicago along the shore of Lake Michigan. Located between Glencoe to the south and Highland Park to the north, it had the advantage of lakefront beaches and quick access to the main arteries into the city: the Edens Expressway, the RTA bus lines, and the Chicago and Northwestern Railroad. Rivercrest was smaller than Highland Park, which had thirty thousand people and was a town in its own right. It was about the size of Glencoe, ten thousand at the last census. It considered itself a close-knit village.

Like most of these suburbs, Rivercrest had no history. It was all new. Fifty years earlier, the area had had three farmhouses, a dairy that supplied milk to Chicago, and a very large pig farm. Today it was one of the ten richest suburbs in the United States.

Henry Ax was Chief Public Safety Officer of Rivercrest, an excellent job. In Rivercrest, policemen were not shot at, firefighters did not have bricks dropped on their heads, and paramedics were not mugged for their drugs. Rivercrest had the pick of public safety applicants. Ax had to handle teenagers on weekend rampages, their overanxious parents, an occasional fire, tornado alerts in the spring, and spring flooding with bridges washed out. Every winter Ax and his men were briefly heroes during the bitter cold, when chill factors plummeted to the seventy-below range, cars died, old people were isolated in freezing homes, pipes froze, and medical supplies were halted. Then Ax and his men became St. Bernard dogs, carrying insulin and food.

Ax had been chosen by the village board from an applicant list of a hundred and seventy-nine, approximately thirty of which were well qualified. He had been here six years. The village was happy with its selection. And he was happy with the town, having almost gotten over the idea that he was opting out of the real job. The real war on crime. The city.

There was very little crime in Rivercrest. Once in a while an entrepreneurial burglar from the big city would come all the way out here to rob a house. But it didn't happen often. There was very little drug addiction in Rivercrest—of the illegal kind. Most of Rivercrest's adult addicts got what they needed from their family physicians. Ax believed that the most common crime in Rivercrest was income-tax evasion. But that was not his department.

Whatever Rivercrest people looked like—blacks, whites, Chicanos, Jews—they were all alike in one thing. Education. If they weren't professional people, they were corporate executives or educators. Ax knew that if every corporation executive, lawyer, doctor, and professor left Rivercrest tonight, it would be a ghost town in the morning.

They were nice to him. He went to club banquets—creamed chicken, limp salad—and talked about public safety in Rivercrest. Mostly they wanted to know how to keep marijuana away from their teenagers. Privately, he thought parents staying home more might help. Publicly, he talked about danger signs. He had lists of danger signs. Concerned citizens' clubs loved lists.

Microsurgeons and microchip magnates did not usually invite him to their homes for dinner, but at public events he knew almost everybody. His position isolated him, but he was happy enough.

Except that he sometimes thought he should have married. He needed someone to talk with sometimes. And especially right now.

What he needed was not a fellow policeman, but somebody who knew him, really knew him, and could tell him whether he was overreacting, whether he was looking for trouble where there wasn't any. It was possible. His underlying guilt at having opted out of the world of real law enforcement, the real danger—jeez, the real world!—might be making him look for serious crime and imagine that he had found it. He needed an honest response, and not from an employee, who might try to tell him what he wanted to hear.

He pulled a sheet out from the bottom of the pile, thinking.

He put the paper from the bottom next to the one he had on top. On the top sheet, he had added an entry after the phone call he had just made. The entry said: DECEASED. He now wrote under it: EVANSTON HOSP, 4:49 P.M. The name at the top of the form was: DUBCJEK, JAMES F.

He squared the two reports so that they lay neatly side by side.

The second form was headed: LINKLETTER, LEMUEL WADSWORTH. The date was April 29. Nearly a month ago. And Ax had been on the scene with that one, too.

Lem Linkletter had been fifty-eight years old, in good health, and a tennis player of distinction in his youth, who could still beat almost anyone he played, even men twenty years younger. He had been a Forest Hills contender in 1948. On Saturday, April 29, he had decided to clean the eave troughs of his house. Linkletter was enormously rich by Ax's standards, though only fairly rich by the standards of Rivercrest. He could have afforded to have his eave troughs cleaned a thousand times over by a professional service. But

Ax was well aware that it was common in Rivercrest for such people to do some of their own work. Ax had been surprised at this during his first year on the job, but no longer. He was now accustomed to seeing suburban matrons lugging manure to their tomatoes, corporation presidents reshingling their own garages, and neurosurgeons rewiring their own basements. One such had burned his house down the weekend of May 17. Ax had been present at the insurance company assessor's visit, and had listened with some amusement when the man said, "Would you let my electrician operate on your brain?" The insurance didn't cover.

Ax had come from a lower middle-class Chicago suburb where having a service do your lawn was the external symbol of really having made it. So the bankers in madras shorts running lawn mowers were a shock at first. But to the banker, he knew, it meant he was a man of the earth who didn't mind soiling his hands, as democratic as the next fellow, and a damn swell guy.

Well, it was okay with Ax. Better than muggers and street gangs. And the bankers and doctors and lawyers appreciated him. They appreciated a job well done—which meant unobtrusively done. The less they saw of crime and the quieter their crime fighters, the better they liked it.

They would not particularly appreciate him stirring up a hornet's nest for no good reason. So he would take a hard-headed look at the facts. Again.

Lem Linkletter had started cleaning the gutters on his house at about 10:00 that Saturday morning. None of his family was at home. The eaves had badly needed cleaning because the maples and other trees had just come out and buds and pollen were clogging everything. Whether a man of fifty-eight should be cleaning gutters on a three-story house—well, if he had been a fifty-eight-year-old roofing contractor,

36

he would have been doing riskier jobs than that. Point was—there was nothing peculiar in all of this.

At 10:45 that morning, Linkletter's body had been found in a tulip bed next to the house by a boy of about twelve or thirteen in a boy scout uniform. The kid had told a neighbor he had been taking a shortcut through Linkletter's yard to get to the community center to board a bus the scouts had chartered to take them on a weekend camp-out. The boy had run off, after giving the neighbor the information and asking him to call the paramedics. The neighbor had not gotten his name.

The scoutmasters had been asked to announce that the police would like to talk to the boy. Nobody had come forward.

Ax had gone to the Linkletter scene himself when the word came in. He went to most things of any importance. The ladder had still been standing against the white siding of the house. Like Dubcjek's ladder. At the bottom, next to where the feet of the ladder dug into the muddy earth of the tulip bed, there had been marks: rectangular depressions blending into the depressions in which the ladder actually stood. It looked like the bottom of the ladder had been pushed sideways about four inches. Maybe the marks had been made by Linkletter himself. Maybe he had slapped the ladder against the side of the house and then kicked the bottom sideways to straighten it up. But to Ax the depressions looked too deep for that. It looked like somebody had been standing on the ladder when they were made.

Who knew? Maybe he had climbed up, decided the ladder needed balancing, and climbed back down to give it a kick.

What bothered Ax was that he had seen the same sort of marks near the feet of Dubcjek's ladder when he was studying it with Samantha Lawton. He had not mentioned it to her. He didn't know what it meant.

Like Linkletter, Dubcjek had been killed by a fall from a ladder.

Like Linkletter, it was a Saturday morning.

Like Linkletter, none of the family was home.

Dubcjek had been found by a neighbor woman, of course, not a twelve- or thirteen-year-old boy wearing a boy scout uniform. The problem was that when Ax remembered the scene, he remembered two boys of that age standing around, watching the police car and the ambulance and the men working on Dubcjek. And they were wearing boy scout uniforms.

Four

Samantha wished they would hold the monthly boy scout award meetings on Saturday night. She understood, of course, why they didn't. The parents would be going out for the evening. One of the intents of the boy scouts was to involve the parents, so naturally Saturday wouldn't do.

But for her the problem with holding these meetings on Tuesdays was that she worked all day. Tuesday was her long day. She taught introductory philosophy at 9:00 and a seminar in logic at 1:00, so it made sense for her to hold office hours that day as well. She saw students from 10:00 to 12:00. And when the seminar was out at 2:00, several students always hung around to talk. Usually a few followed her back to her office, to discuss their papers, or to add arguments they had forgotten to make in class. She understood why this happened. They wanted contact. It was a "subway" college. The students mostly lived at home and commuted to class by the bus or the elevated. They wanted a little personal contact beyond the classroom.

Going to class by bus and back home right after class was not enough like education and too much like going to the dentist. Samantha wished she could spend the day just talking with groups of students, like Socrates, but somehow, in today's world, there wasn't that sort of time.

But to let them follow her to her office and talk for a while— she could do that much for them. The problem was, talking tied her up until well after 3:00. Then she had to race to the train.

"Omigosh, I've got to hurry to catch the three-forty-two."

She'd run to the Chicago and Northwestern station, because there wasn't another train until 4:42 and Tad and Ricky got out of school at 3:30. Fortunately, Ricky usually spent an hour in the computer room after school, and Tad had a habit of running around the playing field for half an hour or so, letting off steam and collecting mud samples on his pants. If she got home by 4:30, Tad would just have had time to raid the refrigerator, and Ricky would be coming down the street. She'd catch the 3:42, get to Rivercrest at 3:57—thank heaven she had found a job in Evanston—walk to the grocery store, spend fifteen minutes picking up ingredients for dinner, and be home by 4:30 at the latest. Supervise snacks with one hand, start dinner with the other. Also change the morning's washing over to the dryer.

But the boy scout meeting was at 7:00, so dinner had to be at 6:00, and she was already tired. It would have been nice to have the meeting on Saturday evening, or even Sunday afternoon, when she could have a day of peace to lead into it. But she understood. Other people would be going out. Going out was what couples did. Not Samantha.

Ricky and Tad ran ahead of her. When they were out with their peers, they always tried to stay far enough ahead of her so that they looked unconnected. At their age, it was not considered quite the thing to admit that you had parents. Well, she understood. They wanted to be independent, or at least look independent.

She understood. She understood. Everybody had a point of view and she understood it. It would be so nice if now and then somebody understood her.

"Samantha!" Sally Winterthur shouted. "Don't stand there daydreaming!"

Sally had a strong voice and considered it a mark of character to use it.

"Hi!" Samantha said, running to catch up to Sally. Ricky and Tad had disappeared into the auditorium.

"Sit with me."

"Sure, Sally. Where's Peter?" Timid, shy Peter.

"Ran ahead. Naturally."

"Naturally."

Sally was wearing calf-length black boots with high heels. The high heels forced her to peck her way along, not walk. Her hair was redder than usual. She wore eyelashes, eye shadow, liner, blusher, lipstick and matching nail polish. Her hair was freshly done and new in style—the latest look with straight pieces of hair sticking up on top of her head. Samantha had known Sally for five years and she still did not know what she looked like.

Samantha had combed her hair before she left the house. She wore her school clothes: loafers, Levi's, a sweater, and a tweed jacket.

They plunged into the crowd at the door.

"Okay, boys. Okay. Settle down! Scouts! Settle down!"

Ira Schultz held up his hand in the scout salute. The boys in the front row stopped pushing each other and sat down. Gradually the quiet spread back through the auditorium.

Samantha looked for Tad and Ricky, but the front rows were filled with bobbing heads.

Schultz said, "Okay! Let's get started." His feet were spread, and he stood onstage in full scoutmaster regalia, including brown shirt, tie, and brown pants, with all the awards he had won as a youth stitched carefully onto his uniform. He even wore brown leather boots. His stomach was large and his legs disproportionately thin. His pants legs were tapered, but the effect was not exactly right. It made him look like a torso held up by a champagne glass.

"This is a proud day for the Rivercrest boy scouts," he said, rocking up and down on his toes. "As you know, we're here to conclude the school year and to report on a lotta successful projects. We're going to give out merit badges and skill awards the boys have earned since the assembly in March. And there sure are a lot of 'em, because we didn't have an assembly in April because of spring vacation. We have the details of the June camp-out and our summer camp. And best of all, as you all know, we're here to welcome to full scouting those boys who have been cub scouts and now are moving up. As you know, to become a boy scout a boy must be ten and a half years old or have completed the fifth grade. We have twenty-two cub scouts here tonight who qualify."

Schultz clapped his hands. The audience, recognizing what was expected of them, applauded too.

"I want to start off with our plant sale, which you all know about. I want you to give a big hand to the man who organized it all, Lee Grey, who is the father of Kip Grey. Lee organized the whole thing from the roots up. Pun intended."

He applauded again, big, moist claps with his cupped hands. The audience applauded. Lee Grey took the steps to the stage two at a time, a slender man who made his scout uniform look well tailored. Brown and lean, like a Doberman pinscher.

"Hey!" said Grey. "This is just a fine bunch of kids!" Everybody applauded again. Schultz stepped back a pace and stood in the at-ease position, hands joined behind his back.

Lee Grey said, "We sold three hundred and eighty-two dollars' worth of plants!" More applause. "We had petunias, impatiens, zinnias, tomatoes, and peppers. I'm sure I don't have to tell you that, because I imagine that everybody here

has petunias in his front yard and tomatoes in the back."
Laughter. "The gals tell me the impatiens are good for shade
and the zinnias are good for sun. I wouldn't know about that,
but I do know that ours are doing just fine! I was able to get
the plants in small plastic flats at way off the usual prices from
a nursery in Northbrook. The owner used to be a boy scout
himself. So we were able to give our customers a discount and
still make a lot of money. So everybody came out ahead."

"Except the local nurseries," said Sally, aloud, to
Samantha.

"Now, with this money, we've been able to buy *six new
tents* for our camp-outs and still have some money left over
for our trip to Wisconsin in July. So we all—"

"Wait a minute, Lee," said Schultz.

"Sure."

"I thought it would be a nice idea for all the folks to see
one of the new tents tonight, so I brought one along. If a
couple of boys would come up and demonstrate it—uh, Kiri
Obisawa and Ricky Lawton."

There was a long wait while Ricky and Kiri struggled out
of their rows over the knees of the other boys. They climbed
onto the stage. Schultz gestured at them and they went back-
stage. Their absence was followed by a lot of bumping and
dragging noise. The audience sat and whispered. Sally said,
"They could hurry this up. What they need is a good
Broadway director."

"Oh, well. Nobody expects it to be perfect."

"It wouldn't take much planning ahead to have Ricky and
Kiri both back there ready to help with the tent."

"I suppose."

"Ira Schultz likes to stand up in front of an audience,
that's why."

Ricky and Kiri backed onto the stage, dragging a mass of

43

bright green plastic fabric. Apparently nobody had explained to them how the tent was to be set up. They fumbled with the aluminum poles and canvas loops. The canvas, heavily impregnated with vinyl, suddenly unrolled itself and sprawled out on the stage, flicking Kiri's ankles and slapping Ricky on the rump as he bent over to grab a pole that was rolling away.

The audience laughed.

Ricky looked around and grinned sheepishly.

"Here, let me do that," Schultz said.

Grey grabbed another rolling pole that was heading for the audience. Schultz seized one side of the canvas and flipped it out flat, as one might a sheet. Unfortunately, all the tent pegs had been rolled up inside. They shot away in a dozen directions. Kiri caught one in midair, but eight or ten others rained into the first row. One flew up and hit Lee Grey between the eyes. He blinked. Boys in the first row scattered for the pegs. Ricky scurried to pick up the pegs on the stage, but put his foot down on a pole, which rolled away. He fell sideways, and caught himself at the last moment. Schultz grabbed hold of Ricky's shoulder, as if to keep him from falling. Schultz then turned sideways, either to give the audience a good view of himself holding Ricky up, or to see whether he still had an audience. In doing so, he backed into Kiri, who was picking up the offending pole, and Kiri, struck from behind in a bent-over position, unbalanced and fell forward off the stage.

The audience gave a long "Ooooh!"

Schultz leaped down off the stage, ready to administer first aid. But Kiri jumped to his feet and scrambled back onto the stage in a jumble of little-boy elbows and knees and legs.

Lee Grey said to the audience, "Maybe we'd better put the tent together later."

Schultz said from the lower level, "Lee, maybe you'd better tell us who won the contest."

The boys gathered the tent pegs and poles together in the canvas section; using it as a sort of a sling to carry everything offstage.

"We had a contest," Grey said, "to see who sold the most plants. We have a first prize, a second prize, and a third prize. For the first prize, the boy gets his choice of a camp cooker—" He paused while Schultz, who was back onstage, walked into the wings to get the cooker. Schultz looked around for someplace to put it down. There was a table in the rear, covered with badges and ties. He went to it, put the cooker on top of the ties, and dragged the whole thing forward, bumping and scraping loudly, so that Grey had to wait until it reached the front to go on talking.

"—or a ground pad for your sleeping bag, which insulates you from the cold and wet." Schultz was offstage, getting the ground pad, but this time he planned ahead and brought the other prize as well. "And a large, rechargeable flashlight. The boy who wins first prize gets his choice. And the second prize winner gets to choose next, and so on. One boy in the troop sold more than twice as much as anybody else. He sold one hundred and ten packs of plants! Wow! That's what I call industrious! And that boy is—" He paused for effect. "—Garvey Fiske!"

He and Schultz applauded hugely, and the rest of the audience joined in, this time with enthusiasm.

"C'mon up, Garvey."

Garvey was resplendent in full uniform—Schultz was very serious about uniforms—with the string of red and yellow beads that signified last year's Wisconsin Trail Hike. He had four metal slides on his belt, which were skill awards, a rectangular metal pin for having passed his community study, a copper arrowhead on his pocket flap that stood for the Hiawatha camp-out, and six or seven embroidered merit badges.

"Now, Garvey, you can have your choice of prizes. The camp cooker, the ground pad, or the flashlight. Which one will it be?"

Garvey walked to the table and silently picked up the camp cooker. He started for the stairs, but Schultz seized his arm and held him.

"One hundred and ten packs of plants!" he cried.

Everybody had to applaud again.

Kiri Obisawa came in second. He had sold sixty-two packs of plants.

D.J. Abbott was third, with thirty-five.

Kiri picked the flashlight, and D.J. was left with the ground pad. Samantha seemed to remember that D.J. already had a ground pad. Then the boys were all released to go back to their seats.

Sally looked at her watch again. "Seven-forty. Over half an hour, and they've got exactly one award out of the way."

Samantha was thinking about Ricky. He had gone to twenty-three houses trying to sell plants. A great many people hadn't been home. Some people, to be helpful, had ordered just one pack of petunias, which they probably did not want. So Ricky, after a lot of work, had sold eleven packs of plants. Could Garvey possibly have done ten times as much work? Was Ricky lazy, or was Garvey a superkid?

"A little later we're going to tell you the other exciting thing we're doing with some of the plant money," Schultz said.

"Oh, good," said Sally.

"But first, I want to introduce Monty Fiske, who, as you all know, is Garvey's dad. Monty has the badges for those who completed the twenty-mile hike at Walton Springs last month."

"Um—I have the badges for the boys who completed the twenty-mile hike at Walton Springs last month," said Fiske. "It's—um—our annual April hike. I mean, if it isn't raining. Otherwise it's a May hike. And we had—ah—twenty-one boys who started out. And we go to Walton Springs because there's a long trail plus there's an access road, so we can put a car at the ten-mile mark for the ones who can't finish. And this year we had—uh—seventeen boys who finished the hike. And their names are D.J. Abbott—"

Schultz stopped him. "Now you boys come up when he calls your names. Sorry, Monty. Go right ahead."

"And their names are D.J. Abbott, Kiri Obisawa, Lome Colby, Garvey Fiske, Tony Camelli, Ricky Lawton—"

Samantha had a moment of fierce pride. And relief, right after the pride. Ricky could hike twenty miles, even without a man in the house, even without a father to go camping with. Here was an event she didn't have to feel guilty about.

But Peter Winterthur had not finished the hike. Ricky had told her that Peter had dropped out after five miles and had had to be helped to the ten-mile car by one of the scout-masters. Ricky had also said that Peter did not want his father to know.

Next to her, Sally was clapping as enthusiastically as any-body. The cruel thing was that she'd have to, of course. Why set a specific distance for the hike? It was one thing to en-courage the boys to do their best. It was quite another, Samantha thought, to make up a specific distance that was so long that some would surely fail.

With the bigger boys onstage, Samantha looked for Tad in the front row, and found him. It was only the back of his head, but she knew him by the lift in her heart. He was gesturing to the boy next to him, bouncing, and pointing at the stage. She knew he was telling his neighbor that the boy onstage was his older brother, the one who had hiked twenty miles.

Twenty miles! That was as far as from here to downtown Chicago! Hiking that distance was an accomplishment he would always remember. Regardless of Peter's feelings, the scouts were giving her son something she could not, and she was grateful.

"Eight-fifteen," said Sally. "This is going to take all night."

Sally spoke so loudly that a woman in front looked around at her.

The boys received a copper disk for the twenty-mile hike. At the cost of several more minutes, Schultz let them all troop off the stage and find their seats before he resumed the program. And it turned out that most of them would be called right back up. Sally groaned.

"Rich Elwin will now present the merit badges that the boys have earned since the last meeting. Rich, as you know, is the father of Dick Elwin, who has been a cub scout for two years and will become a boy scout tonight."

Elwin had an extremely deep voice. He announced merit badge after merit badge, the boy's name, and what it was won for.

It was like counting sheep. Samantha started to doze.

"You can't tell me you're not bored," Sally hissed.

Ricky had won three merit badges—one for swimming, one for lifesaving, and one for first aid. Good. A sense of accomplishment, and something useful, too.

Peter Winterthur had won four. He accepted them gravely. She felt sorry for Peter, who was the color of mushrooms grown in the dark. She was not surprised that his merit

48

badges were for dog care, Indian lore, civic studies, and leatherworking.

Her mind spun off. What would be reasonable survival skills for the modern boy? Finding the house you were looking for when there weren't any house numbers? How to locate safe food in a kaleidoscope world of fast-food chains? The early recognition and deflection of muggers? No, come to think of it, she knew the absolute, consummate survival skill of today. How to find a parking space. "A merit badge in parking," she said.

"What?" said Sally.

"Nothing."

"This is ridiculous!"

"What is?"

"They could just announce all the names and badges at once, and then have everybody come up and get them."

"Yes, I guess they could."

When all the boys had fumbled their way back to their seats, Schultz walked to the rear of the stage and pulled down a movie screen. "Oh, my God!" said Sally.

A bright rectangle flickered on the screen and went out. Flickered and went out. Flickered again and stayed on. "Get the lights, Lee," Schultz said.

The room went dark. On the screen appeared a still picture of three figures around a smoky campfire in daylight. *Okay,* Samantha thought, *slides, not movies.*

The three figures were badly blurred. The fire and the ground around it were clear. The figures must have moved when the picture was taken.

"Okay! This was taken at our May camp-out. Mrs. Pyakoski supplied the chocolate cake you see in the background. What? Oh, okay. No, sorry, folks. That's a cooker lid that fell in the mud. We have a better shot of Mrs. Pyakoski's cake later on. And it was delicious. Let's see. This one is just before the hike. See how fresh everybody looks." There was a wave of laughter from the boys. "As you can see, here we are all walking along the ridge. All in a line and everybody in uniform. Doesn't it look nice! That's Dan Camelli carrying refreshments for the five-mile rest stop on his back. Thanks, Dan!"

In the next picture, everybody and the background and foreground were all blurred. The boys were a blur only a mother could recognize, and Ricky was not in it.

"Okay, this as you can see is the hot dog roast. And there's Mrs. Pyakoski's cake. Thanks, Mrs. Pyakoski!"

"If I were Mrs. Pyakoski," Sally said, "I would give him a cake and tell him to stuff it up his regulation pants."

There was some shuffling around behind them. Then a new voice said, "Okay. These are shots of our summer camp at Pickerel Lake, Wisconsin. We'll be going there this year again, and we want you all to see how much fun it was."

Samantha recognized the casual, slightly ironic voice. Lee Grey.

"Most of you have signed up, but some don't have their applications in. So get going, boys. Lean on your parents."

The first picture showed seven boys standing around a campfire holding toasting forks. The boys in front were out of focus. The next picture was of two boys in a canoe—Ricky and Kiri.

"Christ! We saw all these last fall!" Sally said.

A picture of Peter came on the screen. Monty Fiske was helping Peter out of a wet shirt. They were standing on the bank of a creek. Kip Grey, dripping wet, was wading out of the water, and two other boys stood on the far bank, laughing.

"I wonder what they'd been doing," Samantha said.

"Peter said Monty Fiske tripped and fell and knocked Peter and Kip into the water."

There was yet another picture of a hot dog roast. Then a marshmallow roast. Then a mess in a frying pan.

"This is our sloppy joe dinner," Grey went on, "being stirred by sloppy Dan Camelli. Actually, he didn't spill a drop. But when we got it in the buns, every time you took a bite, it squirted out the other side."

There were pictures of boys in canoes. One showed a group of canoes, easily eight of them, far out in the lake. The boys' heads were as small as flyspecks above the tiny crescents of the canoes. The next was the same view, but without the canoes. Just a flat sheet of water, with a far shore faintly visible in the distance. The horizon line was tilted.

There were pictures of hikes. Seven or eight shots of the backs of boys, in which the featured objects were blue or green backpacks. Then a long series of campfires at night, flames brightly orange, people invisible.

"Shit, this is amateur night," Sally said.

"These people aren't photographers. They're just guys interested in scouting."

"They probably can't get their friends to watch their home movies." The lights went on. "Thank God," said Sally. Ira Schultz led the applause for the slide show. "Well, now," he said, "we're going to talk about one of the most exciting projects we've had for a long time. I'd like to tell you about it myself, but it makes sense for Dan Camelli to do it. As you may know, I've donated my back garden for the project. But Dan, besides being the father of Tony Camelli, is a teacher of biology at the high school, and that means our project has full scientific support and supervision. Dan?"

"Thanks." He ran his hand over his thick dark hair. "I'm going to make this talk—" he grinned at the audience "—very brief."

There were a faint, collective sigh and a few laughs.

Samantha smiled. People smiled at Dan Camelli. He was boyish in his enthusiasms, and she was glad Ricky could be exposed to him. Frederick came into her mind, and she resolutely put him out.

"We have a beehive. It's in Ira Schultz's backyard, and it's functioning very nicely. With the help of a man who raises bees—and who donated the swarm to us—the troop installed it last Saturday.

"Bees are nice little creatures, industrious and clean. They're social insects, of course, and they really are a wonderful example of cooperation. When a bee first hatches, she becomes a nurse to the larval bees. As she gets older, she does a stint as a hive builder, then finally a forager. In the hive, they all have their jobs, and everybody works and everybody cares about the survival and safety of the hive. In a way it's a kind of metaphor for our troop on a camp-out, with everybody chipping in voluntarily in the effort to make it work.

"Anyway, the bees will give us a lot of other benefits, even if you leave out the metaphor. All the boys who help in caring for the bees will earn a merit badge in beekeeping. With a few additional study aids, the bees will contribute to earning other merit badges, such as animal science, botany, food systems, insect life, nature, and even plant science from the pollination point of view.

"Last but most fun, sometime in late July, after we get back from summer camp, the bees will have made enough honey for us to take some. We started out with a large swarm, so they should be able to give us maybe ten or fifteen pounds by then. Mrs. Pyakoski is already working on some menus for a cookout, including barbecued ribs with honey-sweetened barbecue sauce, honey-vanilla ice cream, honey-sweetened lemonade, and corn muffins with honey. Anybody who's interested in working on this should call her.

"Just one more thing and then I'm through. We have asked every boy who is working with the bees—everybody in the troop—to bring in a note from his doctor that he is not allergic to bee stings. Now, we don't expect anybody to be stung. Honeybees are very gentle. We had a demonstration of this on Saturday when our bee expert made a beard of bees on his own face. Just the same, we want no accidents. Anaphylactic shock is a potential result of a bee sting in a person who is allergic to bees, and it is often fatal. So—I hate to be rigid about this but I'm going to be. Get the doctors' slips to me soon. We hope all you parents will come to see our little honey-producers. They're just as busy as bees out there."

Walking home, Tad was happy and excited. Ricky was indignant. Samantha felt peaceful, blessed by the soft spring night.

"Mom!"

"What, Ricky?"

"I *asked* you something."

"I'm sorry. My mind was wandering. What was it?"

"I said, was it fair?"

"Was what fair?"

"About Garvey. A hundred and ten packs of plants. Was it fair he won?"

"What did he do wrong?"

"I *told* you. His father fanches—franchises—all the Surf and Turfs—"

"The restaurants?"

"Yeah, yeah. In Chicago. Whatever. Anyway, Garvey's dad got them all to buy petunia plants. To plant, you know, out in front of the restaurants. So he won. Is that fair?"

"Gee, I don't know." Samantha did not want Ricky to be

disaffected with the boy scouts. She needed them right now, with Frederick gone, and she thought Ricky needed them. But she could not allow herself to be dishonest with the boys. One step on that road, and all mutual trust was in jeopardy.

"I think, Ricky, that it depends on what's important."

"What do you mean?"

"If you were going to reward the boy who did the most *work*—well, I don't think Garvey did the most work."

"That's for sure!"

"But if *you* had gone to a house that just happened to want three dozen flats of petunias, you would have sold a lot without much work, too. I mean, there's an element of luck in this."

"Yeah. I can understand that. But—"

"Wait just a second. Now—if the purpose of this sale was to raise the most money possible for the new tents and the beekeeping equipment, then Garvey raised the most money."

"Yeah." Reluctantly. "I guess so."

"Personally, though, I think it would have been better if his father had asked him not to enter the packs in the contest that his father really sold *for* him."

"I think so, too."

"Were you upset by this?"

"You mean for myself? Nope."

"What then?"

"Kiri sold sixty-two packs. And he told me he had to go to eighty-nine houses to do it."

"You're angry for Kiri's sake."

"You bet! It took him five weekends. Kiri should have won. It wasn't fair!"

The man took off his scout shirt and hung it neatly in his closet. He stood looking at the suits and shirts ranged in front of him, but he did not see them. He was looking at boys' faces in his mind's eye.

He was going to have to change boys again. If he used one too long, somebody might notice.

This was not a new idea to him. He had seen the problem coming for several weeks and had been studying the other boys. He wanted a boy scout, not a cub scout. The younger ones were too unpredictable. But he didn't want one who was too old, either, or at least not one who was too large. If the boy looked like an adult, it defeated the whole purpose. He had studied them all carefully again tonight. And it seemed to him the one he had singled out on the hike last week would do fine. A vulnerable boy, but not erratic. Not too big, but strong, well-muscled, and healthy-looking. Ricky Lawton. Ricky would probably require a lot of preparation. It was an advantage that there was no man in the house at Lawton's, though. And Ricky's mother worked. That ought to make her less attentive to details, less likely to notice absences. You never knew what might attract notice. You couldn't be too careful. All in all, Ricky Lawton was just about right.

Five

The first goal of the hive was architecture. To store pollen, to hold nectar while they evaporated it to make honey, and to rear new workers, they needed wax cells.

The bees hurried, singly, by twos, and then by dozens, to a spot at the top of the brood combs. They leapt to the roof and clung there. The bees that followed clung to them. First a few, then many, then an entire cluster of bees, bound tightly together by the strength of their gripping legs, hung from the ceiling of the hive.

The cluster of young bees began to sing, a hum, a hymn. Inside the ball the temperature began to rise. Pressed close upon each other, the bees generated heat, trapped their own heat, and intensified it. Slowly, the ventral plates issued thin, transparent flakes of real wax, soft from warmth. A hundred flakes of this wax weighed less than a grain of rice.

The architects seized the tiny bits and formed them into hexagonal cells. Then, once the walls were built, they pushed their own bodies into the cells and pressed and shouldered the wax until each cell was smooth and strong.

The builders had scarcely shaped the first cells when the queen, surrounded by her handmaidens, came to inspect them. She touched them with her feelers, scenting their freshness, their cleanliness, approving their size. Then, decisively, she laid the first egg.

A hum of joy arose throughout the hive. At that instant, life in the new home had begun.

The wax generating speeded up. The workers sang. The architects worked harder, thousands of them shaping the wax. They had to hurry. The colony needed every worker it could produce to take command of spring and summer, for the bees knew in their bodies that, as surely as the trees were blooming now, so also winter would come.

"The primary governing body of Rivercrest," Ricky said, "is the village board. It's an elected body. Its chief executive officer is the village president."

"And who," the man asked, "does the day-to-day work?"

"Oh, sorry. I guess I left that out. The village board hires a city manager, and he administers the daily needs of the village and the accounting and so on."

"Good!" The man rose. "You get your Community badge. You always do a good job on these, Rick."

"Thanks."

"Hey, Rick! You want to see a trick?"

"Sure."

"I'm going to show you I can make your arms rise up with my mental magnetism. You stand in the doorway here."

"Okay."

"Now face your palms toward your body. No, just let your arms hang at your sides. Now, with the backs of your hands press out against the doorframe. Keep your arms straight. That's right."

"Do I have to close my eyes?"

"No. No secret moves on my part. Just keep pressing out. You'll just keep pressing for a minute or so."

"Okay."

The man watched Ricky.

"Okay, Rick. Now when I say so, you drop your arms

57

down and step forward. And I will cause your arms to rise up of their own accord. Okay, step forward."

Ricky stepped out of the doorway, and as if by magic, his arms rose out from his body.

"Wow! How do you do that?"

"Can't tell you. It would take all the fun out of it."

It certainly would, he thought. Everybody's neuro-muscular system was set up this way. But natural as it was, *it felt* as if the arms were being compelled to rise up by an external force.

Ricky said, "Gee, you're great!"

"Glad you liked it." The man escorted Ricky out of his study, through the living room, where his wife was reading, and to the front door.

"Well, thanks for coming, Rick. Earn some more badges."

"I will."

"I'd better go. I smell something burning. Do you smell it? Like smoke, but pretty faint?"

"Yeah, I guess so. Just a little bit."

"Bye, Rick."

"What were you talking about?" his wife said. "There's no smell of smoke."

"Isn't there? That's good."

Samantha pulled a dress over her head and wiggled it down. Dan Camelli had asked her to dinner and, still wondering whether she should go, she had accepted. Her indecision was caused by a feeling that her dating—dating anybody, even Dan Camelli, whom the boys knew and liked—would make the boys feel abandoned. Certainly it would make it clear to them that she did not intend to reconcile with Frederick.

By itself, letting them know that she was not going to take

Frederick back was not a bad thing. The impending divorce was hard on them. But it was a fact, and it would be realistic for the boys to begin to accept it.

The problem was, she knew the boys' feelings were not that simple. They hoped, though they might not believe, that their world would change back to the way it had been six months before. That was understandable. She knew their father's rigidity had troubled them. His sarcasm had alienated them. But he was the father they knew. He was the world as they knew it, and now they found themselves rushing into an unknown future.

She wanted predictability in their lives. Keep an even keel. Never for them the uncertainties she had felt as a child. Never for them an unpredictable mother.

For a moment she regretted accepting Dan's invitation. He had taken her to a movie once, a month before, and he had taken her, with Ricky and Tad and his son Tony, out to pizza last week. The pizza evening had been pleasant, but she had passed it off as boys' night out in talking with her children, even though she knew it was Dan wanting to see her. That had not been entirely honest, and she believed she should have been frank.

She had wanted to go to dinner, have an adult evening. She had not been out on a date, except for the movie with Dan, since she dated Frederick in college.

The doorbell rang. Samantha was not ready. With one shoe on and another in her left hand, she limped into her bedroom where she could see the clock: 7:00. Dan had said 7:30. Dan was not the type to get there early—too courteous. "I just couldn't wait to see you, beautiful lady"? Nope.

"Ricky? Would you see who that is?"

"Okay, Mom."

But more faintly, from downstairs, she could hear Ricky say, "Tad, you go get the door."

"Mom said you."

"I'm watching a program."

"So'm I."

The doorbell rang again.

"Ricky!" Samantha called. "I mean it!"

Tad said, "See?"

Samantha hastily finished dressing. The shoe was on, and she didn't wait to check her hair in the mirror. Turning off the bedroom lights, she heard Ricky call.

"Mom? Mom!"

"What, Ricky?"

"It's Dad!" His voice was full of enthusiasm.

Uh-oh.

She heard Tad's feet as he ran out of the television room. They were happy.

I am mature, calm, and unemotional, she said, deep inside her head, as she came to the foot of the stairs. *Frederick doesn't bother me any more. We are only separate people, not a struggling dyad, and Ricky and Tad will see no tension.*

"Frederick."

"Oh, my, all dolled up! Going out?"

The boys stared at her, too, used to seeing her in Levi's or pants. She felt like a freak.

"I'm not all dolled up!" *Dammit, he's been here thirty seconds and already I let him get to me.* "Yes, I'm going out. But I have half an hour. Would you like to sit down?"

"Now we're all formal. Certainly, duchess, will you pour the tea?" He sat, hiking his pants legs to preserve the crease.

The boys stared, not liking his tone. Samantha felt guiltily pleased. The boys would see that Dad was not fun.

"I'm sure you don't have time for tea," Frederick was

60

saying, in his arch, mocking voice. "Shall I take time for a cigarette?"

"Ricky is baby-sitting for Tad, nominally. Actually they're reciprocally sitting each other. If you want to stay for the whole evening, you're welcome to."

"Oh, yes, Dad!" Ricky said. "You can play poker with us."

"Or watch TV," Tad said.

Ricky, however, already saw the withdrawal in his father's eyes. "If you don't want to play poker, we could just talk."

Samantha bit her lip. Let Ricky find out about his father in his own way, at his own pace. She was not going to say anything.

"I made a water molecule for school," Tad said, "with M&Ms for the electrons and neutrons and protons. Red ones for the protons and blue for the electrons and—"

"I'll see it some other time, Tad," Frederick said.

"Oh. I could bring it down. It's in my room."

Samantha looked at the ceiling, away from the enthusiasm in Tad's face. There was a small beige spider crawling across the plaster, just above the floor lamp. Suddenly it lost its upside-down grip on the ceiling and fell. Samantha almost gasped, but the spider stopped six inches from the ceiling and hung there on its safety thread, the light of the lamp casting its shadow on the ceiling above. Then, slowly, it climbed back up, the fuzzy shadow spider and the real spider drawing slowly together, becoming one.

Samantha took her eyes away from the creature. If Frederick saw it, he would kill it.

"Okay, Dad. Next time," said Tad, hiding his disappointment.

"Boys," Frederick said, "how would you like it if I came back here to live?"

61

"Oh, *yes,* Dad!" Tad said.

Ricky, a little more cautious, said, "Could you?" and then looked at Samantha.

She closed her eyes. Frederick wanted to put her in the wrong. She was keeping him out of the house. She was keeping their boys from having a father. "I'm sorry, but I don't think it would work," she said.

Frederick stood up, abruptly but gracefully. Couldn't he stumble just once? Make an awkward move?

"Well, see you later, all." He moved toward the door. Samantha followed.

"Want to make sure I leave?"

"Frederick, I already invited you to stay all evening if you wanted."

"To baby-sit."

"They're your children."

"So they are. But it was you I wanted to see. I want to move back."

Samantha turned to see where the boys were. Ricky was tickling Tad. They would not hear.

"Why?"

"I want you, Samantha."

"You don't really."

"Yes, I really do."

"Just as decoration. The well-equipped executive has one wife and two children."

He stepped out on the porch.

"You're mine," he said. "You'll realize that, eventually."

"Mom?"

"Mm-mm." Samantha had not combed her hair before she ran down to meet Frederick.

"Can I talk to you, Mom?"

"Sure. Follow me around, though. I'm looking for my comb."

"Okay."

Samantha looked on the bed, not really thinking that she had left it there, but it had to be somewhere, after all, and it wasn't in the bathroom. Or on the bed, either. Or the dresser. She stopped a moment and thought, instead of searching further. Doing so, she caught sight of Ricky's face. She held out her hand.

"Honey, I'm sorry. Please talk. I'm only looking with my eyes. I can think about you at the same time. And hear what you say."

"Um. Well—"

That instant she knew for certain the problem was serious. And if there was one thing she had learned about child raising, it was that communication was on their terms. When a child did not want to talk about something, you could ask questions from now until the peanut butter froze over and you would get no answers that made sense. But when a child was ready to talk, he was ready right then, and if you missed that single, precious, psychological moment, it was irretrievable.

Forget the damn comb. She'd find it when the doorbell rang or go looking tousled and trendy.

"Here, Ricky, sit."

She sat down on the bed. And waited.

"It's just that I was wondering."

"Uh-huh?"

"Do you think," he said, rather formally, "that you and Dad will ever get back together again?"

Oh-ho! This question he had never asked, in all the months since Frederick had moved out.

So he's seen the finality in our faces. Or in mine?

"Ricky, I want to be as honest with you as I can. About your Dad, I don't think so. I think we've come to the end."

"I don't understand why."

"Sometimes I feel, Ricky, that it's like a matter of taste. We just don't feel the same way about each other that we used to. As if something that was fun isn't fun any more."

"But I don't like that!"

"No."

"It's irrational!"

Irrational? "It's not exactly irrational. Nonrational, maybe."

"What do you mean?"

"Irrational kind of means—refers to things that are unreasonable, almost crazy, actions that aren't based on good reasons or sound judgment."

"So—then that's what this is."

"No, it's more nonrational. A kind of thing without real reasons. It's like if I said that my favorite color was blue and you said your favorite color was red. Neither of us would be wrong. There's nothing crazy or unreasonable about liking red or blue. It wouldn't be irrational. Because neither of us has to have reasons for our tastes, because they're just that— matters of taste. You couldn't give me real arguments, for instance, to *prove* that red was better than blue."

"No. Not really."

"It's all right that we have different feelings, because we're entitled to our tastes."

"And you've lost your taste for Dad?"

That's about it. And I hadn't thought about it quite that way before.

"I guess so."

"But you used to like him!"

"I know. That's what makes it hard. But people change."

"They shouldn't."

Her face, she thought, must have looked sad, because he took her hand, a gesture for which he would usually have thought himself much too old.

"Well, listen. The best I can do. I am here with you and Dad is nearby. You won't lose us. You know, you're the most important thing in the world to me."

He said, with an impish smile, "More important than Tad?"

"Now don't start *that* silliness. You know perfectly well that you are the finest boy in the world and Tad is the finest boy in the world."

"That's impossible! There can't be two finest boys in the world." He giggled. "Say, that really is irrational."

"Nope. It's logical."

"How can it be?"

"Mother's logic."

Six

Frederick liked driving in the early evening, when headlights were coming on. It made him feel isolated and remote.

He was annoyed with Samantha, but he told himself she would come back to him. This was a cute play on her part, going out with other men. But he knew who she was dating. That high school biology teacher. Biology teacher! Christ! You don't make money teaching in high school.

"Green garden peas," said Samantha. "What else? Pink garden peas?"

"Green parking-lot peas," said Dan.

"And here's Italian lasagna."

"Sure. That distinguishes it from Hungarian lasagna and Japanese lasagna."

"Why do you suppose they use so many adjectives?"

"Lack of self-confidence. But, in spite of their menu, the lasagna is good. Take it from a Camelli."

"Sold. I don't make lasagna at home much because Tad doesn't like the ricotta in it. He says it's squashy. He's against anything squashy right now."

"That's not so bad. How many things can be squashy?"

"Lots. Jell-O is squashy. Squash is squashy, of course."

"Of *course*."

"Liver is squashy. Cottage cheese is squashy. However, ice cream is not squashy. And mashed potato isn't squashy, either."

"Makes perfect sense."

"It does?"

"To a person whose son is currently against slippery, it does."

"Oh. I suppose." More seriously, she said, "Dan, this is nice."

"Naturally it's nice." He grinned at her. "What did you expect?"

She liked him. He was cheerful. Even his hair was cheerful. Springy and rebellious. Probably difficult to comb into place. Dan Camelli was a lumpy man, with no particular concern about how his clothes looked. Face and shirt both happily lived-in. And by God, she was glad of a man who could sit down without hiking his pants to preserve the crease.

A contrast to Frederick was what she needed right now.

Of course that brought up, unhappily, the question of how she had ever been attracted to Frederick in the first place—

"You're very thoughtful," Dan said.

"Is that a gentle way of asking me what I'm thinking?" *I can't tell him. He'd think I was more serious about him than I am, if I compared him to my husband.*

"No. I'm not prying, Samantha. I just thought you looked like you had a hard day."

"No, not really."

And then, to deflect the personal question, to get away from Frederick, and the fact that he had come to the house tonight and disturbed her peace, she said, "We had a freak sort of accident in the neighborhood Saturday. Our neighbor—a nice man, too—fell off a ladder and was killed."

And as the words left her mouth, Samantha realized that she was *not* evading, that she was not talking about an unrelated subject to get away from Frederick, who made her uneasy. *This* made her uneasy, this death.

67

It's been in my mind all week.

The realization shocked and frightened her. Unexpectedly, she was glad to have Dan there to talk with about it. He would tell her there was no menace.

Menace? How silly!

She tried to back away from it.

When she hesitated, he said, "That's sad. Was he a good friend?"

"He was a good neighbor. And his wife, too. But not so terribly close. It was more that—"

"What? What was it?"

"I suppose I'd better tell you. Talking might help."

"Fire away. You're talking to a world-class sophomore boys' advisor."

"Well, I'm not a world-class sophomore boy."

"We'll pretend."

"Okay. What was so strange—it happened like this. It was Saturday morning, and I don't know about you, but my Saturday morning starts very slowly."

"Likewise. Mine are thicker than Mrs. Butterworth's syrup and not nearly as rich."

"So I was moving sort of slowly around the kitchen. I heard a scream, but I thought it was on television—"

"Natch."

"Then I heard another, and I thought that Tad had fallen out of his tree house."

"Right. Having kids is like that."

"But Tad was still in the tree. So when I heard another groan, or moan, I went next door. Jim was lying at the foot of his ladder, and there was paint all over, like black blood—"

"He was painting—?"

"Painting his shutters. Anyway, he was lying on the con-

68

crete of the driveway, and when he opened his eyes, I could tell by the way they looked that he was badly hurt."

"That would have been disturbing."

"No. That wasn't what—it was a shock to see that he'd had an accident, and it was sad that he was hurt, but that wasn't it. When I went up to him and he opened his eyes, he said, 'Why?' "

"What's wrong with that? He was stunned, he wondered why he was lying on the ground."

"No, no. He looked at *me*. Me specifically, and he wanted to know why."

"Why what?"

"Well, I don't know. It was as if I'd done something to him. Then I told him I'd get help, and he said, 'No!' Then he asked why again, and he stared at me like he was terrified of me."

"He *was* terrified. But not of you. He was hurt and he may have known he was very, very badly hurt. If he was frightened, and you were there, and he had to look somewhere, it would seem like he was looking at you as if he were afraid of you."

"But what happened next—I appreciate what you're saying, and you want to make me feel better. But then I went closer. It didn't seem possible that he was really afraid of me. And he said—" She put her hand to her cheek.

"He said what?"

"He said, 'Get away from me!' "

Dan stared at her. "It doesn't make sense," he said, "unless—"

His face didn't change, but she could feel the intensity of his desire to help her, the way you could feel that the oven was on without looking. She said, "Unless—?"

"He must have meant that you should stand back and not

try to move him. He probably thought that you were going up to him to do something. You know—put a folded jacket under his head, or sit him up. Like people do. If he realized he had a back injury or a neck injury, he may have known that moving him could kill him. It wouldn't have been any wonder he shouted at you to get back."

"Maybe. You make me feel better." It was like taking off heavy boots. She felt lighter.

"I hope so. After all, you didn't hurt him. You were there to help."

And yet there was a residue of uneasiness. There had been in Jim's eyes an accusation that was personal. In his expression. Facial expression was a kind of speech that you clearly recognized when you saw it, Samantha thought. But there was no way to explain it to another person who had not seen it. No more than you could make another person feel your nightmare if you told him details about it after you woke up.

And something else. Something she couldn't get hold of. Something about Garvey—

"It's been a week since then," Dan said. "And you haven't talked with anybody about this?"

"Well, I couldn't very well worry the boys. It was bad enough that they saw him lying there in the paint and blood—"

"What about your husband?"

"Oh, I wouldn't talk with *Frederick* about it."

"You told me you have an amicable sort of separation. He visits the house—"

Like smallpox visits a house. That's not fair. Like dust. Like old age.

"Frederick isn't a person you talk with about things like that. He mocks any fears I have."

"Mocks?" Dan asked.

Dan was reacting to her use of the word "mocks." He wondered what kind of man Frederick was. But all Samantha's attention was arrested by a different word. "Fears." Why had she spoken of fears? Jim's death was sad. His questions—even call them accusations—were distressing or mystifying or depressing. But what was there to fear? Jim's death was in the past. There was nothing that could come out of it to threaten her.

She locked the front door but left the porch light on. Since Frederick had moved out she left a light on, front and back.

The trouble with being fourteen years married and the mother of two children was that it limited the reasons for saying no to a man. A blushing maiden could always fall back on timidity ("No, John, I'm frightened!") or a general principle ("I'm waiting for Mr. Right").

Samantha smiled at herself. She did not think very many of her students—just a guess, just a guess—used reasons like that. She had the impression that "Get lost" was more popular than explanations.

How had she got onto the subject of sex with Dan? She hadn't meant to. Yes—he was complaining that, as a biology teacher, he had to teach some of the sex ed courses. "They run six weeks, or else," he said.

"I don't think I even *know* six weeks' worth of information about sex," she had said.

"We teach it very, very slowly."

"I should think so. What if some child had a misunderstanding?"

"The mind boggles. What if he missed a major piece of information? What if the teacher skipped a section? Think of the consequences. Think of the lawsuits."

"When Ricky had the seventh-grade sex ed unit, he said it was extremely dull."

"Intentionally, I'm sure. They do American government with great fervor and a call for class participation. Field trips. Extra-credit projects. What the Constitution means to me. They don't do the same with sex ed."

Samantha walked into the dining room, on her nightly patrol of the perimeter. The house was built as a hollow square, with a courtyard open to the sky in the middle. Because there was no access from outside the house into the central courtyard, she left those windows and doors unlocked, but every night checked the outside entrances, the front and back doors, the sliding glass door in the playroom, and the windows.

The dining room led into the pantry. The pantry led into the kitchen. There she made a left turn and entered the breakfast room, turning out lights as she went. The breakfast room led into the playroom; the playroom, with another left turn, into the study. The study led into the large living room which ran the entire length of the front of the house and incorporated the vestibule and front door. The far end of the living room had two matching arches at right angles to each other—one that led into the dining room and one that framed the lower end of the stairway. Samantha paused there, at the foot of the stairs, and looked back through the dining room to the darkness where the kitchen slept.

She would not be able to keep this house after the divorce. Not on a college teacher's salary. Not unless Frederick decided to pay for it so that the children could stay in their home. And when she stopped to consider it, she wasn't in the least regretful. It was a house designed for show, built to be unique. It was a sculpture, to look at, not to live in.

And worse, it was disorienting. There was no repose here. You could walk around it, and around and around, and never get to a resting place. She had lived here fourteen years, since they were first married, and Frederick's father had helped them build it—helped in the sense that he paid for two-thirds of it as a wedding present. Frederick worked for his father's business but never could have built the house on what he was paid then.

Frederick had wanted the house. It was better than other people's homes.

Samantha didn't want it. It should have memories, but the good ones existed in spite of the house and the bad ones seemed rooted here.

It was the restlessness of the place that troubled her. She did not feel safe here. It was foolish, but she could not feel protected in a house where there was always open space at her back. If she sat in the study, she might face the living room, but then the open playroom was behind her. Even with her back against a wall, she always had the sensation that space stretched away in two directions and that she did not have them both under observation. It was not a retreat, not her own cave, but a tunnel, a squirrel cage in which she had been running for years.

With her back to the stairs, she looked down the long expanse of the living room. It was sixty feet long, and Frederick's great source of pride. It was too long. There were always drafts at her back.

She had the feeling here of being exposed. She felt as if someone was watching her. From the dark kitchen? Or from the far, dim corners of that long living room?

This was foolish. There was no one here.

Then she heard a softly drawn breath behind her.

She could not turn. There was someone behind her on the stairs. No, it must have been illusory, the echo of an appliance in the kitchen turning off or on. The refrigerator made a noise just a bit like that when it was defrosting.

73

Then she heard a quiet footfall.

She spun, saw a figure towering behind her, and gasped. And just as suddenly laughed, an explosion of relief. Tad was there, silhouetted against the light on the stairs. He wore red-and-white striped pajamas.

"Did I scare you, Mom?"

"You sure did. I didn't hear you coming."

"Well, I live here, too," he said, with a little-boy shy smile.

"I'm very much aware of that. But you looked so much larger. Because you're standing a few steps above me."

"Yes, I imagine so," he said, judiciously. He came on down the stairs, growing shorter with each step, until he stood beside her. "I was thinking that this might be a good time for a cookie."

All the usual answers went through her mind. It was late. She was tired. Why wasn't he asleep? How could he be hungry, since he had had a big dinner and also a snack before bed? He had already brushed his teeth. But what she actually said was, "Let's go see what there is. I'd like to have a cookie with you."

Seven

The railroad station that served Rivercrest belonged to the Chicago and Northwestern system. The building was a miniature Rhine castle, with a cylindrical tower, a tiny pointed turret that rose all of twenty feet in the air, and two arches at ground level swooping down from the north and south walls like the wings of a swallow in flight.

Under both the north and south arches of the Rivercrest station hung oval boards with the word Rivercrest in raised Old West wooden letters of chocolate brown on a beige background. On the green in front of the station were WPA-style concrete letters spelling Rivercrest, each letter two feet high, cast in cement studded with pea gravel.

In the bicentennial year, 1976, the town had attempted to gild the lily by spelling out the name Rivercrest on the green itself in red petunias on a background of white petunias surrounded by a frame of blue petunias. The effect had been colorful. But the word was unreadable.

There were two causes of the problem. In the first place, the Rivercrest green was only fifteen feet long, the rest of the space having been paved with asphalt in the 1950's the better to roll luggage wagons. Fifteen feet was just not enough room to spell out the ten letters of the word Rivercrest properly in a medium as difficult to control as petunias. Which was the second part of the problem. Petunias sprawl. The member of the Rivercrest Garden Club who had advised petunias came in for a good deal of criticism in the *Rivercrest Review*, but she retorted in a snappy letter to the editor that petunias were the only flower that came in red, white, and blue, did not require much care, withstood drought, bloomed from the first warm days of spring, and even stood the light frosts of early fall. Asters, which had the right colors, could not stand heat. Portulacas tolerated heat and drought but did not come in blue. Ditto for geraniums. Impatiens ditto also, nor could they stand full sun, and they would need constant watering. The Village president did not dispute the horticultural points, but he had heard once too often that the words on the green looked like Arabic, or Japanese, or a pile of confetti. The conclusion the board reached was: Never Again. Glencoe could to it, but Glencoe had only seven letters in its name and a green thirty-five feet long.

Therefore, this May morning, an employee of Rivercrest named Herbert Bloodgood was planting geraniums in two huge concrete tubs. These tubs stood in front of the railroad station, not on the green but on the asphalt, and would hold the only flowers the railroad station would display this summer.

He had four flats of a dozen geraniums each—all bright red. There were a couple of bags of peat moss lying next to the flats and a spill of moss around one of the tubs. The station's hose lay next to the moss, and it had a sprinkler nozzle on one end. Bloodgood had turned off the flow of water by tightening the nozzle down, but a thin spurt of water shot out from one side nevertheless. It struck the concrete tub and ran down, became a trickle that crept under some of the spilled peat, across the asphalt, where people now stood waiting for the 7:42 train, over the edge of the asphalt near the tracks, and formed a slowly growing puddle around the sharp white ballast stones under the track.

Few of the forty or fifty people waiting for the 7:42 noticed the water. People were bunched in two positions on the walkway, at the two points where the doors of the first and second cars usually stopped. The water ran between the feet of the northern group. Two men, one with highly polished shoes and one with unpolished handmade shoes, moved aside. A woman in sandals felt it trickle between her toes and stepped back. Three teenage boys and a girl, taking the train to New Trier High School, saw the trickle and padded their sneakers in it. Several other teenagers stood about catatonically, seeing nothing.

The splashing of the three teenagers caused a woman in tweeds, carrying a briefcase, to move forward out of the way. A thirteen-year-old boy with freckles leaned forward to see the action. A few friends greeted each other. But in general the crowd was quiet. Most of them were thinking about the problems they had to handle in the coming day. Most were only half awake.

Clarendon Briggs was fully awake. He was one of those running over the problems ahead of him. He stood at the front of the northern group, the trickle of water running directly under his soft Italian loafers. He never noticed the water. In his mind he was playing out the board meeting in advance. He had called it for 9:00 because he knew it would be very, very long. And yet, despite the length of the meeting, they would all just be going through the motions. There were three men on the board who opposed the resolution and three in favor. He, as chairman, would cast the deciding vote. And everybody knew how he would vote.

The bylaws read that the chairman voted only in case of a tie. If he did not attend, or chose to abstain—but he was not going to abstain—the vote would fail. The bylaws required a majority vote to carry.

Briggs sighed. The reason the meeting would take hours

was that its real purpose was to give all the members of the board a chance to speak their minds. Fully. And this was more important than it sounded—boring but important—because then no one would feel railroaded and because if everybody had said every single thing he could think of, there would be less indiscreet grumbling in the halls afterward, less rehashing with outsiders, and less chance of (God forbid) legal challenge later to the board's decision.

For the decision, as Briggs was keenly aware, was emotional as well as financial, and the opposition went deep. Briggs and Carrie was one of the largest department store chains in Chicago, and one of the oldest, founded in 1862. One of the present Carries, Henry, was the great-grandson of the founding Carrie. There was also a great-great-grandson, Harold Carrie. There was a Carrie in-law on the board, in addition to Harold and Henry Carrie. There was a Briggs in-law, and himself. The other two board members were bankers. The bankers, unemotional and uninvolved, believed that selling out to a national chain was timely and financially advisable. And in Clarendon Briggs's opinion, they were clearly correct. The stores had enjoyed six good years in a row, the just-completed fiscal year the best in their history. They would never get a better price. The conglomerate that was wooing them had originated in California and wanted a Midwest division. The multiple they were offering was very fair. And if Briggs and Carrie turned it down, it might well be offered to Carson, Pirie, Scott, or Marshall Field.

The Carrie faction wanted to hold on to the business. They liked going to work each day, walking into a large emporium with their name on it. They believed that there was intrinsic value in having their own place—Briggs smiled faintly at this—and did not understand that Briggs and Carrie was a business and that only financial considerations were important.

Briggs himself had no children. His wife preferred tennis over nursery schools. Harold Carrie had two sons, currently at Andover, whom he wanted to put into the business in a few years. There was no guarantee that a conglomerate would hire them. Guarantee? Briggs smiled again. The older Carrie boy had found sixth-grade math at the local grade school difficult, which was why he had been shipped off so fast to Andover. Metroscope would be unlikely to hire him to clean ashtrays in the men's room.

The tracks began to sing. The last-minute arrivals at the station were now running, not walking. At the cross-street over Green Bay Road, the red flasher went on and the warning bell sounded. After five seconds, to let cars and pedestrians clear, the black-and-white striped barricade arms swung down. Briggs pushed toward the front.

In the distance, where the tracks met, the headlight of the train grew and brightened. He could see the blue of the engine and then, as it came closer, the orange and brown stripes of the Regional Transportation Authority on its side. The ground trembled and the tracks hummed.

Briggs and the group around him, inured by years of familiarity to the roar and the juggernaut weight of the engine, edged forward, already calculating where the second-car door would stop.

As the engine drew toward the station, Briggs felt a push, two hands, just above his kidneys. He was so astonished— this was wrong!—that for half a second he did not move to save himself.

Half a second was too long. As he twisted to right himself, he was already overbalanced. Turned partway around, he fell facing upward onto the tracks. At the side of his vision the engine appeared and grew so rapidly that its bulk came into his sight like an explosion. He had a hundred thoughts in an instant. Of the meeting, and missing it. Of his suit, which was new and now ruined by stones and water, for his mind, even in mortal danger, did not switch so easily from the demands of daily life. He thought this event impossible. He was not the sort of person who was pushed in front of trains. And he thought that such a thought was idiotic. And over all the thoughts, which he knew to be trivial, his soul screamed NO!

But it was the end. There was thunder and then a shriek of brakes.

Where the water from the hose pooled among the stones, it turned pink and then slowly red.

The young boy scout had lowered his hands before Briggs's body touched the track. While the crowd was still screaming and fainting, he walked away.

"Did this coffee take too long?" Samantha asked Henry Ax. She had a pot of coffee on a tray, cream and sugar, two cups, and two plates of cake.

"I make my own schedule. It's the advantage of being the boss."

"Stop me if I'm wrong, but does that mean you work more hours than anybody else?"

"Sure. Set a good example."

"Cream and sugar? This is applesauce cake. I don't usually sit home and eat cake in the afternoons. You give me a good excuse."

"You work?" he said, then hoped he had kept the surprise out of his voice. She raised an eyebrow and he knew he hadn't.

"I teach. At Kenmore College."

She was smiling at him; he wondered whether she was really amused or annoyed. But, living in a house like this, certainly she didn't have to work. He changed the subject. "This is a lot better coffee than I get at the office."

"At my office all we have is a thing to heat water."

"I'll bet ours is worse. It's an urn that goes all day. Makes forty-eight cups at a time. People keep coming in and out all day, drinking it. Switchboard people, public safety people, village board secretaries, buildings and grounds people. But the last few cups you could use for fingerprint ink."

I'm talking too much, he thought. *I don't want to ask her about her son. It should be about time for the kids to get home from school, shouldn't it?*

"Is this your day off, then?" he asked.

"Half day. Are you here about Jim Dubcjek?"

"Yes. Can I go over what happened that morning with you?"

"Sure." She looked closely at him. "Do you always take this much trouble with accidents?"

"Depends." *Damn. I sound evasive. This isn't going to work. She's too bright.*

"Depends on what? It *was* an accident, wasn't it?"

"I don't know for sure."

"What else could it be?" she asked.

"Mrs. Lawton, it probably *was* an accident. But it had some odd features. I'd really appreciate it—it would relieve my mind at least, if I could get as much information about it as possible. You were the only person on the scene. The only adult, anyway."

Ax hitched his shoulders. He wasn't trying to hurt anybody. He was only asking for the truth.

"It's my job," he said, "to be sure."

"Where do you want me to start?"

"When you got up Saturday morning. If you will. Please."

"Um. Well, the kids were up before me. On Saturday they

81

do that. On school mornings I have to call them half a dozen times, but on Saturday morning suddenly they're insomniacs. Anyway, um, Ricky was watching television when I got down. It was a really nice morning and Tad had wanted to go out, but he knows he's not supposed to leave the house until I get up, because I want to know where he is."

"Sure." Ax noticed that she said this matter-of-factly, but her concern came through. She loved those kids.

Ax took Samantha carefully through her morning. He liked her. He realized it at once, and the more they talked, the more he became afraid of what he might discover. He had come here specifically to find out whether her son had been outdoors that morning, whether Ricky had had a chance to—to what? To sneak up suddenly and hit the bottom of Dubcjek's ladder?

And at the same time, he was too much of a professional to warn her. He had to let her tell about that Saturday morning in all innocence, not knowing what he was after. And if it turned out that way, he had to let her incriminate her son.

"I thought it was the kettle, but it wasn't."

"Then what?"

"I thought Tad had fallen out of his tree house. But he hadn't."

"Then what?"

"When I heard the scream, I looked out."

"Wait. Why didn't you think it might be Ricky?"

"He was still watching Jacques Cousteau. Hooked."

Thank God. "Okay. Then what?"

"Garvey came around the side of the house. But he looked all right, too. Garvey always looks all right."

Garvey?

"Who is Garvey?"

"A neighbor boy. He comes over quite a bit to play."

"Is he a friend of your older boy or your younger boy?"

82

"My older boy. Ricky. You may have seen Garvey when you came to the accident. He's Ricky's age. Thirteen."

Not Ricky—Garvey!

"Why do you ask?" she asked.

"Um—which side of the house did Garvey come around?"

"Dubcjek's side."

Ax saw Samantha's face turn expressionless in an instant. *She realizes.* But he had to nail it down.

"Let me get this straight. First you heard a scream. Then you looked out. Then you heard another scream. Then Garvey came around that side of the house—"

Samantha said in a half-whisper, "The houses are fairly far apart. There are some bushes between us and Dubcjek's—a few—just a few—"

They were both silent.

There was a scraping sound at the front door, then a lot of giggling. The door slammed open, hit the wall, and bounced back.

Ax saw Samantha's face change from blankness to eagerness.

Three boys stumbled in. The larger two were wrestling, ignoring the small boy, who ran around them in a circle. The wrestlers fell against an umbrella stand.

"Hold it!" Samantha called. "Regroup!"

The three boys stopped.

Samantha turned to Ax. "These primitives are Ricky and Tad Lawton and Garvey Fiske. Occasionally, they are civilized." Samantha was smiling. "Boys, this is the Rivercrest chief of police, Mr. Ax."

Ax studied the two older boys. Two sets of freckles. Two heads of light brown hair. But one face was more open than the other. He was not sure which was which.

The little boy was staring with eyes wide.

"I know you're Tad," Ax said, "but which is Ricky and which is Garvey?"

"I'm Ricky," said the boy with the open expression. *Maybe not so much open,* Ax thought, *as trusting.* The other one, Garvey, stayed quiet and looked at Ax with narrowed eyes.

"Mr. Ax wants to ask—" Samantha began, but Tad said, "Mom—"

"Wants to ask you about the accident—"

"Mom!" said Tad.

"Tad, just a minute."

"Mom, *please!*"

"All right. All right. What?"

"Can I see his gun?"

"Oh, for heaven's sake!"

Both older boys and Ax started laughing, and in a couple of seconds Samantha did, too. It was so natural a laugh that Ax found it hard to believe in the frozen-faced woman of three minutes before. He caught Ricky's eye, and Ricky shrugged, excusing Tad, and making a friend of Ax.

"Actually, Tad, I don't have a gun."

"You don't? *All* policemen have guns."

"On TV. Right?"

"Sure."

"Actually, I do *own* one." He could see that he rose in Tad's estimation immediately. "But it's not with me. I figured you weren't going to mug me." Tad giggled and made a mugger face. "The patrolmen here carry guns, but Rivercrest isn't a high-crime area, and it's been months since any of the men used one. And then the officer didn't fire it, he only took it out."

"Why did he?"

"Well, there was a suspect we thought might have put a—" *Oh, hell. That's what comes of talking before you think, I can't tell a ten-year-old about a dismembered body in polyethylene bags sunk in Skokie lagoon.*

"Um—there was a body that was found over in the lagoon, and then a couple of days after we found it, there was a man wandering around in the same spot—"

"Oh! You mean the Baggie body murder?"

"What?"

"This body was all cut up in little pieces. And a fisherman caught one of them on his hook, when he was fishing, see. And he pulls it in and looks at it and goes *AARRRGH!*" At this point Tad stuck out his tongue and retched, extremely realistically. " 'Cause the bag he caught was the one with an arm in it. So he called the cops when he was done barfing—I mean he called you guys—and you came and found the rest of the pieces in big Baggies. And the body was in one, and one arm was in one, and a leg was in another one, or maybe half the body was in one—"

"Tad!" said Samantha.

"It's all right, Mom," Tad said in a lordly manner. "He can stand it. He's a policeman! Anyway, we call it the Baggie body at school, because it was all packed up in Baggies, see?"

"Perfectly," said Ax.

"Um—where were we?" said Samantha.

"I wanted to ask Garvey and Ricky about the accident Saturday morning."

"Well don't start for a minute," said Tad loudly. "I'm going to get a cookie. I'll be right back."

But Ax started. Garvey might take a notion to leave any time.

"Garvey, you came around the house that morning about that time. Did you see Mr. Dubcjek painting?" According to Samantha's evidence, at that time Dubcjek was lying on the concrete driveway.

"I don't remember," Garvey said.

"Well, he may not have been on the ladder, either. He might have already fallen. Did you see him on the driveway?"

"I don't remember."

"If he was hurt already, he might have called out. Did you hear anybody call?"

"No."

"Don't be worried that you should have gone for help or anything, if you did hear him. Injured people can sound like cats mewing, or things like that. We're just trying to fix the time. Do you remember any sounds?"

"No."

"Any people around? Or animals?"

"I don't remember even if I went around that side of the house or Battenberg's side or anything. I don't remember anything."

"You can start now," said Tad, coming back with a glass of milk in one hand and four cookies in the other, one held between thumb and first finger, one between the first and second finger, one between the second and third, one between third and fourth.

Ax knew he would be better off if he spoke with Ricky, too. He did not want it to appear that he was only interested in Garvey.

"You two went outdoors, didn't you, Ricky, about the same time your mother went to see who was hurt?"

"Yeah, I guess so."

"Did you see anybody else outside?"

"No. Just Tad, up in the tree."

"Did you hear Mr. Dubcjek call?"

"I guess so."

"You guess?"

"Well, at first I thought it was Tad."

"So you didn't do anything about it?"

"We thought Tad was yelling at us. He always wants to play with us. And if we don't want to, he follows us."

"Well, I *wasn't*. See?" said Tad.

"So how was I to know that?"

Samantha said, "That's enough." She turned to Ax. "Do you need them any more?"

"I guess not."

Ricky jumped up, released from being polite. "I suppose Tad took all the cookies."

"I did not. Boy, you're always wrong about me. You just go look." He said to Ax, "Have you ever been a younger brother?"

"No; I hate to admit it, but actually I'm an older brother."

"Oh. Well, you wouldn't understand, then. But it's 'stremely difficult."

"I can imagine. I really can, you know. People can imagine a lot of things that they haven't been."

"Well, Ricky can't," said Tad.

"Thanks for the coffee and cake," he said at the door.

He watched her make the decision to say one more thing, to talk about the accident. And he saw her glance around to be certain that the children were all in the kitchen.

"Kids are like that," she said. "They can walk right past something you or I would notice, and they just don't see it. But if there's a stickbug on the grass, they'll see that instead. Kids think like that."

He was not going to argue the point. He wished he knew what she would think about when he had left.

He said, "What did your husband say about the accident?"

"I doubt if he knows. Unless he read about it in the papers. And *if* he did, I don't think he'd care. He never spoke with the Dubcjeks."

"He wasn't here that day?"

"He isn't here most days. We're separated."

"Oh," said Ax. The muscles inside his cheeks wanted to smile, but he fought them successfully.

Samantha stood inside the door. She was utterly still, and the expression on her face, if the children had seen it, was serene. But in her mind, she was repeating, *There's nothing strange going on. Even if there is, it doesn't touch us. It hasn't got anything to do with us. But there isn't anything, anyway. Our life is reasonable, and stable, and Tad and Ricky are perfectly safe.*

Three deaths, Ax thought.

Three falls, though that wasn't the most important thing they had in common.

Three accidents with a strange similarity, a subtle similarity, almost a flavor of similarity. In the case of Dubcjek's and Linkletter's falls from ladders, if there was a killer and if he had been seen, he might say, "I was just steadying the ladder for him. I was just trying to help." If someone pushed Briggs in front of the train and was seen, he could say, "I saw him start to lean out. I was just trying to grab him."

A flavor of similarity.

A woman in tweeds, carrying a briefcase, who had remained with a few other sickened commuters at the station, told him there had been a boy at the station, a boy somewhat younger than the others who went to the high school on the train, with sandy hair and freckles, about five feet tall. She noticed him because she was familiar with the rest. He had vanished along with the other teenagers and several adults before Ax arrived—probably, she thought, to take the Nortran bus.

A tired, elderly man carrying a stack of library books had

also noticed the boy. "Too young for New Trier High School, I thought."

"Where," Ax asked, "had the boy been standing?"

"Just behind the man who fell."

In all three deaths, a thirteen-year-old boy near at hand. Near enough in the last case to give that push.

Assuming you could figure out why a junior high school kid would want to push a department store executive in front of a train.

Eight

The streets of golden wax in the colony of bees hummed with the song of thousands of workers.

A few hours after midday on their thirteenth day in the hive, the humming ceased.

The silence started in the area of new cells, where the queen's handmaidens fell quiet, paralyzed by a catastrophe they had never known in their short lives.

The queen was dead.

She had just deposited one waxen egg in a cell and started to the next, when she had paused, arched her back, and died. She clutched the comb in the unfeeling grip of stiff, dead legs.

The silence of the handmaidens spread quickly through the hive. The nurses on the brood combs turned to look. The architects, close by at the new work, stopped their humming. The guardians at the gates sensed the change of temper inside the hive but did not desert their posts or even turn around. Each worker, landing on the lips of the hive with pollen baskets stuffed full of primrose-colored grains, hurried happily in and then cocked her head, listening to the silence.

To the workers, who lived only a few weeks, the queen was a link to the unimaginable past. She was also the life substance of the hive, the only one who could produce new bees.

Though they had never faced this crisis before, the bees immediately began the series of actions that could bring another queen into being.

While the handmaidens stood motionless around the dead queen, two large workers approached the body. They seized it, pulled it from the comb, and carried it to the threshold. It was difficult to work the body through the opening because it had stiffened, and because the hive entrance was purposely made small enough to keep her from escaping. But damaging her was not a concern now, and they forced the body through. As she left the hive, every individual knew it, except the oblivious young in their cells.

On the platform outside, the workers picked up the body of the queen and rose into the air. For such an important individual, she was very light in weight, but they flew clumsily and heavily with the unfamiliar burden. They flew to the bee cemetery, many yards from the hive, hovered over it, and dropped her.

She fell softly. The body sank among the grasses where hundreds of her daughters had also lain.

From among the grass roots, the ants who lived on dead things crept out to assess her.

The architects left off the creation of new hexagonal brood cells. They scurried to a part of the comb where new brood cells were already waiting, clean and empty. With tiny flakes of wax they began to build up a different type of cell on the foundation of an existing one. This cell was longer than the usual type, and it was hexagonal only at the base. As it grew longer than the other cells, it became conical. Before it reached its maximum length, other workers crossed to the comb facing it and cut away some of the cells there, as if they knew the shape the architects were going to build, even though, creatures of this summer as they were, they had never seen one. When the new cell was finally finished, it protruded into the cutaway space, across the intervening gap between the combs.

The architects built three such cells, all alike.

When the three long cells were ready, the nurse bees removed three eggs of different ages from ordinary cells and cautiously carried them to the queen cells. Each egg was as perfect as it could be. If these three potential queens died, it would be too late to select new eggs, for by then the last of the old queen's eggs would be larvae too old to be fed royal jelly and changed into queens. If these three died, the entire colony would die.

Tad's favorite color was yellow. In every drawing he made, he thought of some way of using lots of yellow.

Each Saturday morning at ten, Tad went to art classes at the community center. Quite often Miss Brophy, who taught the class and was herself a moderately successful portrait painter, would let them paint anything they wanted. Tad liked those assignments best. Now and then, however, Miss Brophy set them a specific thing—a human model, a still life, or like today, a specific scene to imagine. Today they were to imagine their family on a picnic, and then paint the scene. They were working with watercolors today, which Tad always found hard to control. Sometimes they ran; other times they puddled and made dark patches where you wanted it all smooth. He preferred felt-tipped markers, which were much easier to control. But he had to admit you couldn't get a nice shading with them. Or mixed colors. Maybe Miss Brophy would let him outline in marker after he painted the scene in watercolor.

After some thought, he decided on the setting. The family would be at the beach. That would let him use lots of yellow, for the sand.

He got right to work. Miss Brophy circulated around the room, making encouraging remarks to each child. She particularly liked Tad Lawton. He was gentle and cheerful and he had a real talent. He laid color on as if he loved it, as if he *tasted it* and each color had a different flavor.

While Tad was making the decision to paint a beach scene, Ricky and the other older scouts were arriving at Ira Schultz's backyard. They were going to watch Mr. Swan demonstrate handling bees. Beekeeping equipment lay spread around on the upper part of the long lawn, some seventy-five feet from the hive. The Schultz garden was very wide, very deep, and thickly surrounded by dense bushes and several flowering crab apples. In the center rear was the beehive, shaded by a large pear tree which had just finished blooming.

"All this stuff isn't necessary every time," Swan said, "but I'm going to show you the right way to do it." He pulled off his boots and put his feet through the legs of a jumpsuit. "Now a lot of the time, working with my own bees, I just put on a heavy shirt and maybe gloves. Maybe the hat with the bee veil. But, see, I can get away with that because I know how to move and what to do and what not to do."

Zipping the suit, he jammed his feet back into the boots. "See, I'm getting the suit bottoms real tightly tucked into the boots. That's 'cause bees, if they get on you, they crawl *up*. So what you don't want to do is leave an opening at the bottom." He chuckled.

"Now, here's the bee veil on the hat. And the important thing is it snaps to the neck of the shirt. You don't want any of the little fellers crawling under the edge of the veil, because then where will they go?"

"Up. They'd get in your mouth and eyes," Kiri said.

"Right! And that's what you don't want, most of all. See,

93

now, the gloves go over the sleeves, so there's no gap there, either. Now this thing here is the smoker. It makes what they call cool smoke, and that makes the bees quiet."

Ricky asked, "Does the smoke hurt the bees?"

"Nope. It just makes 'em sleepy. You don't want to hurt your bees. They're your little gold mines. Now I don't use the smoker all that much, because these are gentle bees. Little puff maybe now and then." He made the smoker puff. A bluish gray cloud formed around it.

"There's two rules when you're working with bees. First one: Move slowly. See, bees, they're used to enemies that move fast. Like mice trying to steal honey, or maybe badgers or bears. If you move real, real slow, they act like they don't even know you're there. See?"

The boys said they saw.

"Now the second rule is, don't squeeze a bee. This is real important. If you squeeze a bee, they all get enraged. It's like every bee practically knows what's happening to every other bee, and if one is hurt, then watch out! And you need to know about it, because you'll be taking the supers off—the supers are the top boxes of the hive, remember—to get at the honey and check on the brood comb and see if the bees are healthy—"

"What could make them sick?" Kiri asked.

"Oh, there's lots of diseases bees can get. There's nosema. That's bad enough. It's a microorganism that gets in their digestive tracts and multiplies there. Makes 'em swell up and die."

Kiri said, "Yuck!"

"But the worst is foulbrood."

"What's foulbrood?" Kiri said.

"There's two kinds. American foulbrood is the most serious disease bees get. It's caused by a bacillus. When the larvae are nine days old, the nurse bees cap the cells so they can change into adults. If they have foulbrood, the larvae look okay and the nurses think they're all right and cap them. But pretty soon the caps get a tiny hole in them. And inside, where the young are supposed to be turning into adults, they are really being eaten away by foulbrood. They turn dark and pretty soon the cap falls in. If you stick a match in the cell, the larval remains come out like a long, gluey string."

Ricky shivered. He didn't want to listen, but he listened. He saw in his mind a baby bee, ivory colored, almost transparent. It turned grayish and sick, and then blackness spread up from its abdomen and it dissolved.

Kiri, always practical, said, "What can you do about it?"

"Well, believe it or not," Swan said cheerfully, "you give them antibiotics. Sulfathiazole with powdered sugar is a good preventive. Or if you have Italian bees, they get European foulbrood, and you can prevent that with terramycin that you mix with powdered sugar and sprinkle over the brood frames. The Italian bees can keep ahead of foulbrood by themselves, usually."

"How?"

"They check the larvae and as soon as they see one is diseased, they pull it out of the cell and throw it away."

"What if that doesn't work?"

"You going to be a scientist, kid?"

"I think molecular biology," Kiri said.

"Oh, yeah? Well, if nothing works and the bees are still sick, you have to destroy them."

Ricky said, "How do you do that?" and was immediately sorry he had asked. He didn't want to know. He wanted the bees to stay well.

"Burn the hive."

"With all the bees inside it?"

"Yup. They're diseased, and if you don't destroy 'em, the foulbrood could spread to other hives."

Ricky closed his mouth and swallowed.

"Now! I want you kids to come with me down to the hive, but stop about ten feet away and stand still. What are the two rules of beekeeping?"

"Don't squeeze a bee!" some said.

Some yelled, "Move slowly!"

"Right. Very good. Now stop and stand right there. You can see pretty well from there, can't you?"

He puffed smoke around the hive. Then he lifted the lid off the top. "This here's the super for the honey.

"There isn't much activity up here, yet. The bees haven't got to it. Been working on the brood comb, I don't doubt. Now I'm gonna lift this super off and don't *any* of you guys move."

He set the box carefully on the ground.

"Don't squeeze a bee!" they all shouted.

"Now don't get rambunctious. Here's the grid we put in so the queen can't get up into the honeycombs and lay eggs. She's just enough larger so you can keep her out. You don't want to eat larvae with your honey—"

"Gross!" Peter Winterthur said, from the back of the crowd.

"—and you want the larvae to grow up and get to be adult bees that'll go out and gather honey for you. So you want them separate. Now I've got the grid off and you can see the brood combs. See all the bees clustering over the combs? Those whitish areas are where the cells are capped with brood in them. They've got some honey started in here. They fill the cells with honey that's pretty liquid, but they fan their wings over it and evaporate it, and when it's right, they cap it. Lot of

96

bees in here, huh? When I put the grid and honey super back
on I have to be very careful—to what?"

"Not to squeeze a bee!"

"Notice you can hardly see the combs, there's so many
bees crawling over 'em. Say, what's this?"

Oh, Lord! Ricky thought. *Not foulbrood!*

"Do you boys see—no, don't come close!—do you see
those little cone-shaped things sticking out of the comb?"

Some of them did; some of them didn't.

"Well, those are queen cells. And the trouble is, if the hive
is making queen cells when it can't possibly be overpopu-
lated—um. I'm looking to see whether I can see the queen
and her entourage—no. That means—let me get this grid
back on—um. That means the queen is dead."

The boys muttered among themselves as Swan gently lowered the honey super back on the hive. He squatted down to
check that there were no bees caught between the boxes as he
lowered it. Slowly he reached for the top lid and did the same.
Then he backed cautiously away. To Lee Grey, Dan Camelli,
and Ira Schultz, he said, "You and me and the boys got to
have a powwow."

Mrs. Schultz was pouring grape Kool-Aid. The inside of
her white pitcher was stained with it.

"Can't we just let the queens hatch?" Kiri asked.

"Sure you could," Swan said. "But it'll take twenty-one
days, if they were just put in now. And they weren't put in
there long ago, 'cause they're not capped yet."

Swan had turned down the purple Kool-Aid, but now accepted an iced tea from Mrs. Schultz. His tea was in a glass.
The boys' Kool-Aid was in paper cups.

"That's what happens in the wild, isn't it?" Kiri said.

"Yes. But in the wild they don't have to share their honey

with humans, either. Now you only got a certain amount of summer, you know, and if you want them to produce fast, they need worker bees *now*. This is when most of the trees and stuff around here are flowering."

Scoutmaster Lee Grey said, "You're our expert. What do we do?"

"My notion is this. I think you should buy a new queen—a mated queen—right away. They don't cost much. I expect if I call the Wheaton Farms Co-op today, you could pick up an Italian queen there on Monday."

"Why Italian queen?" Dan Camelli asked.

"They're more disease-resistant. Like we were just saying, they resist foulbrood, clean up their own act. They're just a little bit less docile, but not so much as to matter."

"Then why do you have this kind?" Kiri asked.

"Good question. My first bees were given to me, and what I have now are their descendants. Caucasian bees. But I have two hives of Italian bees that I bought. I'll be keeping the Italian swarms now, when I have a choice. Course, like everything in nature, you don't always have a choice. There's winterkill and stuff like that. I had a dog run into a hive once and knock it over. They stung him to death, too."

After a moment, Dan Camelli asked, "Would an Italian queen be compatible with the bees in the hive?"

"Much as any. No new queen is compatible. They'll know by the scent she's not one of their own, and they'll kill her if they can."

"Then how can it work?"

"You get your new queen in this special little box with an opening in one end. Can you boys guess what the opening is plugged with?"

The boys looked at each other.

"Beeswax?" Kiri asked.

"Nope! Sugar candy! It takes the bees in the hive about two days to eat through the sugar and get to her. And by that time, they're used to her scent and they think she's one of them, so they don't kill her."

"And she just takes over?" Kiri asked.

"Yup! Just as if she was born there. Starts laying eggs and the handmaidens feed her and groom her and everything."

"Wait a minute," said Ricky, who had been thinking about what he saw in the hive. "What about the other queens? The ones we just saw? I mean the new queens?"

"Well, one way is you can just pick them off."

"You mean kill them?"

"Right. Most beekeepers pick off queen cells regularly so that the bees don't swarm. When a swarm leaves, the hive that's left behind is weaker for a while and doesn't produce as much honey."

"But isn't that—isn't that squeezing a bee?" Ricky did not want the queens killed.

"Smart boy! You and I'd think so. But the bees don't. Squeezing a bee only riles 'em if it's adult bees. When you nip off a queen cell, they don't even react to it."

"What's the other way?"

"The other way is to let the new queen take care of it. And believe you me, she'll take care of it."

"The lake waves are very real," Miss Brophy said. "Is it the beach at Lake Michigan?"

"Yes. At my grandfather's."

"Who's this?"

"My brother."

Miss Brophy pointed to a ring of round objects around the boy's head. "Is he juggling?"

"Yup. He's juggling deviled eggs."

"And this—"

"My mom. She's balancing a pitcher of lemonade on her head."

Miss Brophy chuckled. His mother was smiling happily. "And this fellow here balancing on one hand is you?"

"Sure! I almost can, too!"

"And this is your father?"

"Yup."

"It's a lovely painting, Tad. I don't think it needs outlining with markers."

"I don't either, now."

Miss Brophy stared at it another minute. There was real talent here. But the father in the picture unsettled her. He was standing almost out of the painting, up against the white edge of the paper. Standing vertical and rigid, with his arms at his sides. And wearing a three-piece suit.

Nine

At noon that Saturday, and every Saturday, the man called his broker. His broker had the telephone number of a customer for him and a list of times over the next days when the number could be called. "That's Winnetka," the man said. "Four-four-one is Winnetka code."

"Can't you handle it? It's serious money."

"I can handle it, but not any farther afield than that. Rivercrest, Highland Park, Glencoe, maybe Winnetka."

"You take on more area, you could make more money."

"I could take more chances, too."

"A *lot* more money."

"Farther away is too noticeable. If I'm seen, maybe somebody remembers it." He didn't mention that the boys he used would be more noticeable, too. They were most invisible nearest home—they could be seen without being noticed. He kept his methods to himself. "I'm firm on that," he said.

"You know your business."

The man sat for a while at the breakfast table, thinking. His family was out of the house. At lunchtime a fine drizzle had started, and he did not want to go out. He thought it would be perfectly safe to make the call from home. Then he took a second look at himself and was horrified and a little frightened. He must not start cutting corners on safety. It would be unprofessional and even foolish to let a wish for trivial comfort throw his principles out the window. He got up, took his notepad, a raincoat, and some dimes, and went out to his car.

He drove south out of Rivercrest by Green Bay Road, down into Glencoe, where there was a phone booth at the corner of Green Bay and Park. He left his car two blocks away at Park and Greenwood, and walked back. He did not feel silly taking these precautions. It was businesslike and realistic.

The phone at the other end was answered on the second ring.

"Hello?" A man's voice, but light and hesitant.

"I am the person you've been trying to contact."

"Oh." It was spoken on a descending note.

"Is something wrong?"

"I didn't think you'd sound like this. I wasn't—I didn't know."

The man smiled to himself. He wondered how any intelligent person could imagine his kind of business could be carried on year after year by a maniacal moron. "Who," he asked, "is the subject?"

"The subject? Oh—Meyers Campbell."

"Who lives at—?"

"Nine-six-four Jeffrey Lane."

"That's Winnetka?"

"Yes."

"Now I'm going to ask you some questions about Mr. Campbell. It is essential that you be as accurate and thorough as possible."

"Yes. I understand."

"His job?"

"Lawyer. At Jensen and Crock. Downtown. He does estates and trusts."

"Uh-huh. Working hours. Vacations. Days off."

"Um—hours. He's a—um—workaholic." The man produced this as if he had just thought of the word. "Works all the time. Into the evenings. Weekends. I mean, he takes one long vacation a year, but that's it." There was a hint of resentment in the voice, directed at Campbell's Stakhanovite capacity for work.

"How does he get to work? What kind of transportation?"

"The railway. Chicago and Northwestern."

No good. Not twice in a row.

"Where does he eat lunch?"

"Doesn't. He takes an apple and yogurt. Eats in the office." Again the tone of resentment. The man had it pegged now. This person resented perfection in Campbell. Hated Campbell's superiority.

"Tell me about Campbell's household. What sort of home is it?"

"Big. White stucco. You know the kind. Winnetka's full of them."

"Describe the downstairs windows and doors. Pretend you're walking around the house and tell me what you see."

"Can't you do this yourself?"

"You want it clean and you want it safe, right?"

"Yeah."

"I'm the expert. Tell me."

"Um—okay, I'm standing by the front door. It's heavy, very solid, but it's got a pane of glass on either side. You might break those if you wanted to get in." The man in the phone booth smiled, but said nothing. "Okay, I'm turning right and going around the house. I'm passing two big windows on the front. Really big. Six feet wide."

"How close do they come down to the ground?"

"Not very. Six or seven feet. The basement comes up above ground level maybe four feet."

103

"Any basement windows?"

"Little ones. Barred."

"Go on."

"Well, on the side—it's the north side—there are four sash windows. Pretty large, too. The front two are the dining room and the back two are the kitchen. They're about the same distance above ground as front windows. Going around back—this is the side—it's more complicated. The ground level rises, the windows are closer to the ground. There are two pantry windows, first. Then the back door, the kitchen door, really. Beyond that is the terrace. It's raised, it's right on the level of the rooms inside, and it's made of big chunks of slate. There are two sets of French doors that open onto it from what Meyers calls the sunroom. Beyond that are the windows to the library. Then going around to the south side there are four windows like on the north. They go to the library, then a bathroom, then the side of the living room. At that point, we're back around to the front of the house, and there are two big living room windows on that side of the front door."

"Bushes?"

"Around the house? Quite a lot on the south side. None by the terrace. The north side has a brick walk next to the house. But the back garden is long and grown up in back, so the neighbors behind and on both sides can't really see into the back garden."

"Who lives in the house?"

"A couple who take care of Meyers." He sounded annoyed again. "They're different from the usual couple in one way. It's the husband who cooks and the wife who does the garden and minor carpentry and repairs."

"Their days off?"

"Every other weekend. A full weekend from Friday night

to Monday morning, and they only have to be back Monday morning in time to make breakfast for Meyers. It's set up like that because they go to visit their daughter in Ann Arbor."

"What about this weekend?"

"What?"

"Where are we in the cycle? Is this a weekend they're in the house or in Ann Arbor?"

"Oh. Ann Arbor." So his customer was very close to Campbell.

"And this is regular?"

"As regular as the sun rising."

"Anybody else living there?"

"No. His wife's dead. No children."

This wasn't his son, then. You never knew. An heir, probably. "Tell me about Campbell himself, now. Does he putter around the house? Put up screens? Paint the wood trim? Fix the roof?"

"Oh, God, no! That's Burton and Maria's job. Maria, mostly. Big jobs, he hires somebody."

"Does he like to drive? Fast cars? Motorcycles?"

"He drives. But not fast, and he doesn't really enjoy driving."

"Hobbies?"

"Work. Well, he reads a lot. Fishing. That's about it."

"Tell me about the fishing."

"He takes a full month in northern Michigan in July." There was a note of resentment again, this time because Campbell did not work in July. Campbell just could not win with this guy.

"The Michigan trip. Where to, exactly?"

"Upper peninsula. He takes camping gear and drives to a village and walks. He's got a tiny cabin up there god-awful miles from nowhere. He packs in with some flour and sugar

105

and dried fruit and crap like that. And then he just sits there in a rowboat and catches bass every day. And eats them! Talk about getting away from everything! There's *no* one around the dreary place."

"Okay. So much for hobbies. How's his health?"

"Fine. Just great. If it wasn't—"

You wouldn't be making this call. Right.

"All he's got is high blood pressure. And that's under control."

"Under control how?"

"He takes pills."

"What pills?"

"It's called Corgard."

"That isn't one of the most common things for high blood pressure. Do you know why he takes that, specifically?"

"The first couple of things they tried didn't bring down his pressure enough."

"Uh-huh. What size dosage does he take?"

"Well—we talked about it once. I think he said a hundred and twenty milligrams. They're light blue. It's a tablet, but a long tablet. You know what I mean?"

"I think so. Does he take anything else? Antacids? Laxatives? Diet pills?"

"No, hardly even aspirin. He got on a sort of health kick. Apple and yogurt for lunch—"

"Does he see any women?"

"Well, there's one he's dating. I don't know how seriously."

"Where do they go?"

"Movies, I think. Or dinner and a movie."

"Fridays? Saturdays?"

"Saturdays. Oh, and a lot of the time they go to a museum Saturday afternoon downtown and dinner after."

"Mm-hm. That'll do for now. My broker tell you my terms?"

"No, not really."

The bastard was hoping he would quote a figure less than the contract price. Try to save money, even in something as important as this. People will try anything.

"Yes, he did. You leave off the fifty-percent deposit where he told you by ten tonight. My terms are completion of the project within four months. The other fifty percent on completion."

"Why four months?"

"You want this clean, safe, and if possible you want it to look like an accident. You don't get that kind of a result from a ham-fist with a bazooka. Remember, I'm the professional here, not you. You want it done sloppy, you can easily find somebody sloppy. And they're the kind you read about in the papers later."

"No, no. I've been told about you. I understand. Four months. What if it doesn't come off?"

"If it's *impossible,* though I've never yet had this happen, you get your money back. That's what professional means. I've got my reputation to think of."

With a hissing shout, Ricky kicked and recovered, landing with feet widely planted for balance, elbows out, hands flat.

"Heiss!" he shouted, and did it again.

His weekly tae kwon do lessons were on Thursday nights, but he practiced half an hour every day. Today, he was practicing with Tad on the back lawn. When he practiced, it was in some ways very boring, because he had to repeat the motions again and again. He usually solved this by making up little stories for himself while he kicked and recovered, over and over.

He pictured that burglars had entered the house, big men in dark clothes and stocking masks. They had trapped his mother in a corner. Suddenly, Ricky appeared from behind them.

"Heiss!" he kicked out at the first one. The blow landed just behind the thug's knee, and he went down like a stone. The other whirled. He had a gun!

"Heiss!" Ricky kicked the gun out of his hand.

"Heiss!" He kicked him in the solar plexus, and the thug fell, gasping for air.

"Ricky, you've saved us all!" his mother said.

The first thug staggered up. "Heiss!" Ricky lunged again, in the roundhouse kick, swiveling his hip as his leg shot out.

"How long," said Tad patiently, "is this going to go on?"

"Until I get it perfect." He kicked out again, from the hip, putting power into the snap as the leg straightened out over Tad's shoulder. Tad didn't flinch. He knew his brother wouldn't hurt him.

"I'm going to make green belt," said Ricky.

He kicked again, exactly the same kick, with a little more power.

"That's a dolyo chagi," he said.

"I know."

Ricky kicked again, but this time turning the other way. "That's a pondi dolyo chagi."

"I know."

"And that," he said, spinning, "is a di frigi. Wheel kick."

"I know. You *told* me. Anyway, I don't believe you know Chinese."

"It isn't Chinese. It's Korean. I told you that, too. You didn't remember that."

"I did, though. I'm just testing."

Ricky stood front and punched out directly from the shoulder with clenched fists, quick, sharp, hard blows to the air at shoulder height. He beat a tattoo for thirty seconds, fifty or sixty blows.

"I don't know Korean, really. But we have to know what Mr. Yun means when he calls out commands. And numbers, because he calls out pushups."

"Why in Korean?"

"Because the Koreans invented tae kwon do."

"Why do you want to learn tae kwon do?"

"Why don't you go back to work on your tree house?"

"Because I don't want to. If you don't have any reason, just come right out and say so."

"Because I want to."

Tad grinned. Ricky smiled back at him.

"Teach me Korean numbers," Tad said.

"Hana, tul, set, net, tah sul, yasul, il goh, ya doh, ah ho, yul."

"That's not how. You know I can't remember that. Teach me right."

Ricky took Tad by the shirt collar. Taking him by the hand would have been too much of a show of affection. With Mom at their grandparents' house, he was in charge of Tad. "All right," he said, "listen."

He marched across the backyard to the house, chanting in time with his steps, "Hana, tul, set, net, tah sul. That's up to five. Let's you do it with me."

They went up the steps chanting "Hana, tul, set, net, tah sul."

In the kitchen they said it a few more times, while Ricky got a bowl of grapes out of the refrigerator.

"If you're going to learn this, pay attention. You say it now. I'll give you a grape for every one you get right."

109

"Hana, tul," said Tad. Ricky gave him two grapes and ate two himself.

"Set, net, tah sul," Ricky said.

"Hana, tul, set, net, tah sul," Tad said.

"Good!" Ricky gave him five grapes and ate five. "Again."

Tad shouted words and Ricky gave him grapes and ate grapes. They both shouted and laughed and counted until all the grapes were gone and there was nothing left but the bare stems.

The man was back home fifteen minutes after leaving the phone booth. His wife was still out at a goodbye coffee for a neighbor who was moving to Arizona. Although he did not expect her back soon, he went into his den to do his research. If he took his research materials into the living room she would ask what he was doing. Oddly, if the very same books were in the den she found them entirely unremarkable.

He was a man with a broad range of interests, and admired himself for that. Also, he felt that the work he put into researching his jobs justified them. If something took time, effort, study, and attention to detail, it must be respectable.

And he liked the actual research. He had a strong background in the sciences, and he liked the technical challenge. There was a sort of puzzle to be solved. He felt a thrill when he knew he was within sight of an answer. For this one he rejected a railroad accident. He had promised himself never to repeat a method within a twelve-month period, and he regretted breaking his rule in the two falls from ladders. The first one had been reasonable and, of course, being the first, had not repeated any preceding accident. But with Dubcjek, he had seen no other way out. Dubcjek took no medication, did not clean tools with gasoline, did not ride motorcycles, and was always with his family, rarely alone. He worked in

110

Rivercrest, which was rather unusual itself, and he walked to work, which left no opening for a transportation accident. As if that weren't bad enough, he was a dentist, in partnership with two others, and both of the others got to work earlier than he did. Two technicians and the cleaning woman were always still at work when he left. The man was never alone.

Except when he was doing household repairs and his wife went to the store, and then only if his wife also took the girls.

It had been risky, but had passed, thank God, without notice. Never again.

They'd asked for it, though. Both of those guys. Trying to save money by doing your own work was the kind of thing that could get you killed.

This Meyers Campbell assignment was an interesting puzzle.

Tampering with the car was out. That kind of thing could be traced, and what was worse, with a slow driver, as Campbell seemed to be, it was likely to be ineffective. Causing some guy to run into a fire hydrant and flood the business district was not the purpose here.

Now, that yogurt he ate every day in the office for lunch was a possibility. It might work to introduce botulism into the stuff. Slip into his house the evening before, say a Saturday evening when Campbell was out with his lady friend and the couple wasn't back from Ann Arbor, and put the bacteria in the container. Not he himself, of course. His nearly invisible assistant would do the actual job.

However, the man thought botulism didn't grow in an acid medium, and yogurt was acid. Salmonella was a more common kind of food poisoning, and it grew in acid foods, but salmonella was rarely fatal.

He turned to the *Columbia-Viking Desk Encyclopedia* and looked under "botulism," but he found only a little more than

111

he already knew. "Toxin attacks nervous system; fatal respiratory paralysis common sequel unless antitoxin serum is given." Nothing about food. The wonderful thing about botulism, though, was that because it was uncommon, doctors often misdiagnosed it at first, and therefore started the serum too late.

He turned to *Basic and Clinical Immunology* by Fudenberg, Stites, Caldwell, and Wells. This one had too much information. There was an entire table with the sources of infection, toxin types, mechanism of action on the human body, and the use of antibodies and vaccines, but it was not much practical help, beyond detailing the symptoms: ". . . blocks presynaptic release of acetylcholine, resulting in impaired breathing and swallowing, diplopia, and flaccid paralysis."

He tried the *Merck Manual*. This was better. There were four pages of useful detail, including the encouraging information that the disease was fatal in sixty-five percent of the cases. It did not specifically say that the bacterium favored non-acid foods, but it gave a list of the foods more likely to be infected: string beans, corn, spinach, olives, beets, asparagus, seafood, pork products, and beef. These were all non-acid foods. That meant that the appearance of *Clostridium botulinum* in yogurt would be very unusual. And the unusual attracted attention. It was no good.

This was a shame, because it would be particularly subtle to introduce botulism into the yogurt Campbell might take with him on his fishing trip. Yogurt didn't spoil rapidly, so Campbell might well take a couple of containers along for the first few days, even without refrigeration. And if he developed paralysis in the north woods with no one around to help, confused and ill with no doctor around—the mortality rate under those conditions must be about a hundred percent.

But it wasn't possible, and it was no good worrying about it.

Still the fact that he would be miles from help *on* that fishing trip suggested another idea.

Meyers Campbell was taking Corgard for hypertension. It didn't sound like taking his medication away would necessarily be fatal. But it was worth looking into.

He got out the *Physicians' Desk Reference*. He found Corgard listed in the Product Name Index in the front. It gave page numbers for a picture of the tablets under the Product Identification heading and for a complete discussion of the medication under the Product Information heading.

He turned to the Product Identification first. This was a section of thirty-five pages of color pictures of medications. Corgard came in four sizes. They were blue, and the 120-milligram size was long and light blue, just as the voice on the telephone had said.

The man now went into the much larger section at the back of the book where the pharmaceutical products were thoroughly described. Corgard, it said, was a beta-adrenergic receptor blocking agent. Okay, a beta-blocker, then. He knew people who took them for high blood pressure. He read through the Clinical Pharmacology section without finding much that interested him. He read the Indications and Usage section. Nothing. He had started on the Warnings when his eye saw that it was interrupted by a box of type outlined by a black line. It was headed "exacerbation of ischemic heart disease following abrupt withdrawal." After abrupt discontinuation of the beta-blocker, exacerbation of angina and, in some cases, myocardial infarction had occurred. Physicians were advised to reduce beta-blockers slowly over a period of a week or two, if they had to take a patient off the medication.

This was encouraging.

As if to drive the point home, under Dosage and Administration the physician was warned that he should caution the patient against "interruption or discontinuation" of therapy without talking with the physician. Good.

It was a possibility, but it was far from a certainty. The next step was to find some medication closely resembling Corgard that he could substitute for it. And if possible to find something that, if taken in place of Corgard, would make Campbell's blood pressure worse.

Back to the Product Identification section. He started looking through the pictures for some long blue tablet that resembled Corgard, and on the first page he found one. It was called Ogen. Unfortunately, it was somewhat smaller than Corgard. He wasn't sure Campbell would notice the difference.

Looking up the page number of the description in the Product Name Index, he turned to the back of the book with enthusiasm.

Ogen was estropiate, whatever that was. He skimmed down, catching a warning against use of the drug in conditions of increased blood pressure. This looked good, until he realized what an estropiate was. It was estrogen. Under indications for use, he found symptoms of menopause, vaginitis, ovarian failure, and female castration. Shit.

He could just about see himself going to a doctor and asking for some of that! Talk about being conspicuous!

Back to the Product Identification section. Four pages farther along there was a tablet (he had now found that they called this particular long tablet "capsule-shaped tablet") that was perfect. The exact size, shape and color of Corgard. It was called Naldegesic. He turned to the index.

It was not listed. There was nothing in the Product Information about it.

He thought that meant that the thing was nonprescription. If so, it would be easy to get hold of. And under the picture it was called a decongestant analgesic. Some decongestants raised blood pressure. He knew that from warnings on labels of his own.

But still, if it was nonprescription, it was not likely to be very strong or very dangerous. It would serve the purpose of substituting for Campbell's Corgard without his knowledge. But not the purpose of making his blood pressure much worse.

He kept paging. Niferex, on the next page, was blue, but it was also too dark and had rounded corners.

Campbell would be sure to notice. Valmid was the right size and color, but it was a capsule. So were Theobid and Cyclospasmol on the next two pages. Os-Cal-Gesic was a tablet and the right size, but the color was a little too greenish.

Two pages after Os-Cal-Gesic he found Elavil. It was light blue, the right size, and a capsule-shaped tablet. He turned quickly to the back of the book.

Elavil was called an antidepressant with sedative effects. He sent his eye down to the Warnings section.

Elavil was said to block the effects of certain antihypertensive drugs. If used in patients with cardiovascular disorders, the patient should be closely watched. Under Adverse Reactions he found three that were important: myocardial infarction, hypertension, and stroke.

Eureka!

And to add to the feeling of success, the light blue long tablet that matched Corgard was the large amount, 150 milligrams.

Best of all, the effects of the tranquilizer would lull any suspicions Campbell might have that his Corgard wasn't working. With any luck, he would be so happy from the tranquilizer that he wouldn't notice any adverse symptoms until it was much too late.

Now, the man knew the only problem was to get a doctor to prescribe him some. He checked the Indications carefully. He would have to claim depression with some anxiety. Temporary depression would be the best, so the doctor didn't become afraid he was an addict. Something like "It's inventory time, and I always develop this terrible anxiety—"

Well, he would work that out soon enough. The important thing was—he had the method.

He put the reference works away in the bookcase and lined up the spines as if they had never been used. He had a pretty good idea how to get his hands on that drug.

Ten

In past years, Samantha had graded the Logic 305 final papers at the end of the year. And as soon as she handed them back, the offended students would trickle in.

"Why did I get a C-plus, Mrs. Lawton?"

Samantha would repress the desire to say, "Because the paper was ill-thought-out, turbidly written, and wretchedly researched." Instead, she would take it page by page.

"In your first paragraph, you should have explained *why* you're disagreeing with Max Black's—"

"But I did."

"Where?"

"Right here. Where it says, 'notwithstanding Black.' "

"That's not a *why*, Mr. Phelan."

Now she required all papers three weeks before the end of class, and the final classes consisted of an all-criticism of the papers, two each day. It was extremely effective when a fellow student, who felt no need to be polite, said, "Left Black out because you couldn't think of an answer, huh?"

Class discussion improved not only the worst but also the best papers. The rewrites were a joy. And she could grade them at her leisure.

So by exam week she felt let out of school. It was surprising, really, how much of a lift she got from the end of the rigid schedule of classes.

Frederick was at the house two evenings during that week to see the children. Or he claimed it was to see the children.

As always, he didn't have much to say to them, and tended to hang around the kitchen and criticize her cooking or her housekeeping. Even this didn't destroy her feeling of well-being. The first time he came, she spoke casually with him. The second time she took him in to see the children and went out herself to do some evening grocery shopping.

And one night she went out to dinner with Dan. He was cheerful, and at the same time he was willing to let her go on being impersonal. She wondered how long that would last.

Thursday morning she came downstairs to start breakfast, delighted that she didn't have to be at school early.

At the foot of the stairs, she stopped. There was a strong draft blowing across her face. She could feel her hair stir in the cool air.

Standing perfectly still, she mentally walked around the house. Into the kitchen—had she closed and locked the windows last night? Yes. And the kitchen door? Yes, she had, and hit her bare toe when she slammed it. Through the kitchen and into the breakfast room. Had she forgotten to close the breakfast room windows? No, in fact they hadn't been open all day. The playroom—what about the sliding glass door? She always checked it before going to bed, because it seemed to her the easiest way for a prowler to get in. Anyway, she would never have left a huge thing like that open without noticing. Library and living room windows? She had checked them; it was a habit. But they hadn't been opened because yesterday had been cool and breezy. Dining room the same. That brought her full circle.

She heard Ricky slam the bathroom door upstairs. If there was a prowler, she had to find him before the children came down.

Looking from one side to another, she went through the dining room and pantry into the kitchen. Everything was in its proper place. She moved cautiously to the basement door. She was frightened to think of going down there to search for a prowler, and yet she had gone casually up and down with the laundry last night. She felt no draft of air from the basement stairs, so possibly there was no window open down there in the cellar. *Maybe I don't have to go down.*

That was cowardly. She ran down the basement steps before she could have another attack of fear.

The basement was very large, like the house, and like the house, it formed a hollow square. She raced through the laundry room, the small room where they kept suitcases, the large space where the ping-pong table and pachinko games lived, the furnace and water heater areas, and the wine cellar. She looked into the pool room—hammers with claws, sharp chisels, saws with shiny teeth. Nobody.

Back upstairs, she paused in the kitchen. She could still feel a strong draft. But she did not *have* to think anybody had broken in; air currents were unpredictable. Maybe Ricky had left his bedroom window open and some sort of chimney effect had stirred the downstairs.

She walked quickly into the breakfast room. Its double window was intact. But as she stood there, she felt outdoor air pass coldly over her ankles, and the curtains at the breakfast room window rose slowly toward her and settled back.

She stepped through the arch into the playroom. For just an instant, her perceptions were confused. She wondered why the room sparkled so. Then, in a second level of confusion, she thought the morning sun was striking dewdrops on the floor. Then she saw the glittering material for what it really was.

Glass. The whole sliding glass door of the room had been shattered. It was safety glass, so it had not broken into shards, but into small rounded chunks that caught the early morning sun. The oblique light fragmented and spattered all over the walls and ceiling.

The door frame was utterly empty. The room stood open to the outdoors. Someone could be in the house. Samantha ran across the crackling glass into the library. There was no one crouched under the desk, and no closet to hide in. From the library she ran into the living room. Circling the furniture, looking behind it, she hurried on to the vestibule inside the front door and threw open the coat closet. No one.

There was no one downstairs. God grant there was no one anywhere, but she had to check upstairs. She grabbed a steak knife from the silverware drawer in the dining room, noticing but not caring much that the silver had not been stolen. She hurried—but quietly—up the stairs. There was no need to alarm the boys.

If she found a prowler, she'd shout to the children to run, and then keep him from following them. There was no attacker hiding in Ricky's closet, or her closet, or Frederick's nearly empty closet, or the guest closet, or the linen closet, or the storeroom. Nobody.

Samantha grabbed cereal bowls and slung them on the table. She had cereal and milk out by the time the boys walked into the breakfast room, and she prayed they would be too sleepy to look behind themselves into the playroom.

"Tad, you can't have taken much time to wash," she said.

"I wasn't very dirty."

"Cereal?" Ricky said.

"I didn't have time to make eggs this morning."

Once the glass was swept up and the opening covered with plywood—there was a board-up service in Winnetka, wasn't there?—the opening in the wall would look less threatening.

The coffee was still too hot to drink, and Samantha was astounded to find that she was shaking. She felt violated. During a night that had been normal and apparently secure, her walls had been breached. Any menace could have entered. A hundred pounds of glass—these doors were heavy!—had crashed to the floor and she had never known, because she had been asleep.

How frail was the idea of security. And how very limited were one's senses that warned of danger.

She telephoned Glenmore Glass—"Emergency Board-Up Service, Fastest Replacement." They would board up today.

Then she called the village hall and asked to speak with Henry Ax. In the half minute she waited for him to come to the phone, she decided there was nothing he could do, anyway. But by then it was too late to hang up.

"Has something happened, Mrs. Lawton?"

So she told him.

"I'll come over."

"That door certainly had a lot of glass in it."

"Uh-huh. And I never heard it break."

"Any idea when it happened?"

"Not really. I locked up at a little after eleven, came down to make breakfast about quarter of seven."

"Great! That gives us a range of merely seven or eight hours."

"Sorry. Maybe it doesn't mean much. Maybe a bird flew into the window."

"You're kidding. Big Bird from Sesame Street would have trouble breaking that stuff. You were thinking a forty-pound eagle doing sixty miles an hour, maybe?"

"Maybe I was trying to look on the bright side."

"Besides which, between eleven and seven it was dark, and

there aren't that many night birds, and owls have very good night sight."

"Right."

"And if a forty-pound eagle *did* hit that glass door, you would have found him on the floor this morning with a terrible headache."

"All right. So it wasn't a very good idea."

"You *wish* it had been an accident."

"A big dog running around in the dark?"

"Never." He picked up some of the rounded chunks of glass. "They made this stuff to last."

"All right. I don't believe in the dog, either. I just don't like to think of somebody out there—um—*hating* us."

"Of course not. And what makes it worse—" He stopped.

"What were you going to say?"

"It isn't important."

"Look, Mr. Ax, if you're afraid you're going to worry me, don't. I have a right to do my own worrying. I'm an adult, and I'm here alone in charge of two children. Keeping anything back is unfair to me."

"I suppose. Well, look at this. Glass all over, and no sign of a rock or a brick."

"Yes. I saw that."

"But see—what it means is that somebody threw the rock, or brick, and then came in and got it and took it away with him."

"Why would he do that?"

"Just offhand I can think of three reasons. One is that whatever he broke it with was connected with him. It could identify him, like a hammer with his name etched on it. The second reason is that he needed it—a crutch or a tire jack, that sort of thing."

"And the third?"

"He may have wanted you to know that, whatever he broke the window with, he came into the house to retrieve it. To let you know it *wasn't* just a rock hurled, on impulse. In other words, to frighten you."

Samantha stared at the glass on the floor.

After a second, Ax said, "You make sure nothing was missing?"

"Pretty much. Nothing that's valuable is missing. I don't have any jewelry to speak of, and the silver and television are still here. Somebody could take a can of soup or some dirty laundry and I might not notice. But worn-out size-ten Levi's couldn't be worth much to anybody. In fact, looking around the house, I don't see any signs that anybody even went into any other rooms."

"Does that make you feel better?"

"It did at first. But after I thought about it, it only made it seem more irrational."

Samantha suddenly turned, went into the kitchen, and sat down on a chair.

Ax said, "Did you eat breakfast?"

"Coffee."

"Stay there and don't move. I want to go out and see if I can find any footprints. Then we have to feed you."

She watched him step over the glass on the playroom floor and through the empty doorframe. Outside the sliding door was a flagstone terrace. Ax studied the doorframe all the way around. He shrugged and began moving in arcs across the terrace, each arc a little bigger than the last, until he reached the grass edge. This he patrolled more slowly, walking on the flagstones but looking down into the grass.

After he had studied the entire grass verge of the patio, he stepped onto the grass and quartered the backyard.

Samantha hated to sit here as if she were in the midst of a

Victorian faint. But just for a couple of minutes it was so nice to let somebody else cope—

She stood up when he came back through the playroom door and into the kitchen.

"You have a remarkably clean terrace, and your lawn grows aggressively. Now if you just had some bare spots out there, I might have found some footprints."

"Sorry. If I'd known, I could have had the kids wear a bare spot."

Ax smiled. "Now let's see what you've got in the refrigerator."

"All the usual."

"Eggs, cheddar cheese. Fine. Where's a bowl and fork?"

"Hey! Wait a minute! I can't let you make me breakfast."

"Why not?"

"Um—" *Turn it into a joke.* "Because if Rivercrest hears that the Public Safety Department gives this kind of service, where will you be? Cooking breakfast house to house. You'll never get anything else done."

"Then we'll have to keep it secret." He had already located the fork and found bowls in the bottom cupboard near the stove.

"A detective, I see. Or does your wife keep them there?"

"Nope. I keep them there. I live alone." He whisked five eggs. Samantha got the percolator and a can of coffee. She filled the pot with water and spooned in the coffee, then added an extra scoop. He probably liked it strong.

Ax said, "You sit down."

"I'll feel like an invalid in a minute."

"What would be wrong with that?" He had butter bubbling in the pan.

"Well, I'm not an invalid."

"Then it won't matter, will it?"

She blinked and sat down.

He put two pieces of bread in the toaster and punched it down. He worked, Samantha thought, very efficiently. Not exactly the graceful, no-move-wasted sort of efficiency, but short, vigorous, impatient moves. His rusty-brown hair was as tightly curled as a scouring pad.

He had chopped the cheese while the eggs were cooking. Now he scraped the cheese from the board with his hand and scattered it over the soft omelet top. With quick movements of the pan, pushing it forward and then quickly pulling back, he rolled the omelet over on itself. He had heavy shoulders for that kind of delicate action, she thought. And yet he looked right doing it.

Julia Child has heavy shoulders, too.

She laughed.

"What's so funny?"

"Oh, I was thinking about Julia Child."

"Oh." He tipped the omelet out on a plate. The toast popped up. He put the omelet on the breakfast table and went back for the toast, which he buttered in two or three fast sweeps of the knife.

"Now eat," he said.

"Who was that cartoon character a long time ago who kept holding a handkerchief to another character's nose and saying, 'Now blow?' "

"Elmer. Unless it was Henry. Now eat."

Ax took a knife and divided the omelet between them. He picked up his fork and speared a good-sized chunk, which he put in his mouth.

"My goodness, this is delicious," he said. "Henry, how do you make this? May I have the recipe?"

Samantha laughed. "It *is* good. If you're trying to cheer me up, you're doing a good job. I was shocked when I saw the

125

broken glass. Now I think I was too shocked. I mean, so somebody threw a brick in the door. Nobody was hurt. Nothing was taken."

"That's really the breakfast talking."

"What do you mean?"

"If you get real hungry, and then you eat, you get happy. It doesn't mean there isn't any problem."

"Nobody came in—"

"Look, I don't think you should get *scared*. I just think you should get cautious. Because you don't know—and I sure don't know—why this happened."

"But how am I supposed to go about being cautious? I can't sit down here watching the windows all night. Or board them all up so they won't break."

"No, you can't."

"So what then?"

"You can make certain you lock up well every night. Leave the back porch and front porch lights on. Watch for strangers hanging around, and tell your kids to watch for strangers and let you know if they see any. If you do see anything unusual, call me. And I'll have the patrol car come by here a few times a night."

"I don't think that's necessary—"

"They have to be someplace. And this place is someplace."

"Sophist."

"Do you plan to tell your husband about the glass door?"

"I plan to tell the insurance man. *He* might be some help."

"I wish I could think of some less abrupt way of saying this—but I can't. Will you let me take you to dinner tonight?"

"Dinner?" *Silly answer. Of course he said dinner.* "I'm sorry. I can't—"

"I hope it's not like being asked out by the butler," he said suddenly, harshly.

"What?"

"I mean, some people here think the police are hired servants, right?"

"What kind of person do you think I am?"

"I don't know. I'm trying to find out."

"You think because I live in this—this—this stupid *showplace*, I'm going to look down on you?"

"I don't know."

"I think it's an insulting idea!"

"Don't get excited—"

"And I think you might have waited for me to answer your invitation first. I hope—" She got to her feet. "I hope you don't prejudge everybody you meet in your work. And speaking of work, I work! I don't sit around here eating bonbons and playing canasta or whatever it is you think I do all day. This is my ex-husband's idea of a house. Not mine. When I was a kid we were—we lived in a normal house. It was square, with a room on each corner, just like everybody else's. And my father was a foreman in a company that made air conditioners. And *he worked!*"

"I didn't say you didn't work—"

"And anyway, I *hate* this damn house!"

Samantha sat down and covered her face with her hands.

"Hold it," Ax said. "I admit what I said wasn't fair. Sometimes I'm a little hasty. I asked you out without thinking about it. I mean, I had thought about it, but I blurted it out before I meant to. I mean, I wasn't ready. Oh, hell! And then I thought you were going to say no. I thought you were horrified."

"Well, you thought *wrong!*"

"Yeah! And here we are arguing like two married people. Drink your coffee."

127

"I'll drink my coffee when I'm *damn good and ready!*"

Samantha was furious, and a second later she was laughing. Ax laughed. Samantha laughed until her eyes watered. "You know what the funniest thing of all is?" she gasped.

"No. What?"

"I used to think I *loved* this house."

"I believe it."

"Look, when all this started, I was going to say that I can't go out tonight because Ricky is having another boy over for the night. And you may think it's odd, but while I would leave Ricky and Tad home together, I won't leave the three of them alone. You'd understand this if you had children. When Ricky has a guest, he forgets that Tad exists and neglects him, which is normal but not desirable. And either Tad will get into a mess by himself, or he'll tease Ricky and Peter until they get mad at him. Either way it doesn't work."

"Okay."

"But if you're free tomorrow night, I can go."

"Hooray!" Ax said. "Now eat."

Eleven

"No more pencils, no more books, no more teacher's dirty looks!" said Tad.

Samantha put the appetizer plate down in front of the boys. "Do they still say that?" she asked. "I thought you had to be as old as I am to know that one."

"How old *are* you, Mom?" Tad giggled, glancing at Peter.

"So old—I'm *so* old I don't say how old in mixed company."

She, too, looked at Peter Winterthur. He was Ricky's guest, but Tad liked him and kept trying to impress him. Right now Tad was showing that he could tease his mother and she didn't mind. Well, that was all right. Samantha herself was conscious of trying harder when Peter was around. Peter was so much less spontaneous than Ricky or Tad that Samantha found she smiled more widely, talked a little louder, and let the boys do slightly more outrageous things than usual, to loosen Peter up. Not that it worked. She wanted to be saying—without words, which would frighten him—"It's okay, Peter. We won't hurt you."

Peter was a little taller than Ricky, a quiet, indoor creature. He tended to blink when exposed to the daylight of people's eyes. He was constantly alert to avoid making a wrong move. At dinner, he watched Ricky and Tad as they served themselves from the appetizer platter. Then he served himself just the same way. He would not enter a room in the Lawtons' house unless one of the boys went first. Samantha knew that his mother forbade Peter to use their living room. It was carefully furnished by what Sally called a "name decorator" in white carpet and crystal. So perhaps Peter had to distinguish between rooms that could be used and rooms that could not be used. Poor Peter. As far as *her* house was concerned, Samantha believed the children lived here, too.

Frederick should have married Sally.

Samantha had intended to sit at the table and eat with the three boys, but she decided her presence would only make Peter unbearably self-conscious. So instead of sitting down she went to the stove and pretended to fuss with the pizza.

Out of the corner of her eye, she could see them taking cold vegetables and dipping them in the cheese dip. This method of serving was one she had privately dubbed "Mom's sneaky psychological technique." Rather than turn the dinner hour into the nagging hour, she put out a platter of fresh vegetables arranged around a central bowl of dip or even salad dressing, and they'd go through enormous quantities of rabbit food. It worked, in part because the arrangement reminded them of adult party appetizers. Second, it was colorful and pretty. Third, she put it out at the beginning of a meal when they were hungriest. But mostly, it worked because it was voluntary. It was not like heaping quantities of spinach on their plates and ordering them to finish every bite. She'd had enough of that as a child. Today she was serving carrot sticks, a green pepper cut into thin strips, radishes, and cucumber sticks. All the carrots were gone already, and most of the cucumbers.

"Milk, apple juice, or grape juice?"

She had timed the pizza to give them a good ten minutes with the vegetables. In the meantime, she poured two milks and a grape juice. Covertly, she observed Peter. He was a very picky eater, one of those children who limited their world to hamburgers and pizza, and Samantha considered such behavior a form of fear. Peter was very timid about the unknown. He had, however, latched onto a couple of cucumber sticks and was nibbling them quietly.

Tad and Ricky were both shouting about the end of school and the coming summer vacation. Samantha wondered whether Ricky liked Peter because Peter would listen quietly while Ricky talked. Would that be a bad thing, if so? She had known marriages that seemed to survive on the same nourishment.

Samantha cut the pizza in wedges at the stove, then put the whole pan down in the center of the table. She put out two spatulas so the boys could get at it from both sides. Then she discreetly withdrew to the living room with a glass of white wine.

She was feeling very competent tonight, very confident. In a way, this troubled her. It was unsettling to think that swings of mood affected her perception of facts. Jim Dubcjek's death had thrown a web of uneasiness over the days since. It was not only sadness, but a kind of restless anxiety, because the event had been inexplicable. For all that he had been working on a ladder, he should not have had an accident. He was a careful man. He was about as likely to fall as she was to scald herself in her bath tonight. Yet the uneasiness had faded to some extent. That was normal; you didn't go on thinking about a thing forever. She would put the shattered glass door out of her mind, too. Now she felt she had overreacted this morning, and this disturbed her, too. Either there was a threat or there wasn't. She was not going to indulge in the wide swings of mood that her mother had.

Samantha had been at great pains in the morning to keep the children from seeing the shattered door, but when they came home from school in the afternoon, they could not avoid finding the great sheets of plywood over the gap. She told them the facts, hoping they wouldn't be frightened.

"I'll bet it was the Mafia," said Tad enthusiastically, apparently eager for them to come back. Then he went outdoors to work on his tree house.

"No, it was a giant bird that swooped down to carry us all away," Ricky said. "Or maybe a white wolf. Yeah. Say! It's really a *werewolf*. Maybe I'll turn into a werewolf at night and go out prowling. And when I got home last night, you'd locked all the doors, so I crashed in—blam!—through the glass, and then turned back into myself and this morning I don't remember a thing about it. By the way, can we have pizza for dinner? Peter likes pizza."

So much for protecting their delicate sensibilities. And now she felt optimistic and in good control of events. It was absurd, really, to have moods. Facts were facts, and logic demanded that the same facts be interpreted the same way. Besides, she was not a person who had mood swings. When her mother had run from the heights of frantic anxiety to profound depression, Samantha had refused to be drawn along. Samantha did not fluctuate. She was consistent, even if it meant being unemotional. She was dependable. Even during the problems with Frederick—the estrangement, the filing for divorce—she had been sad and angry, but there had been no wild swings of mood, only a grim determination to hang on.

And to be a person the boys could rely on. The boys must have at least one parent they could count on.

It was one of those nightmares that lies very close to the waking surface. Samantha was almost awake enough to think about it critically, to know it was not real, yet not awake enough to fight the fear.

She dreamed that she was living with Frederick again, that

he was lying beside her here in bed. And yet was not quite Frederick. She told herself that she knew him well, that she had known him for fourteen years. But as she lay there next to that other body, she thought that if the lids that covered those eyes, those apparently sleeping eyes, should open, it would not be Frederick's eyes that would look into hers, but yellowish eyes with a vertical pupil. She knew every crease of his face, and those long, distinctive, tapering hands that lay under the blanket. She could touch them now because she knew them so well.

Something about the texture of his skin had changed. Under the cover of the skin, had the bones of the face slowly altered?

Samantha stirred. She wanted to reach out and reassure herself that he was the same. But she did not dare. She knew that he would be different. The skin would be cold, not warm, not human, the tactile equivalent of a salamander's skin. Frederick would be almost the same. And that was the worst thing. He would be almost the same, and just a little bit different. Almost—not enough to be quite sure. But something—not quite Frederick.

She gasped, unable to catch her breath. For an instant she thought she was smothering. She drew in an explosive breath and cried "No, no!" in her sleep.

Then she sat up and said "No" once more, half awake. Then she was fully awake and heard the word "No!" still in the air. "No! No!"

What was happening? Had she waked from one dream level into a higher level of dreaming? Was she still lying in bed somewhere, in true reality?

"No! No, don't!"

It was Peter's voice. Samantha swung her legs out of bed, not quite steady, and hurried to Ricky's room. She turned on the hall light, then pushed open Ricky's door. Ricky was in bed but sitting up, his hair caught by the spill of the hall light. Peter was on the floor in his sleeping bag.

Peter was twisting and turning and had wrapped the sleeping bag around his body in a spiral.

"I talked to him, but he won't wake up," Ricky said.

Samantha put on the light. "I guess we'd better try harder."

"Isn't it supposed to be dangerous to wake them up?"

"That's sleepwalkers, and I don't think it's true, anyway."

She knelt down next to Peter. The boy was now mumbling "No" and throwing his head from side to side. His forehead glistened with sweat.

"Peter? Peter, wake up."

Ricky came over to help. Samantha took Peter's shoulder and gently moved it back and forth.

Peter screamed.

Samantha and Ricky recoiled. Samantha called, "Peter, wake up!"

"Come *on*, Peter," Ricky said.

"No, no! I don't want to go!" Peter said.

"Peter. It's all right."

"I don't want to go on the camp-out," he said clearly. And then he was awake. He stared at Ricky and Samantha with huge eyes.

"Hi, Peter," Ricky said sensibly, in a normal voice. "You've been having a bad dream."

"I didn't mean to. I'm sorry."

"Don't be silly," Samantha said, "you can't help dreaming. And my guess is you can't go back to sleep right now, either, after a dream that bad. How would you both like some cookies and milk in the kitchen? Get the taste of the dream out, so to speak."

"Sure!" said Ricky, always ready for food. "But I'd like cocoa."

Samantha sighed. Cocoa took longer. She'd have to heat the milk. "Okay, come on. Peter?"

"Okay."

They trooped to the kitchen, Samantha uneasy but with her own nightmare half forgotten. Only the emotional after-taste of it remained. But—what did Peter mean, he didn't want to go on the camp-out? They all loved scouting.

The boys had to spend only an hour at school, just to pick up their report cards and, she supposed, to chalk up another day in order to qualify for state aid. There were a certain number of so-called child days each school had to tally. She wondered how many child days she herself had logged.

Sally Winterthur had dropped off Peter's camping gear while the boys were at school.

"Sally, has Peter said anything about not wanting to go on this camping trip?"

"Nope. Not at all."

"I think he's—he seemed unhappy about it last night."

"Oh, don't listen to him. It's probably because they're doing another one of their damn hikes. He feels funny because he can't keep going as long as some of the kids."

"You mean it really upsets him? Sally, if it makes him feel this bad, maybe he shouldn't put himself in that position."

"Oh, nonsense. It'll do him good."

"Sally, he was really *miserable.*"

"Forget it. I can't do anything about it, anyway. I have to admit I noticed he wasn't very eager. You don't feel good, you know, when your kid is unhappy. He's scared of something, you wonder about it."

She had noticed. "That's what I mean."

135

"But Carson is absolutely firm on this. I mean, he says that's it. It's time the kid learned to fit in."

Samantha hesitated, afraid that saying more would make trouble for Peter.

"And Carson says either Peter gets out there and hikes his goddam best, or he'll paste him one."

"Oh."

"He says let the boy scouts help make a man of him."

Samantha drove the boys and their gear to the Community House. There were three frame packs, each with a bedroll and ground cloth tied on. When Tad put his frame pack on, he disappeared under it, like pictures Samantha had seen of Plains Indians carrying all their possessions on two saplings tied to their backs.

She knew the boys did not want motherly attention, so she did not wave. She had said goodbye in the car. She waved instead at the fathers, Monte Fiske, Ira Schultz, and Lee Grey. Schultz was wearing his badges and regulation tan Bermuda shorts. Big Bermuda shorts. Lee Grey looked lean and fit beside him.

She sent a smile and a wave to Dan Camelli, who was wearing a scout shirt, but with Levi's and no special effects. He grinned and waggled his head, but his arms were full. He had several dozen bags of hot dog buns, his hands locked together under them, making a sling. She did not expect him to come to the car. She pulled out of the parking place, smiling, and another car with two campers pulled in where she had been.

She was still smiling as she drove home. There were two days ahead of her with no child care. Any longer and she'd miss them, but two days was a fine breather. She had a date tonight with Henry Ax. And Dan Camelli was away with the scouts, so she would not have to explain anything or turn him down. She was uncomfortable with turning people down.

On My Honor

She was still smiling when she drove in her driveway. When she took the turn into the garage, she saw Frederick's car in the back and Frederick there, waving at her.

Twelve

"Frederick!"

"Good morning, Samantha."

"What do you want?"

"That's not very welcoming."

"Listen, Frederick, I'm tired, I was up in the night and I've made breakfast and assembled camping gear and delivered the gang to the boy scouts. I'm in no mood for games. I am looking forward to sitting down for a few minutes and decelerating."

"I'll sit with you."

Sighing, Samantha let herself in the kitchen door. Frederick followed. She poured boiling water over instant coffee in two cups, left both black, and handed one to Frederick. He raised his eyebrows at the instant, but for once refrained from saying anything. Samantha led the way through the breakfast room, playroom, and study into the living room, determined to sit there because it was the most formal room in the house. You entertained guests you scarcely knew in the living room.

"What happened to the patio door?"

"What?"

"The patio door is boarded up. I assume you noticed."

"Somebody or something broke it."

"One of the kids?"

"No, Frederick. I am taking perfectly good care of the children. They are not raging out of control. They do not

138

have vandals for friends. It happened during the night. Maybe an animal."

"Did you call the police?"

"Yes."

"Anything missing?"

"No, Frederick. I would have called you if anything valuable had been taken."

"Call the insurance?"

"Yes."

"In the night, huh? What you need is a man around the house."

"If somebody threw a brick through the window at three A.M., you'd be asleep upstairs like the rest of us."

"Sure, but if the prowler came upstairs—"

"Drop the subject! I don't want to talk about it!"

"My, aren't we touchy?"

"We are touchy because our houseguest had a nightmare and we were up fixing cocoa in the middle of the night. And we were annoyed enough to have *shot* a prowler if we had seen one. Is there anything else you wanted to talk with us about?"

"Yes, there is."

"I shouldn't have asked."

"I want to move back."

"We've talked this into the *ground*—"

"Mother is upset."

"I know she's upset. She had me to lunch. Scallops and leeks with complaints and demands."

"You don't sound like yourself."

"Not enough of a patsy?"

"She likes you."

"Frederick, this kind of dishonesty is exactly the problem with you. She does *not* like me. She's willing to put up with me rather than have the disgrace of a divorce."

"You won't have my income; without me—"

Samantha got up. Suddenly she could see a use for this circular house. She could run into the dining room, through the pantry, through the kitchen, breakfast room, playroom, study, back into the living room, and around again. Why hadn't she ever thought of it before? How many circuits of the house would make a mile?

How many miles would she have to run to forget Frederick?

"Frederick, the papers are filed. The divorce is going through. Let's not fight. You'll be just as happy without me."

"What is it you're trying to get from me?"

"Let it *go!*"

"You're either stubborn or stupid."

"Call me that if you want. Marriage includes liking, after all. You spend all your time trying to change me."

"Samantha, listen, I love you."

She watched his mouth form the words. "No," she said. "I can't believe it any more. You say things you think I want to hear."

"If you divorce me, I won't support you. Don't expect to live like this."

"I don't *want* to live like this!"

"You can't fool me. It's a good line, Samantha, but everybody wants money."

She was going to walk away from him, but the phone rang, making it possible for her to leave gracefully rather than angrily. She answered it in the study.

"Samantha?"

"Yes?" she said cautiously.

"Is somebody there with you?"

It was Henry Ax. "Yes," she said.

"Oh. Your husband?"

"Yes." Henry certainly wasn't stupid.

"He isn't bothering you, is he?"

"No," she said, lying.

"Pick you up at seven?"

"Sure. Thanks a lot."

"Bye."

She hung up gently and went back into the living room. Frederick wasn't there. She went through the dining room, pantry, and kitchen, looking for him. As she came into the breakfast room, she saw his car pass the window, going down the drive.

Frederick had left.

Good.

In the hive, a hundred bees clustered around a small packet, just a few inches long, with wooden sides and a screen top and bottom. A hole in one end was plugged with sugar candy. The object had been mysterious to the bees the day before, but had become familiar with the passage of hours. Most of the candy plug was gone, too. The bees had licked it away.

Inside the screened packet, the new queen twitched her feelers, sensing the bees outside. Then she moved to the sugar candy and licked it. On the other side, two worker bees licked it also. The candy was worn so thin now that it was transparent. As they licked, a tiny hole appeared, and in the halo of paper-thin candy, the head of the new queen appeared. For a brief second she paused; then she put a long, jointed foreleg through the opening.

They got to the campsite in Wisconsin, just north of the Illinois border, at 1:00 and had time to eat lunch, unpack the gear, and set up their tents, all in daylight.

Dan Camelli felt good. He liked camping out, but the winter camp-outs were more like endurance tests than real pleasure. Now, in early June, the forest preserve was beautiful.

It was good, too, to have this kind of thing he could do with Tony. They could camp together, with the scouts, and yet not be in each other's pockets all the time. When he and Tony spent an evening together, bowling, for instance, he was often conscious of being a father trying to make up for the fact that the child had no mother. He didn't think Tony felt that way, exactly, but Tony was aware that Dan wanted to make a special effort. For that matter, they were both making a special effort. Tony stayed around the house more in the evening than most boys his age. Once Dan had said, "Listen, Tony. You don't have to stay home and take care of me if there's something you'd like to do."

Phrasing it that way had an element of role reversal, which Dan had intended.

Tony said, "Dad, I like to know you're okay. And besides, aren't you my best friend?"

Dan marveled that a thirteen-year-old could be so mature. He remembered himself at that age as being thoroughly confused and not very reliable.

But then, his mother hadn't died, either.

There was another aspect to the question, "Aren't you my best friend?" besides the open affection. There was an element of, "Aren't you all I have now?"

Tony was on the other side of the stream, helping Ricky Lawton set up their tent. Dan watched for a minute, studying the efficient way his child moved, the unconscious grace.

Someday he'll leave me, too. In five years he'll leave for college. What will I do without him?

Dan Camelli had backed into the position of being food

handler for the scouts. The other men assumed that, because he was the head of what was blandly called a single-parent household, he knew better than they how to cook and how to negotiate the intricacies of a supermarket.

Garvey Fiske and Kiri Obisawa were his assistants today. He handed Garvey the ice chest.

"That too heavy for you?"

"Nope."

Kiri took the plastic bag containing frying pans, spatulas, matches, maple syrup, pancake mix, and packaged butter.

It was interesting, Dan thought, that the four men who regularly led the troop all had different interests, specialties almost, that didn't overlap.

Ira Schultz was the only one who no longer had boys in the troop. His boys were twenty-two and seventeen, but Ira had stayed with scouting even after his children had outgrown it. Ira was the purist in the group. He had been a scout as a child, and still kept his enthusiasm for the symbols. He was the one who demanded full uniform on the boys, and the memorizing of the creed and the oath.

Ira was a tall man with a big stomach and lots of fat on his shoulders. He walked as if he were climbing uphill. He liked to carry the cook tent and poles—ten feet of rolled canvas—all by himself.

Right now Ira was supervising setting up the cook tent. He and four boys were pitching it directly over one of the campground's picnic tables. The tent was so big they would have room to walk around the table once it was set up. The food supply would go on top of the table, out of the way of prowling animals of the night. Unless, of course, you considered teenage boys prowling animals of the night.

Kiri and Garvey carried their bundles over to the cook tent.

"Put that down," Ira said, "and give these fellows a hand.

143

Put a little tension on the ropes for them. We want it nice and tight."

In his nonscouting life, Ira was in wholesale dental supplies. To Dan, Ira was such an avid outdoorsman that he would have expected him to be a landscape architect or run a road-building firm. He wondered if Ira had inherited the business and just moved into it after college, taking the line of least resistance.

Across the stream and up the slope from Dan and the cars, Lee Grey was supervising the layout of the sleeping tents. Lee was the opposite of Ira in appearance. On Ira, clothes always looked bad. Lee was slender and elegant, even though canoe trips and backpacking had revealed a hard set of muscles underneath. On Lee the scout uniform looked custom-tailored, or at least L.L.Bean's best. Dan wondered fleetingly whether Lee made his wife Naomi taper his tan shirts. He had a feeling Lee would be firm about what he believed a wife should do. Like Ira, Lee was quite exacting about certain aspects of scouting. He didn't care so much about uniforms and oaths, but he liked technical matters to be properly done. He was very concerned right now about the placement of the tents. They had to be on high ground in case of rain. The openings could not face into the prevailing wind. Altogether, Lee was very technologically oriented. Which, given his job, might be odd or not. He was in advertising with a major Chicago firm, and he specialized in chemical-company accounts. Dan wondered whether this entailed drafting and layouts and artistic decisions or technical, scientific knowledge and the ability to describe uses for a product. You could always count on Lee to talk about reasons. If the scouts were discussing fire prevention, Lee would be right there with flame points and combustibility. Ira would be more likely to know the scout rules for dousing a campfire.

Lee's son, Kip, was one of the scouts. Kip was a swimmer, a hiker, and a body builder.

The fourth scoutmaster was Monty Fiske.

Monty Fiske's big interest was in crafts. He taught the boys whittling, woodworking, lanyards, and knot-tying. Because there were no crafts available right now, he and Dick and Kip and Peter were digging fire pits for the dinner which Dan would help them cook. Monty had an event set for tonight. They were going to have a knot-tying contest. Monty had brought lots of rope.

"I thought square knots, diagonal and shear lashings, timber hitch and half hitch. How does that sound?" he'd said to Dan.

Dan, who knew granny and square and nothing more, said, "That sounds good to me."

"I've donated two lightweight frying pans for the prizes."

Monty Fiske was in restaurant supplies.

When Ricky had finished helping Mr. Grey set up the tents, he wandered away from the center of activity, down to the meadow where the stream widened. He had thought of asking Mr. Camelli whether he needed help with dinner, but he was uneasy with Camelli. In the old days, Camelli had been his favorite among the scoutmasters. For one thing, he was the only one who didn't think a uniform had to be perfect. Schultz was likely to get after you for wearing Levi's with the scout shirt, or having your badges sewn on wrong. Ricky had not wanted to ask his mother to sew on his badges for him. He was much more aware of how hard she worked than she realized. He had sewn on two badges himself, poorly. The thread kept leaving lumps on the surface of the fabric, not like the smooth way it worked when his mother did it. Schultz

145

told him it was a sloppy job, showed it to the other boys as an example of how not to do it, and asked him to have his mother redo it.

It was Camelli who had come to his rescue. He had said, "Ira, let's be glad Rick's being independent." When it was put that way, Schultz couldn't really complain. He was supposed to respect effort. He had given in, but Ricky knew he hadn't liked it. Schultz wanted them identical, neat, and military.

"We've got to look like a troop, fellows."

Camelli thought it was what they learned, not what they looked like, that mattered. And look at Camelli today, wearing Levi's and a red quilted vest over his scout shirt.

Rick did not want to approach Camelli. He was uneasy about Dan's relationship with his mother. The only way he could think of to cope with his ambivalence was to avoid the cause of it. So he walked down to the stream and away from camp.

It was not a very large or fast stream. It was stony along the bank here, but widened out into a marsh not much farther along. In the eddies, beds of reeds and debris had formed a spongy, dark soil.

Ricky liked snakes and salamanders and frogs and turtles. He thought he would go look among the reeds. A lot of people, Ricky knew, thought snakes and amphibians were slimy. It was a silly prejudice. He had heard that there were not even any poisonous snakes in Illinois except the massasauga rattler. And it was supposed to be unable to inject much venom. In a way, Ricky was sorry about this. He would have liked a small element of risk.

He got down on all fours at the edge of the reed bed. The ground was resilient and springy, and only a little moist, not saturated enough to come up over the rubberized bottoms of his boots. He did not mind getting his hands muddy. He tried to keep his knees up, knowing that Schultz would not be pleased if he got them wet.

Rick was an Indian, creeping up on a herd of buffalo. No, he was a Ninja, a Japanese guerrilla, creeping up on a band of outlaws. That was better. He reached for the *shruken,* the flat steel throwing star, in his pocket, then realized he did not have it with him. The scouts were not allowed to bring weapons.

Deprived of his daydream, and rudely flashed back to reality, Rick tried to recapture the feeling of excitement. He fell to his knees and lunged through a clump of reeds.

He came face-to-face with Garvey Fiske.

Garvey looked up, surprised, from what he was doing. Ricky looked down at it. Garvey was kneeling in the springy grass, holding a frog in his left hand. The small green body tried to slip out of his grip. The legs, sticking out of the edge of Garvey's fist, kicked at the air.

"Hey!" Ricky said. "What are you doing?"

"Be quiet. They'll hear us."

Ricky had caught sight of the cigarette lighter in Garvey's right hand.

"Let that frog go!"

Garvey had jammed a firecracker in the frog's mouth. He jumped back as Ricky leaped at him, and flicked the lighter in his hand. The fuse caught.

"Stay back. It's gonna blow."

Garvey tossed the frog a few feet away. Ricky wanted to run for it, but he was afraid of the thing going off in his hand. He took half a step, but it was too late. The firecracker exploded with a sharp crack.

A blob of something brown and slimy struck Ricky's arm. He ignored it and walked forward. The frog lay in the mud, its head blown apart, its legs still kicking, twitching, in a disjointed rhythm.

"Wow!" said Garvey.

Ricky said, "That's disgusting." He paused a second. "And you're disgusting."

"You some kind of bleeding heart?"

"What'd you want to do a thing like that for?"

"It's only a frog!"

"He wasn't hurting you any."

"Jeez, you're no fun."

"That's right. I don't think this is any fun. I think you're sick."

"What's sick is getting all shitass about a goddamn frog!"

Ricky turned and walked away.

"Hey! You going to tell?"

"No." Ricky glanced up at the camp. Nobody seemed to have heard the firecracker. It had been deafening to him, but maybe the grasses muffled it. "If you want anything to do with me, though, you better start acting like a human being."

"Then I *don't* want anything to do with you."

Ricky turned away again. Without looking back, he said, "Fine." But he felt ill. As he walked up to the camp, the image of the broken frog stayed in his mind.

Samantha had gone to the basement to get the laundry folded before she had to start her shower. She hurried down the stairs. Three steps from the bottom, her foot went out from under her. She gasped and clutched at the railing. Sitting down hard on the stairs, she saw a pencil roll down the last step and drop onto the concrete floor with a click.

Her wrist hurt where she had twisted it grabbing the

railing. But the accident could have been much worse. If she had broken an ankle, it would have been difficult for her to climb back up the stairs for help.

If *she* had broken her ankle, with the kids away for two days—

She heard the phone ringing upstairs.

"You may have wine," Henry Ax said, magnanimously. "I'm strictly a beer man, and I don't care who knows it."

"Seems like the kind of thing you couldn't hide for long. I'm delighted that you're comfortable in your uncouthness. Personally, I'm very couth, but I'm going to have beer because it tastes good."

"That's right. Don't let the snobs wear you down."

Samantha flexed her sore wrist. "I've had such a day—and don't ask. Now, if I wanted to forgo the beer, what do they have? Coke. People drink Coke with pizza. Is that because the full-bodied richness brings out its flavor, do you think? Or is Coke just for sausage pizza?"

"You bet it is," Ax said. "With vegetable pizza, you drink white soda pop, like Fresca, maybe, or 7-Up."

"No, I think they're for anchovy pizza. The light, lemony, flinty flavor goes with fish. And its amusing presumption and naiveté counters the saltiness nicely."

"I've needed these lessons in proper service. What about orange soda?"

"Lord, no! Orange soda doesn't go with pizza at all. It goes with—it goes with Twinkies!"

"You're right. I wasn't thinking."

"No, I was wrong. Really, orange soda goes with hot dogs."

"Only if you leave off the mustard."

Their pizza came. They'd ordered green peppers and extra

cheese, but it came with pepperoni and onions. They laughed and told the waitress that they'd really meant to order pepperoni and onions.

Thirteen

For a while after dinner, the boys ran around in the woods shining flashlights at each other.

Ricky crept through the dark, tracking people without a flashlight. It was more exciting and more like a Ninja to follow people, using their own flashlights as beacons, than to shine one himself. Also, he could see better without the flashlight, because his eyes had become used to the dark. With a flashlight, you saw only what you caught in the beam.

There were other reasons why he wanted to be alone in the dark. He didn't want Garvey or Tad to find him! Tad could play with the other ten-year-olds. Ricky knew that he would play with Tad at home but not in public. It was one of the things you had to do to be one of the crowd. Like not crying in public and not wearing snow pants or rain hats if you could possibly help it. It was one of the things you had to do to be manly. He was pretty sure Tad understood.

Garvey was another matter. He tried not even to think about Garvey. When he did, he realized that he had always seen cruelty in Garvey, an enjoyment of teasing, but he had put it out of his mind. People who lived near you, if they were your age and not absolutely repellent, you got along with.

Not any more, though. This time he was repelled.

Ricky got tired of running. Somehow tonight he could not really believe he was a Ninja. He sat down in the middle of a trio of small oaks where he wasn't likely to be found, and quietly allowed himself to become aware that he wasn't happy.

For a moment he wished his father were here. But he realized that wouldn't work. His father had never liked camping out. Even at a picnic, he resented ants and mosquitoes, and when it came right down to it, he had not liked the picnics much, either. As long as he was being honest with himself, Ricky admitted that his father was not much fun.

His mother was more fun, more flexible, more ready to play, more willing to accept discomfort if there was something interesting to do.

But a boy couldn't take his mother to camp-outs. The scouts did not permit mothers on camp-outs. He thought this was unreasonable, but there were a great many unreasonable rules in the world. And besides, he couldn't expect to take his mother around with him in general. It wouldn't be considered tough or masculine. He needed an adult male friend. He had been sort of friendly with Mr. Camelli, until a couple of months before, when Camelli decided to take his mother out. Now he wasn't so sure. Most of the time now, it seemed he didn't have any friends at all.

While he was thinking, the bell rang for the boys who were taking merit badge exams to come to the camp.

Ricky had completed a unit of leatherwork. In his tent he had a belt and a pair of slippers that he had made for his mother. He went to collect them.

Three minutes later, he was ducking into a scoutmaster's tent.

"Samantha—this is going to sound funny, but what do you know about Garvey Fiske?"

"What do I *know?* Henry, you make it sound like he was a member of the Mafia."

"I'm asking for your safety—"

"Safety?"

"I just want to find out. Let's put it that way."

"All right. But I want you to tell me what you're thinking. Garvey is in Ricky's class at school. Same age. In the scouts with him. He's in a different room this year, but last year they had the same advisor. His parents are the Montgomery Fiskes. They have money. You never see his mother around. I mean *never*. But his father is a scoutmaster. Garvey is a fairly able student, according to Ricky, but talks back to teachers. What else can I tell you?"

"Do you like him?"

"Like him? He's a child. Well, I like kids if my kids like them. If they help my children have fun. Does that sound self-centered?"

"It sounds child-centered. Every boy needs a mother like that."

"I can't stand too many compliments in one night. I'll get tipsy."

"But do you *like* him?"

"Um—Garvey was this kind of child when he was younger: There are slides on the preschool playground. All us mothers had made a firm rule that only one child should get on the little platform at the top of the slide at one time. So they wouldn't be pushing at each other up there, see, and push somebody off."

"Yes."

"But that meant there was always quite a line of kids on the ladder part waiting to get to the top. Garvey was the kind of child who would intentionally step back a step, onto the fingers of the child behind him."

"Oh."

They looked into each other's eyes a moment. Samantha said, "Okay. I'm not proud. I'll ask straight out—why do you want to know about Garvey?"

153

"I'm probably making a mountain out of a—the problem is, I've let a series of coincidences get to me. Coincidences happen all the time in life, don't they?"

"Now you really *are* making me frightened."

He was shocked. "I am? I don't want to. I just said it's probably foolishness on my part. Male menopause."

She laughed. "You're too young for male menopause. I think you're even too young for midlife crisis."

She toyed with a fork, making parallel tracks on the table-cloth. "I don't believe an experienced policeman notices something strange and it's just a series of coincidences. Now, if you were to think of an old friend and right then he telephones, that I believe in. But this is police work you're talking about. Right?"

"Very right."

"Criminal?"

He hesitated. "Yes."

"What?"

"Murder."

"I was right. I am frightened."

"I didn't mean to do this to you."

"I am not a Fig Newton. If cut, I heal, and I have a right to have my own fears. Tell me what it's all about."

Ax thought, *In for a penny in for a pound.* Maybe he couldn't carry this all by himself any more.

"A couple of months ago, a man in town who liked to do his own work around the house decided to clean out his gutters and downspouts. The day was a bit windy, but not too bad. He did the windy side of the house, the north, first, by the way."

"Uh-huh."

"Then he did the east side. Then he started on the south, which was the least windy, you see. We've reconstructed that far because a neighbor to the north saw him start and saw him

154

move to the east. But on the south side—and only the south side—there are a lot of trees between him and his nearest neighbor. At his house no one was home. Wife at aerobics, sister-in-law working at the bank. Brother downtown. So nobody saw what happened."

"I'm getting uneasy already."

"Well, when he was found, he was lying in a tulip bed on the south side of the house with his neck broken." Ax leaned his arms on the table. "Now at first, we didn't think much of it. A boy had found the body, I thought, from what the neighbor to the south said, and I thought the boy had gone to the neighbor's house to report it. We couldn't locate the boy later, but that happens. People don't want to get involved. When I got curious because of Dubcjek, I went back to talk with the neighbor. It turns out that he had gone out to his trash cans. He noticed the boy in Linkletter's yard, looking at the body. As soon as the boy saw him, he came over and asked him to call the police."

"That seems proper."

"Yes, but it could also mean that the boy did not intend to report it until he was seen and knew he had to act in a normal way."

"He might have been so scared that he didn't know what to do until the adult appeared."

"Maybe."

"What did the boy look like?"

"He looked about thirteen, with sandy hair and freckles. Wearing a boy scout uniform."

"Oh."

"All the people who could possibly have benefited from Linkletter's death were absolutely, provably elsewhere."

After a pause, Samantha said, "Is that it? I see that it's very much like Jim's accident, and the boy sounds like—"

"Like Garvey. But that's not all."

"Go on."

"You and I know Garvey came around the Dubcjek side of your house at the very time Dubcjek was calling for help. Why didn't he see him? Or hear him? Why didn't he call for help?"

"I can't believe—maybe he was scared."

"Garvey?"

"Well—"

Samantha picked up the fork again, looked at it, and put it down. She moved the spoon and then put it back.

"And that isn't all," Henry Ax said.

"Please go on."

"You remember the death of a man on the C&NW track a week ago?"

"Yes. Clarendon Briggs. He was on the library board when I was. He kept wanting more books on golf. But he didn't fall from a ladder."

"No, he fell in front of a train. It was the morning train that some of the high school kids take to New Trier. So there was a big, mixed crowd. After the accident, a lot of the people waiting for the train left the scene to go to work some other way. The point is, it was later that evening before I talked to most of them. I had them try to remember who else was on that platform. Two adults remembered a boy who looked a little too young for high school. Then I got hold of some of the high school kids and they said there was a younger kid there. At that age, they don't pay much attention to younger kids. Most of them didn't know who he was—"

"Go on."

"But one of them thought his name might be Garvey Fiske."

★ ★ ★ ★ ★

Ricky Lawton lay in his sleeping bag. Near him, Tony Camelli slept. Ricky was worried. He did not understand what was happening to him, and what made it worse was that he couldn't be sure anything was happening. He felt, without being able to prove it, that he couldn't remember parts of the evening.

It was harder than he would have thought, trying to remember whether parts of time were forgotten.

He remembered the campfire and the sing-along very clearly. The scoutmasters had told stories. Ira Schultz had talked about his uncle, who lived on a Wisconsin farm as a child, with no indoor plumbing or running water, and the only water from a hand pump that froze sometimes in winter. Schultz had been interesting for a while, but he had gone on too long. Lee Grey told some of his experiences in Vietnam. He told them how to hide in a jungle, how to disappear into underbrush without making sounds, how to look like a rock or the shadow of a tree instead of a man. He had held everybody's attention and had the sense to quit while he was ahead. Monty Fiske had told a ghost story. He admitted frankly that he had not made it up himself. It was about two men who were boating down a river and stopped for the night in a large marsh. In the dark, strange humming sounds came out of the sky, and when they looked around themselves in the morning light, they found depressions in the earth, like something made by the suckers of a giant octopus. When night fell that evening, the humming sounds were closer than before—

Ricky had felt that mysterious force, reaching for him. Peter Winterthur had shrieked once, during the story, and most of the boys moved closer to the fire.

Dan Camelli, to lighten the mood, had told four short,

157

outrageous Paul Bunyan stories, and everybody had laughed. Then they had gone to bed. He had snuggled into his sleeping bag, taking his shoes in the bag with him, as the scoutmasters had taught them to do, so the shoes wouldn't be cold and damp in the morning.

If he could remember that part of the evening, how come there was a gap earlier? He remembered perfectly well running about in the woods; he remembered ducking other people's flashlight beams. After that, he had gone to camp to make his report. He was quite sure he had done it and earned the merit badge. He had the leather work, after all, to prove it.

Sometimes when his mother forgot something she considered obvious, she said it was old age creeping up on her. But he didn't think she believed that. And if it wasn't true for her, it certainly wasn't true for him. Why else did people forget things? Drink. He knew about that, but the scouts definitely did not serve booze at their camp-outs, so that wasn't it, either.

He simply did not remember how he got from the woods to the campfire. It was as if his brain had clicked off for a little while, the time he was making his merit badge report, and then clicked back on. He had no way of guessing how long.

Well, he certainly was not going to ask people what he had been doing between merit badge and campfire. They'd think he was crazy.

Was he crazy?

He didn't feel crazy, that was for sure.

Then a formulation occurred to him. It was a phrase he had heard several times from his grandmother—his mother's mother. "I'm out of my mind with anxiety." Occasionally the same idea came in the form, "I'm so worried I can't remember where I'm going."

Ricky was not as fond of his grandmother as he thought he ought to be. She reacted to things only as they affected her. If you made noise at her house, she never asked whether you were having fun. She'd say, "Are you trying to upset me?" If she telephoned and heard that Ricky or Tad was sick, she'd say, "Oh, dear. Now I'll be up all night worrying." She'd call every day to find out whether they were better. This should have implied concern, but it didn't to Ricky. If he talked with her, she would say, "Now tell me you're better. You don't want me to worry." And Rick always wondered if this meant that he was supposed to lie. After a while, they developed a rule in their house: If you were sick, you did not tell grandmother.

But her theory that worry could block mental capacity might be true. And it fitted in with another thing she said. She often told Samantha, in the children's hearing, that divorce "would be terrible for the children."

His mother always got very expressionless when this happened. But one thing his grandmother said made some sense right now: "This is going to cause them psychological stress."

He had been worrying about the divorce, hadn't he? No doubt about it.

He didn't want his parents to get a divorce. He wanted everything to be the way he remembered it at age seven or so. And it wasn't. So he was undergoing worry and psychological stress.

He said it aloud, to see whether it sounded reasonable.

"I have had a memory lapse due to worry and psychological stress."

It sounded wonderful. Perfectly reasonable and very scientific. It had a fine, technical ring to it.

He accepted this and drifted slowly into a sleepy, less troubled state. Thoughts of the day merged gradually into a dream where suckers came into the camp and sucked his brain dry of the juices of life.

★ ★ ★ ★ ★

Alone in his tent, the man looked out through a triangular opening at the stars. He was mildly, cautiously, satisfied with Ricky. Soon, Ricky would be ready to use. He was resigned to the idea that it was too dangerous to go on using Garvey. Briggs was the last. It was unlikely but possible that some dim-witted policeman would stumble on Garvey if he was present too often at accident scenes. Just as Garvey had replaced last year's boy, so Garvey was now to be replaced.

Unfortunately, the Lawton boy needed to be handled differently from Garvey. He would take a great deal more time and attention.

Garvey's great value lay in the fact that he had almost no moral sense. Therefore it was not necessary to make up complicated fact situations for Garvey. Ricky was quite different. He was a mass of foolish scruples.

It would be all right. He would make it work. Thank goodness this had happened after he had a lot of experience. Because Ricky would have to be handled very, very carefully.

It was nearly midnight when Henry Ax walked Samantha to her door. At Samantha's request they had dropped the subject of Garvey. She wanted to think about it.

"What was that?"

"Something in the bushes," Ax said.

"A cat, I suppose."

"Big for a cat."

She put the key in the lock. A breeze stroked her bare arms.

"Lock up well," Ax said.

"I will."

"Look, Samantha. Would you like me to come in?"

Suddenly, shockingly, she wanted to ask him in. Take him

in. Keep him through the night. *The children are out and it's lonely in this squirrel-cage house.*

"No. But thanks."

"Call me if you need me."

The campsite was silent, except for the breeze. A sliver of moon, a nail paring, hung just above the rushes of the marsh. There was enough light to pick out the ridge of tents on the hill.

The same late breeze that had stirred on Samantha's skin forty miles away troubled the rushes. They leaned over in obedient waves, like water on a shallow pond.

A flap opened on the tent of one of the scoutmasters. The small, pale face of Peter Winterthur peered out, scanning the campsite. It was light enough, between the hard light of stars and the luminous fragment of moon, so that he could see the slope. No one was moving.

A voice from inside the tent whispered, "You won't tell anybody. You know what they'd do to you."

The boy shook his head. His shirt was askew, and he straightened it. He looked out again, making sure, then slipped sideways, letting the dark tent flap fall closed behind him.

In the thin moonlight, tears shone silver on his cheeks. Next to the glistening tear tracks, his skin was dull.

Putting his feet down flat, without scuffling, he made his way across the open center of the clearing to his own tent. Once he started, he moved rapidly, but without a sound.

He edged into his own tent, hardly dislodging the flap. It made only a faint swish of sound, lost in the sigh of the breeze. The boy eased into his sleeping bag as sinuously as a snake, leaving all his clothes on, not even removing his shoes until he was all the way inside, when he pushed each off with the other foot.

There was no sound from his tentmate except deep, regular breathing.

Only when he was fully settled, with no one to see and no one to hear, did Peter make a sound. Lying still in the sleeping bag, he gulped, a single sob.

Fourteen

The new queen studied her domain. There was a duty she had left undone. There was another queen in the hive.

She walked directly up the face of the brood comb. The handmaidens scampered after her, trying to surround her, face her, and keep her guarded, but she moved so fast they could only trail after in a ragged body. The queen, led by her sense of smell, plunged into the darkest and most protected part of the hive, the center of the most central brood combs.

Here the three daughters of the old queen, chosen by the nurses to be queens, lay in their cradles of wax. They were of three different ages. The youngest had just been sealed in her cell, well supplied with bee bread, to make the change from larva to queen.

The queen stood on the cell, peering at the fresh seal. Then she forced her jaws into the seal and with a great wrench, tore it from the wax around it.

Within was a pale, soft, formless creature, the youngest queen. While the handmaidens watched in silence, the queen dipped her head into the cell, and pulled it out. With a single bite, the queen cut her in two.

The pieces fell writhing to the hive floor, far below.

As if eager to be done with this butchery, the queen attacked the second queen cell more quickly. She bit through the guarding cap and pulled the developing queen from the protecting wax cradle. This one was older and larger, begin-

163

ning her metamorphosis, but still soft and pale. The queen severed her in two bites.

At the third cell that held the oldest child, the queen paused. Perhaps she sensed this cradle held one more nearly a true queen. Using her jaws like scissors, she uncapped the cell. When she tore away the cover, she revealed a young queen, wrapped in a white silken cocoon. The reigning queen took hold of the cocoon and, wrenching it from side to side, worked it out of the cell. It fell to the floor of the hive.

She rushed down the comb, trailed at a distance by hand-maidens who hung back, fearful.

On the floor of the hive she approached her rival. The young queen was not yet fully formed, but inside the silk shroud there was the distinctive shape of a bee. The queen took a grip on the silk, tearing at it, now unwinding it, now impatiently cutting through the skeins.

At last, lying on the floor of the hive was a pale naked thing, formed like a bee, but white. Only her eyes were black. Her legs and feelers, not yet adult, were soft and moistly folded across her body, fragile and transparent, and her wings were crumpled across her back and thin as a film of water. A ghost bee. She unfolded her feelers, searching for meaning in what was happening.

This sign of life was a goad to the queen. She lunged at the helpless princess. In one bite, she severed the waist. In another bite, she cut through the neck.

The slender legs unbent and moved, but the work was done.

Without a backward glance, the queen turned away from her executioner's work and walked up the face of the comb toward the brood cells.

Architects had already arrived to inspect the queen cells. After a moment's study, they went to work, cutting the extra-large wax cells into manageable pieces. They would chew it down to soften it. By tomorrow the wax would be new cells for brood and honey.

Samantha was happy with her quiet Saturday at home. Henry had said she was on a treadmill lately, and he was absolutely right. She'd had no time to sit and think. It wasn't that she wanted to sit and think in order to solve anything, particularly. It was just that an occasional quiet moment felt good. It must be like dreaming—fallow moments must give the mind a chance to sift out emotional husks and chaff.

Right now Tad and Ricky would be cleaning up after breakfast at the camp. They'd be about ready to hike. She smiled. Then she thought that to be able to smile to yourself all alone in a room because you'd thought of your children was a great blessing indeed.

She wondered how they would get along after the divorce. She believed that Frederick, with his immense pride and his desire to strike back at anyone who had hurt him, would sell the house and give her as little money for the boys as possible. Would her salary be enough?

We'll get along.

I certainly won't run home to mother.

Talk about sifting out pieces of chaff! Her mother was unresolved business, undigested trouble. It was a lump that never changed. She kept going back to it, turning it over, looking to see whether it had developed any cracks anywhere that would allow it to be broken down into more digestible pieces. The problem was always resistant.

When Henry had mentioned having someone to talk with, her mind had flashed with regret to her mother. Some people must actually *talk* with their mothers, share hopes, share doubts. She was glad Henry hadn't asked her about her

165

family, because she wouldn't have wanted to explain and would have had to find a way to duck the question. It was better to keep that particular undigested lump out of the daylight.

Her mother was psychotic.

Her mother had had her first psychotic episode when Samantha was four. Samantha had no memory of it. It had happened, she knew, just after her younger sister had been born, and the doctor had said it was a postpartum depression, which would go away. When it had lingered, the doctor had said she was neurasthenic.

Possibly he was old-fashioned, or possibly he was not so old-fashioned as kind. He may not have wanted to label her crazy. At any rate, "neurasthenic" made Samantha think of the languid heroines of nineteenth-century fiction, who took pride in being extremely sensitive.

Her mother apparently recovered, although, looking back at it, Samantha realized that her mother had never been completely normal. There were extreme fears—paralyzing fear of automobile accidents, panic at losing her keys, terror of trying anything new. She would not move a picture from one wall to another.

When the second real psychotic episode had hit, Samantha had been eleven and the terms had changed. Neurasthenia was now hopelessly outdated. Her mother was having a nervous breakdown. That, too, was a kind name for it. It sounded like the glamorous complaints Hollywood actresses talked of when they didn't want to do a certain picture.

The trouble was that at home it was not glamorous. And what made it worse was that the family was told nothing. They were not told how to deal with it, how to react to irrational statements, or whether their behavior would make it worse or better. Samantha's sister believed most of her life that she had caused it. It was her fault because it had started just after her birth. Not one of the psychiatrists that treated her mother ever told the girl differently.

With no information on how to handle his wife, Samantha's father, who was a kindly man, decided that the family should simply do anything her mother asked, carry on by themselves, and let her mother do anything she wanted. He called this "keeping an even keel."

It was agonizing for Samantha because she never knew when she walked in the door after school whether her mother would be in a frenzied high or a depressed low.

And yet at the same time, Samantha had absorbed the idea that this *was* a true illness, and not her mother's fault. To make demands on her, even to resent her behavior, was like kicking a man on crutches.

Samantha kept thinking that if she found just the right combination of words, she could break through to her mother. It would have been easier not to hope. The frustration of trying to reason with her mother was enormous, and Samantha got used to going to bed with headaches, eating with indigestion.

But in later years, she thought that she had been right to make the effort. If she had simply given her mother superficial answers and babied her, never uttered an honest word, there would have been no relationship at all.

She had been right to try. When she finally decided it was hopeless, she could console herself she had not given up without a fight.

So Samantha went to school and came home, and didn't date, and didn't bring friends home. She studied and did well and won a scholarship to college.

And freedom.

When Samantha married Frederick in her last year in college, a year after her father's death, her mother came to the wedding. But she was as sure as ever that nothing could possibly work out. She had been too nervous to give the wedding for her daughter herself, as etiquette demanded. And Samantha had not wanted her to. It would have been staggeringly difficult to arrange anything at all in the face of her mother's incessant anxiety attacks.

Frederick's mother, Anne, loved to plan parties. Samantha told the Lawtons that her mother was not well, and that was that.

Samantha and her mother now had a cautious relationship. Whenever that old impulse to reach her mother led her to blurt out a piece of information, she regretted it. Sooner or later, it would return as a peg on which to hang cobwebs and gravecloths.

Samantha sighed. Thinking about her mother provided no solutions. There were only implications.

Rule one: Be rational, for the boys.

Rule two: *Talk* with the boys.

Rule three: Keep an even keel.

She went out to the kitchen and got a croissant and a cup of coffee. This morning she had brewed coffee, the first time in months that she had done that for herself, with no company coming. Possibly she was recovering.

The phone rang.

I hope it's not Frederick.

"Hello?"

"Samantha? I've been worried about you."

"Hello, Mom."

"Why haven't you called? I thought something was wrong."

"No. Everything's fine."

"How are the boys? Are they very upset?"

Damn it; people have divorces without disaster. "No. They're as happy as clams at high tide. In fact, they're on a camp-out this weekend they've really been looking forward to."

Uh-oh. Big mistake, and the words just out of my mouth.

"A camp-out? You mean *overnight?*"

"Two nights," Samantha said, grudgingly.

"In the cold?"

"It's the middle of June. It was sixty-eight here last night."

"Well, I still have the furnace on. And anyway, the ground can be very damp."

"They have sleeping bags and ground cloths and tents. The scoutmasters teach them how to keep warm. It gives the boys a sense of self-sufficiency. Listen, Mom, they get *enjoyment* out of this. Let them have some happiness."

"I'm sure I'd be the last person to deny them any happiness. Life is so short and there are so many terrible things that can happen to people. Is it safe where they are?"

"It's a regular state campground."

"Is there a river?"

Lie. Lie. I can't.

"A little stream."

"People have been known to drown in bathwater. You remember Mrs. Cantrip and her water lily pool. How do you know they'll be careful?"

"You know, Mom, I don't think the boys really *want* to drown."

"That's not funny."

"I didn't mean it to be funny. The boys are very reasonable people—"

"They're just children. What if they wander in the night? What if they started sleepwalking?"

169

"It would be the first time. Mom, don't try to worry me—"

"Are they due back Sunday?"

"Yes."

"Well, I want you to call me the minute they get home. You let me know they're all right. I'm going to be terribly worried about this until I hear."

Monty Fiske had worked it out so that he didn't have to hike the ten miles. They always needed someone to drive a car to the halfway point with refreshments. The halfway point was also where they left the boys who couldn't go any farther, and they were planning to let all the cub scouts stop there. So he had volunteered to drive the station wagon to the Miller's Creek Junction.

There was no problem getting the job. Ira Schultz was the gung-ho scout type who thought there was nothing finer than to march at the head of a long line of troops. Lee Grey actually liked the muscular activity, the feel of stretching himself. Although in fact he never seemed to stretch himself. Lee Grey, the man most likely to walk up Mount Everest without once breathing hard! He was the sort of man Monty most despised—the kind to whom everything came easily.

Nothing had ever come easy to Monty. He worked hard. And got little enough gratitude, too.

He and Dan Camelli packed the large cans of apple juice in the car. Camelli was another he didn't like. Everybody else loved Camelli. Camelli helped out. Lent a hand. Carried his own weight. He camped to be with his son and to help the scouts. Monty thought that nobody could be that sincere unless he was stupid.

Dan said, "Want me to get one of the big bags of trail mix, too?"

"Hey, that's a good idea."

"They won't be having lunch until Black's Forge."

"Yeah. Great!"

He slammed the tailgate of the station wagon. Camelli could toss the bag of dried fruits and nuts on the front seat.

When Dan came back with the bag, Monty said, "Some kid gets sick on the hike I'll have to bring him back to camp. If that happens, I'll leave the food at Miller's Creek Junction and go back for the leftovers later."

"Good," said Dan, and he slammed the front door.

Dan watched the car bump slowly out of the campground.

You're going to get to the junction in fifteen minutes, Dan thought, *and then just wait. What do you come on these campouts for?*

Fifteen

Ira Schultz formed up the scouts on the slope in front of the tents.

"Shoes tied?"

"Yes, sir!" they shouted. They knew he liked shouted responses.

"Ready?"

"Ready!"

A dappling of eager faces on a green field. The awards and belt buckles and polished boots and young eyes glinted in the sun. The uniforms were tan, but the blue-and-white ties and red and blue and gold merit badges were bright confetti against the shirts.

"Well, this is only ten miles, so everybody should be able to make it. You're a good group, and I'm proud of you all." Peter, tucked in the center of the group, prayed not to fail. "We'll have drinks at the junction and be at the forge for lunch. Ready?" he asked, louder than before.

"Ready!" they all screamed.

"Let's hike!"

The boys had been back home less than an hour before Samantha knew there was something wrong with Ricky.

Tad had won first prize in the knot-tying contest in his age group and was full of the excitement of victory. Ricky was apathetic.

It wasn't like Ricky to be tired after a weekend. Tad often

was. Ricky was usually recharged. Also, he did not quite have the aura of a tired child. He went out in back during the afternoon and practiced his tae kwon do moves, but he did it mechanically, with no enthusiasm.

It was puzzling.

"Want to see a timber hitch lashing?" Tad asked her.

"Listen, who was it who helped you learn these knots?"

"Sure. I know. But would you like to *see* one?"

She watched Ricky covertly. It was as if this was not her boy, or as if a part of him was missing. But of course that was ridiculous. Studying him, she decided that he had a guarded quality. He was protecting something in his mind.

She concluded that a disturbing event had happened at camp. Having got that far, she had two choices: ask and don't ask.

Samantha believed that the less you ask a child the more you are told. It took only a few probing questions for a child to feel his privacy was being violated, and after that he would close up. There was no response more impenetrable than, "Gee, I don't know."

Her technique was to be available. But it didn't work today. At their late lunch, Ricky ate his tuna fish sandwich and stared at the backyard while Tad talked. During dinner he stared at his plate, then the wall, then the clock.

It weighed on Samantha, and it was even a little frightening.

"Ricky? How was the forest preserve? Starting to get green?"

Boy, that was silly. We've had leaves for a month.

"Oh, sure. I guess so."

"Anybody fall in the river or get hurt?"

"Nope."

"Amazing." She forced a small laugh.

173

"Well, Peter Winterthur burned himself on a hot dog stick, but it wasn't bad."

All right. Isn't honesty my policy with the kids?

"Ricky, I'm just beating about the bush. Let me be frank, here. I've noticed that you're sort of subdued. I was wondering whether anything bad happened."

Ricky had been thinking all day about his blackout. He had an uneasy feeling that it had happened once before this weekend, sometime in the recent past, and that he had forgotten it or not understood what it was. It scared him, and he was not sure that the cause he had deduced was adequate explanation. He'd had a friend in third grade, who had since moved to Dayton, who had developed epilepsy. He'd had blackouts. As it happened, he was fine once he was put on drugs, but during the long process of diagnosis he had told Ricky about the blood tests, the X rays, the hospital, and the needles. Ricky wanted no part of it. He definitely did not want his mother to take him to the doctor. Especially since it was probably nothing. Also, he did not want to worry her. It had only happened once, or maybe twice. If it happened again, *then* he would think about telling her.

"No, nothing bad."

Samantha had tried to put Garvey out of her mind since she talked with Henry Ax, but she had not really succeeded. He was as hard to dislodge as a piece of dust under an eyelid.

"Um, Ricky. What do you think of Garvey?"

How did she know about that? Ricky wondered, shocked. The frog. His utter disgust. Maybe she didn't know, but sensed—he couldn't talk about it. It was still too painful. But he wanted to reassure his mother, too, unaware that he was about to mislead her, to divert her from the real menace.

"I'm never gonna play with Garvey again! I'm not going to see him any more! Ever!"

★ ★ ★ ★ ★

On Monday morning the man made an appointment with a doctor in a suburb five miles southwest of Rivercrest. He told the woman on the phone it was "not quite an emergency, but I'm new to the state of Illinois, and I was taking medication, and I can't refill the prescription here. So it's sort of—" he paused and laughed charmingly "—important, but I don't feel right to claim it's an emergency."

The office nurse was sympathetic and gave him an appointment for Wednesday morning.

Wednesday morning he was careful to reread the entry in the *Physicians' Desk Reference* for Elavil. Under Indications it said: "For the relief of symptoms of depression." Good.

He moved down to Contraindications. Elavil was contraindicated in people with known hypersensitivity to the drug. No problem.

Under Warnings he found useful material. Elavil could "impair mental and/or physical abilities required for the performance of hazardous tasks such as operating machinery or driving a motor vehicle." All right, so he would not be a commercial airline pilot, depressed by the seriousness of his responsibility. "In patients who use alcohol excessively, it should be borne in mind that the potentiation may increase the danger inherent in any suicide attempt or overdosage." That was all right, too. He would be a near-teetotaler. Not quite, because that would be less believable and might suggest a rigid personality. Lord only knew what would set off a doctor's warning bells.

"Use in pregnancy." Skip that.

He closed the book, reshelved it, lining it up with the others so that it did not look recently used, and left for the appointment.

175

★ ★ ★ ★ ★

In Downer's Grove, he parked three blocks from the doctor's office and walked. He had stopped on the way and noted two houses next door to each other, numbers 311 and 315 Hartley Avenue. That meant there was no 313.

The office nurse said, without apology, "The doctor is running a little late."

"That's just fine," he said. "I'm way behind in my paperwork and I brought my briefcase."

He smiled at her and she smiled back. He had used a dark hair coloring this morning, the kind that rinses out. And he had combed his hair back instead of to the side. But he didn't think she'd remember him anyway. She had the air of the professionally sympathetic, actually bored.

She handed him a sheet to fill out with personal data.

"Who recommended the doctor?" he read to her. "I'm embarrassed to say I found his name in the phone book." Which was true. "This place is on my way to work." Which it wasn't.

"It happens. He won't mind. He hardly even looks at these things. It's for billing."

"I'm self-employed," he said. "And I like to pay at the time of service."

"That's all right with us."

He knew it was. There was a sign on the desk, "Please pay at time of service." A great many doctors were doing this now, and it certainly would not be noticeable that he had paid cash.

He filled out the form with a false name—he had picked Eugene Patterson for no particular reason. His address was 313 Hartley Avenue. And he entered a plausible but fictitious Social Security number. He took care to vary it in every way from his own, but he knew the doctor's office would never use it, because he would make no Medicare claims and would have paid by cash when he left. For his next of kin, he entered his wife, Rosemary Patterson. He liked the name Rosemary, and he had never met one.

He had marked up scrap papers from his briefcase for fifty minutes when he was called into the examining room.

"Take everything off, Mr. Patterson, and put this on."

He ripped the paper gown getting into it. He was resigned to having every part of his body prodded—"Throat to asshole," he muttered—because he had no serious illnesses, and because when the doctor had satisfied himself of this, he would be more willing to prescribe what the man wanted. For a moment, he was afraid that all this trouble was for nothing, that the doctor would not give him the medication that he wanted. He might have some bias against Elavil, for example. Maybe one of his patients had reacted badly to it. Accident or suicide. Who could know? Or the doctor might think some newer drug was better. There was a limit to how much he could press the doctor for this particular drug before making him suspicious. If the doctor was stubborn, the only thing to do would be take the goddamn Mellaril or Valium prescription, save it in case he ever needed it, and go to another doctor for the Elavil.

He'd hate to take the time. And yet, the fact that he was going to such lengths satisfied him. It felt good to expend the time, study, and effort.

"Well, you're in generally good health, Mr. Patterson," said the doctor at the exam's conclusion. "Your blood pressure's a little higher than I'd really like, but it's not in the treatable range yet. Do you eat a lot of salt?"

"Well, I guess I do. But I suppose it's mainly habit. I could cut down."

Demonstrate how sensible you are. Not a crazy type.

"Good. That might help. What about exercise?"

"Um—some of the year I get a chance to walk to work. That's about a mile each way. This time of year, I'm just too busy. In fact, that's why I came in. We moved the store here last February from Oklahoma and I haven't seen a doctor—"

"So what is the trouble?"

"Nerves. I hate to admit it. I ought to be able to control these things—"

"Oh, well, Mr. Patterson, everybody is under stress at times."

Just what I hoped you'd say.

"It's only this particular time of year. I'm in rugs. Oriental, Scandinavian, Indian. Rugs, not carpets; you get me?"

"Yes, of course."

"They don't move as fast in the early summer. People are going away. Camps. Summer homes. Europe. It's not like fall when everybody at once decides to get their interiors looking good. So we do inventory in June and July. And, God, it's a bitch. And frankly, I don't like to admit it, but I get tense. I work maybe fifteen hours a day. And weekends. I get frazzled, and then I get depressed. That's the long and the short of it. My doctor in Oklahoma City prescribed Elavil. A hundred and fifty milligrams. I just ran out, and I find I can't get the prescription filled here just by showing them the bottle."

"That's right. You can't. Why Elavil?"

Oh-oh. He doesn't like it.

"Well, we tried something else first, but it didn't work so well. It made me drowsy."

Don't get too cute, here. Don't name one; it might be too similar to Elavil. Be vague.

"Which one was that?"

"I can't remember the name. It was a small white tablet. Anyway, we switched to Elavil, and it's been fine. What he usually did was give me a prescription for forty-five of them, just to get me through inventory. I don't need them the rest of the year."

He wants to give me something else. Push the button that gets him into a positive attitude. Make him the healer.

"I must admit, Doctor, that I'm embarrassed about using artificial assistance at all. You'd think I was some fool menopausal woman."

"Mr. Patterson, it's no disgrace to need help once in a while. We all do sometimes. Probably the Elavil gets you through a genuinely stressful period."

Whew.

The doctor pulled over his prescription pad.

"Do you drink, Mr. Patterson?"

"Only at rug-buyer conventions." He laughed. "I'm sort of a teetotaler around the house."

"Good. I don't want you to drink while you're taking these. It's important. It could be really dangerous."

"The conventions are all in the fall. I couldn't take time for one now, anyway."

"Here you are, Mr. Patterson. I'd like to see you in about six months to check that blood pressure."

"Fine, Doctor." He took the prescription with a casual gesture.

"And cut down on the salt."

He paid the office nurse in cash on his way out. He figured the cost of the visit was one one-thousandth of the fee he would earn for his work.

Samantha put aside her fears. She was absolutely determined to keep an even keel, not to fall into the sequence of irrational terrors that had plagued her mother. Worry looking for an object. She decided, through sheer mental force, that there was nothing wrong with Ricky but distaste for Garvey and nothing wrong with Garvey but a passive sadistic streak. This was bad enough, but not a cause for terror. She was glad that Ricky had decided not to play with him. Ricky was a kind person, a gentle person, and she was glad of it.

Tad, the artistic one, would start painting classes at summer school this week. Ricky was taking soccer and his regular tae kwon do course. Then Tad and Ricky would go to the scouts' summer camp in Wisconsin for a week. She planned to be utterly lazy. One week of absolutely nothing!

The man called his customer.

"Can you go away for ten days? Between now and when Meyers Campbell leaves for northern Michigan?"

"Um, actually, I was going to, anyway."

"Far?"

"The Tetons."

"That's fine. Make sure people out there see you every day. I would suggest, too, that *if* you're going to see Campbell at all between now and then, don't go to the house. Meet him at a restaurant or something."

"Yes. All right. You—uh—got the deposit?"

"I wouldn't be going ahead otherwise. Do you have any connection with a pharmaceutical company?"

"What? No."

"Work for a drugstore?"

"No."

"Come in contact with drugs being shipped, marketed, or disposed of? Shipping company? Post office? Medical group? Live with a nurse?"

"No. No contact at all. I'm a—"

"I don't have to know that. Do you take any drugs?"

"Aspirin. Synthroid."

"Have any leftover medication in your medicine cabinet?"

"No prescriptions except a few tablets of erythromycin."

"Any Elavil?"

"No. I don't even know what it is. Is it a tranquilizer?"

"Doesn't matter. Goodbye."

"Wait! Why do you go into all this?"

"It's why you're paying so much. I guarantee there's no way you'll ever be connected with this. Didn't my broker tell you?"

"Yes. I just—I wondered. It wasn't what I expected."

"The point is that nobody else would expect it, either."

The next Saturday the man picked Ricky up at eleven in the morning, ostensibly to go to Evanston to buy a dozen camp cookers for the scout camp, help carry them back, and pack them for the trip to Wisconsin.

Ricky rode happily down Green Bay Road. He was thinking about bees. This afternoon, after they got back with the camp cookers, the patrol would go and see the bees. Today they would be taught how to use the bee suit, and they'd be allowed to go right up to the hive and look inside.

Ricky daydreamed a bit about how it would feel to be a bee. The hive would seem very large, and the maze of combs would be like the ranks of buildings in downtown Chicago. But you'd be able to run up and down the sides of the buildings. And the rooms inside, the offices and hallways, would be filled with golden honey.

He felt the hum of the hive around him, and the scent of honey and flowers. It was warm with the gentle humidity of moisture evaporating from nectar, from richly scented cells of honey. And golden grains of pollen, packed in wax, stored for winter even in the warmth of early summer.

Ricky began to dream. Then the man next to him spoke, and the dream took over.

They drove down a street in Winnetka. The man stopped on the block behind Meyers Campbell's street. They talked a minute. Ricky got out with a small bottle in his pocket.

He was wearing his scout uniform.

Ricky crossed through the large side garden of a house. The garden was so large that it was unlikely that anyone in the house would notice him.

Ricky crossed the backyard through some flowering shrubs and came to a small stand of trees. From this he knew he was in back of the house he was seeking. He walked out of the trees and directly across the back lawn to the flagstone terrace at the back of the house.

He did not know that the person who lived here was out for the day with a lady friend, nor that the couple who took care of the house were in Ann Arbor, Michigan. He knew nothing at all, except his goal.

There was no furtiveness in his manner as he crossed the terrace to the French doors. He put both hands on the center, where the two doors came together, and pushed. The doors moved an inch. He pushed harder. They moved, stuck, then unstuck, and swung inward undamaged.

Ricky stepped through.

From the doorway he could see the front hall beyond the bright room in which he stood. He walked calmly into the front hall and turned to the stairs. Glancing neither right nor left, he climbed the stairs. At the top he looked for a bedroom that showed signs of use. There was one room with a light blue shirt on a chair, and a pair of discarded socks on the bed. He entered the room. On the side facing the street was a bathroom.

Ricky went directly to the medicine cabinet.

Without hurrying, he read all the labels. When he came to a small brown plastic bottle labeled Corgard he took it down and poured the contents into his hand. He counted them. There were thirty-eight. He made a small pile of them on the shelf.

Ricky took the other bottle out of his pocket. He poured all the tablets in it out on the counter. There were forty-five. He took thirty-eight of them and put them in the Corgard bottle. Then he swept the Corgard tablets and the remaining Elavil into his hand and poured them into the bottle he had brought with him. He put the Corgard bottle back into the medicine cabinet and the bottle he had brought into his pocket.

He closed the medicine cabinet.

Downstairs, he backed out of the French doors and pulled them together after him. They had outdoor handles of ornate brass. With a good tug, the doors shut firmly. He turned the handles to a closed position. He turned and walked away across the terrace.

They had picked three boys from the troop to look into the hive today, Garvey, Peter, and Ricky. Dan Camelli thought any more people walking back and forth might make the bees nervous.

"We don't want to get 'em riled up."

They had only one bee suit, so it was one boy at a time. Ricky suited up first. Mr. Swan was not here to give advice. Ira Schultz and Lee Grey had decided that Camelli knew enough about bees to supervise.

Camelli wore only a flannel shirt and Levi's and high boots. He went to the hive with Ricky and, when Ricky was in position, slowly lifted off the top. Checking to make sure there were no bees on the lid—"Don't squeeze a bee!"—he put it on the grass, picked up the smoker, and gave the hive a few puffs.

"That's enough to gentle them down, I think."

"Ready?" Ricky asked. Half his mind was on the bees, and he was excited to be able to look into their secret home. The other half of his mind was worried. He felt, but could not prove, that he had experienced another memory lapse this morning. He did not remember coming back from buying the camp cookers. He didn't remember anything about Winnetka. He felt as if he had missed Winnetka and wakened somewhere in Glencoe. It couldn't have been more than five minutes, though.

"Ready, Rick," Camelli said.

Rick forgot his worry and gazed into the hive.

He looked down into bank on bank of combs, with tiny golden bees swarming across the ranks and files of honey cells. Lush sections of filled honey cells bulged from the combs, and a scent of honey and flowers filled the air. Some of the cells were capped with convex waxen lids, pregnant with reserves for winter. Many were uncapped, filled with honey that was on the brink of oozing from the cell, but stayed miraculously on its lip.

"See the bees near the open cells there?" Camelli said. "They're all lined up and fanning air across the honey with their wings."

Ricky heard Peter say, "I don't want to do it."

Lee Grey asked him, "Why not?"

"I just don't *want* to!" Ricky could hear panic in Peter's tone.

"Oh, well, Kiri can do it, then," Grey said, exasperation in his voice. "He's next on the list."

Dan said, "I'm going to lift this honey super for a minute, Rick, so you can see the brood comb. There's a guard between them to keep the queen from coming up here to lay eggs in the honeycombs. In the wild, bees have honey and brood next to each other."

He lifted the honey super slowly and carefully. Ricky leaned forward, unaware that he was moving. His mouth opened with wonder.

The heart of the bee city lay open to him. He saw cells with tiny grubs, just hatched from the egg but still smaller than a grain of rice. He saw the capped cells where the young bees were making their final transition from baby to adult in the privacy of their wax-and-pollen cradle. He thought he saw, but couldn't be certain, the queen deep within the hive, surrounded by handmaidens, all facing her, all waiting to serve her.

He saw workers bristling with pollen, hurrying to deposit it and fly back to the summer world of fragrant flowers. He smelled the sweetness and the moist warmth.

Ricky did not hear Peter's or Dan's voice. His mind was among the bees. *This is what happened to me in the car,* he thought. *I was dreaming this, and I fell asleep.*

He wrenched his mind away from the bees, enough to feel relief.

I didn't have a real blackout. I fell asleep and dreamed I was a bee. So I don't have to tell Mom. Everything is perfectly all right.

Sunday evening, Dan took Samantha into Chicago for dinner. They walked from the station.

Samantha said, "Uh—Dan?"

"Oh-oh, serious tone of voice. What's the matter?"

"Just trying to be honest."

"Dear John stuff. Disaster. I knew it."

Samantha laughed. "No, I just wanted you to know I had a date last weekend."

"You mean while I was knocking myself out on ten-mile hikes and camp sing-alongs you were out frittering?"

"Once."

"Who with?"

"Henry Ax. He's the—"

"Police chief. Good heavens."

It was an extremely urban street. There was trash in the window wells of basement apartments. Gaily painted prostitutes lounged on the street corners as if window-shopping for the most presentable customers.

Taxis roared away from stoplights and braked to a sudden stop, shuddering, just short of bumping into the cars at the next stoplight. Pimps in pastel plumage sauntered by like kings.

"This makes me feel better," Samantha said.

"For God's sake, why?"

"I wonder—I think it's because everything's on the surface here."

"What are you talking about?"

"The evils are on the surface. You can *see* them."

"Samantha, you're being very obscure. Evils on the surface compared to where?"

"Rivercrest."

They settled into leather and wicker chairs in the open courtyard of the Acapulco Restaurant. The sky was purple above; street sounds were clear but distant. Dan ordered slushy margaritas and when the waitress had left, said, "What did you mean about Rivercrest?"

Samantha wished that she had not said anything. She didn't know why she had even made the comparison. Surely Rivercrest was as accessible to the eye as anyplace else. If anything, it was a little dull and stodgy.

"I guess I was thinking about what Henry said."

"What kind of things did Henry say?"

"You sound tense."

"I don't mean to. But if he's trying to impress you with his—his—the importance of the cases he handles—"

"I don't think that's it."

"He's in charge of a small, law-abiding suburb. With all the crime there is in urban centers, that sort of job is pretty much a cop-out."

"I imagine you're not making a pun," she said, rather grimly.

"Oh, great. I've made you angry."

"Look, Dan. It's not as if *you* teach at an inner-city school, either."

"Oh, I've copped out, then?"

"It was your word, not mine."

"Hold it. Hold it. Wait a minute. Let's both take a breath."

"All right."

"I don't want to make you angry. And you don't want to make me angry. I hope."

"Granted."

"So, all right. Let's assume that the suburbs need cops just like they need teachers. I shouldn't have suggested otherwise. Fair enough?"

"Fair enough."

"Now just exactly what scary stuff does Henry Ax imagine is going on?"

"Imagine?"

"I take that back, too. Just give me the facts."

Samantha told him.

Dan said, "I think he's overreacting. I'm a biology teacher, not a statistician, but there's one thing I know. The smaller the sample, the harder it is to know what a normal rate of anything is. He can't possibly be sure there are too many accidents in Rivercrest in a statistically significant way. You could have five fatal accidents one year and fifteen the next, and your percent change is huge, but the total number of cases isn't many."

"He's not saying just that the number is larger. He's saying there are peculiar similarities—"

"The similarity being that a boy of about thirteen was seen a couple of times. Not seen to *do* anything. Just seen. There are probably a hundred thirteen-year-old boys in Rivercrest. And boys go everywhere."

"And that these accidents happened to very, very careful people. I knew Jim. He was extremely methodical."

"When somebody gets killed, it's always his first fatal accident."

"Oh, but you're begging the question. It makes a difference whether it's a person who's already had a lot of careless accidents or whether he never has."

"All right. I admit to that, in theory. But I don't admit there's anything strange going on. People, even careful people, do have accidents."

"Dan, tell me something. Straight out, tell me what you think of Garvey Fiske."

"I think Garvey is a little shit."

Samantha's mouth fell open.

"You wanted it straight," Dan said. "I could have wrapped it up better than that. But that's my bottom line."

"Okay."

"Garvey is sly. He's cruel to small animals and small people. He sniggers at sexual allusions, and he's one of those kids who see double meanings in everything. They all do some of that at his age. I see it all the time in school. But most kids are interested, and nervous, and trying their wings. Garvey sniggers as if sex were another way to degrade people."

"Ricky told me last week he's never going to play with Garvey again."

"Good decision. You've had the problem of living close to him. Tony never liked him in the first place, and we live far enough away so it wasn't a concern."

"Henry thinks it was Garvey at those accidents."

"I'm not very clear on what Ax thinks Garvey did. Does he think the kid is going around murdering people for no particular reason?"

"Sadism is a reason."

"Look, I dislike Garvey. And it costs me some to say that. Kids should be helped, not hated. But even Garvey is not *that* sadistic. He's the kind of mild sadist we sometimes charmingly call a tease, and he's nasty. But he's no mass murderer."

"I thought, if they were accidents, real accidents, he might have just watched and—um—enjoyed it?"

"And not wanted to admit it afterward? I think that's a pretty good description of the little monster."

"How did Garvey get this way?"

"I don't know. I can't figure him out. Or his father."

"Monty? What's wrong with Monty?"

"I don't understand him. He comes to scouts. He's a real force in organizing camp-outs. But he doesn't seem to *like* any of the events. Doesn't like hiking, tries to get out of rock climbing. Complains about the cold in the winter and the flies and mosquitoes in the summer. Doesn't like swimming. About the only thing he has real enthusiasm for is crafts. Woodworking, knot tying, that sort of thing."

"He probably comes because he thinks it's good for Garvey."

"They hardly speak to each other."

"Well, you know how boys at that age don't want to be

seen with their parents. Tad and Ricky always walk ten steps ahead when we go to school."

"Yeah. Yeah, but it's not as true on the camp-outs. The boys usually want their fathers to see how great at fire-building and all that stuff they are. 'Look, Dad! I hiked twenty miles!' "

"And Garvey doesn't?"

"Garvey doesn't go anywhere *near* his father."

In Winnetka, Meyers Campbell was packing his car for the drive to the upper peninsula of Michigan. He wanted to get an early start in the morning. He was very selective about what he would take, because it all would have to fit in a backpack that he would carry several miles in to the camp on the little lake. He planned to have one of the guides pack a load of staples—flour, pancake mix, sugar, powdered juices, powdered milk, dried egg, canned ham, cooking oil, and dried fruits. To these foods, he would add the clear lake water, and with them he would eat the fish he planned to catch.

It was exactly the way to cleanse your mind, open your soul, and recharge your body.

He was whistling "Singin' in the Rain" as he packed, and when he realized this, he smiled. "Hope that doesn't mean bad weather."

His housekeeping couple had the keys and the run of the house. His lady friend was spending three weeks with her mother in Atlanta. Everything was taken care of.

"Better not forget these." He slipped his bottle of Corgard into his backpack and zipped it up.

Samantha put Garvey and even Henry out of her mind. She and Dan ordered tamales and the hottest salsa. Their mouths flamed; they drank Mexican beer and laughed and ate more hot sauce.

Sixteen

In any large organization, there is usually a small group of people who do the actual work. Monday evening, the men who did the real work for the scouts met at Izzy's Delicatessen in Rivercrest for dinner and a discussion of plans for the summer camp.

Izzy's Deli was known among Rivercresters as Delizzious. Delizzious was the functioning heart of Rivercrest if ever there was one. In January, when Izzy and his wife went to Sarasota for two weeks, downtown Rivercrest was not only cold but lonely.

Izzy's Delicatessen was not large, and it was three times as long as it was wide. Far in the back, the cook worked in splendid isolation, behind a wall with a three-by-three-foot opening. There was a counter just in front of the wall, where customers were served at bar stools. Several customers, like Karl Bartlett, who owned the ice cream parlor, Glade Morrison, a mailman, and several other people who worked in Rivercrest in the hardware store, the drugstore, or the town offices, always sat at the counter. Some of them thought it was faster than sitting in a booth. Morrison did it because he could leave a smaller tip. Craig Selleck, the youngest of the public safety officers, sat on the stools because he thought it was more masculine. To him, the booths were for women.

In the front of the store was the deli counter. Behind glass there was a ten-foot display of chopped liver, chicken salad, tuna salad, coleslaw, potato salad (mustard or German), half-sour and dill pickles, beef roasts, tongues, turkey breast rolls, nova, gefilte fish, cheeses, and tubs of black and green olives. At the end of the glass was an electric slicer going back and forth, back and forth, all day long, pausing only when a salami or turkey breast had to be substituted for roast beef or tongue or pastrami. On the wall was a board with hooks, from which descended thirty or forty salamis, hard sausages, and beef rolls, all hanging from the strings tied around their ends.

At the front end of the glass counter was the cash register, flanked by a display of Joyva halvah on one side, a sloping display of cigars—El Primo, Bolivar, and others—and in front of that a chest freezer filled with frozen blintzes.

In the store window, on sheets of shiny paper, there were displayed for the passerby glossier items than pickled tongue: plump bagels and bialys, cinnamon rolls sparkling with sugar, fat loaves of dark rye, and shiny butter-top white rolls.

Izzy's was made for the senses. It was noisy. The cash register had a juicy rumble when the drawer slid out and a solid thwack when it swallowed payment. From somewhere behind the rear wall came hisses and sizzles. Coffee bubbled; the orange-drink machine belched when the spigot was pushed. The meat slicer moved back and forth with a hungry sigh.

And the smells! Coffee and lime phosphate, hot pastrami and roast beef and frying potatoes. Mustard, relish, and onions. Sour pickles, and sweet Coke and chocolate ice cream. And each odor separately distinguishable, a symphony miraculously accessible to the human nose.

Waitresses filling orders yelled, "Beef for barbecue" or "Ham for Denver" at the front where the slicer worked, or, "Toast a bagel" at the cook in the back. All the customers heard all the other customers' orders.

Izzy's was made for rubbing elbows, anyway. It was predi-

192

cated on the assumption that, if you had wanted peace and privacy, you would have had the sense to stay home and make your own peanut butter and jelly. The double row of middle booths were so cheek-by-jowl that, if a lady in one booth smoked, a gentleman in the next booth inhaled Virginia Slims. Every conversation in the place was audible everywhere else—unless it was drowned out by the noise. Everyone talked. Women, men, schoolteachers, housepainters, teenagers with their own argot. Babies cried.

There was a "good" restaurant in Rivercrest. It had amply separated round tables, white tablecloths, subdued lighting (Delizzious went in for plenty of fluorescent), cloth napkins, quiet waiters, and paté, fresh salmon, and spinach salad. It dozed under a giant oak a block away from Izzy's, which put it outside the center of town. It was well patronized, in a quiet way. But it was not the heart of Rivercrest.

The four scoutmasters had chosen Izzy's as a place for a working dinner, without even considering any other restaurant. You could go there in whatever you happened to be wearing. You could shout for more coffee. And if your conversation got loud, well, everybody in Izzy's might hear it, but in the general noise nobody would care.

Dan Camelli arrived first and picked a booth on the side, in back near the coffee machine.

Ira Schultz came in next, hunching his way through the door, swinging across the floor with his big stomach in the lead, cuffing Izzy on the shoulder, who was five feet four and thin; Izzy reeled and grinned.

"Hey, Ira! Wife throw you out?"

"Meeting friends. Don't poison us!"

Dan thought, *Male talk.* His mind flashed to an interview with an astronaut he had seen on television, Interviewer: How do you go out there and get in an experimental ship, knowing you could be killed? Astronaut (arms down but held out from his sides slightly, gunslinger style, feet eighteen inches apart): Well, Chet. It's my job.

"Dan!" Ira gave him a slap on the shoulder. Behind Ira, Dan saw Monty Fiske and Lee Grey.

"Sit down, guys."

"Lazy life, huh, Dan?" Ira rumbled, squeezing into the opposite bench. "They let you out of school."

"You kidding? I've got summer school. Imagine entire class of kids who failed biology."

Fiske sat next to Dan, Grey next to Schultz, with Ira taking up two thirds of the bench. Schultz ripped open a pack of Marlboros, tapped one out for himself, and offered the pack around.

The waitress said, "Want menus?"

"Not me, dear," said Ira. "Know it by heart."

"Anybody else?" She was wearing an Izzy's T-shirt, no bra, Levi's, and a cardigan sweater wide open in the front. Lee Grey grinned at her, Monty Fiske stared at Ira's cigarette, Ira stared at the T-shirt. He said, "I'll have breast of turkey on rye and a cherry phosphate."

Heavy humor, Dan thought.

"Turkey, white meat," said the waitress, unimpressed. "Coleslaw? Potato salad?"

"Nope."

"Reuben, side of coleslaw, the rye bread without the seeds, and a hot tea," Monty Fiske said. He glanced at Ira and back at the waitress. "Please," he said. Ira did not notice.

Lee Grey said, "Pastrami and Swiss on dark rye and coffee, please."

Dan said, "I'd like a barbecued beef and a side of coleslaw. And coffee, please."

"Four kids we don't have swimming ratings on," Lee Grey

said. "And I'm sure as hell not going to take them on the canoe trip without it."

Dan said, "School pool's still open."

"Trouble is, I'm working late every night this week. I can call 'em and tell 'em there's a problem. See if they want to take the test. But I can't be there this week to give it to them."

"I'll do it," Monty Fiske said. "You arrange it. I'll go with them and give them the test."

"Free swim is Wednesday night," Dan said. "That okay with you?"

"Yeah, any night this week except Friday."

"Trouble is," Lee said, "the little monsters put it off and then go into fits when I won't let them out in the canoes."

They reviewed the food plans. Like every year, conversation degenerated into a discussion about what the boys wanted to eat as opposed to what they ought to want to eat.

"If they won't eat it," Ira said, "it won't make them healthy, no matter how healthy the stuff is itself."

Dan said, "Listen, they're out there in the wilds. The nearest pizza place is a fifteen-mile hike through swamps. They get so hungry they'd eat squirrels. If you have good food that tastes reasonably palatable, they eat it. They might even learn to like it."

Lee said, "It's not as if we have to feed them bran and bean sprouts three meals a day. We could just cut down on the cookies and hot dogs and candy and crap like that."

Schultz said, "They won't like it."

Lee said, "Wait a minute. Could it possibly be that someone here at this table wants doughnuts and so he can eat them himself? Or put it another way—are we willing to set a good example?"

"All right," Ira said. "You win. Partly. But you gotta remember that we want those kids coming back again next year. They've gotta be happy with their meals."

"You want a compromise? How about canceling the candy and soda pop order," Grey said. "And get in fruit and juice instead. Keep the cake and doughnuts. It's a good time of year for fruit anyway. Shouldn't be too expensive."

"Let's cut out the hot dogs," Camelli said.

"That's going too far."

"If we're done with the vital stuff," Camelli said. "like what has to be ordered and paid for, I'd like to bring up a general point."

Schultz yelled, "Coffee!" at the waitress. "Is this so general I need another phosphate?"

"I've been thinking about the boys after this summer," he said. "You know, one of the main problems in scouting is the attrition rate around the age of thirteen or fourteen. Cub scouts we've got plenty of. And most of them go on to be boy scouts for a couple of years."

"That's because the program is a good one," Schultz said.

Lee said, "Go on, Dan."

"We do well up to about age fourteen. By the time the kids get into high school, very, very few are left in scouting. How many senior scouts do we have? Four? Four in the entire village!"

"It's always been that way," Schultz said.

"It's high school," Grey said. "More homework. Girls. Getting themselves into college. It all saps their energies."

"Girls especially," Schultz laughed. "Little energy sappers."

"No, that isn't the full explanation," Dan said. "I know of fifteen high school boys who are taking tae kwon do lessons three nights a week. That doesn't get their homework done or introduce them to girls. And I know fifty or sixty who are in computer clubs."

Schultz said, "So?"

"So, the reason those things are popular is because they're real things. You really learn something. It's a grown-up activity."

"And we aren't?" Schultz said, grimly.

"Not enough. Scouting has a lot of real instruction. But most of it has to be done during summer camp. Canoeing. Trail finding. Survival camping. All that stuff is good, and it's real. And they're the most popular activities we have for the older boys. But too much of what we do during the year is silly. Indian dances, assemblies, merit badges, and the uniforms."

"They can't make senior scout without merit badges. They want 'em."

"The ones who *stay* in scouting may want them. But by that time we've lost nine out of every ten boys who started. I'm talking about *keeping* them."

"By giving up merit badges?"

"By doing real things, whether we give badges for them or not. The hive has been a good thing. I don't believe any of those boys realized that an ordinary householder without a farm could keep bees. But we need more of that sort of thing and fewer of the make-work badges. Lanyard-making is pretty silly and they know it. And community studies! They visit the fire house and a village board meeting and get a badge for it!"

"They'd never see a village meeting otherwise."

"They'd see one and have more involvement and more suspense and more realism if they developed a project for the village—park improvement, for instance—and presented a proposal to the board and tried to get them to accept it. These

197

are fourteen-year-old boys. They're not children anymore. In some societies they'd be full citizens. You can't treat them like cub scouts and expect them to like it."

Schultz's voice was cold. "You'd give up ceremonies? And awards?"

"And copper bangles for everyone who went on such-and-such a camp-out. And ties for the jamboree. And a lot of the competitions. There are more than enough competitive athletics at school. And contests. That isn't anything we do especially well. We could get into wildlife conservation. Park management. Planting projects. These kids care about the place where they live. Let's make use of that."

"Well, I'm certainly glad that nobody's here from the national organization to hear you say that. So you think we're outmoded, do you?"

"Indian dance ceremonies probably looked a lot more exciting in the days before television. Kids needed simple amusement. It's a different world, Ira. Now they need involvement."

"Shit, that's not scouting. Scouting is badges and uniforms and awards!"

Lee Grey leaned back smiling. Monty Fiske said, "Actually, Ira, I think Dan's right, to a certain extent."

Dan was amazed. He had always thought of Monty as ineffectual.

Lee Grey said, casually, "Dan's got one good point. Almost an unbeatable point."

"Which point was that?" Schultz growled.

"That boys leave scouting about the time they enter high school. After the age of fourteen, as far as attracting scouts, we could hardly be doing any worse."

"Well, hey! I'm not going to sit here and listen to this. This isn't our own private organization. It's a nationwide thing. I went into scouting as a little boy, and I loved it. Those uniforms and badges have years and years of tradition behind 'em, and I want to see 'em go on forever."

His voice was rising. Some people in the middle row of booths looked over, avid to see a fight.

Dan said, "Ira, I don't want to hurt your feelings. But the national has always encouraged local interests. It'd be a fairly modest change—"

"You call us outmoded and that's modest!"

"Hold it!" Lee Grey said. "Now wait right there. Ira, you don't have a right to get mad at Dan. He's made this statement to us out of respect for our views. That's good enough for me."

Ira growled something under his breath, and Grey continued.

"Dan's been a good worker for the scouts, and he volunteers for a lot of the hard work, not just the fun stuff. I think he's earned the right to speak. It's a free country, isn't it, Ira? Freedom of speech?"

Ira nodded. Dan knew Grey had intentionally used on Ira a phrase he had to approve. Dan wondered whether Ira was maybe not too bright.

"So let's give Dan the courtesy of at least thinking about what he said."

Courtesy, thought Dan. Lee Grey was a bigger smoothie than Dan had realized. The things you found out about people when you stirred up a fuss.

"Dan's not suggesting revolution, Ira. He's not saying that we junk everything tomorrow. He didn't even use the word 'outmoded.' So let's kind of take it home with us, okay?"

"Fine with me," Monty Fiske said.

Grey said, "Ira?"

"Oh, yeah. Shit, why not?" He turned to Dan. "I didn't

mean you couldn't talk, you know. But there's a lot of good in ceremonies. And you don't want—um—baby with the bathwater, you know?"

"I know," Dan said.

The check came. All four dinners had been added together.

"Let's see," Monty said. "I had the Reuben and the coleslaw. No, I had tea, too."

"Tea for two," said Schultz.

"And the tax divided by—anybody got a pencil?"

While Dan collected money for the check, six blocks away Samantha had taken her after-dinner coffee into the living room. Distantly, she could hear the voice of the television set, but she could not make out the words.

Ricky's strange reserve continued, but she believed she now knew the reason for it. Garvey had done something horrible. Samantha wondered how any action by Garvey could change Ricky for such a long period of time. But obviously it had, so she put it out of her mind.

A whole evening with no homework! What luxury!

She picked up the evening paper.

One headline caught her eye.

GRISLY END FOR PERFECT FAMILY

William McDonnell came to work as a volunteer in the Forest Grove Retirement Home that Saturday morning, as he had done for the past eighteen months. His co-workers say he seemed much the same as usual, engaging the elderly residents in the outdoor games that had become his specialty. No one suspected that he had left at home a grisly sacrifice.

Samantha paused. The hair on the back of her neck moved. Her spine felt cold.

In Forest Grove the McDonnells were known as a perfect family. Marie engaged in volunteer work for the girl scouts. William was a Village Board member, a Little League coach, and a volunteer organizer for the blood-drive, as well as a visitor at the Forest Grove Retirement Home.

But the center of William McDonnell's life was his family. Blonde, blue-eyed Susan, eighteen months, and brown-haired Timothy were picture-perfect children, with the wholesome good looks that might be used to advertise vegetable soup.

"I never saw anybody that spent so much time with his children," said Grover Genio, a neighbor. "Except for Saturday morning at the Retirement, he was with them the whole weekend. Croquet. That was his latest thing. He made a croquet court on their back lawn."

"You could always count on him if we needed somebody to set up for a meeting," said Edwina Finch, director of the Grove Playschool, which Timothy, the older McDonnell child, attended. "Pour coffee. Set out the cookies for parents' night. Of course, Mrs. McDonnell came to help out, too." (Please turn to GRISLY, p. 10. col. 4)

Samantha shivered. She turned to page ten.

Forest Grove is a suburb out of glossy magazines. Manicured lawns, freshly painted houses, flowering spring trees. The McDonnells' house was as perfect as any, with white clapboard siding, gray shutters, and a gray roof, surrounded by a split rail cedar fence and pink crab apples in bloom.

But something happened in this picture-perfect world. Something dark and final.

Police must speculate what happened between Friday night, when McDonnell, his wife Marie, and Timothy and Susan were last seen alive, and Sunday, when their bodies were discovered by Rev. Cormlinson, pastor of the Forest Grove Lutheran Church.

The family was seen by neighbors at the Waukegan Road Happy Pizza, having a Friday night out. According to observers, they were talking and laughing.

Police theorize that the family went home and that Timothy and Susan were put to bed, for their bodies were found clad in pajamas. Marie McDonnell probably stayed up to watch a television program. Sometime that evening, William crept up behind her, carrying the small hatchet the family used to split kindling, and struck her from behind, splitting her skull. He probably went directly upstairs then, for the children showed no sign of having wakened.

Both were found lying in their beds, Timothy with his neck severed, Susan with her head split open like her mother's.

Because of the condition of the bodies, police believe that the children's and Mrs. McDonnell's deaths occurred late Friday night or early Saturday morning. William McDonnell then dressed in the casual clothes which it was his habit to wear to engage in games at the Retirement Home. Chris Clanfield, chief of the Forest Grove Police, says, "We think he went to the Retirement Home that morning so that nobody would guess that there'd been trouble. This would give him more time to do what he thought he had to do."

He stayed three hours at the Home, as he always did, coaching and playing games.

"He was just as cheerful as he always was," said Leon Drecker, retired owner of M&D Drugs in Forest Grove, and a resident of the retirement home. "He played shuffleboard, and then some of us did aerobics with him."

McDonnell then returned home, put his car in the garage, and closed the garage door. Sometime during that Saturday afternoon, he started the car, plugged the crack at the bottom of the garage window with a cloth, lay down on a blanket on the floor, and died.

When police entered the garage Sunday afternoon at the request of Rev. Cormlinson, they found William McDonnell dead. In his hands were pictures of his wife and children.

Rev. Cormlinson spoke for many of the McDonnells' friends. "It's a pity that when a man is so troubled, those around him may never know. If only he had reached out to us, we might have been able to help."

Samantha's hand clutched the side of the paper convulsively, her knuckles showing white. Deep within her mind a shadow moved. She felt that some primitive instinct for danger was trying to communicate with the civilized, rational part of her mind.

We spend our days, she thought, *reading the faces around us. And we have no notion of how often we are completely wrong. It's as if the words in a book writhed and changed just after we turned the page.*

Very rationally, Samantha told herself that she was specially vulnerable to such fears because of her mother. She had seen the difference between her mother's social mask and her real, shadowed mind with writhing terrors. Samantha knew firsthand that masks existed.

For that reason, it was all the more important not to give in. Samantha methodically unwound her fingers from the newspaper. She dropped the paper on the coffee table, picked up the cup, and finished her coffee. But deep within her mind the fear lived, caged by reason.

By noon the next day, Meyers Campbell was settled in his camp on Bear Lake, forty miles south of Lake Superior. He had driven from Chicago north through Wisconsin. The upper peninsula of Michigan lies over the state of Wisconsin, so that, even though southern Michigan is just forty miles from Chicago around the tip of Lake Michigan, it is a shorter trip to drive to the Upper Peninsula through Wisconsin.

Even so, it was a drive of three hundred miles. He did not reach Coppertown until nearly dark on Monday, and to attempt to pack in to Bear Lake at that hour after a day's drive would have been foolish. Instead, he had stopped for the night at the Timber Line Motel just outside of town and a block away from the intersection of U.S. 45 and M22, four miles north of Agate Falls.

Milt Vanderkamp was the owner of the Timberline. He had built it himself, twelve separate cabins made from joined pine logs, each with its own pine bathroom and real fireplace. Milt had managed and even cleaned it himself since 1959, when his wife Ellen had run away with a botanist from the University of Michigan who had been staying in Coppertown while investigating the role of the prevailing winds in the reproduction of white and red pine.

During the ski season, Milt employed one Henrietta Camploops to help him clean. She was a twenty-five-year-old who had four children to support. She was solid Dutch stock, blond, pink-faced, and big-breasted. Too fleshy for urban tastes, she was not bad at all in Coppertown, and made Milt wish he were forty again. Or even fifty. But summers she was not needed, and he did his own maintenance.

Milt and Campbell shook hands.

"Bass good this year?" Campbell asked.

"Bigmouth. No smallmouth. Not worth the line. Dolly Varden's been pretty good in the streams. But you're not a fly man, are you?"

"Used to be. I've got a touch of arthritis in the knees."

"Oh, ya?"

"The cold in the rivers goes right through waders."

"Ya."

"Copper Kettle still open for dinner?"

"Supper. Ya."

"Thanks, Milt."

"You betcha."

The next morning Campbell left his car with Milt, who would put it behind the office and keep an eye on it.

There were no roads where Campbell was going; he bought some eggs and bread at the local IGA. It was still early when he and David Heartline, a Potawatomie Indian, had breakfast at the Copper Kettle and left with packs on their backs. It was eight miles to the lake, with packs a trek of half a day.

The cabin was waiting for him, unchanged since last year, which was hardly surprising since scarcely anyone had passed that way in the intervening months. From November to April it was locked in snow. During January, snow cover on the level ground had been ten and a half feet.

When they arrived, David Heartline accepted coffee, but after it was made and drunk, he would not stay to rest. He turned around and began the eight-mile walk back to Coppertown.

Campbell puttered around for a while. He did not intend

to fish that day, though he checked on the old rowboat that he had left jammed under the cabin. He made a mental note to caulk a crack in the stern that evening when he had unpacked the caulking compound.

He distributed his few belongings around the cabin. By then it was dinnertime. He made scrambled eggs and a Swiss cheese sandwich, which he ate with great relish.

Campbell had been in the habit of taking Corgard just before bed. His doctor had said it didn't matter when he took it. The stuff was slow to build up in the blood, so there was no need to split the doses and take one in the morning and one at night like faster-acting drugs. Campbell had taken one last night at the motel. The fact that it was not really Corgard but Elavil he had not noticed. There was no obvious effect from the discontinuation of the Corgard. The only effect of the Elavil was that he felt rather mellow. This he attributed to his delight in being in the country.

He laid his sleeping bag out on the bare cot. Then he swallowed his medication for that day.

Seventeen

Ira Schultz did not give Camelli's proposal the consideration he had promised. He had work to do. Ira had inherited his dental supply company, not from his father, as Camelli theorized, but from his wife's father. He had spent fifteen years working for old man Plankstein before the old man died. Plankstein had suffered from blood pressure high enough to blow out an inner tube, and for years had thrived on it. In their office, his ruddy face was everywhere; his portly belly sidled into Ira's field of vision when Ira was at his desk, at the water cooler, or brewing a pot of coffee.

He had hated to see Ira spend time getting the coffee going. It wasn't work.

"Learning to be a short-order cook? It should help when I fire you."

"A supplier comes in, he wants a cup of coffee, Dad."

"He comes in, he wants to sell supplies, Ira. Go get orders."

Plankstein had three daughters, Hilda, Sara, and Susanna, but no sons. "God gave me this to bear," he had told Ira, in front of the girls. "No son." Then evenly distributing the sour rasp of his tongue, he said, "And only sons-in-law to try to kick into shape. No one to carry on the name."

"I have my own name to carry on," Ira had said.

"What's that to me?"

Ira had half wanted the old man to die. He had fully wanted him to retire. It happened one Friday morning with crust on the snow and frost flowers on windows.

207

Hilda, the oldest daughter, had been three years divorced from a periodontist she had met working in the business. She had asked both sisters and their husbands to come to the house, to confer with her and the older Planksteins on a family matter. As it turned out, she hadn't wanted conferring as much as moral support, or perhaps just somebody else around for her father to yell at.

All seven of them had stood around looking at the fire, which the old man kept calling "a real fire." Hilda had made her announcement.

Hilda was going to marry a Catholic.

The blood pressure which had supported the old man so long had shot higher. A vessel had blown in his brain and he had fallen to the floor as if deflated.

If the old man could have spoken, Ira knew he would have said, "See!"

Hilda's new husband was a chemical engineer who wanted nothing to do with wholesale dental supplies; Susanna's husband had never been interested in the first place. He was a gastroenterologist, a choice of specialty that invariably had sent old man Plankstein into dry chuckles and scatological remarks.

Ira had been left holding the business. Oddly enough, now that he was his own boss, he felt trapped. Ira liked to get outdoors. He liked scouting. Ira had grown up on the southwest side of Chicago. If it had been left to his mother and father, he would scarcely ever have seen a tree, much less learned to hike and camp out. When he was a boy, the idea of sleeping outdoors without walls or locks or window glass—out in the world!—had seemed inexpressibly romantic. Nothing between himself and the sky! Air that smelled of pines. Look up and see the stars. His mother could not understand it.

"Your father works his life out to give you a roof over your head, and you go out and sleep on the ground?"

If he said the air was fresh outdoors, she said it was cold and wet. If he said there was great freedom, she said, "Freedom is to have a door to lock so a burglar doesn't come and get you."

In the way of children who know they are not understood, he dropped it. If his mother herself asked why he went camping, he said, "All the other kids do."

That she understood.

Unlike Ira, Monty Fiske had been born into a family that was really rich. And as a child he had been much more deprived. Fiske and Braden, his father's business, was a very large Chicago real estate corporation. During the years of Monty's youth, his father had been engaged in expanding the firm's activities into other cities. He opened offices in Terra Haute, Indianapolis, Michigan City, Elgin, Waukegan, and Milwaukee during the time that Monty went from age two to thirteen. His father had been busy opening the office because Braden, the other partner, had been busy acquiring new buildings for the firm to own. This was a fairly new idea in a time when most real estate companies thought in terms of selling property rather than owning it.

Monty's mother had been the belle of the fifteen debutantes, Eloise Montgomery. By 1942 she had married, was the wife of an absentee husband, mother of a baby boy, and a citizen of a country harrowed by World War II. She had found that fun and parties were not what they used to be. But she had been an extremely resourceful young woman. She had moved methodically, first convincing a hungry middle-aged surgeon to perform an operation not often done at a time except in cases of dire physical risk. She had her tubes tied. She had then consoled herself consoling sailors, soldiers, and Marines. Bright and self-interested, she had soon been able to discern every rank in every branch of the service from its uniform. She had preferred the upper ranks.

Little Montgomery Fiske had grown up in a twenty-four-room brick pile in Winnetka. He had had a nursemaid who was supposed to see that he came to no harm. There had been a cook who made breakfast, lunch, dinner, and snacks for him, but was taciturn otherwise, her medium of expression having been the stove. A gardener had manicured the lawn for him to romp on.

Monty had been absolutely miserable.

At ten he had driven his bike—the finest postwar two-wheeler money could buy—down the steep beach road, through the ravine, and smack into the side of the boathouse. With a child's flexibility, he had broken only his arm and collarbone, but the family physician believed it was an attempted suicide.

After that, Monty had also had the best psychiatrist money could buy, and his parents had left for Barbados the day he came home from the hospital.

School had been pretty good for Monty. It had gotten him out of the house. But in scouting he had been really happy. In scouting he had been engaged in a cooperative effort with the other boys. It had taken several of them to pitch the heavy tents they used at that time. Cooking had been cooperative, and canoeing.

He had been needed.

Monty Fiske did some thinking about Dan Camelli's proposal. He agreed that ritual wasn't necessary, and in scouting it was always done pretty amateurishly. Ritual had never helped him much. He had been sent to church, his father's Episcopalian church, with the cook.

Nor was he fond of uniforms. He had no conscious

memory of his mother's sailors and soldiers. But he didn't like uniforms.

He thought it might be a good idea to hire a tae kwon do instructor to keep the boys interested. The more boys in scouting the better.

Lee Grey was precisely neutral on the question of form versus content in scouting. He had said exactly what he believed at the meeting, that high school boys have less time for scouting. In Lee's view, at that age tits and ass were beginning to obsess them, and spending a whole weekend with other boys was not their idea of fun.

Even so, it might be easier to get older boys if older ones weren't thrown in with the younger ones so much. One of the foundations of scouting was that older boys taught the younger ones, thus passing on the torch. To Lee, this was one of those ideas that sounded better on paper than it really worked in the field. Its result was to make the older boys baby-sitters for younger ones. The older boys would learn more information faster if they went at their own pace.

As a kid, he had dropped out of scouting himself at age thirteen. He had wanted real challenges. His school had offered fencing and he had gone into it with swords flying. And competitive swimming.

Lee Grey was competitive.

His father, William, had been quarterback for University of Michigan in 1943 and a Marine in Pacific by late 1944. By 1946 he had been a salesman for Krieger Chemical. By 1950, at the age of twenty-eight, he had been vice-president in charge of marketing. At thirty-four, he had been senior vice president. In 1960, at the age of thirty-eight, he had become president of Krieger, by virtue of incessant work, willingness to step on the other vice-presidents, and the timely action of the president, who had gone drinking and dining with an expensive call girl one hot June night, missed a turn on Sheridan Road, and run into a sycamore tree at seventy-two miles an hour.

Lee Grey's father had been president of Krieger for seven years, during which time he tripled their sales. Then a major chemical company, which William called a "world-class conglomerate," had offered him their presidency. He had taken it, and just six months later had been involved in a world-class scandal, stemming from the bribing of a Pentagon official.

William Grey shot himself.

By that time Lee was twenty-two. His entire experience of his father had been like his experience of every athletic coach he had ever met. Winning was the thing. You won by being "a great competitor." That meant, at the very least, that it was always more important for you to win than for anybody else to win. One of the best qualities was "heart." Heart meant that no matter how many times you got knocked down, you got up and tried again. Lee Grey no longer even remembered that he had gone through a stage of wondering whether this made sense, whether, if you were knocked down often enough, it didn't mean you were in the wrong sport. The thought had been completely swamped by his desire to please his father. Lee believed that merit badges were a good idea, as well as the other forms of scout competition—model-races, knot tying, swimming, whatever. People could be motivated by trying to beat other people.

He wished his son, Kip, were more competitive. Maybe he'd better come down a little harder on the boy.

In Ira Schultz's backyard, the bees had settled into a routine. The new queen was not only accepted, none of the

212

workers remembered a time when she was not there. Her children, now eggs or young larvae, would soon hatch out as adults. She had even laid a dozen male drone eggs. In a few weeks, all of the citizens of the hive would be her children.

Tuesday afternoon, June 30, the man went to a phone in Kenilworth and called his broker in Chicago. He was given a phone number in Winnetka.

The man called and got a male voice. He said, "I was given your number by Gary in Chicago."

"Sure. What would you have done if my wife answered?"

"You should have thought of that when you gave us this number."

"You caused the problem by not wanting to meet. Gary said you wouldn't meet me."

"And I won't. It's for your protection as much as mine. There is no way anybody ever can say we were seen together. I work safe, which is why I'm expensive. Take it or leave it."

There was an intake of breath, dry as sawdust. This guy had not expected anybody educated, the man thought, or anybody who would tell him what to do. It was important not to act hungry. It made you more valuable.

"All right. What now?"

"I will ask some questions. Make sure your answers are accurate. Any mistake at this point is yours."

"I won't be dictated to—"

"Do you want this done right?"

"Of course."

"Amateurs are cheap. And sloppy."

"I realize that."

"Answer the following questions. Or—I have other calls I can make."

When the man hung up, he found that he was literally rubbing his hands. He was getting better and better at this. Maybe he could expand. Conservatively, of course. Maybe he should test out a few more boys.

Eighteen

Samantha got into bed but she couldn't relax. All day Ricky had been distant and cool to her. Was it just because he was becoming a teenager? She didn't really believe it. She had an unusually good relationship with him—or did all mothers think that? Were they all stunned when the children became teenagers and changed, and began to pull away emotionally?

When she finally started to drowse, she found herself picturing hurrying Ricky and Tad into the car—right now, in the middle of the night—and driving away. They would just drive and drive and drive until they were far away from here. They would find a place that felt safe. Then they would stop.

It was a very strange idea, quite unlike her, and completely impractical.

As she sank into sleep, Samantha became afraid. She was surrounded by demons. People changed shape. Familiar people who were warm, affectionate, and reliable melted under her very eyes and became malevolent.

She was dreaming about Frederick's last night at home. Half asleep, she tried to fight it off. But reality of today faded and the past became reality.

He had come home late. She had thought for some time that he was researching some new product line, though he was being secretive about it. He wanted to spring it on his father—a full-blown, completely researched idea that would

215

make money for the company and prove he was his father's equal. He resented being in his father's shadow, being paid and evaluated by his father.

The children were in bed. She waited downstairs for Frederick. Because the house was built as a hollow square, all the inside windows looked into the courtyard. It was late winter, and this inner space was filled with damp, grayish snow. When they had first finished building the house, Samantha had suggested that they plant a tree at the very center of the courtyard, a straight, tall tree reaching up to the sky. Frederick had simply ordered three expensive dwarf weeping cherries. They were delivered and planted before she could say no.

The cherries wept in the spill of light from the windows.

Frederick came in looking smug.

"I've got it," he said.

"What is it?"

"A speller-dictionary-thesaurus. You can hold it in your hand. Bright digital display screen—but the point is, I'll show him this time."

"He'll be proud of you."

"He'll be envious."

"Frederick, he really loves you more than—"

"Forget it. I know him. Anyway, now that I'm over this hump, I want to discuss something with you."

"All right."

"It's time the boys went away to school. Ricky's not a problem, but he'd like military school, anyway. It's Tad who really needs it. He's too soft. Military school would whip him into shape."

For an instant Samantha was too astonished to think. She simply said, "No."

Frederick said, "Then we can entertain more."

Samantha said, "No."

"And get the house cleaned up. Get the toys out of the sofa cushions. Get the—"

"No. My boys stay with me."

"Listen, I never intended to get bogged down in decades of child rearing."

"It certainly doesn't impinge on you much. You don't pay a lot of attention to them."

"Thirteen years is enough."

"I won't send them away!"

"What if I tell you to choose between them and me?"

Samantha sighed once and said, "Then I would just have to choose to keep the boys."

"I'm not joking."

"Neither am I."

"You'd let me move out?"

"Things have been—it may be best all around."

"Samantha, I'm on the verge of making millions. If I leave and you have to survive on a college teacher's salary, don't expect me to help. You'll be poor."

"Frederick!"

"You can't turn your back on that kind of money, Samantha. Nobody would."

"I'm supposed to keep on living with you because you're rich?"

"Sure. Why not?"

"I'm talking about living, not about spending. Am I losing my mind? Everything you say is crazy!"

"Oh, no it isn't. You have romantic ideas about life. But this is real. Money is real."

"Frederick, did you always feel this way?"

"Of course."

"But remember when we used to talk about what we wanted out of life? You were talking about a home and a family and warmth and—do you remember when we first met, all we said about mutual trust?"

"Sure I do."

"And the importance of a family?"

"Sure!"

"Well, did it mean anything to you?"

"Of course it did. It was what you wanted to hear. I was trying to make you happy."

Slowly, she repeated, "You were trying to make me happy." She stared at his hands, at his face, then hands again. He was smiling, unbelievably, smiling.

She tried to remember what he had looked like when they first met, but the memory eluded her. She was not sure now whether they had ever met.

Is this Frederick? Have I met him at last?

How many errors can I make about the nature of the world?

In the morning Samantha found a letter from her mother in the accumulated mail. It contained, as usual, a clipping from her mother's hometown newspaper but not an obituary, the sort of thing her mother sent most often. It was a report of a Ferris wheel accident at an amusement park in Texas.

The headline read, "Two Killed, Six Injured." There was an AP photograph of the ride, its girders bent, flying on its side on the ground. A great many people were standing around staring. The ride was named "The Whizzer." The two killed had been boys, fourteen and sixteen years old. Those injured had also been children.

There was no letter. Her mother rarely got up enough energy to write a letter, but she had written on the white margin of the paper, "I thought you'd be interested because the boys like to go to fairs."

The boys like to go to fairs. Yes, most boys like to go to fairs. Samantha held the clipping, trying to understand. What went through the mind of a person who would cut out this article in preference to all others and mail it? In preference to crafts projects, and new books and good things to do? Her mother was not actually suggesting that she stop taking the boys to fairs. They only went to one or two a year, anyway. And there was no suggestion that they stop going on certain rides.

Samantha thought she knew what her mother was really trying to communicate: that life was not just unpredictable, not merely dangerous, it was subtly booby-trapped. Grisly death waited everywhere, hidden even in cheerful things. Samantha's mother had always believed that Samantha did not realize how dangerous, discouraging, and hopeless life really was. She had been trying for years to convince Samantha of it.

Her mother must have believed that if Samantha became as depressed as she was, then they would at last see eye to eye.

In her own dark fashion, her mother was trying to reach her.

Nineteen

Ricky lay on the sofa in the playroom, in front of the new glass door. He had turned the television set on, because he knew if he just lay there staring into space Tad and his mother would ask what he was doing. Then Tad had come in and started watching. Ricky was not watching, and he'd turned the sound down farther than usual.

Ricky figured he was in big trouble. There were the occasional memory gaps, and in addition he was becoming less certain about the in-between times, the times when, he supposed, he did not have blackouts. How did he know for sure that he didn't? Two things really scared him. One was that he was sick. The other was a horror of what he might have done when he was blacked out. From a decade of watching television, he had learned that people did very strange things when they had blackouts. He did not believe he turned into Mr. Hyde. In fact, he casually pictured himself running around with long teeth snarling at people, and he almost laughed.

What horrified him was that he might have done something embarrassing.

What if I took off my clothes?

What if, someday, I wet my pants?

Even just falling down asleep with people watching was embarrassing enough. He felt his face get red with shame at the thought. People would talk about it and feel sorry for him. Poor Ricky Lawton. Fainting fits.

Fits. He wished he had not thought of that word. Was it

possible that he fell on the floor and thrashed around and foamed at the mouth? He tried remembering whether his clothes had ever felt as if they had been thrashed around in, but he couldn't tell. For one thing, it had taken him a while each time to realize there had been any blackout at all. Besides that—he smiled, faintly—his clothes always looked thrashed around in, anyway.

Tad was sitting on the floor watching the TV.

"Tad?" he said.

"What?"

"Do I do anything funny sometimes?"

"Don't talk. I can hardly hear the television. Why can't I turn it up?"

"Turn it up if you have to. Do I ever act strange?"

Tad giggled. "You act strange all the time."

"I'm not kidding about this."

"Why do you want to know? Think you're losing your mind?"

This was too close to the truth.

"Naw."

"I guess not. You have to be old, anyway, to lose your mind. Like Gran. It doesn't happen to kids."

Ricky opened his mouth to correct this statement, but then he thought it might be to his advantage to let it stand. "No, I was daydreaming," he said.

"So what?"

"So nothing, I guess."

That left it completely incomprehensible from Tad's point of view. But it told Ricky something. Tad could hardly have noticed Ricky doing anything extremely odd, or he would have mentioned it. It was scant information, but what there was of it was encouraging.

His mother had been looking at him speculatively lately.

221

But that was probably because he was preoccupied. She'd certainly tell him if she thought he was sick.

The best thing to do was wait and see. Don't panic.

These were lush days for the bees, these first days of July. They sped out of the hive each morning as soon as it was light, small amber bullets directed at the finest new flowers of the day. There were tubs of pansies on corners in the village center, marigolds and geraniums in front of the bank. The florist had planted great tubs of tuberous begonias that grew fat, luscious stems filled with sap, thick leaves so heavy with pigment that the veins were red, and huge heads of moist, flesh-colored flowers, spongy with internal juices and dripping in the early morning with dew.

Izzy's Deli faced south and had a big box of zinnias: stiff, dry plants, their stems all vertical, tough, and a military gray-green. They were red, orange, yellow, and pink. Their leaves stood out at right angles from the stalk.

The bees visited all the flowers. They forced their bodies so hard into the necks of the petunias that they could not turn around and their legs were pressed to their sides. They had to back out, wriggling, covered with pollen. They clung to the petals of the geraniums in front of the railroad station, and clung tighter with all six legs when the train swept by and the draft it pulled after it made the flower heads bob and dance.

Pollen and nectar flowed into the hive. The cells bulged with honey being evaporated to the proper consistency and pollen being packed tight and capped. The population of the hive was rising fast. The brood cells were filled with eggs, larvae, and, under their cap, pupae changing into adult bees.

But unknown to the busy nurse bees, under some of these caps, a deadly change was taking place. A bacterium had invaded the hive. A few of the young, hidden from the eyes of the nurses, had failed to make the magical metamorphosis from clumsy larva to winged adult, and instead had undergone a hideous deterioration.

The clear, light, infant flesh, which should soon have turned to the golden brown of the adult honeybee, was dying. In this necrotic change, the flesh became grayish at first, then darker as it began to rot. The shape of the bee disappeared, liquefied, and in a few days became a sticky, blackish, amorphous mass.

Somewhere deep in Samantha's mind, an infection of doubt had set in. On the surface, lighted by daylight, she seemed well. She believed that she had overcome her fears.

But because the fears were not irrational, only inexplicable, they did not dissipate. They formed pockets of blight.

Samantha would have said that she was fine. Better than ever. And in one way it was true. She had cleared her mind of Frederick, and now wanted to live through the completion of the divorce, the final grinding out of the legal papers by the mechanism of the state. She also wanted to retain continuity for the children, keeping an even keel and enough of a friendship with Frederick so that civilized contact was possible.

She went to dinner and a movie with Dan on Monday night and went bowling and had pizza with Henry on Wednesday.

Both men were aware that Samantha was putting something out of her mind. Dan, with perhaps too much sensitivity, chose not to pry. He assumed it was the slow progress of the divorce, and he went carefully about amusing her, making sure she had a good evening.

Henry, more impatient and more abrupt, would have asked her straight out what was on her mind, except that he assumed it was the same as the problem on his mind, the series of accidents he was coming to view as murders.

"Been making notes on Garvey for me?" he asked, making a joke of it, swirling the beer in his heavy glass stein.

"What? No, actually Ricky hasn't been seeing much of Garvey."

"Thought you were going to be my undercover agent," he said, still smiling.

But Samantha answered very seriously. "I'd tell you anything, if I knew anything. But I really think we were exaggerating."

"We were?" He was astonished. "Why do you say that?"

"Garvey is no killer. We were really considering that—I mean, that he could be a murderer, weren't we?" She smiled at this, uneasily.

"Yes, we certainly were."

"Well, that was silly, of course. We had a couple bizarre events, and we just rushed to a foolish conclusion."

"Have you any new reasons?"

"No. Just that it doesn't make sense. He's a child."

"And children never kill?"

She pushed her beer mug away angrily. "I suppose there have been some. But I think it's very rare."

"Garvey is not exactly a child anymore. He's five feet three and a hundred and ten pounds."

"He's a child! He's just as much of a child as Ricky is!"

Oho! thought Ax. Instead of asking her what happened to her critical faculty, he changed direction and proceeded slowly.

"So Ricky hasn't been seeing him at all?" He let his voice trail off, hoping she would fill in some details.

"Except at scouts, no. Ricky's been playing more with Peter." Abruptly, her unconscious forced up a bubble from the pocket of doubt, past her censoring system. "Of course, I wonder sometimes about Peter. He's been so nervous."

"About what?"

She was dismayed that she'd spoken, but her mind spit out another piece of half-digested fear. "Oh," she said hastily. "Nightmares and things. When he stayed overnight, he had a bad dream and said he didn't want go on the camping trip with the scouts."

"Kids get silly fears," Ax said carefully. "About camping out in the dark, that sort of thing."

"Oh, I know it. Ricky came back from the last one absolutely exhausted. In fact, ever since then he's been—"

Henry Ax said nothing.

"The kids are all tired," she said, hastily. "A long school year and then camping and running around in the dark and telling ghost stories and God knows what else. It's no wonder they're—acting odd." He let her drop it. Garvey, Peter, and Ricky. All with some kind of problem. All scouts.

The following Saturday Tad and Ricky would be leaving for one week at scout camp. Ricky had been there the year before, but it was Tad's first time. Samantha hoped the weekend camp-outs had prepared him for it. He had never been away from home that long.

She wrote names in the backs of shirts, pants, and underwear with a laundry marking pen. She wrote on the bottoms of the socks, but it wasn't very readable. The boys stowed their clothes in duffel bags. They wanted to take all their favorite shirts and didn't care at all about underwear or socks.

Ricky was still quiet and withdrawn. Samantha hoped that summer camp would snap him out of it.

Twenty

"Why aren't you eating your cauliflower?" said Carson Winterthur.

Peter raised his head. "Um. I was feeling sort of funny." He hoped his dad would just let it drop.

"Do you have a stomach ache?"

"No, sir. Not exactly."

"Then eat your cauliflower."

Sally said, "Wait a minute. What's 'not exactly' mean?"

Peter wished he could eat alone.

"Answer your mother, Peter."

"Well, I was sort of feeling—um—not hungry."

"Why?"

Peter started to eat his cauliflower. Maybe that would end the discussion.

"Answer your mother, Peter," Carson Winterthur said, in his "dangerous" voice. Peter knew that voice. It meant you were getting yourself into trouble fast.

"I don't want to go on the camp-out!" he said.

"Why not?" said his mother. "I thought you loved scouts."

"Oh, yeah. I like the model-car racing. And some other stuff."

"What other stuff?"

"Well, we were doing tree classification with Camelli. That was good. And the bees are kind of scary, but they're real interesting."

"So why don't you want to go on the camp-out?"

226

"Um—I just don't like camping out, I guess." He was sorry he'd mentioned it. Maybe he could've just got real sick the morning they were supposed to leave. But his mother would take him to the doctor, and there wouldn't be anything wrong with him, and his dad would be madder yet.

"He's just trying to get out of the hike. Peter, I'm only going to tell you this once. I intend you to make an effort. You hike with the rest of them, and you camp out even if it's cold. I don't want any more mollycoddle behavior around here. Is that clear?"

"That isn't it, Dad—"

"Yes, that *is* it. And I don't want to hear any more about it. You get out and hike with the rest of them. Do you understand?"

"Yes, sir."

Henry Ax had decided there was no point breaking down Samantha's defenses if he had no solution to propose. However, before he dropped the subject, he had asked her for the names of scoutmasters. She gave them to him with the look on her face a Victorian lady might have had when asked for the location of the bathroom: she told him, but she didn't want to think about what he was going to do with the information.

Ax went to the office early Thursday morning to set up appointments with the scoutmasters. He also arranged meetings with the police chiefs of the three adjoining suburbs. He had met all three of the men at regional conferences, so as long as he didn't blow it by presenting his questions in a way that sounded paranoid, it should be all right. He saw Dan Camelli first. Dan brought in some beer. "Have one of these."

"Oh, great. Thanks." He took a swallow. "Good beer."

"Moosehead."

"And it's nice and cold."

There was a short silence. Henry thought maybe he should have worked out a set of questions. But every time he had a scenario for an interview all planned, one of the answers would start a new line of thought, and he never got back to the script.

He took his usual way out of a dilemma—hit it directly in the face.

"I hate this," he said. "You're going to think I'm crazy."

"Try me."

"I want to tell you about three recent deaths."

"All right," said Camelli, calmly.

Henry Ax told him about Dubcjek, Linkletter, and Clarendon Briggs. As he talked, he watched Camelli's actions. That was what he had really come for, unless he got lucky and Camelli had some real piece of information.

"You see the similarities? If there's anything you know about Garvey, I'd like to hear it."

"You've been bothering Samantha about this."

"She was involved from the time she found Dubcjek's body."

"She needn't have been involved. You didn't have to worry her about the rest."

"I don't believe she's worried; what she's doing is trying not to think about it."

"No wonder. She's living alone. Somebody broke through her door in the night, and you get her thinking there's a homicidal kid in the neighborhood?"

"I'm not trying to scare her, dammit! If Garvey is dangerous, she has a right to know—"

"Ricky isn't having Garvey over these days, anyway."

"I know. And I just hope that doesn't make him mad. This is not my imagination. Somebody pushed Briggs in front of that train!"

"You don't know that."

228

"Briggs was a careful man. He'd never fallen—"

"In front of a train before? I imagine most people fall in front of a train only once."

"All right, all right. I did start to say that, and it was stupid. But Briggs was not accident-prone. He was a cautious man. And I feel certain, inside, where I get scared, that Dubcjek's and Linkletter's ladders were bumped. There's something malignant out there, and it's real, and if I don't stop it, no one will."

Camelli stared at Ax. "You *do* mean it."

"I don't usually go around trying to make a fool of myself." In fact, he had been surprised at how strong his conviction was, when challenged. Sometime in the last few days his doubt had vanished.

"Well, you may believe it, but I don't," said Camelli.

"All right, I can accept that. But I wish you'd accept that if I think there's a serious danger, then I have a job to do."

"All right."

"Tell me a few things. Ricky Lawton has stopped seeing Garvey. He hasn't said why. Samantha thinks Peter Winterthur is having psychological problems. Ricky himself has been noticeably withdrawn since the camp-out a couple of weeks ago. All three are boy scouts. Is there anything about their scouting experience that could have upset them?"

Camelli laughed. "They may have been upset when our fearless leader was eaten by a bear for breakfast on Saturday. Oh, I suppose I shouldn't make fun." For just a second he remembered a feeling of disquiet at that last camp-out. But there had been no reason for it.

"I'm trying to take this seriously," he told Ax, "but I think it's silly. The scouts are a very fresh-air group. Very open. To tell you the truth, Peter is having some problems, but they're family problems. Somebody in his family is leaning on him, but what an outsider can do about it, except provide an outlet, I really don't know."

"Samantha said he had a nightmare about the camping trip. Didn't want to go."

"Well, that's pretty typical. It's practically axiomatic among teachers, for instance, that the kid who has trouble at home doesn't want to go to school. He thinks something bad will happen at home while he's gone, like divorce. In other words, it's the home, not the school, where the trouble is, but it looks as if the kid hates school, you know?"

"Yeah. Okay."

"You asked about Garvey. Garvey is—um—a little insensitive. His father is one of the scoutmasters. They don't seem to get along well. These kids come in all sorts, just like people."

"And how is Ricky?"

"Ricky is in the middle of divorce. The thing some kids are scared of has already happened to him. You can hardly be surprised if he's strange right now. Ricky is a very, very nice kid, and he's going to pull out of it."

Ax smiled. He didn't feel like smiling. He had learned nothing. "Look," he said, "try to think that I don't usually go off half-cocked. You don't have to believe me, but I've had a lot of experience, and to me something is wrong. Do one thing, if you will."

"What's that?"

"Keep your eyes open. I'm not a scoutmaster. You watch for me."

Henry stood up. Dan said, "All right. I can hardly refuse. You do one thing too, though." He stood up.

"Okay."

"Don't lay this on Samantha any more. No omens of doom from you. She's had enough real-life doom lately."

Henry had already made that decision himself. "Well," he said casually, "that's probably the best thing."

Dan caught Ax's eyes for a second. There was a challenge in them. Ax was first to break contact. He turned to the door.

"Thanks for the beer."

Behind him, Camelli said, "First you catch your boogeyman—"

For the rest of the afternoon, Ax interviewed the police chiefs.

The first one he saw, a stringy, older man with forty-two years in law enforcement, three years from retirement, thought Ax was losing his grip. He didn't come right out and say so, but he asked whether Rivercrest gave its officers enough vacation. When he started talking about northern Wisconsin rivers that offered good fishing and suggested he look up some nice motels for Ax, Henry thanked him, said he'd think about it, and left.

The second man was the sort Henry liked. Low-pressure, scholarly, and willing to talk, he kept an office full of reference books, and took Henry's problem seriously.

But he didn't see anything to worry about. "You can start seeing peculiarities in any data if you look for it, Henry. There's *never* been a case without loose ends. There's never been a case without coincidence, if you get enough of the facts. Hell, *everything's* coincidence if you go at it from the back end. Guy happens to take his wife's car to work and that's the very day the tire blows. If she had used it around town, it wouldn't have been going sixty on the highway and no one would have been killed."

"I know it, but look at the threads that run through these accidents."

"Henry, you had any *other* accidents this year?"

"Well, sure. A lot. But these have similarities."

"It isn't enough, Henry. Let me tell you something that happened to me. We had three separate accidents in the village in one month involving silver Mercedes. Three! In one month! I thought—naturally—we had a maniac. There's a guy out there who's taking revenge on silver Mercedes. Never mind that Mercedes in my town are as common as Fords. I figure we've got a guy out there whose wife or kid was run down by a silver Mercedes. Right? So we pushed the investigation. I mean, no automobile accident, not even Chappaquiddick, has been so carefully gone over. Every piece of each car. I mean, we had the parts *x-rayed.*"

"What did you find?"

"Oh, it was worth it. Now, the first accident was caused by exactly what it looked like. Terminal stupidity. Seventeen-year-old kid borrows his dad's car to take his girl for a ride. During the ride, she tells him that she's breaking off with him. So he drives the car straight into the abutment of the Green Bay Road underpass. Girl told us so when she came out of the coma three weeks later. The boy died.

"Second one happened because the driver fell asleep at the wheel. This guy is making a hundred and ten thousand a year as a customer's man for Bache, but he's gotta run a string of ice cream parlors, too, 'cause otherwise he might run out of money, am I right? So he gets home from work, eats dinner, then goes out, visits all the ice cream places, he should let the help know he's got his eye on them. Last one closes at midnight in Morton Grove. He's coming home, falls asleep, crosses the center line, head-on into an A & P truck. Christ! Melons all over the road. And slippery! Cantaloupes and watermelons. We had the trucks out half the night washing it down and the road crew sweeping the goosh off. I swear, it looked like a major disaster—that pink melon flesh all over. And where they swept it," he laughed, "we had melons growing in the median strip the rest of the summer."

"You said it was worth it."

"Oh, yeah, the third one made it worth it. Found a tiny little spring filed through. I'm not sure we'd have noticed it otherwise. Wife driving the car. Husband's a dealer in foreign cars. Husband is screwing his psychiatrist, who, by the way, is a woman. Wants a divorce. Wife says, 'Over my dead body,' which isn't smart. She piled into a tree on the ravine curve. We confronted the husband with the evidence, but the real reason he confessed was his shrink told him to. She didn't like him any more."

"But he took her advice?"

"Yup. Point is, there you got it. Three silver Merccdes. Mercedeses. And one big, fucking coincidence!"

The third man said to Henry Ax: "Yes, I can think of two cases."

Henry felt his mouth fall open. After a few seconds he said, "What were the cases?"

"Of course, you have to remember, these were *accidents*. If there had been anything suspicious about them, I would have really pushed. But if you're just asking about cases involving boy scouts—"

This was a young man, rather pedantic, cautioning Ax with an upraised index finger. A Business Administration type of cop. Ax didn't mind. He'd take information from Richard Nixon's tailor at this point.

"I sure am," said Ax.

A man had returned home late one Wednesday evening, the young cop said. This man always worked late. He owned a restaurant in Evanston. At 11:00 P.M. he drove into his garage, got out of the car, and lit a cigarette. Cigarette, man, car, and garage blew up. The investigation showed the top was not on the gas tank of the lawn mower.

"Our fire investigator said it was possible that fumes had been escaping for several hours, if somebody forgot to put the top on the mower. I asked him if such a small opening could let that much evaporated gasoline escape. He said it was pretty likely, but he thought the fumes would dissipate, too, especially if the garage was open. Naturally, I asked the man's wife whether the garage had been open. Said she couldn't remember. I asked her whether the mower had been used recently. She said she thought Saturday afternoon. So—we looked for other evidence. Not a speck. I went back to our expert and asked him what he would guess if he was forced to guess. He said it was possible that somebody had poured gasoline on the floor to evaporate just before the victim was due home."

"But how would anyone know—"

"You're going to ask how anyone would know he'd light a cigarette. I asked his wife. She said he didn't believe in smoking while driving because it was distracting. So he always lit up the minute he got out of the car."

"What about the boy scout?"

"Well, naturally I interviewed the neighbors. One told me she had seen somebody in the garage about half an hour before the man came home. She thought of calling the police— you know how people will *think* of calling the police!—but instead she decided to watch the garage to see if he took anything, and if he did she'd call the police then. He came out in just about five minutes without anything in his hands, so she knew it was all right. She thought it was all right, anyway, for another reason."

"What?"

"The kid was wearing a boy scout uniform."

Ax let the words hang in the air. After a minute the other man's index finger came back into play.

"You understand, there was no evidence of tampering. Nobody there when the accident occurred, and anybody could have left the top off the gas tank. Nothing."

"You said there were *two* cases."

"The other I maybe shouldn't even mention."

"Why not?"

"The first case was probably an accident. The second one certainly was. Although the druggist had a perfect record, which makes it strange. You don't figure a man's first mistake to be fatal."

"What happened?"

"I'm only going into this because of the scout angle. A man in his fifties here, taking Dicumerol for a heart problem. Dicumerol reduces the tendency of the blood to clot." He cocked his head at Ax, as if to ask whether he was being too technical.

Ax couldn't resist. He said, "It increases prothrombin time."

"Yes. Well. He died very suddenly and his wife, for some reason, looked at his pills. She said they looked slightly different to her, just a little smaller, but otherwise the same color and shape. So I had our drug man look at them. Instead of the blood thinner, it was a substance that can *increase* the tendency of the blood to clot. And the autopsy showed coronary clots.

"Okay, so what did we do? Naturally, I took the tablets to his pharmacist. He was astounded. He admitted that the two tablets looked quite a bit alike, but he said he couldn't possibly have mixed them up. He showed me the bulk packaging they came in and, sure enough, they were very different. One came in big plastic things like gallon jugs and the other in small cardboard containers. And he made the point that the Dicumerol is very common. He fills prescriptions for it a lot. The other was rarely used, and he claimed that he'd have looked twice because it was an unusual drug. He said he couldn't possibly have made that sort of mistake. Of course, he had to say that."

"Um, I suppose."

"He lost his license."

"What about the scouts?"

"Well, naturally, I went very carefully into the question of who had been in the house in the previous couple of weeks, on the unlikely chance that somebody switched the medication. Wife had no access to drugs, and nobody else much had been to visit. No mysterious telephone repairman or anything like that."

"Uh-huh."

"But the victim's son was a member of a boy scout troop."

"Mmm?"

"It doesn't mean anything, of course. But a couple weeks before, the boy's local troop had played host at his house to a neighbor troop."

"Neighbor troop from where?"

"Rivercrest."

Naturally.

Twenty-One

Scenario Number One, thought Ax. Garvey was homicidal, a killer, acting alone. It was an appalling idea, but perfectly possible. The disturbance that Ricky and Peter were showing stemmed from a partial or complete awareness of Garvey's mania. Garvey could have told them what he did to people and frightened them into keeping silent, or alternatively they were not really aware of what he did, but felt an aura of disturbance around him. Peter might have resisted going to camp for fear of being put in a tent with Garvey. And Ricky had already made it clear that Garvey repelled him.

Scenario Number Two: Garvey had collected a coterie of disturbed children around him, a gang of killers. Even so, Ax believed Garvey would be the one who actually killed. It was difficult for Ax to reconcile what he knew of Ricky Lawton with murder. Passive acceptance, maybe. On the whole, he found this idea a lot less likely than scenario number one.

Scenario Number Three: Garvey or other boys might be involved, but at the instigation of an adult. If so, this adult was likely to be a scoutmaster, because the most natural close contact, except between father and son, was between boy and scoutmaster. There were any number of problems with this one. He could not imagine why a scoutmaster would kill people. Unless perhaps, he was insane. But, if it were so, why didn't other scoutmasters get a whiff of the devil in their midst? Could a murderous heart be *that* well hidden?

Ax had spent hours one afternoon looking for similarities between Dubcjeck, Linkletter, Briggs, and the two "accident victims" the chief of police had told him about. He found three: they were all men who lived in Rivercrest or a contiguous suburb, and were all rich. It wasn't enough.

Ax had started out on this quest with a sort of vigilante fervor that belied his training. He now believed he had been right, if impetuous. If he was right, a killer had murdered several people that he knew of, and there was no way of telling how many more, undetected. It was time to put together some facts, carefully.

He wanted very much to talk with the boys involved. But there were problems in interviewing minors. It would probably have to be done in the presence of their parents, and he was afraid he could not do it that way without tipping his hand. Garvey's father was one of the scoutmasters—one he wanted to interview. Peter might already be a disturbed child, and to upset him without good reason would be exceedingly dangerous. As for Ricky, he could talk to him casually at Samantha's, but he refused for his own personal reasons to question him in any way that would upset her. Which left him nothing to ask. He'd have to leave the boys alone and tackle the scoutmasters.

Ira Schultz had told Ax he would see him at home at 6:30. Ax assumed Schultz was having either an earlier dinner or a later dinner. But when he arrived at the square brick house with the rigidly controlled hedge and lawn, he found the family in the middle of eating.

"I can come back later," he said. He was embarrassed, standing in the hall, looking at four people at the table in the dining room.

"No, no, no. Come on in here." Schultz grabbed the coffee pot, his cup and an extra cup, and lurched off down the hall. Ax nodded hesitantly to Schultz's wife and two sons. They nodded back. He followed Schultz.

Schultz went to his den. The walls and bookcases were covered with Jaycee awards, golfing trophies, citizenship awards, several scouting badges and plaques, a framed statement that Ira Schultz had, for three consecutive years, pushed the community chest over its stated goal, and a Blood Bank award for having donated a championship number of pints of blood.

Ira was a man who took community involvement seriously.

"I didn't know it was your dinner hour," Ax said, thinking that Schultz could perfectly well have warned him.

"Oh, don't worry about it. The family's used to it. I'm a pretty involved sort of guy."

He likes it, Ax thought. *He wants the family to see that people need to talk to him in the middle of dinner.*

"So what's this about?" Schultz said.

Ax settled back in a dark brown leather chair with brass studs. Schultz poured him coffee, black. He had forgotten the cream and sugar, so Ax didn't mention them. Schultz had forgotten the saucer, too, and when he pushed the cup at Ax, he slopped some coffee onto Ax's thigh. Ax mashed the hot spot with his thumb and was grateful he had worn dark pants.

He had decided to be vague and watchful. He would throw out phrases that sounded like they meant something, and look for reactions.

"Now, I don't want to go into names," he said. "You can understand that."

"Of course."

"A few boys who are scouts may have been involved in some—um—violent incidents around town. I was wondering—"

"I can't believe that! We have the finest group of boys I've ever worked with—" He knocked into his coffee cup, and upset it over the desk blotter.

"I assure you—"

"Of course, boys do get high-spirited. Break a window, maybe. And firecrackers. We've had a few problems at meetings with firecrackers." Schultz mopped at the spreading coffee stain with a fistful of Kleenex.

"I assure you, Mr. Schultz, that I would not be here interviewing you if it were just a matter of firecrackers."

"Well, no. I suppose not."

"If my suspicions are correct, there is more than one boy involved. Do you know of anything in scouting that could have—uh—united these boys in a cadre?"

"Cadre? Like a gang? You're kidding! I don't even know what you mean." He threw the wad of wet Kleenex at the wastebasket. It missed and landed against the wall with a soggy plop.

"Have any of the boys formed a club?"

"No. We don't permit that. Here, have some more coffee. One of the scout principles is that we are all in it together. There are *no* unpopular scouts and *no* cliques."

"Do any of them stick together a lot?"

"Nope. We don't allow them to be exclusive."

"Are any of the scoutmasters involved in teaching boys paramilitary techniques?"

"No. Well, Dan Camelli made some proposal about tae kwon do."

"Have you been teaching tae kwon do?"

"No, no. It was just an idea. What is this?"

"I don't want to go into detail, Mr. Schultz."

"Well, gee! For a second there I had visions of the kids running around Rivercrest killing people. Ha!"

Ha, ha, thought Ax.

"I mean," Schultz said, "paramilitary technique! We're a very peaceful organization, you know. These are boys from good homes. Not that we wouldn't take a boy from a troubled family. I mean, a boy like that would need us even *more*. But what I'm saying is we have all good boys. The most military thing we do is, we march!" He laughed again.

He looks frank enough, Ax thought. *But anybody who can get really thrilled about giving quarts of blood has to be a pretty good actor.*

"Let me put this to you another way," Ax said. "If you had a bad apple, he would make *everybody* look bad, but it wouldn't be the fault of the scouts."

"No, that's right, it wouldn't."

"Are there any?"

Schultz did not answer immediately. Ax wonder whether he was going to hear that Garvey was a bit wild, but no real problem.

"Can't say there are," Schultz said. "No, sir, I don't believe there's a boy in that group I don't like."

Ax sighed, very quietly. "And what about scoutmasters?"

Schultz thought again. "Well, you know," he said. "I'm not real fond of Dan Camelli. But he's a good man. These guys, you know, they're giving their time to scouting when they could be doing other things. Could be in the Bahamas. Could be out making money. You never get rich being a scoutmaster. You just get satisfaction of watching boys develop. You know there are boys who have never in their lives camped out until they get into scouting? There are boys who don't know it's possible to walk more than a mile. This is a wonderful organization, sir."

"Yes, I know."

"These dads could be out at bars or whoring around, but instead they're with boys."

"Well, thank you, Mr. Schultz," Ax said, rising.

"Out in the fresh air."

"Roughing it," Ax said, nodding.

Ax was pleased that Garvey opened the door at Fiske's house so that he could observe Garvey at close range. But then it hit him like a blow—he *wished this* child to be the killer, the evil thing he sought, all along, so that Ricky wouldn't be involved. He stared at Garvey, half asking forgiveness in his mind for the prejudice he was feeling.

When Monty Fiske came in, Garvey faded slowly down the hall, and this Ax found very abnormal. Most kids were curious about cops.

"Mr. Ax," Fiske said cheerfully, not aware of anything odd in Garvey's quick departure, "sit down."

They sat in the living room, on a sofa covered in burlap. Fiske was wearing Levi's and a sweatshirt, and the bottoms of his tennis shoes were covered with short blades of grass.

"Sorry I wasn't in here when you arrived. I was mowing the lawn."

Ax said, "Nice to have it light this late, isn't it?"

"Yes, you can get a lot done after dinner."

"Mmm."

Ax let the silence hang. If he could make Fiske uneasy without being impolite, he would. After a few seconds, Fiske said, "So what seems to be the trouble?"

"Oh, I thought one of the others might have called you."

"Others? What others?"

"The other scoutmasters. This has to do with the scouts."

Fiske became still for a brief moment. Ax knew it was wariness.

"What about the scouts?" Fiske said.

"Have you noticed any of the boys behaving strangely?"

Ax saw Fiske's breathing stop, his face freeze expressionless. Then he laughed, a laugh like a series of coughs.

"I can't say I have, except that boys of that age behave
strangely all the time. It's a very confused age."

"Oh? Well, possibly. Have you noticed any of them acting
aggressive?"

"Aggressive? No."

Fiske was simply surprised at this, not uneasy. Ax knew he
had taken a wrong turn.

"Emotionally disturbed?"

"I don't think so."

Fiske was cautious again, but not worried. Ax had not
come close to the heart of the fear.

"Are the boys frightened of anything?"

"Not that I know of."

"Guilty?"

This was a bigger reaction. Fiske started, then covered it
with an angry reaction that Ax felt was contrived.

"Damn it! What is this all about? Why catechize me this
way? If you want to ask something, ask straight out!"

"I have reason to believe that a few of the boys may have
organized themselves into a gang."

"Gang? I wouldn't have thought it of these boys. This isn't
a neighborhood for gangs, anyway."

He was bland as a politician accused of nepotism, Ax
thought. Ax knew he had again moved away from the point of
discomfort. It was like playing the child's game where the
person who knows where the secret is calls "Hotter!" or
"Colder!"

"Has Garvey reported any talk about gangs?"

"No."

"Has Garvey shown any reluctance to go on camp-out?"

"No. He loves them."

"How about the other scoutmasters?"

"What about them?"

"How well do you know them?"

"Fairly well. I see them a lot on camp-outs. And we do a lot of planning."

"Would one of them encourage a gang?"

"Never. One of the principles of scouting is that the boys are all equal. No boy is ever made to feel left out."

"All the men are devoted to that?"

"Devoted is a funny word. But I think so. All the men are real scouters. They want to get boys outdoors, and teach them about nature and survival."

Jokingly summarizing this, Ax said, "Not one of them would lead a boy astray?"

Fiske turned white. "What do you mean?"

"I don't know, Mr. Fiske. I'm only asking. Is there anything in particular you're thinking of?"

"This is really offensive! I get the feeling you're just fishing, and I can't imagine why! Scouting is a fine organization. It's a wonderful thing for the boys, and I'd hate to see you cast dirt on it. If you've got wind of a boy doing a—a wrong thing, I can tell you it's on his own and it wouldn't be countenanced by the scoutmasters. I mean, boys get up to strange things; I know that. They can even imagine things that never happened, you know. Make things up for the fun of it. I suggest you give up this random interrogation. We're all responsible citizens, and if you put it in people's minds that we're suspicious in some way, you could be open to charges of slander. What's more, it would be an irresponsible misuse of your position. I would advise you to be careful, Mr. Ax."

"Well, I certainly don't want to upset you," Ax said blandly.

"I am not upset! The point is, you have to be careful what you insinuate."

"I didn't know I was insinuating anything. I'm just asking questions."

"You can insinuate with questions, too. Don't think you can't. You should *not* make people uneasy about a fine and blameless organization. Or any of us who give our time to keep it running. Men go into scouting to help boys."

"No fear of that, Mr. Fiske. I'm keeping my questions in the family."

Fiske got up and pointedly walked to the door.

"Well, whatever triggered this interest, I would advise you of one thing. Boys gossip, but a lot of it is imagination. It's the age for imagination. Don't go off half cocked." Fiske clapped Ax on the shoulder. "Don't be in too much of a hurry to believe their wild ideas."

Ax stood on the curb with his hand on his car door. *What in the world,* he thought, *was that all about?*

Lee Grey was not ruffled by Ax's questions. As far as Ax could see, Grey was not capable of being ruffled by anybody. He sat on his front porch in Adidas and a track suit, stretching his legs out straight, then flexing them, then extending them again.

"Always stretch after you run," he said.

Ax did not tell him he hated jogging.

Grey reverted to the question. "Gangs in the scouts!" he laughed. It was a big laugh, but final, like water gurgling down a drain. "Henry, you can't be serious. That would be against the whole mystique."

"But would it be impossible?"

"Oh, jeez. I suppose nothing is impossible. But you'd sure have a time convincing me there's a gang of thugs in the scouts." Grey may have been running, Ax thought, but his track suit looked sleek and smooth and fashionable.

"What about the scoutmasters?"

"What about 'em?"

"Would any of them lead the boys astray?"

"Lead them astray! That's a hell of a weird way of putting it. Is there anything specific you're driving at?"

"There's a possible connection to some very serious crime."

"You're shitting me."

"I may be wrong, but I assure you I'm not joking."

Grey peered in his face. "No, I see you're not. You're way off base, though. No kidding, Henry, these guys are the most complete bunch of straight arrows it's ever been my privilege to meet. Half of them are scared of even putting pressure on the kids to compete. I mean, there's *soul searching* before we can plan a rope-tying contest. This is a sincere group, Henry."

"Yes. Well, I'm glad to hear it."

"No. No, you're not. You got a bee in your bonnet and you want to prove it, right? Only natural."

"I wouldn't be pleased to find I was right in this case."

"Still, you want to show people you're on the job. Get out in front of the other investigators, huh, Henry? I just think— hell, I bet you're real good at your job, too. But this time, babe, you're way out in left field."

Ax was out of Lee Grey's house by 10:15. He wanted to go see Samantha, but he was afraid that, the way he felt, he'd ask her questions, even if he swore to himself he wouldn't.

There had been a fear of the future growing in him all day. It was as compelling as a persistent pain in the chest. And it had become stronger since he had talked to the scoutmasters. He felt that some time today he had been close to a monster.

246

Brimstone had rubbed off on him. He had breathed its exhalation, but he didn't know when.

He thought he would stop on the way home and buy himself a beer. Maybe that would wash away the fear in his throat. But the beer tasted bitter and the light in the bar was yellow as the smell of fear. He did not like sitting facing the bar with his back to the room, feeling that someone could come up behind him and he would see only a distorted vision in the mirror, his view of reality only a reflection fragmented by pyramids of glasses and rows of bottles. He felt isolated, alone, and vulnerable.

Ax got up and went home.

Twenty-Two

"Is Frederick fighting the divorce?" Dan asked.

"He fights it by trying to talk me out of it," she said. "But the papers are moving inexorably through the great digestive system of the state."

"Don't complete that metaphor."

"Forgot you were a biologist."

"Hell, yes. We know all about that kind of stuff."

They were sitting on Samantha's sofa. The boys, she hoped, had gone to bed, in order to be wide awake to leave on the camp bus in the morning. Dan was going along for the whole week, of course, and he seemed to feel the impending absence, for he said, "You going to see a lot of this police chief while I'm gone?"

"Some, I guess."

With his usual sensitivity to her tone of voice, he said, "Are you deliberately understating that to make me feel better? I mean, if you're going to see him seven nights a week, you can tell me so."

"No. You're sweet, Dan. I've been seeing Henry maybe twice a week, and as far as I know it'll go on that way."

" 'You're sweet' is the kind of thing you say to your great uncle Calvin."

Samantha laughed. She took his hand. "I said sweet because I meant sweet. You're very kind. You know I'm in an early state of recuperation and you don't push me. You're sweet because you're the opposite of sour. You don't crab at me and want me to be different."

"Did Frederick do that?"

"He dictated the way he wanted the house, the yard, my clothes, and our food. After a while, it makes you feel you're not good enough. The idea that you have to be changed makes it pretty clear you're not all right just the way you are."

"You're all right just the way you are."

"See what I mean? You're sweet."

"Sweet? My God, Samantha, I think of taking you home with me. Sending Tony to his grandmother's for the weekend. Carrying you over the threshold—"

"But you haven't pushed. And that's sweet," she said lightly.

"I have at least one scrap of sense left. But I want you to know that I'm on your side. I'm available. If you're worried. If you're lonely. If you need—" he grinned "—someone when you're feeling low in the middle of the night."

"I know, Dan. And I'm glad."

She felt a rush of affection for him, and she knew that if she kept looking at him she would want to touch him. She could almost feel his shoulder muscles under her hands, and she knew how they would harden if he held her, put his arms around her. She dropped her eyes and looked away.

After seeing Dan off, Samantha went to check on the equipment for the camp-out, which they had parked at the back door. Two backpacks, two bedrolls, two duffel bags, two ground cloths—all ready. She looked down at the assembled equipment, thinking that she was feeling well and optimistic—and the whole world spun away from her.

I'm going to lose them, her brain shrieked. *The children. I'm going to lose the children. They can't go on this trip.*

These are just backpacks and bedrolls, she thought. *They're*

249

real. There's no menace in them. The camp is safe. Ricky went last year and no evil happened.

But her mind screamed, *Don't let them go. Don't let them go. Keep them here, no matter how.*

"There's nothing wrong," she said aloud.

But a vision overlaid the pile of gear. She was alone and someone was stalking her. Someone wanted to kill her. And at the same time that she tried to escape the stalker, there was a great, a terrible danger stalking Ricky.

Keep them home!

This is ridiculous. You shouldn't have mixed your drinks this evening, that's all!

Keep them home.

Don't let them near the boy scouts.

She turned and ran up the stairs. Ricky's door was closed, unusual for him. Good. He needed the sleep.

Tad's light was still on. Tad was sitting up in bed, too excited to sleep. When he saw her, he started to explain.

"I couldn't sleep, Mom. So I thought—"

"Tad," she panted, "you can't go."

Get hold of yourself. You'll frighten him.

"Listen, I don't think I want you to go on this camp-out. It's—um—I'm going to miss you too much."

Tad stared at her. He had been looking forward to it for a year.

"Why don't you two stay home, and we'll drive somewhere. We'll go see something exciting. Like the Badlands, maybe," she said hastily, knowing she wasn't making it sound as much fun as she had intended. "We'll do some exploring."

Tad was looking hard at her. "Are you feeling okay?" he asked.

"Yes I—no, I have to be honest with you. I got worried about you going to the camp-out. I started thinking something terrible was going to happen." Even as she said it, the searing vision was fading, the horrible certainty was turning to doubt. What had upset her so badly? She was acting like her mother. "I guess I got excited about nothing."

"That's okay, Mom," Tad said kindly. "After all, you've never been away from both of us that long before."

You've never been away from both of us that long.

She giggled. For every mother who says, "He's never been away from home before," perhaps there was a child who saw it the other way around.

"Tad, you're right. Except for a weekend now and then, ever since you've been in the world, you've been with me. And I like it that way."

She had lost the intensity of that vision of disaster. It lingered as an afterimage, the memory of a light recently turned out. She had been silly, and she said so.

"That's all right," Tad said. "You'll feel better when we're on our way."

Twelve blocks away, in the part of Rivercrest near the C&NW railroad tracks, where the houses were smaller, Ricky crouched out of the lamplight in the shadow of a bank of junipers. He had been there two hours, and if he had been in his normal state, he would have been growing tired. As it was, he was so focused on his goal that he did not feel boredom or the cramps in his muscles.

It seemed to Ricky that he was doing something very adventurous, and at the same time heroic. He was waiting for an enemy. The enemy was out to get him and his mother, and Ricky had to strike first. If his thoughts had been less concentrated, he would have wondered, briefly, whether his mother would check his bedroom and find him gone. But this never entered his mind.

251

The enemy's driveway sloped down an incline into his garage. Ricky had gone in the side garage door earlier, to see whether there was any gasoline in cans or other material that could be used for a booby trap. But he had found almost nothing: a lawnmower with practically no gas in it; an empty gasoline can; four rakes, two of them bent so much that they were unusable; two snow tires; a wheelbarrow; a bag of bark chips; and a bag of vermiculite. He had taken the bag of vermiculite and spilled it near the far wall of the garage. He did not know how this would be useful, but something told him it might.

When he went in through the side door, the big lift-up door of the garage had been closed. He left it that way when he went out so that the enemy, coming home, would not know that anything was wrong.

Ricky watched as headlights came up Elm Street. He looked away from the lights themselves, to keep his night vision, and thought what a fine guerrilla warrior he was. The headlights went on past the driveway, throwing shadows of the junipers on the side wall of the house—a distorted file of bushes that marched in unison, then bent around the corner and, much elongated, rushed away down the back wall.

Vaguely, Ricky thought that might be about the fiftieth car that had passed while he was waiting.

A car came down Elm Street going the other way. This time the juniper shadows hurried, elongated, up the back wall of the house, then, rounding the corner, slowed down and straightened up to march quietly along the side wall.

Ricky got to his feet and stood still behind the bush, in case it should be his enemy. But the car went on past. He was not really conscious of the dryness in his eyes, the cramps in his feet and leg muscles. It was cool tonight, but he did not think about that. He thought about his enemy.

Another car came down the street. The shadow junipers hurried up the back wall again and around the corner. There they froze. The headlights had turned in the driveway.

The shadows were transfixed a second; then the car crawled down the inclined drive, leaving the house in darkness.

Ricky waited. His enemy had come.

Henry Ax got out of the car.

Under Ricky's eye, he left the car door open and the engine running and walked to the garage door. Ricky did not really recognize him. He knew only that this was the man he had been told to get, the man who was a danger to him.

Ax seized the handle of the garage door at the bottom.

Ricky slunk toward the car. He reached out to throw the shift lever from park to drive, so that the car would slide down the slope and smash Ax against the garage door.

But the door skidded up fast, with a rumble. Too late. Ricky ducked down into the junipers.

But Ax was not coming back to the car. He had caught sight of the spilled vermiculite, its shiny flakes glistening in the headlights. He went over to investigate, muttering under his breath, "Goddam cats."

Instantly, Ricky sprang for the shift lever and threw it into drive.

Ax was bending over the pile of vermiculite, looking for tracks. The car started slowly down the slope, without much change in engine sound, its door still open, gaining speed rapidly. After a couple of seconds, Ax became aware of the increased intensity of the headlights. He looked up.

He saw the car rushing toward him. He started to spring to the left, but it was too late. The car had been almost on him when he jumped, and it struck him while he was at an angle, leaning to the left, but still in its path.

The front bumper pinned Henry Ax against the back wall of the garage. The wheels of the car ground forward, slipping a little on the dust of the garage floor, as they pushed against resistance.

Ax screamed, shoving at the hood of the car with both hands, desperately pushing sideways, straining his body to get away from the automobile. The right side of his pelvis fractured. With the lessened resistance, the car drove forward another two inches, mashing the abdominal aorta against the spine and rupturing it. Ax's body spasmed forward and the car drove another half inch, crushing the lower end of the duodenum where it met the beginning of the small intestine. The walls of the duodenum ripped, and the blood from the torn aorta surged into it at great pressure, raced up the stomach and esophagus, and erupted in a sheet of blood from his mouth. The hemorrhage caused his blood pressure to plummet. He lost consciousness and sagged over the hood of the car, mouth now pumping blood more and more slowly onto the metal surface.

Henry Ax was not yet dead, but he had been dying from the moment the major blood vessel ruptured.

Ricky slipped forward and studied the situation. The wheels of the car were still grinding slowly. He reached in and changed the shift lever to neutral. He left the car running, to make it look like an accident. He left the driver's door open.

He looked around. The house, like so many in Rivercrest, was isolated by its landscaping. The sunken driveway and garage acted as a natural sound barrier and screen. But someone might notice the headlights, or the glow from them, if they were on all night. He pushed the light control, turning them off.

Maybe whoever found the car would think Ax had come home by daylight.

A person who had been accidentally killed by his car would not get up and close the garage door, so Ricky left it open. With the lights off and the garage secluded, he thought it was unlikely that anyone would come and investigate. The motor was not loud, and would eventually run out of gas. Most likely, the enemy would not be found until somebody at work decided he was missing and came to check. By then Ricky would be far away.

Ricky took a last look at the enemy. The mouth was still oozing blood, but only a little. The eyes were open and staring and did not move. Ricky could not see any breathing.

Ricky walked up the slope in the shadow of the house. There he stopped to look around. Even from here, he could see the garage roof but not the inside. He could barely hear the motor running.

Ricky crossed in shadows to the house next door. It was dark. He cut across their backyard and out onto the street.

By the time he reached the corner, he had forgotten why he was out. He thought perhaps he had decided to take a walk.

In the garage, Henry Ax's heart began fibrillating. It quivered arhythmically for three or four minutes. Then it stopped.

He was dead.

Twenty-Three

The bus drivers sat inside the two fat yellow buses with the doors closed, arming their psyches against a seven-hour drive with thirty-six ten- to fourteen-year-olds. Geranium petals blew from the community center flower beds onto the legs of the scoutmasters, who were forming up two bus groups.

At the stroke of 8:00, the bus drivers threw open their doors. The buses rocked a little as the kids pushed in. Then the two buses moved, trundling up the street heavily, as if they were pregnant.

Samantha's horror of the night before had passed. Like the memory of a headache, she pictured it but could not quite feel it. Henry Ax was taking her to Chicago to dinner tonight, to what he called "the old neighborhood." She was not to dress up. It was not that kind of neighborhood, he had said.

At home she got into a good, hot bath with bath oil. She dozed, wondering whether you could drown if you fell asleep in the bath. Then the telephone rang. *Don't get up.*

It rang again.

I'm not getting out.

It rang again. Maybe the bus had been in an accident. She got up. Skidding on her own dripping bathwater, she ran to the phone.

"Samantha, dear?"

"I was in the tub, Mother."

"Oh. Have the boys left?"

"Yes. This morning early." She shivered in the cool air.

"Samantha, have you ever checked out that camp?"

"Mom, it's seven hours from here."

"You know, these summer camps can be very dangerous. They say that there are a lot of drownings. I remember reading—was it thirty-one last year?"

"In the whole country?"

"Or three hundred and ten? Or—"

"Mother, it's a scout camp. They're very safety-conscious."

"And food poisoning, too."

"Ricky went last year. He said the biggest danger was poison ivy. Nobody got hurt."

"A friend of your father's died of that. Did I ever tell you? He had poison ivy and scratched it and got blood poisoning."

"What year was that?" Samantha asked grimly.

"Well, it was just before the war."

Quickly realizing that the war in question was World War II, Samantha said, "Mom, that was before antibiotics."

"Well, it certainly goes to show you that nothing's safe, doesn't it?"

They called the festivities on the first night the Pickerel Lake Powwow. There were troops from three suburbs here. The scouts had cleared sticks and branches from their camp-site as they pitched their tents, and had carried all the sticks to a central area near—but not too near—the cook tent and mess hall. They piled them there tepee fashion. Then Ira Schultz formed up a party with one boy from each troop to go with him into the forest to cut some large deadfalls for the fire. Peter Winterthur was chosen, but he didn't want to go. Kiri Obisawa was the second choice. Peter said he didn't feel well, but Ricky believed Peter was afraid to go into the woods with just one man and a few boys.

So Peter was put in the next draft group—one boy from each troop to help in the cook tent in the late afternoon. This duty would rotate, with a new boy chosen to help cook and another boy chosen to help wash up each day. But even so, all of those chosen complained loudly about the assignment, except Peter, who went along quietly.

Ricky got picked for water patrol. He, seven other boys, and Lee Grey went down to the lake with snorkels and masks or goggles. They held hands to make a chain that stretched out from shore about twenty feet. With Lee Grey as anchor man on the end farthest from shore, they waded along with their faces in the water, scanning the bottom for broken bottles, cans, and submerged boards with nails. Grey said, "This may be a wilderness area, but you never know what kind of junk hunters and campers throw away."

They did the entire circumference of the small lake. It took three hours, including a lot of time standing on shore warming their feet up. Ricky enjoyed it. He found he had endurance, and he felt well. Maybe things were going to be all right after all.

This camp-out, he was sharing a tent with Tony Camelli. His first choice would have been Kiri Obisawa, but you didn't get choices. The scoutmasters believed that if the kids got to choose, somebody might feel left out. Ricky had been afraid he might be given Garvey as tentmate. As it turned out, Peter had drawn Garvey this time. Ricky knew from Peter's face that Peter was not pleased. Garvey bullied Peter. But the scoutmasters would not change the assignments. This was wrong. No one should be forced to pal up with Garvey. That was Ricky's view.

Ricky liked Kiri because he was a person who was interested in things. He had fun with almost everything that turned up, whether it was a nest of caterpillars in a tree or a cut on his own hand. He always had questions. Why do tent caterpillars stay together and build a web around themselves? Is it for protection? Wouldn't they all find more food if they spread out? Why wash a cut? Doesn't the bleeding clean it out? What if there are germs in the water you wash it with? Of the scoutmasters, Dan Camelli and Lee Grey answered Kiri's questions with facts. Ira Schultz was likely to say, "You wash it because the Red Cross first aid book says you wash it." Or, "Look up caterpillars in the encyclopedia. You'll remember better if you look it up yourself."

Ricky suspected that people who told you to look it up didn't know the answer. Anyway, looking it up was not better than asking, because if the book wasn't clear, you couldn't ask it to explain.

Tony was on the dinner cleanup crew.

"Yuck!" he said. "I hope they don't have chipped beef!"

"Why?"

"Cleaning it up. Last year, my first day they had it. It gets dried on the plate like glue, that yucky white sauce it's in, you know? It's like Elmer's glue."

"Yeah. Yeah."

"And you can't get it off. You have to soak the dishes a long time and then rub it off. And little pieces of meat get stuck in it. Like throw-up!"

Ricky giggled. "You know what the high school troop called it last year?"

"Yeah, shit on a shingle. I heard 'em. Schultz heard it, too, and he got so mad! Boy! Was he pissed!"

"Well, they shouldn't serve crud like that."

"Maybe they'll have hamburgers."

"Or spaghetti."

"Their spaghetti," Tony said grandly, "leaves something to be desired."

"Yeah. Flavor!"

They giggled. "Hamburgers and french fries and chocolate cake wouldn't be bad," Tony said.

"There's no nutritional value in that stuff."

"Let 'em have nutritional value tomorrow. We just got here."

"That's the gong. We gotta go."

"Wait a minute. I got a Frito in my shoe."

After dinner, which was not chipped beef, but franks and baked beans, carrot sticks, and apple pie, the cleanup crew went to work in the kitchen tent. The rest of the boys had an hour free before the powwow.

This hour gave the scoutmasters time to get ready. They were going to be Indians tonight, in war paint. There were twenty-four scoutmasters, enough for a good show of whooping and dancing. They had decided to do this the first night, figuring that making fools of themselves was a good way to break the ice and get rid of the notion that the adults were going to be sober and bossy during the week. All of them had brought whatever makeup their wives were tired of—old lipsticks, little pots of rouge and blusher and eye shadow that had worn almost to the bottom, and eyebrow pencils in several colors. When they started to dress, eyebrow pencils became the most popular, because you could get clear outlines with them.

"I look like I fell in the franks and beans," Ira Schultz said. He had not developed good control of his rouge. When it wouldn't come out of the pot smoothly, he pulled it out in pieces and smeared it on with his fingers in lumps and streaks.

"No, you look like you fell in the poison sumac," Monty Fiske said.

"Clawed by a bear," said Lee Grey.

"I feel silly," Schultz said.

Dan Camelli had bought his makeup at Rivercrest Pharmacy, because he had no wife to borrow from. "You're supposed to feel silly," he said. "Try some of this black pencil. Make a few zigzag lines."

"This isn't really Indian," said Lee Grey.

"The Indians would have loved this stuff for war paint," Dan said. "They would have traded seven strings of wampum and a deerskin for this green goop with the little silver sparkles."

"Yeah," Grey said. "I'm using something called Toasted Gingerfrost."

"I," said Dan, "have Peri-Twinkle Blue and Perle Taipei Peach."

"Yum," said Lee Grey.

Ricky sat between Kiri and Tony, in a big circle of boys around the fire. He had felt good all day, but there was an underlying apprehension. He had been holding back from his mother facts about his health that he knew she'd want to know.

Ricky trusted his mother. He felt he had betrayed her in not telling her about the blackouts. But he was afraid.

He wanted more than anything to have a father he could talk with. But his father changed so much from day to day it was hard to know how to talk with him.

His father changed faces.

When Ricky's father was cheerful, he was as buoyant as—as Dan Camelli, for instance. He had to admit Dan was one of the better fathers he had met.

The most difficult face Ricky's father wore was the petulant, dissatisfied one. The one where you couldn't do anything right. The one that made sarcastic remarks that hurt, like, "Of course you can't pick up your room. You're the first-born son. You're too important."

What did that mean? He didn't feel important. He just forgot to pick up his room because he was making a clay model of the human eye for biology class.

Or, "I would think almost anybody could sit still at the table for half an hour. Are your mother and I that unattractive?"

You could hardly think of an answer to stuff like that. They weren't anything you could get hold of, exactly. They just made you feel bad.

Ricky stopped thinking when he heard the war whoop from behind the cook tent. He settled himself better on the hard ground and got ready to have fun. Two dozen scoutmasters came whooping around the side of the cook tent, into the firelight. They had their shirts off and had painted war paint on their chests and faces.

Several of them wore saucepans on their heads. One carried a ladle and one carried a spatula. The rest leaped and danced without props. Boys from one of the other troops beat on drums made from the giant-size potato chip cans.

The man in front led the others around the fire, chanting and dipping, until they formed a circle, bending forward, then leaning back on the next beat with a whoop. Kiri said, "That isn't really Indian," but he was laughing and clapping at the same time, so Ricky knew it was an observation, not a criticism.

The boys started clapping in time to the drums and the dance. They gained confidence in the beat and clapped louder. The men circled the fire, which threw their shadows out like spokes of a wheel that went around and around and around. The red and green and blue war-paint picked up the firelight and glittered with color.

Tony Camelli clapped his hands and shouted, "Go, Dad!" Ricky wished his father were here.

He had thought it was Dan Camelli who led in, but now that the men were all circling, there was no longer any lead position, and he couldn't tell who any of them were. The men he had known for years had melted into these creatures, their faces camouflaged by paint, distorted by the flicker of the flames. Where the amber and orange firelight hit them, the red paint glowed brighter and bloodier red, but the blue looked purple and the greens turned black. The faces themselves flickered and dissolved in the writhing light. The bodies, growing sweatier, reflected the yellows of the light and glistened, distorted, with vivid highlights and deep cuts of shadow.

These bodies could be anyone, men he had never known, or men he knew, slightly changed, faces melted, bodies distorted, souls vanished.

Ricky started to sweat, though he was sitting still. At the same time, he was cold and shivering. Everyone around him shrieked and clapped and laughed and screamed. Ricky shivered until the shivers turned to shaking and big beads of sweat stood out on his forehead. Then he knew he was going to be sick.

He jumped up, lurching, running, and made it to the woods, where he was sick among the evergreens.

Even there, the shadows of the tree trunks flickered insubstantially, and in the distance he could still hear the screaming and the beating of the drums.

Samantha locked up the house and went to her room to undress. It was only 10:00, but she was sure now that Henry was not coming. She had thought of calling him, to see whether he was sick, but she had decided not to. If he were too sick even to telephone, the only way she could find that out was to go to his house and break in.

And there certainly was no good reason for that.

Besides, if he had forgotten their date and taken another woman home with him, it would be disastrous. That applied to telephoning, too. She did not want to appear possessive.

Henry was not, as far as she could tell, the sort of person who would just forget a date, however. And she did not really think he had found some other woman in such a short period of time.

By far the most likely thing was that some real emergency had come up. Emergencies were his job. A burglary, a multiple traffic accident, a fire, it could be anything. He probably believed that she, as a reasonable, thinking adult, would know he'd call when he could. He'd expect her to be mature enough to go to bed and not feel insulted or hurt.

Well, all right. That was exactly what she was going to do.

At Village Hall, Charles O'Malley Elfenbein, a Rivercrest public safety officer, was also thinking of Henry Ax. It was unusual for the chief not to show up for a whole day. Still, it was Saturday. And Ax did not have regular hours. Actually, Elfenbein thought it was pretty good that Ax could take a day off.

Elfenbein was married and had a four-month-old baby boy and an eighteen-month-old daughter, which meant two in diapers. Naturally, he was worried about Ax's continuing unmarried status. He hoped Ax was out on a date, an all-day, all-night date.

He hoped Ax was having a lot of fun with a very nice woman.

Twenty-Four

On Sunday morning, Samantha still hadn't heard from Henry Ax. No matter what the emergency, he could not have been kept continuously busy for fourteen hours. Probably she had offended him. She hadn't believed there was a killer loose in Rivercrest. She had hurt his pride.

Well, she couldn't pretend to believe in an idea she thought was far-fetched, could she?

If he was not angry with her, though, what could have happened? Illness? A heart attack at his home? A fall down the cellar stairs? Electric shock? Or he could have been injured on the job, shot by a burglar, struck by a speeding car at the scene of an accident. A fire? An explosion in a ruptured gas main?

Or had one of his parents been injured? Or taken ill?

By noon she realized that she was spinning off disasters that might have happened to Henry at such a rate that her imagination was tiring. It was silly to spend this much energy worrying when she could telephone.

She decided to call his house. If he had a woman friend over, at least noon was not a very embarrassing time to talk.

The phone rang and rang. She let it ring a dozen times, thinking he might be really ill and the sound might rouse him.

But finally she knew it would not be answered. She stood holding the phone for a few seconds, wondering whether he would be embarrassed if she called him at work. Well, she didn't have to give her name. She didn't have to explain why

265

she was calling. And certainly lots of people must call the police chief. In Rivercrest his office was where the buck stopped.

"Is Henry Ax in?"

"No, he isn't. Could I take a message for him?"

The man's voice was courteous and not evasive. Samantha decided Henry had not been injured on the job. There would have been a different quality in the voice.

"Well, do you know where I could get in touch with him?"

"I'm not permitted to give out his home number."

"Oh, I have his home number," Samantha said, not meaning to. Now she was stuck. This man would know it was a personal call. Well, let him, dammit. She was worried now.

Elfenbein, who was on eleven to seven today, said "Oho!" silently with his lips. Not only a lady friend, but a worried lady friend. He heard it in her voice. In his job, he was an expert on worry.

"Have you tried calling him there?" he asked.

"Yes. There wasn't any answer. You mean you haven't seen him today, either?"

"No. But it's Sunday, ma'am. He doesn't always come in on Sunday."

"What about Saturday?"

"Yeah, he's almost always here on Saturdays."

"I mean, was he there yesterday?"

Elfenbein hesitated. He was not certain how much information to give out over the phone. If Ax was out with another woman, and if the woman on the phone was a pest or a girl he was trying to get rid of, Ax might not thank Elfenbein for talking about where he'd been.

Or hadn't been.

At the same time, in his rather expert judgment, this woman was worried, not jealous or irritated. And for that matter, Elfenbein was getting a little bit worried himself.

"Well, no. He wasn't in yesterday."

"This isn't like him. He'd let you know, wouldn't he, if he were called away suddenly? If one of his parents were ill?"

"I would expect him to. Of course, if it was very sudden— who knows? We can all cover for each other here. The place runs without him, even if he doesn't always think so." He smiled.

"But he'd let you know as soon as he could?"

"Unless he wasn't going to be gone long. Were you supposed to meet him at any particular time?"

"He was coming over at seven-thirty last night."

"I see. So as far as we know he's only been missing, um, less than eighteen hours. If he's missing at all, I mean."

Angry, she said, "This isn't just *somebody* who's missing. He's a village official, and we know where he usually is, and we know that disappearing isn't like him."

"Ma'am, could you give me your name and address?"

Reluctantly, Samantha did so. "What will you do?" she asked.

"We don't look for missing persons until they've been gone twenty-four hours, ma'am. Except young children. Tell you what. I get off work at seven. I'll go around and check out his house on my way home."

"Thank you," she said, not really meaning it. She had heard that official tone come into the voice, and she knew it was not going to work to ask him to break procedures.

She'd give Henry another hour. Then she was going over to check his house.

"Hi, Kiri," the man said. "What are you doing?"

"Oh, I was just counting the needles on this pine tree. It has five needles in each cluster. That makes it a white pine."

267

"That's right. Say, hold still a minute. There's a bee or something on the back of your neck."

Kiri, who was wearing bathing trunks and no shirt, held still.

"I don't want to swat him or anything. He might sting. Do you feel him?"

"No."

"Right on the back of your neck?"

"No. I can't feel him."

"He's a little guy. There, he's walking across the back of your neck. Do you feel that?"

"No."

"Walking up into your hairline. Feel that?"

"Nope."

"There he goes. He's flying away."

The man lay in his tent during the after-lunch quiet period, thinking. He was annoyed. Kiri was no damned good. You couldn't get him to believe suggestions. Ricky was biddable but difficult. And he had resolved never to use Garvey again. As of now, Garvey was retired. Period. Safety first.

He wanted to complete his outstanding contract. He had a horror of letting these things run on more than a few weeks, in spite of the fact that he guaranteed completion within four months. The customer might get nervous and give the game away. After all, the customer was an amateur. But before he could get on with the contract he had to decide what to do about The Threat. Henry Ax had been only half the problem.

Ax had been dating Samantha Lawton, and Samantha had been on the scene of the Jim Dubcjek project. He was certain that the two of them had talked.

When Ricky arrived for his instruction in advanced first aid, the man said, "May the force be with you."

Ricky stood still, his eyes unfocused. The man quickly ran through the tests for the depth of the trance. He used first a part of the LeCron scale.

"Ricky, on a scale of one to a hundred, with a hundred the deepest, how deep is the trance you're in?"

It never failed to amaze the man that this actually worked. But every source he had read found that self-evaluation correlated very closely with observation by professionals and with physical tests, such as breathing rate, galvanic skin response, insensitivity to pain, and changes in gastric motility and gastric secretion.

"Eighty," said Ricky.

Then, using a combination of the North Carolina Scale and Long Stanford Scale, he took Ricky through his subjective responses. Ricky reported a fading away of the physical environment, drowsiness, and relaxation.

"Now you see nothing but my eyes, and you hear nothing but my voice. Is that right?"

"I see nothing but your eyes and I hear nothing but your voice."

"Can you see this tent pole?"

"No."

"Do you hear any shouting?"

"No."

Tunnel vision and total concentration.

"Now, Ricky, I want to ask you about your mother. We want to help her. Was she dating that man, Henry Ax?"

"Yes."

Good. He's answering truthfully, and without any hesitation.

"Did Henry Ax ask you anything about scouts?"

"No."

Odd. Maybe he had never had a chance to talk with the children.

269

"Has your mother been worried about Garvey?"

"Yes."

"About scouts?"

There was no answer.

"Is your mother worried about scouts?"

"I don't know. I think so."

"What makes you think so?"

"She didn't want us to come. Tad says she thought something terrible might happen."

"Why did she let you come?"

"Tad said he wanted to."

"I see." She had not tried to question them, then. Possibly she just suspected, and was not sure. In any case there wasn't much time to waste. He had never used a child as young as Tad, but he was going to have to try. A ten-year-old should be easier to put into a trance, but possibly harder to control. There was no other way; this project was certainly going to require both children.

"Ricky, you are now going to wake up. In a minute, when I clap my hands, you will wake up. You will remember that we talked about first aid, and we're going to enroll you in the CPR course. You won't remember anything else, and you won't remember being in a trance. Do you understand?"

"Yes."

"Ready now! Wake up!"

Samantha made one last telephone call to Henry's house. But the phone rang and rang, and though she knew that the ring you heard on your phone was not the ring that was sounding in the house, she had an overwhelming impression of a phone ringing hollowly, echoing, with no one there to answer it.

There's something wrong. I've got to get to Henry.

She started for the car, and then, on impulse, turned around and went up to the bedroom. Frederick had once kept a gun on the shelf of his closet. It was a small automatic. She was not sure she remembered how to use it, although she had fired it once. But the desire to take it along was irresistible.

It had been weeks, she thought, since she had opened Frederick's closet. She did not enjoy seeing the reproach of its emptiness.

She swung open the door. An odd odor penetrated her consciousness just a second too late. There was a sound, a brief scraping noise, and the tail of her eye caught motion. She recoiled. An object flashed into view at the side of her head and struck a sharp blow on her shoulder. A sudden wetness spread down her shirt and Levi's.

She grabbed at the doorframe. A jar smashed to the floor and broke. Glass and moisture spattered her ankle. Her hands clung to the doorframe.

There was a sharp, unpleasant odor. Her shirt lay against her skin with a prickly dampness. On the floor next to her foot lay pieces of glass and a pool of amber liquid.

Samantha stared at it. Her breath was still whistling, her heart racing, but she realized that there was no further threat. She stopped gasping, forced herself to consider what she saw. And smelled.

Urine.

She gagged.

No you don't. Stop and think. They want you to be sick. Sick and scared.

The closet had double doors. It would be easy to walk in using one door and set the trap over the other. She looked, shaky but determined. There was a thumbtack on the inside of the door she had opened. A short piece of string dangled from it.

Of course. The door had been closed, then the string looped onto the doorframe above the door and the jar of urine set on the loop of string. When she had opened the door she had pulled the string, which pulled the jar off the frame. Simple.

Henry had been right.

I've got to get to Henry.

This trap could have been set days ago. All Garvey had to do was put it there and wait. He could be miles away—and *was* miles away—when the trap sprung.

There was no gun on the shelf. She hoped Frederick had taken it away with him. The idea that Garvey might have stolen it made her feel sick.

I've got to get to Henry.

Not like this! Samantha took a bath towel and threw it over the pool of urine in the closet. Let it soak it up. She didn't have time to wipe it. She pulled off the sticky, evil-smelling clothes, gagged, and waited a moment at the toilet, thinking that she was going to be sick. When she had fought it down, she stepped into and out of a two-second cold burst of shower. She wiped what she could with a hand towel and got into new clothes, shivering, while she was still quite damp.

I've got to get to Henry.

In the car she had visions of Henry lying at the bottom of the cellar stairs, his leg broken, without food or water since Saturday. Or even Friday night.

There were no newspapers accumulated on his front porch. But she had never been here before, and she did not know whether he took a newspaper.

There was no mail outside, either, but he had a mail slot, so that didn't tell her anything.

Shivering, she rang the bell. She could hear it ringing, far back in the house. Unlike the telephone, she really could hear this, but it was probably imagination that it sounded hollow and the house sounded empty. She rang again.

Craning around to look through the front window, she could see nothing but the top of a chair. There were no lights on inside, as far as she could tell. She bent over and looked in the mail slot, feeling foolish. A circular, a letter, and the *Rivercrest Review* lay on the inside doormat. That was all she could see. Grabbing the wood that separated the window-panes, she tried to push down the top of the double-hung window. It would not even jiggle.

Samantha knocked, with her fist. Still no response. The silence made her feel colder, and she thought a faint odor hung around her still. She tried the knob, but it wouldn't turn.

At least he takes precautions.

Tensely, she walked around the side of the house. There was a bank of juniper bushes, a driveway that sloped down, and his car. Surely his car hadn't come home without him. He had to be here.

No, not necessarily. Rivercrest was so small that people frequently walked to town. She might almost have passed him. He could be at Delizzious right now having lunch.

She could break a house window and go in and look for him.

He could be in the garage, fixing something. That could be why he didn't hear the doorbell.

I've got to find him.

She walked down the driveway toward the garage and the car.

The car had not been put away quite right. It was at a slight angle. That was odd, because Henry was an accurate driver.

As she got closer, she could see that the driver's door was

open. He must have just come home. Maybe he was un-packing something.

As a matter of fact, there he was, leaning over the hood of the car, fixing something. Or polishing the hood.

But everything was so quiet.

"Henry!"

She could see his head lying at an angle on the hood. It was as if he were listening to something, maybe a problem with the engine. How could he listen to the motor when it was turned off? His eyes were looking toward her, staring at her.

She walked closer.

Why didn't he answer? It was so hard to make people understand. You talked to people and they just didn't hear what you were saying.

How strange! There was a great pool of dried brown blood on the hood of the car. And the only things moving were a piece of his curly hair that stood up into a light breeze and a wasp that was inching down over his open right eye, testing the odors of dead skin and blood as it walked.

For an instant, Samantha did not understand what this meant.

"Henry?"

Then she screamed.

Twenty-Five

"Dad, can I talk to you?"

When Dan saw Tony come into the tent, he knew from Tony's expression there was a problem.

"What's happening?"

Tony sat on Dan's folding camp cot. So he meant to stay awhile.

"Dad, *if I* ask you something, will you promise not to do anything about it unless you and I agree first? It's kind of not my secret. Will you?"

"Um. That's too complicated. I can almost promise, but not quite."

"Why not?"

"Well, let's imagine one of the boys stepped on a dirty nail. You saw him do it, so you know about it. And he admits to you that he hasn't had a tetanus shot in a long time, but he makes you promise not to tell anybody because he's scared to have a shot. So you come to me about it. And I'd have to act. It might be life or death. I'd *have* to do something about it, whether or not you wanted me to."

Tony grinned. "I'll take your best judgment. The thing is, I don't want you to question him because then he'd know I talked to you and—"

"And that wouldn't be good. No, I see that. Suppose you tell me what it is, and we work out together what's best to do."

"Well, it's about Rick."

"Okay."

"The night of the powwow—night before last?—about halfway through the powwow he got up and ran off. I thought that was kind of funny, so I followed him. After a couple of minutes, I mean. I didn't want him to know."

"And?"

"I heard him—um—being sick in the woods."

"I see. Has he been sick since?"

"I don't think so. Not like that."

" 'Not like that.' Like what, then?"

"He's been having nightmares. He says things in his sleep and he screams. What he says is mostly gibberish. I usually can't understand the words. But he wakes up breathing hard and everything."

"Nightmares? Is he scared of the dark here? Or of the woods?"

"He never was on any camp-out before."

"Would he tell you? He might be embarrassed."

"Well, but—after these nightmares he sometimes gets up and goes off and walks in the woods."

"Jeez. I guess you're right. He's not afraid of the dark if he does that."

"It looks to me like he's trying to get away from his dreams, you know?"

"Yeah. Have you talked to him about it? Or have you pretended to be asleep?"

"Would that be wrong?"

"No, no. I imagine you might, so as not to embarrass him."

"Well, actually, both. The first night here he had two dreams, I guess. At least he woke me up twice. He was really scared. So the first time I asked him what the trouble was, but he didn't want to say—"

"What exactly *did* he say?"

"Um—well, something like—oh, I know. I asked him what was the trouble and he said, 'Nothing I can understand.' "

"Nothing *you* could understand?"

"No, nothing *he* could understand. See?"

"I don't see much, that's for sure. Then the next time, what did you do?"

"I figured he didn't want to talk about it, so I just lay there and watched him, you know? So if he was sick I could do something, but otherwise he didn't have to explain all the time. And that was when he went out for a walk. And he did last night, too."

"Oh."

"I mean, this isn't like Rick. If it was Peter, okay, but not Rick."

"I know. Rick is pretty solid."

"So, I mean, what am I going to do?"

"I'm thinking."

"Dad, could Rick have a brain tumor?"

"Whatever made you think of that?"

"Well, I saw this program on *Emergency!* about a little kid—"

"Oh. Well, I doubt it. At least we have to find out first if there's a simpler explanation. Do you think he'd talk with me?"

"I don't know. There's sort of a problem. You know."

"His parents' divorce and his dad leaving and his mom going out with me."

"Yeah."

"Well, okay. I'm not going to just walk up to him and say, 'Hey! What's bothering you?' I'm not quite *that* stupid."

Tony laughed. "I know."

"What I'll do—see what you think of this—is tonight I'll stay awake and watch awhile. And if Ricky goes out, I'll get myself into a position so I'm just casually meandering across the clearing at the same time he is, on an intercept course. I'll just happen to run into him, so it won't be like you told me about it. And if he's upset enough, he may talk."

"Thanks, Dad."

"Thanks yourself. I'm glad you care about Rick."

"Well, sure. Jeez, Dad, I'm not a heartless monster."

"That, old pal, is for sure."

Charles O'Malley Elfenbein was a distraught, saddened man who also knew he was in over his head. He had sent Samantha Lawton home and supervised the on-the-scene with Henry's body. He had ordered the car towed to the forensic lab. The body was taken to the Cook County Medical Examiner, as were the bodies in all unexplained deaths in Cook County, whether in Chicago or not. They'd report their findings, but the actual investigation had to be handled by the local police. Without Henry Ax to take charge, that meant Elfenbein.

All Sunday night and right through to Monday morning he sat in the office—at his desk, not Henry's. He was grieving for the loss of a friend. Henry had been more than his boss. Elfenbein was going to miss him.

He had to handle this as a possible homicide. But he felt very inexpert at suspicious deaths. This was not Chicago, where homicides happened every day.

And, in fact, he did not know how to classify this. There were really no clear pointers to homicide, but if you wanted to call it an accident, there were certainly anomalies. He could not imagine, for instance, Henry Ax putting his car in neutral and getting out of it. Shifting into park would be absolutely automatic.

Nor was it mechanically possible for the car to have

slipped from park to neutral. On Ax's car, reverse was between neutral and park, and it just didn't seem likely that the shift could pop across reverse into neutral. He'd have to ask an expert, of course, but he wouldn't bet on it.

Henry was never careless with his car. Elfenbein knew very few policemen who were careless with cars. They had seen too much blood.

Another problem. The car's lights were off. Not burned out, not failed by a run-down battery, but turned off at the switch. Either they had been turned off after the accident by another person or Henry had driven home in daylight. And that seemed odd to Elfenbein, because he thought Henry rarely went home before dark. Henry worked till 6:00 or 7:00 and then went out to dinner and, like a lot of people who lived alone, lingered over a beer or two. Well, it was possible he had started home by 8:00. But Elfenbein wondered about it.

The autopsy might help with that by fixing the time of death.

Then there was the matter of the fingerprints. There were two that were not Henry's on the gear lever, not very good prints because the plastic was rough. Part of one had been found on the light switch, but the switch was a deeply fluted column and the print was fragmentary. Even without analysis, Elfenbein knew they were not Henry's prints. They were too small.

There was no reason that he knew of for anyone to kill Henry. But if Henry had been murdered, Elfenbein wanted so badly to catch the bastard that his face got hot just thinking about it. He was fearful that he didn't have the skills. He had been trained, he had spent three years in Chicago getting on-the-job exposure, but out here in Rivercrest, he just didn't get the experience.

He knew one thing. In a murder case you looked at people involved with the victim—relatives, lady friends. Samantha Lawton had been after him to find the body. No, that wasn't fair. She only said she was afraid there was something wrong. Then *she* had found the body. And there were those fingerprints. About the size of a large child—or a woman.

Elfenbein knocked. Samantha Lawton opened the door and stared at him with glazed eyes. "You remember me? Yesterday? Charles Elfenbein?"

"Yes. Come in." She looked like she hadn't slept. "I have to ask you some questions."

"Yes. All right."

"I'm trying to trace his movements Friday and Saturday. When you called me Sunday, you said he was due here Saturday night?"

"At seven-thirty."

"And you hadn't seen him all day?"

"No." The woman sounded dulled.

"What had you been doing Saturday?"

"In the morning I took the kids to the bus to go on a boy scout camp-out. The rest of the day, I cleaned."

"All day? On a Saturday?"

"Well, the kids were out, so it was a good time."

"Then what?"

"After seven-thirty, I guess I thought he was late, until about nine. Then I thought some emergency had come up. A fire or a major traffic accident."

"Friday night you didn't see him?"

"Friday night I had a friend over."

"Name?"

"Dan Camelli. He's a teacher at the high school."

"Uh-huh. Okay. Now I'm going to ask you to let me take your fingerprints, Mrs. Lawton. For purposes of elimination.

Since you were first on the scene, we don't know what you may have touched."

"I didn't touch anything."

"Well, I have to do it anyway. In times of stress, people often touch things and don't know they're doing it."

"I don't mind." *She knows,* he thought, *that she's a suspect. And she doesn't seem to care.*

"Thank you," Elfenbein said.

"I'd better tell you something," she said.

"Oh? All right."

"Henry was working on a case. He may have told you about it, but he may not. He believed there had been a series of murders in Rivercrest recently."

"In Rivercrest? We haven't had a murder in three years."

Samantha said quietly. "All right. I can see Henry *didn't* tell you. He believed the deaths of Jim Dubcjek, Clarendon Briggs, and Lem Linkletter were all caused by the same person. A boy named Garvey Fiske. He thought there might have been other deaths as well. And he was trying to discover whether Garvey was acting alone, or with other people."

"Those were accidents!"

"Look, I'm not asking you to believe me. I didn't believe Henry myself at the time. But you can find out. Henry must have talked with people. He must have left notes. I didn't talk with him about it much in the last week because—because *he knew I didn't believe him.* But I'm sure he was working on it. When he got a problem in his mind he didn't let up. I should have been more—" Samantha hesitated, trembling "—more sympathetic. But I thought he was making a mountain out of a molehill, and even now, my God, I don't know what to think. But I'm terribly frightened. Do you understand?"

"Yes, ma'am. Of course." Elfenbein did not realize that a bland, official tone had entered his voice.

"Lieutenant Elfenbein, please. This is *true*. Look on his desk. Look in his file. He must have kept notes. You'll find something."

"Thank you, ma'am. We're always interested in any help you can give us."

Walking down the path two minutes later, Elfenbein thought, *Nice looking woman. Intelligent. Speaks clearly and simply. I wouldn't have picked her for a nut case.*

Samantha watched him walk away. She knew he had dismissed her information from his mind.

No one will help. No one.

There was a bowl of tomato soup on the coffee table. It was orange and gelatinous. She thought she must have heated it for herself last evening and forgotten to eat it, but she couldn't remember clearly.

This is what terror feels like.

A vision of Henry's head, lolling against the car, and of the blood, rose before her eyes. She dwelt on it, hugged it. Of Henry himself, dead thirty years before his time, she refused to think. He was still out in her kitchen somewhere, making omelets.

Samantha's phone rang. It was her mother.

"Samantha, I just wondered whether you have a toaster."

"What?" said Samantha, unable to follow. "Of course I have a toaster."

"We had such a terrible fire in town here last night."

"Mother, I have problems right now—" She felt tears in her eyes.

"Two children burned to death, and both their parents. One seven months and one three years old. They say it was the toaster. It shorted out in the middle of the night and caused the fire."

Behave normally. Behave sanely.

"Mother, there must be fifty million toasters in the country. Most of them don't cause fires. You have to have an idea of relative risk."

"I thought," her mother said, with no sign of having heard, "that it would be a good idea if you unplugged your toaster each night before you go to bed."

"Mother, don't you understand—"

"I certainly wouldn't ask you not to have a toaster. I don't own one myself, but I can understand having one. I think if you just unplugged it before you went to bed . . . I mean, in the daytime if you have a fire, you're awake and you can get out of the house."

"Yes."

"Isn't it awful that there are so many terrible things happening in the world?"

"Mmm."

"Such horrible things happen to people."

"Mmm."

"You don't seem to be in a good mood."

"I'm preoccupied. I've got to go unplug my toaster. G'bye, Mother."

Dan pulled on an old sweater. It was one Anne had knitted for him. He patted it down across his chest, thinking of days that were gone, and then focused his mind on Tony. He was very happy that Tony cared so much about Ricky, and he was happy too that Tony came to him when he had a problem.

When he stepped out of the tent, the night air felt cool. The breeze coming across the lake picked up moisture. The night was dark, although the moon would rise in an hour or so. Far across the lake an owl hooted. The sound made the hairs on the back of his neck stand up. Silly, of course. An owl was an owl. It wasn't the soul of a child in torment.

If he moved, he'd feel warmer. He walked quietly across the open meadow that sloped down to the lake. Maybe it was foolish to be out here, past midnight, on an errand that might be useless. Ricky might not take a late walk. If he did leave his tent, he might not want to talk. The project that had seemed reasonable this morning now seemed ridiculous.

He had to be alert tomorrow. There was a whole day of camping, cooking, and swimming to get through, and a bunch of boys to keep up with. Also, if he ran into one of the other scoutmasters out here in the night, what would he say he was doing?

Dan smiled at himself. That was just weariness talking. After all, if he met a scoutmaster out here, what was the other guy doing?

He wandered down to the latrine. He could at least say he got up for that reason.

The latrine area was unsavory in the night air. The breeze from the lake would have been welcome in the hollow, but it did not reach. There was a reek of stale urine and a moldy dampness. Camelli urinated and left quickly.

He scanned the field between the tent area and the cook tent area. Nobody afoot. The woods were quiet except for the stirring of the very tops of the trees. Occasionally, heavy limbs of oaks would creak against each other and groan.

There was no sound of crickets. No fireflies. No night birds.

It might be a foolish errand, waiting out here, but all at once he felt that it was not. Some primitive part of his brain felt evil in the night. Muscles on the back of his neck contracted, responding to a chill that passed along his spine. Nothing moved; no one called for help. But he knew.

Farther up the meadow, in one of the larger tents, Peter Winterthur lay trembling. A man bent over him. There was a spill of faint light through the upper part of the tent flap, where the two pieces of fabric did not quite meet. The lower part of the tent flap was securely closed.

The light was a dim scatter, bounced off the trees and the moisture in the air, originating from the Coleman lantern that burned all night in the cook tent. It did not cast shadows. It was not much brighter than the starshine in the sky and the faint shimmer that meant the moon would soon rise.

There was just enough light for Peter to see the man. But he would have known him anyway. He had feared him for months.

The light was only barely enough to pick up the glitter of tears on Peter's face. The man saw them, and they annoyed him.

"Stop that crying, you hear?" he whispered, a rasp of sound so faint, so low, that it was neutral, neither man nor woman nor boy speaking. Just a ghost of a voice.

"I'm sorry," Peter whispered, even more faintly.

"I'm not doing anything to hurt you."

Peter sniffled and wiped his face on his arm.

"Say it!" the man commanded softly.

"You're not doing anything to hurt me."

The man unzipped Peter's jeans and seized the ankles of the pants, pulling them off in one motion.

Peter lay still. The man folded the Levi's neatly.

The man rolled Peter onto his stomach. He made a caressing motion of his hands on Peter's back; then both hands circled the small waist, his fingers sweeping under the elastic of Peter's underwear. Slowly, gently, he drew the underwear down Peter's legs.

Peter gulped once, and wiped his hand over his eyes. He

closed his eyes, and thought as he always did that if he kept them closed it would be over sooner.

The man's hands laid the underwear down on the folded Levi's.

Peter could hear the man now, could hear the dry rustle of his clothes. Peter caught his breath. He knew from experience that holding his breath did not work, but he did it anyway.

Peter gasped as he felt the man place a fingerload of Vaseline between his legs. Peter had been expecting it, yet he never expected it. In the center of his body, it was always a shock.

He felt the man move his thighs apart. He felt himself stretch as the big penis forced its way in.

On the meadow, Dan Camelli heard a sharp gasp, as if someone, somewhere in the dark, felt pain. But he could not tell where it had come from. He waited, and he did not hear it again.

When it was over, the man dressed Peter. As he slipped on Peter's pants, he said, in a low whisper, "You're not telling, you know."

"I know."

"We've talked about what they'd do to you."

"I know, I know," said Peter, frantic to leave.

"A mental hospital, probably, where they put electrodes on your head and give you electric shocks."

"I won't tell. I never told, did I?"

"No, and that's smart. They'd call you names. All your friends. You know that."

"I know that."

"Look around, before you go out."

Dan Camelli saw motion, like a passing shadow, farther up the slope. There were so many tents that he could not tell just where he had seen it, but he thought it was up where the scoutmasters' tents were pitched. He watched and saw nothing. Then he realized he would see motion better out of the side of his eyes, so he looked forty-five degrees away.

He caught movement again, but this time a little farther down the slope. He tried to guess where the person was headed. If it was Ricky, he didn't want to appear to be following him. He wanted to intercept him, as if by accident.

Camelli drifted like a breeze diagonally across the meadow. He kept his eye slightly away from the figure and saw it twice, as it passed into the visible area between one tent and the next, then the second and a third. They were on a collision course that would bring them together near the cook tent. Good. It was a reasonable place to be heading and a place to talk without waking other people.

Camelli put on a little spurt of silent speed, fearing he might be too late. He slipped past the large supplies tent, glided out the far side, and came face-to-face with a boy. The boy jumped, then froze.

"Peter!" he said. He had expected Ricky.

"Um, hi, Mr. Camelli."

Dan could see the trail of tears, like a snail's track, down Peter's cheeks.

"Did I frighten you, Peter?"

"No, sir. No."

"You looked like you were scared of me for a second."

"I didn't know it was you." Peter tried to smile, a wide smile that frightened Camelli. The smile of a dead child.

"Peter, is something wrong?"

"No, sir. What could be wrong?" He shifted feet.

"I don't know. It's just that you look unhappy. Um— Peter, you're bunking with Garvey, aren't you?"

"Yes, sir."

287

"Is he—is Garvey bothering you, or anything?"

"Gee, no."

"I mean, Garvey can get a little bit domineering at times. If you're being disturbed, we can change the bunkmates. Or I'll talk to Garvey. You see what I mean?"

"Yes, sir. But Garvey isn't bothering me."

"Or threatening you?"

"No. All I did was—I came out for a walk. I guess I'll go to bed now. I'll bet Garvey's asleep. He was asleep when I left."

More words than Dan had ever heard from Peter at one time. Something was surely god-awfully wrong. But he couldn't very well secure Peter's confidence by calling him a liar.

"Listen, Peter, if anything gets—um—bad for you, would you please tell me? Or tell one of the other counselors? Or even tell Tony. Don't keep it bottled up. Huh?"

"Yes, sir. Well, I guess I'll go to bed now." Peter moved sideways two steps and then turned around.

"Peter?"

"Yes, sir?"

"You don't have to call me sir. Goodnight."

Camelli watched near the cook tent, watching to make sure Peter made it safely back to his tent. He had a sense of not having handled the interview very well, but he couldn't imagine what else he should have said. Was there a magic combination of words that could have made Peter trust him?

The child reeked of fear.

But Peter had not been Dan's reason for coming out tonight. He decided to move closer to Ricky and Tony's tent. He had been staying away so it would not appear that he'd been hanging around if Ricky came out suddenly. But it was very late. Camelli simply could not spend the whole night outside and expect to look normal in the morning. He resolved that if he didn't catch Ricky in the next half hour, he would go to bed.

He moved around behind Tony and Ricky's tent so that if Ricky came out the flap, Dan could fade back into the distance and intercept him somewhere farther away.

Dan stood still until his knees began to ache. When he bent his legs his knees made a popping sound. A lattice of silver appeared on the ridge—the moon rising behind the pines. The breeze had gone down, and the dampness increased.

He heard a cry inside the tent. At first he started to move away, but there was no sound of anyone getting out of a sleeping bag, just another moan and a string of disconnected syllables.

The voice spoke a longer string of gibberish. Although the sounds meant nothing, Camelli recognized frustration and urgency in them. Then Ricky said, "I can't remember!"

Dan waited another twenty minutes, but Ricky did not come out and there was no more talking. Once he heard someone sigh and turn over in a sleeping bag. He wondered whether it was Tony or Rick. Finally, chilly and apprehensive, he went back to his tent.

He slipped into his sleeping bag with all his clothes on and lay there trying to warm up, trying to stifle an intense feeling of impending disaster.

What in hell was going on here?

Twenty-Six

The disease did not attack adult bees. Only the young, still pearly in their cells, were invaded by foulbrood.

The adult bees moved swiftly to contain the plague. The undertaker bees pulled the sticky masses from the wax cells, flew them far from the hive, to the bees' cemetery, and dropped them into the grass. The nurses moved in to clean the cells. Patrols strode over the brood combs, inspecting the larvae, identifying and pulling out the dead. Working without rest, they began to catch up with the spread of the infection, to find and remove larvae in earlier stages of the disease, when the tissues were just beginning to dissolve, and then even earlier, when the babies were just beginning to turn the deadly yellow-gray. Ruthlessly, they rooted out those that were still alive, but dying. These could transmit the plague. Like marshals in medieval Europe, inspecting for the Black Death, they patrolled unceasingly back and forth across the brood combs.

Very early Tuesday morning Swan came in from the country to check on the hive, as he had promised to do while the scouts and scoutmasters were away at camp. As soon as he removed the honey super and looked into the brood combs, he saw the signs of foulbrood.

"Damn good thing we put in that new queen."

He went back to his truck. In a little paper cup, he mixed one teaspoon of terramycin and one-and-a-half teaspoons of powdered sugar. He took this back to the hive and sprinkled it

290

over the brood combs. The bees would eat the sugar and the antibiotic.

He set the super back on top. If these had been Caucasian bees infected with American foulbrood, the entire hive would have had to be killed with calcium cyanide. Then he would have burned the dead bees, combs, and honey in a pit so that other bees in the county were not infected by them. The hives might be used again if they were thoroughly scorched with flame, but personally he'd be leery of having them, himself.

It all would have been a bit rough for the scout troop, Swan thought.

Samantha could not stand it any longer. She had spent a long and ghastly night on the sofa in the living room, wrestling with panic that there was danger to Tad and Ricky. She fought the terror—it was too much like her mother's behavior—with everything she knew. The camp had been safe last year. If Garvey was a killer, he had never killed children. If there was a threat to her family, it seemed to be directed against her, not them. Dan was at camp to watch over them.

It didn't work. She woke after a couple of hours' sleep with a dry mouth and tears of fear and anger in her eyes. She had accepted Tad's assurance that he was all right as if that meant Ricky was all right, too. But that was wrong. Tad had never been affected. The threat had always been against Ricky.

Henry's funeral, delayed by the autopsy, would be Thursday morning. It was now Tuesday morning. The need to hurry was shrieking in her mind. She went upstairs, where she picked up a flannel shirt and a comb.

Downstairs, Samantha took all the cash from the coin jar

291

and her secret supply of money in the back of the desk drawer. With what she already had in her wallet, it was enough. If she needed gas or a new tire or dinner, it was enough.

She locked the front door, went out the back door, and locked that after her.

She got into the car and took out a road map of Wisconsin.

The man stood behind the cook tent, where Tad was finishing a banana. Tad looked up at the man and smiled. The man said, "Hey, there's a wasp on the back of your shoulder. Feel it?"

Tad said, "No."

"Crawling toward your neck. It must tickle."

"Oh, yeah! I feel it now!"

"I'll flip it off."

Samantha settled into the drive, trying to sit easily and stay at a reasonable speed. But in bursts of panic, she would gasp for air and feel her hands clench on the wheel.

She could not remember whether she had eaten breakfast, so she picked up a chocolate shake. It tasted odd, metallic and glutinous, but she decided that was a combination of soybeans and fear, and she drank the whole thing.

Dan spent lunch in a state of extraordinary alertness. Kiri approached him, asking whether they could do feeding experiments with their hive of bees. Dan was able to answer, and even to be enthusiastic, and still watch Peter and Ricky.

Ricky looked preoccupied to Dan, but the boy talked with the others. Peter made no effort to talk at all today.

The announcements at lunch were about the hike proposed for next morning.

After lunch, Dan tried to gauge Ricky's mental state indirectly. He asked him, "Ricky, do you think there's anything wrong with Peter?"

Ricky was responsive and frank. "Peter," he said, "has been absolutely *strange.*"

By midafternoon, Samantha had passed Oshkosh, Wisconsin, on U.S. 41 and turned off onto Wisconsin 110 through Butte des Morts. *Hill of death?* she thought. *Mount of the dead?* She picked up U.S. 10 and took it for forty miles northwest until it joined U.S. 51 north.

Suddenly, she noticed her gas was running low. She pulled into a gas station next to a mom-and-pop diner. While the tank was being filled, she took the opportunity to go to the station's rest room. Coming out, she was struck by the smell of french fries cooking and something less definable, possibly custard pie.

Maybe she needed solid food. She tried to balance her need to hurry against her chances of making a seven-hour drive safely on just a milkshake. But when she went into the diner, she knew she could not eat. Even the pie that had smelled so good at a distance looked slippery and sickening. She ordered a coffee and forced herself to drink it.

By now it was 4:00. She had completed slightly over four of the seven hours' drive to the camp. Surely she could make it tonight.

Half an hour farther north, she knew she was not driving well. Her eyes shifted into and out of focus, and normal sounds had a hollow ring, a sure sign that she was half asleep. There were beautiful roadside rests here. She saw one surrounded by big beech trees with bluish silver bark. It also had a broad green lawn, a set of rest rooms, and night lighting which would make it safe, she thought, to take a nap there.

No! I have to get to Ricky!

Then she realized that she had felt the same urgency about Henry. And when she reached him, he was dead.

The campfire and sing-along tonight ended earlier than usual. Tomorrow was an early hike to a small but beautiful waterfall seven miles north.

By 11:00 the activity around the camp had quieted. Dan Camelli, standing in front of his tent, could see a man still cleaning up in the cook tent. His shadow on the tent wall grew larger or smaller, depending on whether he walked toward or away from the Coleman lantern.

It was much warmer tonight. There was no wind whatsoever. In the woods, late fireflies blinked.

Dan's concerns tonight were both Peter and Ricky. How he would handle it if he saw both out at once he didn't know. He would be an opportunist, he supposed, and take whichever came first or looked more important. Rick had seemed better today. Peter had not.

The light in the cook tent went out. Dan stayed in the shadows, making no attempt to see who was leaving the tent. It was better if there were no voices to frighten Peter or Ricky. Dan was certain that, whatever drove Peter out of his sleeping bag, crying, into the night, Peter did not want to be seen.

When the other man had gone, Dan faded horizontally across the field to the evergreens, red pine and white pine, that fringed the east side of the camp. This was the part of the woods closest to the tent that Peter and Garvey shared and not far from Ricky and Tony's.

The pine needles were soft and silent underfoot. There was a faint sighing in the woods as if, even when the wind was not blowing, the trees grew and breathed. The air was spicy with the scent of pine.

Dan wore a dark shirt, Levi's, and a pair of blue sneakers. He had intentionally tried to be less visible in the dark, without wearing a black sweater and pants which would have made him look like a commando.

After half an hour, he sat down on the pine needles. The mosquitoes were busy tonight, and there was no breeze to blow them away. Dan couldn't slap them for fear the sound would carry in this silent night, so he brushed them off. Even so he moved slowly, conscious that motion would make him more likely to be seen.

Tonight he did not feel he was being foolish, staying out in the dark. The sight of Peter's anguished face had driven the idea from his mind. But he was tired. He had not had enough sleep last night, and a day with teenage boys was no way to rest up. His eyes closed.

He opened them suddenly as a bird flapped overhead. There was still no moon. He thought he had napped only a couple of minutes, but he was not certain, and he scanned the camp, looking for motion.

There was none. Everything slept. The bird above him had either flown away or settled silent on a branch. After a time, he heard rustlings under the blanket of pine needles. Some nocturnal animal was going about its dark life, out of sight of predators. He became aware of silent, hidden tunnels, out of sight of man, out of sight of the sun, where things lived their entire lives in the dark. What would the sun look like to them? Painfully hot? Unimaginably bright? Like a laser, or the searing, searching eye of God?

He caught a motion, out of the corner of his eye. Turning his head, he saw it was the flap of Peter and Garvey's tent. Dan held his breath.

A slender shape moved in the shadow. The tent flap fell back into place with the slick scrape of vinyl-covered canvas.

Thin and not very tall, the shape paused a moment as if scenting the wind.

Dan could see the lighter oval of the face. It hung in the air above the invisible darker clothes, unmoving, waiting, listening for sounds. Then it turned and looked straight at Dan. But only in his direction. He knew it did not see him! He held still. The shape was surely Peter, not the heftier Garvey. It faced the woods a full minute, then turned and held its head toward the cook tent area, waiting for its eyes or ears or more secret senses to tell it whether anyone was awake.

Quite suddenly, it slipped away. Dan did not dare to move at once. He waited in the trees, seeing the shadow move slowly and quietly up the slope. Now he knew that it was Peter. His head was carried low, looking at the ground either in sorrow or in caution. His steps were slow, but he did not stop.

When Peter was 150 feet away, Dan moved. He slipped diagonally along the slope between the tents. Not quite crouching, he moved with his body bent forward, so that he was partially obscured by the tents. The back of Peter's head, with its dark hair, was toward him now. If Peter turned, Dan would see the lighter face, and be warned. Then Dan would freeze.

But Peter did not turn. He moved steadily through the dark toward the tents of the scoutmasters. It took him several minutes, moving quietly, but he was making purposeful progress. Dan knew from his motion that he was not just out for a walk. He was going somewhere.

Peter came to the side of a certain tent, stopped, and looked around. Dan had anticipated that when Peter got where he was going he would check again to make certain he was not observed. Dan was ready. As soon as Peter turned, Dan froze, still as death.

Peter swung his head once around to take in the whole camp. Then in one swift motion he ducked down into the tent. Dan kept his eye on the tent and moved closer. He knew whose tent this was.

Dan was relieved. So Peter had found a friend. One of the counselors was already counseling him. So much the better. That was what scoutmasters were for. Dan had not really wanted to force his concern on Peter, especially when he got as little response as Peter had given last night. Dan turned to go back.

An instinct made him pause. Some sense that was not sight or hearing told him there was trouble. Danger. It might have been the furtiveness in Peter's trip across the clearing.

Without stopping to think, Dan acted. If he had paused and wondered, he would have found reasons not to interfere. He would have assumed, as people do when they start to reflect, that things were perfectly normal.

He moved while impulse was still strong. He walked briskly up to Monty Fiske's tent. Saying, "Is Peter sick? I thought I saw him—" he pushed back the tent flap and looked in. "Oh, my God!" Dan said.

Twenty-Seven

Dan went to Tony and Ricky's tent, woke them, and told them he was bringing Peter to stay with them for a little while and to ask him no questions. He put Monty Fiske in the cook tent. Monty walked in circles around the inside of the cook tent, asking Dan to let him explain. Dan told him to stay there or else. Then he took Peter to Tony and Ricky's tent.

What should he do about the boys? There wasn't only Peter to worry about, but Garvey who was Monty's son. Dan did not have to like Garvey to be worried about the effect on him if this got out. Dan had to get rid of Monty and he had to help Peter, and help him fast.

Dan felt sick. He was shaking. He had seen Peter trembling, and Dan had caught it and was shaking so hard he could scarcely walk. His teeth chattered.

He was so angry at Monty that half his trembling was sheer fury. He was also sick with horror at what had been done to Peter. A child! To take advantage of a child!

Dan tapped on the flap of Ira Schultz's tent. There was no response. He tapped again.

"What?"

Dan ducked inside.

"Something wrong?" Ira asked.

"I'll say something is wrong!" Dan plopped onto the ground. His knees would not hold him any longer. "Peter Winterthur was crying, so I followed him. He went to Monty Fiske's tent—"

"Oh, Christ!" Schultz gasped.

"What in hell do you mean, 'Oh, Christ?' "

Schultz didn't answer. Dan repeated, "What do you mean, Ira? Tell me now, you hear me?"

"I just thought—"

"What? *What* did you think?"

"I thought—I figured maybe he'd stop."

"You thought he'd *stop*? God, Ira, *you knew about this!*"

"Well, with Peter going to his tent—anyway, I figured he'd get tired of it."

Dan's chest did not seem to work. He caught his breath, and forced words out between his teeth. "You knew about it and, God help us all, *you didn't do a thing to stop it!*"

"I—Dan, look, it was voluntary, wasn't it? What was I supposed to do?"

"It was *not* voluntary! I stumbled on it because I saw Peter going back to his tent crying last night! Holy shit! You can't *ever* assume somebody screwing a child is voluntary on the part of the *child!* They're just too fucking scared! I don't believe this. I absolutely do not believe this! How long have you let this go on?"

Schultz didn't answer.

"My God! You knew and—"

"You don't have to swear."

"I don't have to *swear!* Is everybody crazy?"

"I couldn't—it would be worse for Peter, wouldn't it, Dan? Everybody knowing? And Garvey. You don't want everybody saying that his father is that type of man."

"Shit! I know what it was! I *know* what it *was,* Ira. You didn't want anybody to find out because—not because of Garvey or Peter, and not for the sake of Monty Fiske, our fucking live-in pederast! You didn't want anybody to find out because of the *scouts.* You didn't want anybody to think badly of your beloved scouting! That's it, isn't it, Ira? Isn't that just the goddam truth?"

When Ira didn't answer, Dan stood up angrily. His head struck the roof line. He bent over Ira, his fists balled.

"Tell me, you chicken shit!"

"I—okay. I did think of that. But it wasn't *our* fault, what Monty did. It wasn't the fault of the scouts. I mean, that kind of thing can happen anywhere."

"But this time it didn't happen just anywhere. It happened here. Right under our noses, where we are responsible for the well-being of the boys! *That's* where it happened!"

"All right. You're upset."

"I surely am upset! I am goddam upset. You and I, you chicken shit, are now going to have to fix it. If it can ever be fixed. Protecting Peter is the first thing. Protecting Garvey is the second thing. You're going to come with me, and you're going to do as I say!"

The road was trying to surprise her. Samantha was driving down a black ribbon, keeping close track of the dotted line down the center. In her present state of exhaustion, that bright line in the dark gave her an enormous feeling of security. But when she was happily dependent on it, it would whip to the left and wind dizzily down a hill.

She had stopped twice more for coffee, but it had not helped much. She almost suspected that her last roadhouse had fed her something decaffeinated, for all the good it did.

Time was playing tricks, too. She was not making the miles she should have been. By now she should have been at the camp. Sometimes she would look at her speedometer and find that she was going only thirty miles an hour. But the trees were rushing by, and the road, when it tried to trick her, lurched away so quickly right or left.

When she found her speed had fallen again, she pushed harder on the accelerator. She was climbing a hill now, cresting it, soaring down the other side. She pushed the needle to forty-five, to fifty. Surely fifty-five was a safe speed, but it seemed so fast!

Now she was swooping into a valley, full of white trees in the black night. White trees! Floating. Ghost trees. How silly! They were birches, of course, and only speeding by as if they were weightless.

One rushed at her!

She swerved. It was not—she felt a thump!—it was not a tree. She had seen its eyes. A dog! Oh, God!

Her brakes screamed. She leaped out of the door, left it swinging free. Running back along the shoulder of the road—surrounded by white trees!—she rushed to the crumpled thing. As she did, two more of the creatures leaped away. Graceful arcs of leaps made with knobby knees. Two fawns! The fawns bounded to the line of trees and stopped there, looking back at her. Their slender, fragile legs were like sapling birches. Samantha stooped to the thing she had hit. It was a doe, a slender, long-necked animal. In the faint light misted back from the car's headlights, she looked amber or golden. She twisted her neck back, trying to arch away from Samantha. Her eyes were deep brown. "Don't die!" Samantha said. "Don't die!" The deer let her head sink. Samantha reached to hold it up, but by the time she slipped her hand under the soft neck, the body was limp. When Samantha looked, the fawns had faded into a line of trees.

Dan took Peter to one of the picnic tables on the meadow. It was dark, but the meadow felt open and he hoped to hell Peter felt freer here.

"Peter, sit. And listen to me. Nobody else is awake except you, me, Fiske, Schultz, Tony, and Ricky. Tony and Ricky don't know what's been going on, and when I've talked with them they won't even mention you were awake tonight."

He paused. Peter nodded.

"Now, Tony and Rick are reliable. You accept that?"

Peter nodded.

"So far, so good. Now, listen. I wish to God this had never happened. And I blame myself for not seeing that something was wrong—"

Peter had made a small sound that Dan could barely hear.

"What did you say?"

"You shouldn't."

"Blame myself? Well, thank you, but I can't help it. Anyway—I'm going to say some stuff straight out because I don't want any misunderstandings or fear on your part. Okay?"

Peter nodded again. Dan could see that he was crying.

"I want you to know that not all men are like Monty Fiske. I wish to hell and back you had told me when this first happened, but I realize it's hard to make a decision when an adult is threatening you."

Peter put his hands over his face. Dan studied him a couple of seconds and went on. He hoped he was doing this the right way. But he couldn't let the child go to sleep with doubts and fears and horror.

"Very few men have this particular disease, that they would victimize a boy. I suppose in some sense he couldn't help it, but I have to tell you, Peter, that I felt like punching him until he was a bloody mess."

Suddenly Peter giggled. Then he hiccupped. Then he stopped and was quiet, watching Dan's face.

"Anyway, Peter, I want you to know that he can't pass on

302

his disease to you. You are not dishonored by this. You've been hurt, and that's all. I don't know what he told you—"

"They'd send me to a—a—"

"Mental hospital?"

"Yes."

"Well, that's a lie. If you feel very upset, you might want to see a counselor to help you get over it. But you're *not* sick, and he *is*. I mean that. Peter, do you understand and believe me?"

"I guess so."

"I hope you do. Nobody can do anything to you for this, and nobody would want to. You and your parents might want to prosecute—"

"Don't tell them!"

"Don't—"

"Don't tell my parents! Don't tell my father! Please? You *said* I could trust you! Don't tell them!"

"I—wait, Peter. Sit down. I won't tell them if you don't want me to. You have my word. But I may ask *you* to think about it again later. Not tonight, though. We'll talk about it when you've had a chance to absorb the fact that Monty Fiske is really gone."

"I won't want to tell them, *ever.*"

"Peter, someday you've got to come to terms with your parents." Peter didn't answer.

"Never mind that now. I won't do anything without your permission. Do you understand?" Peter nodded.

"So—the next thing I want to consult with you about is this. Do you want to stay at camp or go home?"

"Oh, I wouldn't mind staying now." Dan's eyes filled with tears. It all washed over him from Peter's point of view. The horror of being forced to go to camp, knowing that man lay in wait for him. Unable to tell anybody why he was terrified of camp, too frightened to speak, terrified of the very thought of getting on the camp bus. And all of this invisible to Dan, who should have been protecting him.

"I think it's the best thing, too, Peter. I'm sending Monty Fiske home tonight, and if you went at the same time, people might connect it. Not that they'd have any idea what happened, of course, but they'd wonder. Staying, I think, will do one very good thing. It'll give you a chance to think everything out over the next few days and decide what you want to do without any pressure. You can think about whether you want to talk with your parents—"

"I *won't*."

"Or whether you want me to talk with your parents—"

"No."

"Well—" Peter was showing more resolution than Dan had thought possible. And that was good. It was a sign of health. "All right. I glanced in on Garvey on my way here, and he's asleep. So let's just have you slip back into bed. You're sure you'd rather stay than go home?"

"Oh, yes!"

There was nothing to be done for the dead deer. Samantha started toward the woods, thinking she could find the fawns, thinking she could help them. But when she reached the first of the birches and saw how dark it was among the trees, she realized that she could not possibly find them. They could be just a few feet away, but if they were silent, she would never know. She felt they were nearby. She could not tell where.

She went back to the doe. Samantha sighed. She had to push on.

She put the car in gear. When it started to move, the right front bumper shrieked. Then she noticed the car was listing to the right. She had ascribed it to the wheels being on the shoulder of the road.

She got out again, wearily, and went to look.

The right front tire was flat. It had been sliced through by the bumper, which had buckled under when she hit the deer.

All right. She wasn't beaten yet. She got out the jack to change the tire. She pulled at the bumper, to get it away from the tire. It wouldn't move. She jammed one foot against the grille and pulled and pulled until tears came to her eyes. Nothing happened.

The jack was useless. She could have raised the car with it, but she could not pull the bumper away from the wheel.

At 2:30 A.M., Monty Fiske left the campsite in his car, heading for Rivercrest. Dan would tell Garvey in the morning that his father had a case of poison sumac so severe that he had to go to the doctor.

"Don't tell anybody about this," Fiske had begged Ira and Dan.

"I don't intend to," Schultz had said.

"Ira!" Dan had said. "We're going to have to deal with this in the way that's best for Peter. We can't sweep this shit under the rug."

"Publicity about this would hurt everybody," Fiske had said. Schultz had nodded.

Dan had said, "I'm not talking about publicity. But his parents may need to know. Peter may need counseling."

"Dan! Don't tell them, please! It's not my fault! It's something I can't help. It's like a disease."

"Then you should have got treatment instead of a victim."

"Dan, *please.*"

"I'm going to do whatever seems best for Peter."

"He didn't object—"

"Don't tell me that! I saw his tears! Get out of here. Get out before the boys hear us. And before they see me flatten you out."

Camelli flopped wearily into his tent. His muscles ached and his brain longed for sleep. He was not shaking any longer; he just hoped that he'd done the right thing. Should he have called the police? Dumped the whole thing into the criminal justice system? Courts, police questions for Peter, newspaper stories, maybe the six o'clock TV news. "Scoutmaster Rapes Boy." *God, no.* He really did not believe he should have done that. But the responsibility frightened him.

Maybe he could force Monty Fiske into getting psychiatric help. Blackmail him with the threat of a lawsuit by Peter's parents.

Lee Gray would have to know. That was all.

Could Dan take the responsibility for Peter's future mental health and for keeping it from Peter's parents? He believed it was best. But he didn't like it. And he didn't like lying to the others.

But it didn't matter if he was unhappy. There was plenty of pain in this affair. The important thing was to help Peter.

And at least the problem was over. There might be consequences. *Would be.* But the active danger was past.

The truck was filled with crates upon crates of asparagus, which smelled earthy in the dark. The driver of the truck wore a black-and-red plaid shirt.

"Hit a deer?" he said.

"Yes, and my bumper's bent."

The man walked over to the dead doe. He touched it with his boot.

"Yup. Bad for you, good for some others."

"What do you mean?"

"Deer gets hit around here, they always take it to one of the retirement homes. There's two of 'em. The Lutheran and the Baptist. Got any preference?"

"No."

"Just as well. They prolly wouldn't listen to you anyway. Don't consider it your deer."

He walked back to the cab of his truck. Samantha stayed near the deer. She heard the man at his CB. She heard him call himself "Willy-nilly" and call her a lady in distress. She didn't care. Whatever could get her moving—

"Can somebody fix my car?" she asked when he came back. She was fighting hard not to show the urgency she felt.

"These aren't wreckers. Just the sheriff."

"Oh, please. Can't you call a wrecker?"

"Lady, there isn't one single all-night place in this county."

"I have to—I *have* to get somewhere—"

"Let me take a look at your mess-up, here."

They both looked. Samantha's heart sank. It looked bad.

"You wouldn't get anywhere even if you got a tire on. Just chew it right up again."

"I know."

"Tell you what, though. That tire is shot anyhow. I got a chain; I could tow you to the station at Cutlerville."

"But you said there wasn't anything open."

"Isn't. Opens in the morning."

"Oh, my God."

"Lady, morning isn't all that far away any more. Don't look like that. They open early around here. This is farming country. Place'll be open by six-thirty, for sure."

Samantha looked at him. "Mr.—"

"Call me Will."

"Will, that deer had two fawns—"

"Mmm? Usually they only have one."

"Well, she did. Will they be able to survive without their mother?"

"Let's see. Middle of July. Were their spots starting to fade?"

"Yes, I think so."

"Well, you know, they just might make it."

The man was furious with Monty Fiske. In one stupid instant, Fiske had made it difficult for a scoutmaster to be alone with one of the boys. And it was imperative that he get Tad Lawton alone long enough to work on him seriously. He would have to find a way *now*. Today. On the hike. It was always the first session that was the hardest, that required time and privacy. After that, he could plant cues that would make it easier to put the boy under quickly.

He was glad he had taken the chance to work with Tony Camelli before all the shit hit the fan. But neither Tony nor Ricky was as good, as easy, as Garvey had been. Maybe several boys in rotation would be the best thing. Maybe that would get around the danger of one boy's face turning up at accident scenes. With three or four, he might be able to take on more jobs.

But first there was one unpaid job he had to do to make himself safe. And for it, he would need not only Ricky but Tad as well.

Samantha was asleep in her wounded car near the air pump of the gas station when its owner came to open up.

"My golly! How'd you do that?"

"I hit a deer."

"Ah-ah-ah. I can see. Look, there's hair and blood on the fender."

Samantha got up and swayed. "Can you fix it right now?"

"Well, I always say make haste slowly. Do you want it fast, or do you want it to look good?"

"I want it fast. I don't care how it looks."

Twenty-Eight

The Rivercrest scouts, primed with pancakes and orange juice, formed up in their hiking line with their leaders. The men would station themselves at intervals in the pack, one in the front, one in the middle, one in the rear. Tad found a spot in the tail of the line, near some of his friends.

"Hey," said the man to the other scoutmasters. "I'll take the caboose this time."

"Wait a minute," Kiri said. "I have to get my magnifying glass."

Samantha pushed her car as fast as it could take the bumps and dips in the dirt road. Oaks crowded so thickly around that there was nothing on the ground under them but Solomon's seal and last fall's leaves. Every so often her car struck a root that had twisted to the surface. The car would bounce and groan.

Soon she would come to the turnaround where the camp vehicles would be parked. But on this two-track, if another vehicle were to approach, either it would have to back up to the turnaround, or she to the main road.

Well, it would have to be the other car, Samantha thought. She was in a hurry.

Then the turnaround appeared. It was a loop of turkey track, with six cars and a panel truck parked off it, shoved deep into the surrounding woods like spokes on a wheel. She did the same with her car, impatiently pushing its nose into a stand of sassafras.

She jumped out and slammed the door. "The lake should be downhill," she said out loud. The trees ate up the sound of her voice and left no echo. It was like speaking in a dark closet full of clothes.

"Hey, let's start!" Schultz called.

Dan Camelli said, "Ready." He was pleased that they were going ahead with the day's activity. The less anybody noticed disruption, the better for Peter. Ken Abbot, D.J.'s father, was on his way up, to fill in for Fiske.

Today's hike was only seven miles, to the waterfall. They would camp for lunch not far from Timm Hill, the highest point in Wisconsin.

"Head 'em up. Move 'em out," Lee Gray said. "Let's get these dogies out onto the trail."

Samantha found a footpath which did indeed lead downhill. She started running, then forced herself to walk. After a hundred yards, the woods thinned, turning into a mixture of birch and pine, then opening into a clearing. She was now at the top of the slope, where the counselors' tents were pitched. She stood still and looked down toward Pickerel Lake.

Beyond the counselors' tents were the boys' two-man tents, dozens and dozens of them, then an open space, then a wide meadow with the cook tent, the supplies tent, and the meeting area, with rings of logs for the boys to sit on around a blackened center, filled with the ashes of dead fires. Beyond this was the lake.

There were boys moving around outside the cook tent. Other boys stood at the lake's edge, shouting, while four of them raced, backstroke, from one buoy to another a hundred yards away. As Samantha watched, the swimmers turned at the buoy and raced, crawl-stroke, back again.

She could see one group of four boys cleaning picnic tables. Another little platoon was carrying plastic bags of trash up the hill toward her. A circle of boys at the edge of the swamp was watching a counselor point out something on the ground. Behind the cook tent, four others were washing frying pans. *Busy as bees, a job for everyone,* she thought.

Samantha strained her eyes across the clearing. She did not see Ricky or Tad. Or Dan Camelli. Or Lee Grey, or Monty Fiske, or Ira Schultz. Where was everybody?

Breathless and fearful, she hurried down the slope. As she got near the counselors' tents, a man stepped out and saw her.

"Hello?" He smiled, but his face was not pleased.

"I'm looking for Mr. Camelli. Or Mr. Schultz, or—"

"Are you a parent of one of the boys?"

"Yes, but—"

"It was clearly stated in the literature that we don't permit parents to visit during the week. Except for fathers who are counselors, of course."

What about boys who don't have fathers! What about mothers who would like to be counselors? Never mind—

"I haven't come here as—"

"If mothers come to see how the boys are doing, it might make some of them homesick."

"I haven't—"

"And if we let some mothers come, then we'd have to let all mothers come, wouldn't we?"

"Would you *please* let me speak! I have not come here as a parent. There has been a death in Rivercrest that is—that it would be extremely important for the parents who are here— for the *men*—to know about. This is not trivial. Since you don't have a telephone here, I've had to drive up. It has taken me seven hours on the road to get here, and I would just as soon be at home if I could, so I don't care to have my presence characterized as a maternal whim!"

"Oh. You should have said so right away."

"I tried. Are the Rivercrest counselors here?"

Where is Ricky?

"They've just left."

"Left?"

"Today is their hike to the waterfall."

Oh, my God. "When do they get back?"

"They hike to the waterfall, have lunch there, and hike back."

"But when do they get *back?*"

"My troop did it yesterday and we were back by three."

Samantha looked at her watch. Ten-thirty. Good God. Urgency swept over her, making her dizzy with fear. And yet—if they were hiking, surely they were all well and healthy. So far. She clutched her elbows with her hands.

"I'd prefer you not to wait in the camp," the man said. "If the boys see a mother waiting around, they'll wonder why their mothers can't visit."

"This is not a *visit!*"

"Yes, but they won't know that, will they?"

"I'll stay with my car. Or go into the village for lunch."

"That's wise."

"I wonder if I could trouble you," she said sweetly, "to tell Mr. Camelli I'm here, if you see him. I'm Mrs. Lawton."

"Certainly. Always happy to help."

Samantha hid her tears of frustration until he had turned away.

The man trailed along with the ten-year-olds, watching for an opportunity and staying close to Tad. When they were twenty minutes away from camp, the man said, "Look. A sparrow hawk!" And while pointing up into the branches, he tripped and fell over a tree root. He landed heavily and cried out.

"Are you hurt?" Tad asked.

The column of boys and men had stopped at the cry and looked back. The man struggled to his knees, gasped, and sat back down. Boys crowded back to look.

The man said, "I think I'd better rest a minute."

One of the other scout leaders came and stared down at him.

"How bad is it?"

"Not bad. Half an hour rest ought to fix it."

"Maybe we'd all better wait with you."

"No. Don't. Don't make everybody sit around. Tell you what. Leave Tad. He and I'll come along in half an hour, or less. Meet you at lunch."

"Right. Listen up, boys," said the other scoutmaster. "We've talked about this before, but now we have an example. If you have to leave somebody on a wilderness hike because he's injured, leave somebody with him. It's an important—"

"But what if there's only one guy to start with?" Tad asked. "I mean, say two guys are hiking and one of them breaks his leg. And the other guy can't carry him. What do you do?"

"Then you leave supplies with him so he has something to eat. And you cover him up with blankets or put him in a sleeping bag, because an injured man can go into shock real easily if he gets cold. Then you go for help. But boys, what is the most important thing to do at that point?"

"Blaze a trail," said Tad.

"Right! You have to know for sure how to find your way back to him."

He looked at Tad. "You both got compasses?"

"Sure," said Tad.

"Naturally," said the man.

"You know the way?"

"Right up the stream. Can't miss it. Meet you there."

The troop moved off, straggling out again into a long line, and vanished quickly in the thick woods.

"Well, Tad," said the man, "we're going to be here a little while. Sit down and let's talk."

"Now, Tad, I'm just going to test your concentration," the man said. "Do you understand?"

"Yes."

"Are you concentrating? So that you hear only my voice and what I'm saying to you?"

"Yes," Tad said, without inflection.

The man flicked on his pocket lighter. "Do you see that flame, Tad?"

"Yes."

"Did you know that some flames aren't hot?"

"No."

"Well, this is one of them. It's a cool flame. Isn't that interesting?"

Silence.

"Tad, isn't that interesting?"

"Yes. It's interesting."

"I'd like you to have a chance to feel it. Now you hold out your hand."

Very slowly, but with no hesitation, Tad's hand rose up in front of his chest, then reached out forward.

"I'm going to hold this under your hand, and you won't feel any heat. Do you understand?"

"Yes."

315

The man moved the flame under Tad's hand, near the base of the little finger. The flame touched the skin. He left it there only a moment, possibly one full second. He did not want any blister to form, for people to ask questions about. But it was long enough to hurt.

He looked into Tad's eyes. Even without asking, he knew. There was no change of expression, no sign of fear or pain. For his purposes, Tad was going to be just right.

Dan walked into the clearing near the car. Samantha, frantic with waiting, swung around when she heard him and said, "Dan, can you bring me the boys right away? I want to take them home."

"What?"

"I want to get the boys out of here!"

"Samantha, you can't!" He was frightened that at the least disruption, rumors would fly about Peter and Monty Fiske.

"Oh, yes I can! Garvey is a killer, and I don't want my children near him one more day!"

"Garvey! That's crazy!"

"I don't want them near him! Whether he kills them or pollutes their minds! I don't care, I'm going to take them out of here."

"Has Henry Ax been working on you—"

"Henry! Henry—working on me? Dan, I hope to hell you mean well, because—because Henry is dead, Dan."

"Oh, Lord, Samantha, I'm sorry." He walked toward her and took her arm, but she pulled away. "Dead. What was it? An automobile accident?"

"Funny you should say that. Christ, it's funny!" Samantha started laughing, crying, tears running down her face.

"What was it?"

"His car rolled down his driveway and crushed him to death against the back wall of his garage!"

"Shit!"

"I found him Sunday. He'd been dead since Friday night."

"*You* found him. Oh, Samantha, I'm so sorry. I'm so sorry."

"And Garvey killed him."

"What do you mean?"

"Henry wouldn't have left his car in neutral! He was after Garvey and Garvey knew it. He killed him."

"I don't believe it."

"Did Henry ever come to you to ask about Garvey?"

"Well, he—"

"Did he or didn't he?"

"Yes."

"I said he was killed Friday. The night before you all left to come up here. Garvey's last shot at him for a while! He'd be far away when the body was discovered."

"That's not proof!"

"And he's threatening me! Smashed my door, booby-trapped my house! These things are *not my imagination!*"

"Booby-trapped your house?"

She told him.

"Of course," she said sarcastically, "there's a problem with urine. Everybody's got it. So I can't prove it was Garvey's. But in my heart I know."

"Oh, Samantha." He put his arm around her shoulders, but she shook it off.

"Do you believe me or not?"

"I don't know what to think. I believe you, but not about Garvey. I'll be honest with you at least. Isn't that enough?"

"No. I want my children."

"There's no danger to them in all of this. Not even what's happened to you at your house."

"Oh, yes, there is. There's—they—"

"What?"

"I can't say it."

"What?"

"There's an influence. There's evil. Garvey is malign and somehow it's spreading through—oh, Dan, I can hardly say it!"

"What?"

"I think it's spreading to Ricky. He's been so cold. I realize Tad isn't exposed to Garvey. Tad plays with the ten-year-olds. But Ricky's in danger. It's as if he's losing his soul!"

For several minutes Dan was silent. He did not try to hold her again. He believed he knew what had happened to the boys, but he dared not talk about it. He watched her, and he saw resolution in her face. She was going to take Ricky out of camp. What would that do to Peter?

But beyond his duty to Peter, he had a duty to Samantha. He had to reassure her. He spoke slowly.

"Samantha, you have to admit that Ax's death could have been an accident. Leave it aside for a minute and take the booby traps. Those were different things from—they wouldn't have killed you. If you had fallen the wrong way on the pencil, you might have broken your arm. The glass door—the urine—they're a kind of malicious joke. I don't believe a child would understand—"

"What are you saying?"

"I'm saying they were childish acts. The kind of thing that might have been done by a very disturbed child. An abused child, who wanted to hit out—safely, from a distance—to get back at the world."

"Garvey."

"No. Peter."

"Peter! What are you talking about?"

"I want you to take my word for something. There's—I can't tell you what was happening, but it's over. I want you to be reassured, and not to worry. It's all over."

"What is?"

"I can't talk about it. Will you trust me?"

"No. I trust *you,* but I won't take anybody's judgment on this but mine. I'm sorry, but that's the way it is! I don't know what's going on, or what influence may be warping my *own child.* If you know anything about this, you owe it to me to tell me!"

"I've made—it's a commitment that affects a child's reputation. Samantha, can't you just take it from me that it goes a long way to explaining even why Garvey is so—so unappealing a character? And it *doesn't* suggest that he's a killer."

Samantha stared at him. "I'm sorry, Dan. I respect you, but I can't accept that. I have too much at stake."

"Please—"

"If you're so concerned that I'm going to *gossip* with what you tell me, you don't know me very well. I would have expected better from you."

"It's not my privacy that would be breached."

"Dan, look at me. Why don't *you* trust *me* with this?"

For a moment he looked directly into her eyes. He could see her fierce need to know, and it hurt him, because he knew he could not tell her. It was, as he had said, not his secret to tell. He looked away.

Samantha knew immediately what his decision was.

"Dan, I want Ricky." Her voice was cold.

"Samantha, it may make things a lot worse here—"

"I want him to pack and come with me. Now!"

"Please—"

"My children are all I have. I don't care who else is hurt. I have to get Ricky away from here. I'm not going to rely on anybody else's judgment any longer."

Dan hesitated, hoping she would change her mind. "He may not want to leave," he said at last.

"Bring him here."

Twenty-Nine

Dan returned with both Tad and Ricky. The four of them stood in the sassafras grove near the car.

"Aw, Mom, I don't want to go," Tad said. "I'm having fun." Dan could not resist glancing at Samantha. There was no triumph in his look, but there was hope.

"Ricky?" Samantha asked. She didn't care if he wanted to stay. She was going to take him home, today. But it would be much pleasanter if he agreed.

"Um—" Ricky studied Dan, then Samantha, sensing hostility between them, "It's okay with me."

"What is, Ricky?"

"To go home."

It was a long drive. Ricky slept in the car. Samantha drove through the night, energized with relief. She had only one question that stuck in her mind.

When they reached home, Ricky woke.

"Ricky?" she asked.

"Mmm? What, Mom?"

"I was a little surprised you agreed so quickly to come home."

"Oh, well. I wasn't having that much fun."

"What was the trouble?"

"Um—I've been forgetting things and stuff."

"Often?"

"No, just sometimes."

321

Samantha knew he was evading. But she had him out of the danger zone, so things should soon improve.

"Mom?"

"What, Ricky?"

"Why did you come and get me?"

"I was afraid for you, hon."

Ricky thought about that a moment. She expected him to ask why.

"I was afraid, too," he said.

"All right, Tad," said the man. "Tell me how you feel."

"I feel all slowed down," said Tad, slowly and judiciously.

"We talked about the scale of one to one hundred. On that scale, how deeply asleep do you feel?"

"Ninety."

"I see. That's very good. You're very good at this. It's warm and pleasant in here. Does it feel warm and pleasant to you?"

"Yes."

"Now, I'm going to ask you something new. You are deeply enough into your trance to open your eyes and not wake up. Do you understand?"

"Yes."

"Now, when I tell you to, you may open your eyes. Now. Open them."

The boy opened his eyes. He did not look around the tent, or even at the man. His eyes focused at a spot about eighteen inches in front of his face.

"What do you see?" asked the man.

"I see you."

"Do you see a lantern?"

"No."

Tunnel vision. Excellent.

"Now, Tad, I'm going to tell you a story. It's a real story. Do you have a dog?"

"No. My dad didn't want one because they shed."

"Well, you have one now. A little white one with brown patches. It's quite shaggy, and it has brown eyes. Now, Tad, do you have a dog?"

"Yes."

"How long have you had your dog?"

"I don't know. Awhile, I think."

"That's right. Now, your dog is here with us."

Tad's eyes dropped to a spot on the ground. He smiled at the spot, but didn't say anything.

"What is your dog doing?"

"He's just sitting there, watching me. His tail is wagging."

"Ask him to shake hands."

"Shake," Tad said. He put his hand down near the ground. He smiled. "Good boy!"

"That's very good, Tad. But now you are unable to move. You can't move a muscle. And that's too bad, because do you know what's happening? There's a snake crawling in the tent flap."

Tad's eyes went to the tent flap and widened. He stared at the ground where the flaps of cloth came together, eyes wide and afraid. He tried to get up, rocking forward a half inch, but could not move.

"Now the snake is creeping up on your dog, but the dog doesn't know it."

Tad tried to get up. His foot trembled with the desire to step on the snake, but his body would not move.

"Now your dog sees the snake. He's jumping up. He's going to defend you from the snake. Look! He's lunging for it.

He's got it! Wow! He's bitten right through the snake. Killed him. The snake is dead."

A smile of relief came over Tad's face.

"But wait a minute. There's something wrong with your dog. He's staggering. His legs are buckling. Oh, he's falling down. And twitching. Tad—"

Tad gasped. Tears were running down his face.

"Oh, Tad. I'm afraid he's dead."

Tad began to cry, great sobs that shook his whole body.

Complete belief, the man thought. *What I tell him is real. IS REAL. And complete control. He couldn't move, even to save his dog.*

The man let Tad cry for two or three minutes. Just to be on the safe side. It was almost impossible to fake tears, real, wet tears, and you sure couldn't do it for long. Tad was not just cooperating. It was real for him.

"Now, Tad, it's over. In just a minute you're going to wake up. And you won't remember your dog. You won't remember being asleep. You won't remember anything you said or did while you were here. You only stopped in to talk to me about first aid lessons in the fall."

"Yes."

"What did you come to see me about?"

"First aid. I'd like to take first aid lessons."

"And when did I say they would be given?"

"In the fall."

"That's right, Tad. Now I'm going to count backwards from ten. When I get to one, you will be almost awake. When I tell you to wake up, you will feel perfectly normal. And you won't remember about being in a trance. Do you understand?"

"I won't remember about being in a trance."

"That's exactly right. Ten, nine, eight, seven, six, five, four, three, two, one. You are now awake."

On My Honor

In Michigan's upper peninsula, the weather had been clear and fine. The cold water of nearby Lake Superior produced evening fogs, but the days were yellow with sun and scented by evergreens, like retsina wine.

Meyers Campbell had rarely felt so good. He was more relaxed than he had been in months. Now and then he had headaches, but they seemed to dwell behind his eyes, and he blamed them on the bright sunlight that danced on the lake water while he fished.

In Campbell's brain a small artery, the size of a strand of thin spaghetti, had begun to bulge. Like a blister on a poorly mended tire, the patch was distended and shiny.

Campbell's blood pressure was now fluctuating around 220/140.

Because of its distension, the blister was much thinner than the surrounding normal artery. With each heartbeat, it pulsed.

The sunlight was so bright on the unnaturally green cemetery grass that Samantha could see ants going about their scavenging business among the insect dead. Every worm cast showed among the green blades, and cut blades, fresh from last night's mowing, lay among the living plants.

She heard the earth fall upon the coffin, and the voice of the minister. "In sure and certain hope of the resurrection to eternal life through our Lord Jesus Christ, we commend to almighty God our brother Henry; and we commit his body to the ground; earth to earth, ashes to ashes, dust to dust. The Lord bless him and keep him, the Lord make his face to shine upon him and be gracious unto him, the Lord lift up his countenance upon him and give him peace. Amen." Samantha said, "Amen."

Samantha parked her car in the driveway in front of the house, not having enough strength to put it around in the garage in back. She let herself in the front door, and walked through the vestibule, dropping her keys on the small table she kept there. Just at the archway into the living room she stopped. The living-room chair that she kept near the fireplace had been moved. It was pushed back, so that now it faced the coffee table.

She was certain it had not been out of place when she left for the funeral. No matter how tired she might have been, she would have noticed. This was not the position in which she liked the chair, and it was not the way she ever left it.

As she stood still under the arch, she heard a sound in the kitchen. It couldn't be Ricky. He would just be starting home from tae kwon do.

A metallic sound. Not very loud. Not a deep sound, as if something heavy or thick had been bumped. More like a spoon. A spoon touching something. Or a knife.

There was a second sound, just like the first. She pictured it being made by a knife being tapped against the counter.

Then she heard footsteps coming from the kitchen. She backed quietly to the front door, trying not to let her arm brush the arch, trying to keep her shoes silent on the vestibule tiles.

The footsteps came toward her through the pantry into the dining room. Samantha felt behind her for the doorknob. She got her hand on it and started to turn.

Then she saw the figure walk into the dining room.

"Frederick!"

"Oh, *there* you are. I heard your car and kept waiting for you to come in the back door." He had a spoon in one hand, cup and saucer in the other.

"Holy God, you gave me such a scare!"

"Oh, I'm sorry. Awfully sorry." But Samantha saw satisfaction in his eyes.

Her legs felt weak. She sat on the sofa. "I knew Ricky couldn't be home yet, and I heard a noise."

"Actually Ricky is home. He's upstairs."

"How—"

"I saw him trudging along Green Bay Road, so I picked him up. Isn't this his camp week?"

"No."

"Shall I get you some coffee, Samantha?"

"No, thank you. I don't feel well."

Frederick sat down next to her. She thought her dark clothes and air of exhaustion pleased him. She forced herself to sit up straighter and smile.

"So, how have you been?" he asked.

"Just fine!"

"I heard lover boy got killed."

"Frederick, please don't. He wasn't lover boy and you only demean yourself when you act unsympathetic like that."

"But I am. I'm a very unsympathetic character. Been that way for years."

"Christ, Frederick, *let it alone!*"

Frederick studied her. She thought he was looking for flaws. "The divorce will be final in four weeks. If we don't do anything to stop it."

"Well, I certainly am not going to do anything to stop it."

"That's not really wise. Now that you don't have the police chief, you need somebody around here. You need a man around the house for protection."

"Protection? Protection from what?" Suddenly she sat up straighter. Her eyes, which had begun to close, opened wide and stared at him. She heard Dan's voice saying, "childish tricks, really."

"Oh, my God!"

"What?"

"Oh, my God, Frederick. It was you."

"What?"

"*You* broke the glass door. And left that jar of—of—the jar in the closet."

"Oh?"

"And that stupid pencil! I suppose you thought if I broke my arm on the cellar floor, I'd need you back here to supervise the house. Or I'd be so scared I'd think I needed somebody! I should have known. It was so childish. *Childish!* What a goddam cowardly booby trap your mind must be."

She saw in his eyes it was true, but she thought for a moment he would deny it. Then he said, "Well, it was a good try."

"I—I—" she stuttered, but her anger broke the words free. "You can't think ahead—you—one of the *children* could have slipped on that pencil—to think that you could scare me out of here!"

"You'll be out of here soon enough after the divorce."

"Good! Frederick, you never grew up! You live in a wish-world. The way I would have come back to you is—is if you had *changed*. If you were warm. If you showed some sympathy. This is just an act of insanity! It misses the target so badly it's hard to believe you were really trying to do what you say you were. This is hostility; it's not any real wish to have me back."

"Don't reach for it. You're no psychologist."

"Frederick? Oh, Frederick, you wouldn't."

"Wouldn't what?"

"It's too ghastly."

"Oh, go ahead and say it. Nothing's too horrible for Frightful Frederick, the monster of Rivercrest."

"Don't joke about it!"

"Why? What are you talking about?"

"Did you kill Henry?"

"What?" He shot to his feet. "What! Kill that *cop?* Are you *crazy?*"

Samantha might never have really known Frederick, but she could tell when he was lying. She believed him.

Frederick had caught back his fury. He said, lazily, "Really, Samantha. You flatter me. Or yourself. I wouldn't go that far for you. A pencil on the stairs, maybe. I'd only kill for—say—a couple of million dollars."

Samantha didn't answer. After a minute or two, Frederick simply walked through the dining room and kitchen and out the back door.

Meyers Campbell spent all morning Friday fishing and caught a beautiful bigmouth bass. He strung the bass on a line when he came in for lunch and left it in the cold water at the lake's edge. It would make a fine dinner. But he had gone out on the lake at dawn with only a cup of instant coffee and a Holland rusk for breakfast. He had hurried because he had known from the look of the day that there would be good fishing. Now he wanted his delayed breakfast.

He opened a can of ham pieces. This was a time for a full breakfast. Ham and eggs. The eggs were powdered, and though the taste was not bad, it was much more satisfactory with ham. He fried up the ham pieces and then poured in the reconstituted eggs and thought that, cooked this way, you'd never know the eggs weren't fresh.

By noon he had a feast laid out on his pine table. He knew the ham was salty, and as a person with high blood pressure he should not eat salty food, but it wouldn't matter too much. After all, he was taking his medication.

More cautious than ever before, the man invited Tad to his tent in daylight, while the boys on K.P. were helping to cook dinner. Tad was very quick at going into a trance.

"Are you completely relaxed?" the man said.

"Yes."

"Are your legs relaxed?"

"Yes."

"Is your body relaxed?"

"Yes."

"Are your arms relaxed?"

"Yes."

"Is your neck relaxed?"

"Yes."

To Tad it seemed as if he were floating in a pool of warm water. He was free of pain and anxiety. Someone was looking after him. Someone was taking charge. He could let go and everything would be all right.

"Now, Tad, I want you to remember when your mother didn't want you and Ricky to come to camp. Okay?"

"Okay."

"Tell me again why that was."

"I don't know, exactly. She thought something was wrong. Really, really wrong."

The man reflected. He had to do this in more than one step.

"Why would your mother want to keep you home from something that was a lot of fun?"

"I don't know."

"It doesn't sound to me like what a mother would do."

"I don't know."

"Tad, have you ever heard of shape-changers?"

"No."

"They're like vampires. But they don't suck blood. They take over a person's body. Then they look like the person, but they really aren't. Not really."

"Like the Body Snatchers?" Tad moved uneasily.

"Exactly like that." The man watched Tad's restless motion. *Bring this to a close.*

"Tad?"

"Yes?"

"Do you think your mother is really your mother?"

Thirty

Meyers Campbell sat very still in his rowboat in the middle of the lake. His hook was baited, his rod was in his hand, but he did not drop the line into the water.

Before his eyes the shore blurred, refocused, and blurred again. He felt a faint nausea and had a conviction that it would grow worse. What frightened him most, though, was a headache that stabbed through the center of his brain, just behind the eyes. He had to get to shore.

He picked up the oars, fumbling, dropping his fishing rod, then forgetting the rod entirely, grasping the oars finally, but clumsily. He placed one oar blade, then the next, in the water. He was afraid of accidentally dislodging them from the oarlocks and losing them overboard. He pushed down on the tape-wrapped handgrips, lifting the blades in the air, and pushed the handles forward, thinking about each motion. Pushing forward made the blades of the oars move back behind him. Then, he thought, he must lift up on the handles. That would lower the blades into the water. Then he pulled the handles toward him, which made the blades move back in the water, forcing the boat ahead.

The bulge on the artery in his brain had burst. A wall of blood pushed out, pressing against surrounding brain tissue, then slowing somewhat under the pressure of the brain around it.

The backward nature of rowing was almost impossible for a man with worsening brain damage. He began to recite to himself the motion he had to make.

"Raise handles, pull, dip handles, push."

His head pulsed with pain. The opposite shore had long since vanished, it was so blurred, like a view through a window slashed with rain. He could only hope he was forcing the boat in the direction toward the shore and his camp. He had to keep pulling on the oars, no matter what part of the shore he was heading toward. If he fainted out here, he would probably drown.

Every pull on the oars made the pain worse. Every time he dropped his head forward to lower the handles and raise the oars out of the water, he felt as if the pressure in his head would explode his eyes. But he made himself get through another sequence of up-pull-down-push.

And then it didn't work any longer. Had his brain stopped functioning? He was pulling on the oars, but the boat didn't move.

And the oars would not go down into the water.

He was at the shore!

He scrambled out of the boat, falling, going down on his knees in the shallows and reeds and mud. He flopped like a beached fish, but he made it up the bank to dry ground. He would not drown. At least he would not drown.

Through the rain and the mist that covered his eyes, he saw his cabin. Surely he could get that far.

Campbell's legs took their own path. There was some sort of communication problem between his legs and his brain. He did not stop to wonder why this had happened. He was too busy trying to compensate for the starboard list that had inserted itself in his nervous system.

His path described a great half-circle as he approached the cabin door. Dimly, he saw his bed standing in the alcove, across fifteen feet of space.

He couldn't make it. The terror that had driven him this far relaxed as soon as he crossed the threshold. He fell inside the door, the upper part of his body sprawling onto an old rag rug. Now unconscious, he lay with half-open eyes, his breathing noisy and rapid.

Scouts and scoutmasters arrived home Sunday night, heavily laden with dirty laundry and poison ivy.

Dan had been longing for a bed that was soft, and he fell into it like a stone. He just had time to be thankful that the blanket did not wind around him when he turned over, as his sleeping bag did, and to marvel at the complete, not relative, absence of mosquitoes, before he sank into a deep sleep.

When he opened his eyes, it was noon.

It took him another twenty minutes to convince himself to get up. He puttered his way downstairs, only to marvel that he could turn a stove switch and a burner got hot. No need to pile up sticks and light a fire.

Half an hour later, Tony came downstairs.

"Morning, Dad."

"Hey! Tony, look at this!" Dan turned on the burner and it got hot. Tony understood.

"Gee, that's great, Dad! Can I try it?"

"And look at this!"

Dan punched down toast in the toaster. Tony giggled.

They ate toast in a friendly silence.

After a time, Dan became aware that Tony kept glancing at the clock. He watched him do it once or twice more, then asked, "Got any plans for this afternoon?"

"Nope, I'm gonna veg out."

Dan almost asked why Tony was looking at the clock. Then he stopped himself. "Well, here we are having breakfast at one P.M. What'll I do about lunch? Maybe I'll boil eggs for egg salad."

Tony said, "Sure."

Dan watched Tony covertly while he filled a pan with water, put the eggs in and set it on the stove. "Maybe I'll bake some frozen turnovers," he said.

"Mmm-hm," said Tony. But he seemed to be thinking of something else. "I guess I'll go out." Now his voice sounded flat.

"Wouldn't you—well, sure. Okay."

Dan waited, standing at the stove, until he heard the front door slam behind Tony. He rushed into the living room and looked out the window. Tony was walking along the sidewalk.

Dan ran to the hall closet. He got out a straw fishing hat that he could not remember ever wearing. He hesitated a second and then took out a plastic Chicago Cubs baseball jacket, which he had always thought particularly ugly and rarely wore. Then he hurried out the front door, slowing to a natural stroll on the sidewalk. He hoped that if Tony looked back he would not recognize his father in these clothes.

Tony did not look back. He walked south a block, then east two blocks to Green Bay Road. On Green Bay he went south one more block.

Dan thought Tony was going toward the railway station.

Samantha, Tad, and Ricky had also slept late. Samantha glanced into Tad's room when she got up, and he was still sleeping. She had heard Ricky go downstairs just a few minutes before.

She was trying to think whether Tad had been unusually quiet last night when he got home. Well, there was no point in imagining problems.

Brushing cobwebs from her mind, she started down the stairs. Ricky was just ahead of her, crossing the pantry on his way to the kitchen.

"Ricky!" she called. "You hungry?"

She turned. It was Garvey.

"Garvey! *What are you doing here?*"

"I thought Rick might have brought home my fishing pole, Mrs. Lawton." He spoke in his too-courteous voice. Samantha thought it sounded menacing.

"Well, he didn't bring home any fishing pole. How did you get in here?"

"Rick let me in." He pointed to the playroom, where Ricky was watching television.

"Didn't he tell you he didn't have your pole?"

"Sure. I was just leaving."

Samantha let him go, watching to make sure he shut the back door behind himself and that it latched. Then she rushed to it and threw the deadbolt. She felt like screaming.

She knew now. She knew for sure.

Ricky and Garvey. Two sandy-haired boys. About the same height, about the same age, both freckled. Garvey just a little heavier than Ricky.

No wonder Jim Dubcjek screamed for me to get away! He thought Ricky had pushed his ladder! He thought Ricky had tried to kill him!

Glancing down from the ladder when he felt the force of the kick against its bottom. Catching sight of that freckled face as he spiraled, tumbled—he thought Ricky had killed him.

And that meant Garvey had killed him.

No one would believe her.

Thirty-One

Tony's manner of walking alarmed Dan. It told him more clearly than words that this was not just a simple stroll. It took him a minute or so of observation to understand what it was about that walk that made him uneasy. It was *directness*. Tony did not skip, or kick stones, or hop down off the curb and back up again, or lurch along on one foot, or inspect the trash, as boys do. As Tony usually did. He walked rapidly and straight, without looking sideways at squirrels, or barking dogs, or interesting junk left at the curb for the trash collector.

That walk made Dan afraid.

When they came to the turreted station with the geraniums in front, Tony turned east and crossed the road. Dan was puzzled. Not the railway station, then. Then what?

Tony walked quickly one more block and stopped at the corner. Above him was a sign, "Nortran Bus Stop," and the times and routes. Six or eight people were already standing at the stop. Another arrived while Dan watched. There were several women, two of them very old, two men with briefcases, a workman in blue overalls, and a teenage girl. Tony slipped toward the side of the group farther from the corner. When the bus came to the corner, it would drive past this side of the group, then stop. Tony edged next to an old woman with a cane, whose hair was bluish and thin.

Dan moved closer, keeping out of sight behind a large man with a briefcase. He could not imagine what Tony was doing here, but he consoled himself that he knew his son. Whatever his goal was, Tony would not do anything wrong.

As two or three more people came, Dan moved closer to Tony, intending to follow him onto the bus. Dan ducked his head, bringing his hat brim down, and hunched his shoulders, which bunched the jacket up around his neck. Then he scratched his nose. There was not much else he could do to hide.

Dan was hit by a sudden, fierce love for his child. *Thank God for Tony.* Dan edged forward, involuntarily, wanting to hug Tony and at the same time keep hidden from him.

Dan edged closer to Tony, until he was standing next to him.

Tony! Don't you feel me here? What is it that's turned off your mind? You're standing so still.

The bus was coming. Dan could see it a block away.

Tony's foot edged in front of the old woman's cane. The bus came fast, jouncing merrily on its rubber tires. One of Tony's hands came up to his chest, just behind the old woman's back. Only a father watching every tightening of shoulder muscles would have noticed the tensing of Tony's back, the slight lean forward.

Tony leaned forward.

Dan seized Tony's arms at the elbows.

"No, Tony!" he whispered in his ear. The whisper sounded like a roar in his head, and his lungs hurt. Or was it his heart that was in pain?

Bus tires swished past the curb, six inches in front of the old woman's cane. Its brakes hissed as it came to a fast stop. The hissing blended with Dan's whisper and Tony's gasp. Tony whirled around, and Dan, filled with an urgent need to cover up, to keep everyone around from even suspecting, said, through an aching throat, "Tony! I thought we were going to the beach this morning!"

Tony's flat, blank eyes looked at Dan. His muscles were hard under Dan's hands. Then abruptly he *saw* his father.

His eyes cleared, and intelligence came into them. The muscles in his shoulders relaxed.

"Dad! What are you doing here?"

"What are *you* doing?"

Tony's face was puzzled. "I don't know. I guess I was taking a walk."

The old woman boarded the bus. She was the last on, and she moved slowly. Tony and Dan were left alone on the concrete. The doors slid shut with a final pneumatic gulp. The bus moved. It built speed rapidly.

Frederick had been thinking a long time about whether to call Samantha. He had decided earlier today to go ahead, almost picked up the phone, then put it down.

Since his visit to the house three days before, he had been asking himself some serious questions. The first question was whether he really believed that Samantha would come back to him, now. The honest answer was that he didn't think so. It was probably the first honest answer he had given himself in quite a while, and it brought a few others in its trail.

Frederick was not a self-critical sort of person. He believed that most people were essentially selfish and that most of them either wanted something from him or were out to hurt him. But that was not true of Tad or Ricky, was it? If he acted sometimes as if he expected them to criticize him, that was probably wrong.

Therefore, Ricky's manner when he gave him a ride home on Thursday was the result of some other cause. It was not any antipathy to Frederick himself. He dialed Samantha.

"What do you want?" she asked when she knew who was calling.

"You probably won't believe me, and you probably don't care what I say—"

"Frederick, get to the point."

"But I think you ought to take Ricky to a doctor."

In a cautious voice, Samantha said, "Why?"

"He wasn't like himself when I saw him the other day. He's either depressed or he's sick."

"Oh?"

"He could be anemic. Maybe he has a strep throat."

"I'll check on it."

"Samantha, listen. I am not trying to make an indirect run at you. Ricky is the only reason I'm calling."

Slightly less coldly, Samantha said, "Okay. I noticed it too."

"And you'll take him to the doctor?"

"Probably. I appreciate you mentioning it. I'm glad you're—"

"Noticing my own child?"

"You said it. I was going to say 'concerned.' Goodbye, Frederick."

In the den, Samantha replaced the phone. How odd, she thought, that he would finally notice, just when the danger was receding. Well, that was Frederick, always a little too late.

Ricky was in his room and had shown no interest in playing with Garvey. Things were improving.

Upstairs, Ricky was oiling his scout knife. He had just finished polishing the blade, and before that he had spent half an hour with a good Arkansas stone, sharpening it.

"Tony, sit."

The kitchen was full of smoke. The smoke alarm was giving out loud, staccato blasts. Dan turned off the oven. The turnovers were black, and smoke poured from around the oven door. In the pan on the stove, the water had not quite boiled away, but the eggs danced in the last half inch with rubbery, overcooked clicks.

Dan opened the back door to let air in. The smoke eddied visibly through the back-door screen. The air cleared in the kitchen. After a couple of minutes, the smoke alarm fell silent.

They could talk.

"Tony," Dan said gently, "what were you doing?"

"I don't know. Just walking, I guess."

"I mean at the bus stop."

"I must've—I don't remember."

"Tony, listen. I *love* you. I don't blame you for anything. I just want to know what made you do it."

A look of alarm came over Tony's face. "Do what, Dad? What did I do?"

"You don't know?" Dan was already certain of the answer. Tony *didn't* know.

"I sort of don't remember much about this whole day, as a matter of fact." Tony tried to make his chin firm, but it trembled.

"Okay," Dan said.

"Dad, tell me what happened. Don't scare me."

"Tony, you didn't actually *do* anything. You were going to do something."

"What?"

"Push a person in front of a bus."

"*Me?*"

"Yes."

"Why would I do that?"

"Tony, we've got to figure this out."

"I'm scared."

"I'm scared, too."

So Tony accepted that he had done it. That frightened Dan. He wanted Tony to say, "Impossible! I'm not that sort of person!" Tony accepted it because he was aware of the blank in his afternoon.

Should he go to the police? And tell them what? That he had stopped his son from killing someone? If they believed him, it would mean—God only knew what it would mean! Psychiatrists for Tony? Prosecution as a minor for attempted murder? No! He had to figure out what was happening.

Had Tony done anything like this before? Could he have killed a human being? Henry Ax? The thought swept over Dan like an evil gas and left him feeling weak and nauseated.

This was what Samantha had thought of Garvey all along.

And Ricky had been confused and strange. Even Tony had said there was something wrong with Ricky. Could Ricky have killed Henry Ax? Could Tony?

Shit!

He could not go to the police. Face it, he *refused to* expose his son to the police.

The man's hand hovered over the telephone, just as Frederick's had done an hour earlier. He was alone at home; no one would overhear, and he wanted very much to make the call, to get the action started. But it was just past 4:00, and the best time for the boys to go into action would be later in the evening. There would be less chance of callers dropping in at the Lawton house later.

And that being the case, it would be wise to wait a while before lighting the boys' fuse. The best effect was obtained when the signal to go came close to the action.

Too bad darkness fell so late in July.

Well, he would call Tad and Ricky at 8:00.

Dinnertime or cleanup time, a good time to find them at home. And he'd give them 9:00 P.M. as the hour to move.

He drew his hand back from the phone. Eagerness could lead to danger; 8:00 P.M. it would be, and not a minute earlier. And after that—what relief!

He didn't want Samantha Lawton alive another day.

Thirty-Two

"Tony, you trust me, don't you?"

"Are you *kidding,* Dad?" Not a flicker of hesitation, but a big helping of scorn that he should have to ask. Dan's heart felt warmer, the ache less painful.

"Did any of the scoutmasters spend an extra lot of time with you during camp?"

"Um. Nobody extra, as far as I know."

"Schultz? Fiske? Grey?"

"No. Mr. Grey talked with me a while about competitive swimming. I did a merit badge with Schultz and another merit badge with Grey. Nothing with Mr. Fiske."

"Did you stay on and talk with them beyond the merit badge questions?"

"No. I mean, maybe half a minute. Like, 'Thanks' or 'I'm glad I passed,' or like that."

"Did any of them seem to be trying especially hard to make friends with you?"

"No-oo. I don't think so. Schultz talked a lot. Grey is more—um—informative. Mr. Fiske wants to do what he likes to do. I guess they all try to be pretty friendly."

"Did anybody give you pills? Or unusual food?"

"No."

"I just wish I had more to go on. Tony—will you go in and watch television, please, while I make a phone call?"

"Don't you want me to hear the gory details?"

"I'm sorry. You stay if you want."

"In that case, I think I'll go watch some television."

Dan smiled and brought up his hand to touch Tony's arm. Tony laid his hand over his father's.

Tony went to the recreation room. Dan hurried to the front door, locked and bolted it, and then did the same with the back door. It would not keep Tony in, but Dan would hear if he went out. Dan went back to the phone.

The phone book said the Ann Arbor, Michigan, area code was 313. He dialed the information access.

"Information for what city?"

"Ann Arbor," he said.

"Go ahead, sir."

"I need the number of Jan Idema in the psychology department at the University of Michigan."

"I have the university number, sir, but not the extension numbers of the departments, sir."

"Well, give me that."

She did.

"Can you get me the university and ask them for the extension number?"

"You have to call the university for that information, sir. Or if you wish you may call the operator and ask her to place the call for you, and she will request the extension number. But that will be charged as an operator-assisted call."

"Thank you," Dan said, his mind screaming, impatiently, *Assist me!*

He dialed the university number. *Let Jan be in his office. Don't let him be at home. Someone is sure to tell me they don't give out home numbers.*

Jan had a big, happy laugh and a trace of Dutch accent that Dan remembered the instant he came on the line.

"Dan! I haven't heard from you in months!"

"I'm sorry. I should have called."

"Well, now you have. That's good enough."

"I'm afraid I called for a favor."

"Good! Tell me."

"I want to describe a situation to you, but for some reasons, some—hell, I'm doing this badly already. I want to avoid giving the person and place too clearly. It's not that I don't trust you, it's a difficult—"

"Dan. Simmer down. I'm happy to operate in complete ignorance of who, when, and where. I do it all the time. Just go ahead."

"Okay. Thanks. There's a person here who has done something completely out of character—" He described what Tony had almost done, cautiously, anonymously, soft-pedaling the fact that the act had been intentionally homicidal. "The accident could have been serious," he said. "Could this person be drugged?"

"Could anybody have given him food, water, or a pill or injection in the previous twelve hours?"

"No."

"Did anyone have *complete* control over him, full-time, in an institution for example, for the preceding several weeks?"

"No."

"Then no. Anyway, Dan, even in an institutional setting where you can both drug somebody and talk constantly with him, programming a person is not as easy as the tabloids make it sound. You can drive him nuts with drugs, easy!—but programming him to do a specific act at a specific time is something else again. Besides, he would have acted nuts when he got out."

"What would it be when the person seems normal right up to the moment this *thing* happens?"

"No previous mental illness?"

"No."

"Could somebody have got at him for brief periods?"

"Yes."

"Did he seem inattentive to outside stimuli just before the incident?"

"Yes."

"What about hypnosis, Dan?"

"I—can children be hypnotized?"

"Holy cow, yes! They're *much* more easily hypnotized than adults, the darling little beggars. In fact, they're so much easier that some people think we're all easily hypnotizable as kids, but we lose it as we get older. So we're talking about a child, are we?"

"Well, yes. Listen," Dan said hopefully, "I always thought children couldn't concentrate enough to be put in a trance."

"Oh, maybe children under five or so that can't focus their minds very long. I have doubts even about that. But whatever, there are other ways. Babies, for instance—you can stroke them and rock them and hum to them. Just like Mother used to do to make you sleep, huh?" Jan laughed cheerfully, a big laugh that made the phone vibrate.

"But Jan, you can't just walk up to a kid and say, 'Here, let me hypnotize you.' I mean, you can't hypnotize a person against his will, can you?"

"Well, in the first place, adults resist more than children do. But even with a child—no, I don't think a stranger could do it very easily. The child wouldn't trust a stranger. Trust is a big factor in entering a trance. That's probably one reason why children are easier to hypnotize. They haven't learned to distrust yet."

Trust, like a boy might trust his scoutmaster.

"Jan—"

"Want to hear something funny? In the old days, the ability to be hypnotized easily was called 'hypnotic suscepti-

347

bility.' But that didn't have the right PR value. Susceptibility sounded like a weakness, like catching a disease. Now the hypnotists—perfectly legitimate people, mind you, who use it for surgery where drugs could be risky, and dentistry, and all kinds of fancy good things—now they call it 'hypnotic responsiveness.' See, that makes it sound like a *talent!*"

"But, do you mean a person—"

"Can just walk up and hypnotize you? No. But you can do it and not call it hypnotism. There was a case out near you, recently. A young girl was killed, and the police got the notion that one of the boys who lived nearby had done it. He was upset, of course—so would you be if a friend of yours got killed. And they kept asking him questions, and he just couldn't remember what he had been doing late that night. Turns out he was probably asleep, but never mind that. Well, the police got in a psychologist who was supposed to help the boy relax and remember. Well, let me tell you, he relaxed that boy and relaxed that boy. Never used the word 'hypnotism' as far as I know, and he claimed he was not trying to hypnotize him. But, by God, it *was* hypnotism, even if you called it ham and eggs and a side of hotcakes. During these 'relaxation' sessions, he suggested to the boy, maybe not intending to, that the kid had killed the girl. And sure enough, within a few hours, the boy thought he remembered smothering the girl with a pillow that had been left near the body."

"So he did it, after all?"

"Well, no. Actually, the girl was strangled with a ligature that had been pulled tight around her neck, not a pillow at all. Hypnosis had made him 'remember' an event that never happened. Courts are beginning to realize this. When hypnotists work with crime witnesses now, the courts are starting to require that the sessions be videotaped. That's so they can go over them later to see whether the hypnotist suggested details to the subject that he later seemed to remember. Because it's so very, *very* easy to suggest to a person under hypnosis what it is you want him to remember."

"If you wanted to hypnotize a—a young teenager—without him knowing that he'd been hypnotized, what would you do?"

There was silence on the other end for a few seconds. Then Jan said, "This is important to you, isn't it?"

"It couldn't be more important."

"All right. What I'd do—that is, I wouldn't do it, because it wouldn't be ethical. But assuming I'm an unethical person, what I'd do is this. I'd start very cautiously. First, I'd test to see how hypnotizable the kid was. There are dozens and dozens of ways you can do this. One is Chevreul's pendulum test. I'd pretend it was a sort of game. I'd say, 'Kid, I've got a trick here. See this pendulum? It's magic.' And I'd have a lead weight or a golf ball or whatever on the end of a string. I'd say, 'You hold this by the end of the string.' What kid wouldn't, just to see what would happen? Then I'd tell him, 'You try your hardest to hold that steady, so it doesn't swing. You try now. But that pendulum is going to start swinging on its own. It's going to start swinging forward and back, now. Forward and back. Forward and back.' And by God, Dan, let me tell you, seventy, eighty percent of the kids you try, that pendulum will start swinging forward and back. Then you can say, 'Now the pendulum is going to swing around in a circle. It's starting to swing around in a circle. Look at that, it's swinging in a circle.' Now, you will find if you try this on a lot of kids, some will get into it more easily than others, and they're the ones who are likely to go most easily into a trance."

"Holy shit. It's as simple as that?"

"Matter of fact, you can try it on yourself. Get a pendulum

and try to hold it steady, but in your mind *picture* it going around in a circle. I'd bet you five bucks it will swing in a circle. These are called ideomotor motions, but the point in this case is to test whether the kid imagines it swinging because of your suggestion. The purpose is to tell whether the person to be hypnotized can enter into another person's ideas. There are so many ways to test this, I'm sure you don't want to hear them all. There are even ways of screening big groups of people for the best hypnotic subjects."

"How?"

"You get your kids, say, sitting around you in a circle, and you say, 'I smell a new odor coming into this room. It's a sharp odor. Maybe like ammonia. Can anybody smell it?' And some of them will say they do. You say, 'It's faint, but it's there.' And one may say it smells to him more like cleaning fluid. Another one will be sure it's ammonia. And some, of course, may not smell it at all. That last type is not your best subject."

"Yeah."

"Then you have a good potential subject close his eyes and you can make him believe an ice cube is a hot piece of metal. You get a sort of ascendancy—Dan, are you all right?"

"Sorry. I just groaned."

"Do you want me to go on with this?"

"I *have* to."

"Will you tell me what the trouble is?"

"I will later, if I can. But, Jan—under hypnosis a person can't be made to do anything that he wouldn't do normally, can he? He wouldn't do anything against his moral sense?"

Jan sighed. "I don't know what you're up against here, but I'm afraid the answer is he can. People who can be deeply hypnotized, and even most of those who can only go into a medium deep trance, will do things that in a normal state they would consider wrong. You *must* realize this, Dan. You've heard of proper ladies taking their clothes off at parties in response to a posthypnotic suggestion. You must have."

"I always thought that only worked with people who had a suppressed desire to do it anyway."

"No, it's not as simple as that. People will do things they otherwise would believe are wrong because they've entered so thoroughly into a different picture of reality. They no longer see true reality around them. For instance, if you can convince the woman that she is getting ready to take a bath and there is no one in the room, she will take off her clothes."

"Could a person be convinced—" Dan's voice stumbled. "Could—"

"Dan, are you sick?"

"Not exactly. Could a person—"

I can't ask this.

"What, Dan?"

"Could a child be made to commit murder?"

"Jesus Christ, Dan!"

"Tell me!"

"I wish I could say no. Wait. I don't want to do this in my own words. Hang on and let me get a book."

Dan hung on to the phone. He squeezed it.

"Here it is." Jan's voice, concerned and tense. "This is from *Modern Perspectives in World Psychiatry.* I'm quoting. 'With some cunning and indirect suggestion under hypnosis, the deep-trance subject could be made to follow about any suggestion within his powers: and the truthful answer to the other old question "Can the hypnotized subject be made to perform acts contrary to his moral code?" is a qualified *affirmative.* Numerous statements in the literature taking an opposite view would seem to be more public relations campaign by hypnotists than a scientific observation.' End of my quotation."

351

Oh, my God. How long has Tony been exposed to this? What has Tony done?

"Dan? Are you there?"

"Yes."

"Do you want to talk about what is wrong?"

"Not now. Jan, assuming a—a person—had been under the influence of a hypnotist, how could you break him out of it?"

"Well, if just the sense of reality, *real* reality, intrudes strongly enough, that'll often do it. And of course the effect doesn't go on forever *if* you remove the hypnotist."

Remove the hypnotist.

"But what about suggestions that the hypnotist has made that the subject is supposed to carry out later? Posthypnotic suggestions?"

"That can go several ways. If the suggestion is physically incapable of being carried out, that breaks the sequence, of course. Once in a while another hypnotist can break the rapport. But that is terribly difficult. Harder than you might believe. And subjects who can enter deep hypnosis have a spontaneous amnesia that is *very* resistant about everything that went on during hypnosis. If that's reinforced by a suggestion from the hypnotist that the subject forget everything that was said during hypnosis, you may *never* get him to express what happened. But Dan, if you remove the hypnotist and make the posthypnotic suggestion impossible to carry out, the whole episode may fade away into the past."

"Yeah." *Remove the hypnotist.*

"The thing is, Dan—are you there?"

"Yes."

"Thing is, children enter into this so well. The ability to be hypnotized depends on the ability to become *imaginatively involved* in the hypnotist's fictional world. And children imagine so beautifully. Watch them play. A stick is a jeweled sword. A frying pan is a mighty shield. Just sitting on the living room floor, a kid can see himself lost on Mars. Adults can't do this very well. It takes a damn good movie to get me to suspend disbelief. Imagine what a hypnotist who was a bit of a storyteller could do with a child."

"I'm imagining."

"Dan?"

"Yes?"

"Are you going to be all right?"

"I'm going to try."

"Call me back, Dan, when it's over."

"I'll do that."

Thirty-Three

As she was starting dinner, Samantha had an idea.

"Tad? Would you like to make cookies with me?"

"I don't know. Not right now."

"What are you playing?"

"Micronauts."

"I can see that. I mean, why are they all lined up?"

"They're hunting."

"What are they hunting?"

"See that piece of scuzzy stuff?"

Samantha looked at a brownish fuzzy lump a few inches in front of the lead Micronaut. She had assumed it was a simple piece of lint.

"Oh, that? Yes, I see it."

"It's a micronasty, and they're going to catch it."

"What will they do when they catch it?"

"They'll pull it apart, and they'll pull it into littler and littler pieces until it completely disappears."

Samantha shivered. "Why will they do that?"

"It was pretending. It was pretending to be a nice little puppy."

Just after 6:00 P.M., Tony left the television set and went into the kitchen to check on his father. He found Dan with his elbows on the table, his chin sunk in his hands, his eyes closed.

"What'cha doing, Dad?"

"I'm thinking."

"You look it."

"Do I look like I'm making progress?"

"Nope."

"My impression exactly. Tony, I just can't figure this out. Why and who? I don't even know which is more important, why or who? And I think I've got to work fast. There's no telling what else he may be planning."

"Can I help?"

"I don't think—yeah, maybe so."

"Shoot."

"Tony—at camp, you say none of the scoutmasters spent especially long periods of time with you. But did any of them ever act in ways that seemed odd to you?"

"Jeez! All of them!"

Dan smiled, but he said, "Like what?"

"Well, Schultz used to go over in a corner of the cook tent and burrow around in the trash, and I thought that was funny. One time I watched him and I found out what he was doing. He had a stash of vodka under the ground cloth and he'd go over after dinner and take nips of it. And one time I heard Grey grunting and stuff in his tent. I thought he might be sick, see, and all alone in there, so I peeked in the flap and he had this thing with wooden balls that rolled on sort of thongs and he had his back to me and he was rolling it over his stomach, trying to roll the fat off. I mean, he isn't fat, he's really strong, but he was trying to *keep* the fat off, I guess."

"That isn't quite what I had in mind," Dan said.

"What *did* you have in mind?"

"Lord, Tony, I wish I knew."

He did not dare leave Tony in the house alone. He didn't know what Tony would do if the person who was using him came by or called on the phone. But Dan couldn't sit here any longer, either. He had to take action.

Remove the hypnotist.

His hands ached to remove the hypnotist.

Dan's neighbor, in this less affluent part of Rivercrest, was a man of about sixty. He was tough. A retired Marine, he jogged five miles a day and worked out an hour every day with weights. In the best days of summer he took his weights out to the backyard and worked with them there. Three days a week he swam at the YMCA.

Dan called the man Grange, short for Grainger. Grange's wife was dead, and he lived alone. In the winter, when Grange went to visit his daughter and son-in-law in Dayton, Dan kept his eye on the house, picking up stray mail and sometimes shoveling the walk to make the place look lived-in. He had never particularly asked Grange to return the favor. Dan phoned him.

"Grange, could Tony come and spend the evening with you? I have to go out, and I think Tony's in danger. I'll explain later. It's important to have somebody I can trust to watch him."

"Henry Ax, I beg your pardon. I've been wrong," Dan said aloud. Henry had been right, and Dan had all but made fun of him. Partly out of jealousy, because Henry was seeing Samantha, and partly out of sheer disbelief, he had not even really paid attention to what Henry had been saying. Now he wanted to remember. What exactly had Henry thought was going on? Who had he suspected?

Somebody in the scouts, of course. Some scoutmaster.

Why? Why take a boy and make him kill?

A psychotic? A psychopath? Serial killers, he had heard, are usually psychopaths. Paranoid schizophrenics kill on a short-lived impulse. Was that right? Call Jan Idema back? No, Jan would have left the office. And anyway, there might not be time.

It didn't feel reasonable, anyway, that whoever had set this in motion was a total crazy. If Henry was right and there had been other cases, then this was systematic and well organized. In fact, it would require technical knowledge, and knowledge of hypnosis, and research into the habits of the people to be killed. That did not sound like a nut.

Why use the boys? Why use scouts, specifically?

Well, a boy would not be suspected of murder. He'd have no motive, and besides that, people don't think of children as killers.

And scouts even more so.

A boy scout, especially in his uniform, looked so innocent.

And of course, while the boy was killing, the man would have a solid alibi. And no connection to the murder. Very businesslike.

Businesslike!

A contract killer, of course. And one with a perfect gimmick. It could have been going on for years, undetected.

Not Monty Fiske. He was sick and weak and almost pitiable.

Organization, cool-headedness, planning. Not Ira Schultz, clownish, clumsy Ira, with his big belly and big pants.

Lee Grey.

Lee—sleek as a carnivore, hard-muscled, alert. Lee the competitive. Lee the smooth, cool-headed and cold-eyed.

Dan started out from his house on foot. He was too angry to drive. He couldn't focus his eyes on pedestrians or anything but the flame of his anger.

It was now 6:30.

Grey's house was five blocks north. He was there in minutes.

Grey's wife Naomi answered the door.

"Is Lee home?"

"No, and he's supposed to be. Come on in."

Naomi's mouth was angrily compressed. "I'm sorry," Dan said, though he wasn't. "Am I interrupting something?"

She all but stamped her foot. "The roast is drying out. We have a deal. I cook. He's supposed to be home by six to eat. I can't be sitting around here forever waiting for him."

"Oh?"

"It's not your fault. Let me get you a drink."

He was about to say no, when he realized he had a few minutes to find out what Naomi knew. "Let me pour one for you, and you sit and relax. How about that?" He pointed his head at the credenza, loaded with bottles and glasses.

"Sure, Scotch."

He came back with a large one for her, smaller for him. He hid the upper part of his glass with his hand.

"So, Dan, what do you need to see Lee about?"

"Scouts. The money. You know."

"Oh?" She looked at him, waiting.

"The *extra* money."

"I'm glad *somebody* has some."

"Well, just some odds and ends."

Okay, so she probably didn't know. In fact, why should Lee tell her? It would make him hostage to another person. If they were ever divorced, she might talk. Might talk anyway. A person as cautious as the mind that had planned this would keep it all to himself.

"Personally, I think it's time for Lee to get out of the scouts," she said grimly.

"Why?"

"He's spending too much time on it."

"Oh."

"And on work. Look at this! It's nearly seven. Dinner's been ready an hour and he's not home! I have a meeting later!" She held out her glass. Dan took the broad hint and refilled it.

At 7:15, Lee was still not there. Dan wanted to hit his hands together, to run out and look up and down the street, to telephone Lee's office. He sat quietly.

At 7:20, a car pulled into the driveway. The back door of the house slammed open. Dan heard Lee's voice calling to the house in general: "Shit! A twelve-car pile-up. Can you beat it? Right at the rush hour. Fire trucks and ambulances up the ass—"

He saw Dan.

Naomi gestured at Dan and said, "Uh—he's been waiting—"

"Dan! Sorry to sound so pissed off. The Edens was stopped *dead!* I was just a half a mile short of the Dempster exit, but you can't get off the fucking thing unless you abandon your car and climb over the fence. Christ! Honey, get me a drink."

"Lee, Dan's been waiting, and dinner's drying out, and—"

"Well, just get me a drink, dammit, and I'll *talk* with Dan and then I'll *eat* the damn dinner!"

Naomi left, fast.

"Can we talk in your den?" Dan asked.

"Sure. Why not?"

Dan felt a creeping uneasiness as Naomi came back with the drink and he followed Lee to the den. Its cause was the expression on Lee Grey's face—exasperation, annoyance with the other drivers, the highway, his wife, and probably Dan, too. And a complete lack of interest in whatever Dan had come to say. In fact, he had the look of a man who was trying to be polite but was actually tired and bored.

Dan was afraid he had the wrong man. And that meant—

"So, Dan, what's the trouble?"

Of course, he might be a superb actor. In for a penny, in for a pound. There was no way to do this but head-on.

"Lee, have you been using the scouts to kill people?"

Samantha was putting away the dishes when the phone rang.

"Can you get that?" she called.

She heard Rick run to the telephone in the study, which was next to the playroom, but she could not hear what he said.

Ricky said, "Hello?"

"Ricky?"

"Speaking."

"May the force be with you."

Ricky's casual stance straightened. His eyes, which had been scanning the desk surface, rose and focused about eighteen inches in front of his face, as if he saw a vision there, in the air.

"Yes," he said.

"Is Tad there?"

"Yes."

"Then you may wait one hour and go ahead with our plan. It will be dark then."

"Yes."

"Now put Tad on."

Ricky slowly lowered the phone to the desk, not banging it. "Tad!" he called.

"What?"

"Telephone."

Tad came in and picked up the phone. Ricky stood next to him and waited.

"Tad?"

"Yes."

"May the force be with you."

"Yes."

"In one hour you will proceed with our plan."

"Yes."

"Hang up now."

Tad and Ricky walked back into the playroom and sat down facing the television set. There was a clock on top.

"Who was that, Ricky?" Samantha called.

"Scouts."

"What did they want?"

"We're gonna check on the bees tomorrow."

"Oh. That's all right, then."

Lee Grey stared at Dan with stupefied incomprehension. His mouth was half-open. A second or two passed, and then the urbane Lee Grey asserted himself. "What in hell are you talking about?"

"Maybe I've made a mistake."

This was not acting. "Dan, you're fucking scaring me. Are you all right?"

"Sure. I've gotta go. I've gotta talk to somebody."

"Wait a minute! Have you been *taking* anything? Are you on some kind of drugs? Dan, I got a doctor who's very good as this kind of thing. He got my wife's sister off Dalmane, and I mean this is a person who between air and Dalmane would choose Dalmane every time—"

But Dan was already leaving.

"I'll see you later, Lee. Sorry I bothered you."

Dan walked fast. It was nearly 8:00, and the sun was getting low. He ran one block, then walked one block, then ran one block. He was soon out of breath, and a pain was growing in his side. He jogged another half block. The pain got worse. He was short of breath.

He knew what the trouble was. It was fear. He would be breathless even if he stood still.

He kept walking.

Thirty-Four

Dan was running when he hit the slight rise to Ira Schultz's house, but he slowed there to a walk. He did not want to be puffing and gasping when he met the man.

Schultz had a very large front lawn, a concrete S-curve path to the front door, and a row of low bushes that hid the backyard from the street. Over the tops of these bushes, Dan saw the plume of a sprinkler leaning slowly back and forth. Even while he watched, catching his breath, he saw the plume sink, make one last spurt, and go off. Dan knew that the backyard was larger than the front and surrounded by bushes. He hoped it was Ira out in back, alone, turning off the sprinkler. It would be much harder to meet him indoors, with his wife and children looking on, asking what the trouble was.

Dan's heart was pounding and his palms were sweaty. These were symptoms of fear, but the only emotion he was conscious of was a red, consuming anger.

He strode across the lawn and pushed through the bushes into the backyard.

The sun was so low now that its light was broken up by the large trees in the back of Ira's yard, and its color was deep orange. Dan stood for a second looking down the back lawn. Ira Schultz was near the beehive, holding a pair of pruning shears, his body outlined by the reddening light behind him.

"Hello, Ira," Dan said, and even at that distance, even in

363

the distorting light, he knew. He read guilt from the firming, defensive stance of Ira's body, silhouetted against the fiery sun.

Dan had found the man.

As Dan walked across the wide lawn, Ira relaxed his body. He wore big floppy shorts and no shirt. "Well, Dan?" he said.

"Don't bother," Dan said, "I know all about it."

Ira's eyes searched Dan's face. All at once, with no downward flick of a glance to give warning, Ira stabbed upward with the pruning shears, straight at Dan's heart.

Dan had no time to jump back, and only a split second in which to turn, bringing up his left arm. The steel blades punctured the white shirt he wore, cut through the top of his arm, and came out through the fabric on the other side.

It had taken enormous force to strike such a blow with a tool whose points were quite blunt. All at once Ira, with his big, flapping Bermuda shorts and his big stomach, was not ridiculous any more. Ira had weight, but he converted it to force. Big and fast, bathed in orange light, he bore down on Dan again.

Dan pivoted. The shears flashed past his shoulder. He kicked at Ira's kneecap, hard and quick, but Ira danced back. Blood ran from the wound in Dan's upper arm down over the knuckles of his left hand. Ira lunged again. Dan jumped, and the steel shears narrowly missed his neck. He felt their passage in the hair on the back of his head.

He turned and drove his foot sideways into Ira's big belly. Ira backpedaled so fast that the kick only forced some air out of his lungs. He coughed once, and then laughed.

With a chill, Dan realized that Ira was not only taller and heavier than he, but also faster. And he was armed. And he was not wounded.

Dan was going to die.

"Not so tough, are you, Camelli?"

"Ira, it doesn't make sense to kill a man in your own back-yard."

"Who can see? It sure doesn't make sense to let you get away. I'll think of something to do with the body later. I'm an expert. I'm almost infallible."

"It isn't going to work, Ira." Dan talked, thinking fast. "Too many people are onto you."

"No. Only two and one's dead. The other will be soon."

"What do you mean?"

"The police chief is dead. Samantha Lawton should be dead—" he looked at his watch "—um—in a few minutes."

Dan punched forward with one fist, but Ira was faster, batting Dan's hand out of the way, then slicing across with the shears. Dan leaped back.

"You should have been exercising, instead of teaching school, guy. Now me, I work out at the gym three nights a week. Makes a difference, doesn't it, boy?"

Ira lunged at Dan with the shears point-forward. Dan twisted. The blades ripped across his shirt and skidded along the skin over one rib. They tore a shallow gash, and the pain blinded Dan briefly. He staggered back nearer the beehive.

Ira stepped forward in a wide-legged, aggressive stance. He meant to finish Dan off now, and Dan knew he could not duck fast enough, could not run fast enough, and did not have the weight to match Ira's.

Dan lurched to the side and chopped his hand down in a hard blow against the beehive. Then he took one quick step away from the hive, in the split second before the bees surged out.

Dan held very still.

His blow had driven the upper box of the hive sideways. From this new opening and from the hive door, a stream of bees erupted, amber bullets, shooting out too fast to see, spinning up into the air above the hive and hanging there, an angry cloud. The cloud buzzed with a venomous fury as more and more bees poured out; the cloud thickened, darkened, and its angry roar increased. It looked for an enemy.

The red light of the dying day danced on the cloud of furious bees. As their wings moved, they shimmered in the glow—scarlet wings, now catching the light, now losing it. It was a blur of red bodies, red humming wings, a pulsing, venomous cloud of primitive poison.

Ira had stopped dead when the bees emerged. He was frozen in horror. The cloud was only three feet from his head, and he stared at it, transfixed.

"My equalizer, Ira," Dan said, carefully, hardly moving his lips. He was no less terrified than Ira, but the difference was that three seconds earlier he had thought he would surely die.

Ira said, "Aahhh."

"If you don't move, they won't sting you. They don't really see you if you don't move."

Had he only bought time?

Dan did not mention that it was fast motion that the bees perceived. Very, very slowly he moved his left foot backward. Infinitely slowly. As slowly as an ice cube melting, he thought in those long seconds, as slowly as bread rising. His goal was to get gradually, imperceptibly, beyond the reach of Ira's arm and Ira's pruning shears.

"I can't move," Ira said, "but neither can you."

"Right. But that still leaves me better off, doesn't it? Somebody will find us."

"Oh, yeah? My family is out of town. Nobody will see us here."

For the first time since he came into the yard, Dan was able to study Ira.

"My God, Ira," he said, revolted, "those children *trusted* you!"

"Move your lips too fast, boy, and those bees are gonna get you."

"Ira, people have died! And Lord only knows whether those boys you used are ruined forever. Don't you *care?*"

He had no sense of whether he was reaching anything in Ira, whether there was a core of humanity to reach, but the horror of it had to be spoken.

Ira said, "So?"

"Holy shit, Ira!"

Inadvertently, Dan had leaned his body forward, and he saw the red cloud of angry bees shift in his direction. He froze. Through clenched lips, he said, "What did you do it for? Just money?"

As if amazed at the question, Ira said, "Of course, money!"

"For God's sake! This is—shit, I thought Monty Fiske was evil. With his nasty little perversion! I tell you, it seems like a *sincere* little perversion compared to you! At least he had a genuine impulse. It was a human sort of desire. However warped it was, it was the real thing. Disgusting, but a real thing. You—you aren't even tragic!"

"If somebody offered you enough money—"

Ira had been edging one foot forward slowly while Dan was talking. Dan slipped his right foot slowly back, gliding cautiously over the hose. Ira still held the shears with their points toward Dan. Dan wondered whether Ira could drive the shears into him in slow motion. He and Ira were still fighting, only moving so slowly that the battle could hardly be perceived.

"If somebody offered you enough money, Dan," Ira said, trying to distract him.

Suddenly, Dan realized that his equalizer, the bees, would not last indefinitely. If several minutes went by and they didn't see any motion, they would conclude that the threat had gone, and they would return to the hive. Or if the sun went down with no further threat—and sunset was only minutes away—the bees, who were creatures of daylight, would go back in their hive. Then Ira could fall on him with the shears.

Ira was going to kill him, after all.

Dan stepped back a little faster. The cloud of bees hummed and several scouts shot toward him. He froze.

"Now-now-now! You almost bought it that time, Dan-baby!"

Dan didn't answer.

"Matter of fact, maybe you should. It would sure save me a lot of trouble."

"If you kill me, you'll be found out."

"I doubt it. Bees would make it simple, though. The great biology teacher came over to do a little experiment. See whether—oh, maybe whether—bees fly at night. He must have miscalculated someplace."

There were a few bees on Dan's arm now. He looked down and saw three or four on his pants legs.

There were bees on Ira, too. There were some crawling on his bare legs and some on his bare chest. One landed on Dan's cheek and crawled toward his nose.

He hardly dared breathe. He did not dare talk.

Ira, too, had stopped moving his foot.

"Itches, I guess, don't it, Dan?" Ira said. For some reason, the bees on Ira were mostly on his ankles, legs, and chest, which were bare, while Dan's were on his arms and nose. Dan longed to taunt Ira, but he was momentarily paralyzed. The dozens of bees on Ira's bare legs must itch, too. Must be making him nervous, though he didn't show it. Crawling up under those big, flapping Bermuda shorts. *Bite him in the balls, you guys,* Dan shouted silently.

"Couple more coming up your neck, Dan!"

Dan felt them. There were more landing on his arms and neck by the minute. The bee on his nose was making its way across one nostril, its busy legs brushing the sensitive inside of the opening. If he sneezed, the bees would sting him to death.

If the sun set, the bees would go into the hive and Ira would kill him.

Dan turned his eyes cautiously toward the west. The sphere of the sun was just touching the horizon. He did not have much more time.

Dan looked at the hose, lying on the ground between him and Ira. It was within reach. Very, very slowly, he folded his knees down. He tried to feel whether there were any bees on the backs of his legs. He thought not. There were dozens on his arms now, several on his face. One was crawling toward his eye.

He bent and let his hand fall slowly toward the hose.

Ira, red in the darkening sun, laughed. "You flip that thing, boy, they'll be on you before they touch me."

Dan's hand touched the hose. Slowly, slower than human muscles want to move—he could feel the muscle fibers tense and release, faint jerks in the tendons—*don't let the bees notice!*

If only Ira did not understand in time.

Slowly, but in one continuous motion, he pushed the hose forward six inches. Because it was stiff, it buckled, forming a bend. Then, while Ira was still laughing, he turned the part of the hose he held in his hand, flipping the curve of the hose over, up against Ira's leg. And against the dozens of bees that swarmed on it.

It struck Ira's calf and hit the bees on bare skin just above Ira's argyle socks. He realized what Dan had done a second too late. His eyes widened in awareness and an instant later at the pain as several injured bees sank their stingers into Ira's ankle.

Ira had not quite time enough to control his reaction. He gasped and jerked his foot back. He realized instantly that he should not have moved, that he should have endured any pain to stand still, but it was too late.

The bees on his legs and chest drove in their stingers as far as they would go, throbbing with poison, pushing them farther and farther, until the poison glands and stingers were so imbedded that they were torn from the bees' abdomens.

The cloud of bees was upon him.

Ira shrieked in agony. Dan wanted to stand up, to run, but he was just inches from a hundred thousand enraged bees. Bent over, one hand near the ground, knees scarcely able to hold the position, he forced every muscle in his body to stay rock-still. The swarm, furious at the scent of their injured fellows, struck at Ira's arms, legs, chest, and face. Ira's eyes opened, stark white around the pupils, and his mouth emitted an inarticulate scream which changed to rasping gasps.

The bees were on his eyes now, in his hair, on his bare chest and bare legs. Between his fingers. On his lips. In his nose.

Ira arched backward and forward. He started to run, but he could not see, and he jumped and staggered. Shrieking, he tried to scrape away the bees with his hands, but the hands themselves were covered with their bodies, and for every sheet of dead bees he scraped away, others shot through the air to take their place.

Shuddering, twitching, Ira wiped the bees from his eyes. Dan could see the eyes, hot and red, filled with hate.

Ira, coated with bees, seething with bees, turned toward Dan. His mouth opened to curse Dan, and the mouth was filled with bees.

Dan knew what Ira was going to do. Dan could not run, or strike, to save himself. He could only steel himself.

He hoped Ira would die and fall to the ground before he reached him.

But Ira came on, a seething red mass. He fell, and Dan fiercely hoped that he would not stand up again, but he rose to his feet, impossibly, and took another step. His eyes were swollen shut now and covered again with bees, but he knew where Dan was and there must have been just one thought left in his mind—revenge.

Dan watched the mass of heaving death approach. He gritted his teeth.

The manlike shape was nearly on him. It staggered again, fell to one knee. But its arms reached out in a tortured spasm, and the puffing hands, bubbling with bees, closed around Dan's ankle.

The bees that were trapped between Ira's hands and Dan's ankle drove their stingers into his flesh. Dan was still half crouching. He had expected the burning pain, and he held rigid. The agony from his back muscles was swamped in the searing pain of the venom that shot into his ankle. The pain traveled up his leg and invaded the center of his body.

But he held rigid. He wanted to gasp and to scream, but he dared not even breathe.

Bees from Ira's hand and arm swarmed over to Dan's leg. Dan could feel them, running among the hairs, looking for a place to sink their stingers.

But they didn't. They searched, but did not sting.

Now Ira's body was still. Dan did not move.

The bees waited.

If anything moved, Dan knew, the bees would kill it.

If a mouse ran across the lawn that moment, the bees would kill it. Or a dog. Or a child.

But all was still in the garden. There was no sign from neighboring houses that anyone had heard Ira screaming.

Dan could feel the blood trickling from his arm wound. But the bees were not attracted by blood, and he hoped the motion of the blood was too slow to enrage them.

He held absolutely still. He was afraid he might blink. He was afraid the pain in his leg would make him twitch. The pain was so intense, he was afraid it might make his leg weaken and he would fall down.

After a few moments, he felt such a desire to blink and was so afraid to do so, that he slowly closed his eyes and kept them closed. He held that position, body crouched, not knowing how much time was passing. When his muscles shrieked with the strain, he gloried in it, because it meant he was holding his position. Every part of his body hurt. He stayed still.

Thirty-Five

It was dark.

Samantha stood in the archway between the dining room and living room. A slight draft from the stairs behind her stirred the hairs on the back of her neck. The dining room was dark. The stairs were dark. Samantha felt a desire to turn all the lights on.

Silly, of course. Nothing could go wrong now; the three of them were alone together. The rest of the world was locked out.

The windows to the inner courtyard of the house were black, even though the living room lights were all on. The center of the house, she thought, was dark. A black heart.

At the far end of the living room was a matching arch that led into the study. The study was dark, too, but beyond it she could see the glow from the television set in the playroom, which spilled onto the study rug as a long bluish triangle. That knife of faint light made the den appear even darker.

Although she had locked all the doors and windows earlier in the day, her ears were keyed to every creak and rustle of the house. Small sounds. If danger came, she thought, it would herald itself with small sounds.

She could hear the sound of the television set from here and was happy to know, at least, where the children were. They must have compromised on a nature program.

"The garden spider," the narrator said, "waits in the

corner of her web, eight legs resting on strands that she has woven fresh that morning. The slightest vibration will be carried to her sensitive nerves—"

Samantha shivered. As long as she was up, she might just as well check the front and back doors.

The front door was locked. She opened it to test the automatic lock, which was on, then closed it and reset the bolt.

The back door had its lock, chain bolt, and floor deadbolt in place. She glanced into the playroom, imagining that the sliding glass door might have broken silently, but it was intact, and the broom handle that she had wedged into the groove so it would not slide was in place also.

"The fisher spider walks on the surface of still ponds, using surface tension to keep himself from sinking. He studies the living creatures below him in the water. They do not appear to notice him, skating above them on the surface, in a different world. When he sees a particularly juicy morsel, he strikes."

There was a sound, a faint rustling. Because of the shape of the house, she could not tell exactly where it was coming from. Standing now in the kitchen, she might hear a noise from the study echoing around the corners and sounding as if it came from the playroom.

If a sound was produced in the side of the house directly opposite where she stood, she might hear it as if it came from either side.

But it didn't really matter, did it? They were locked in, and nothing could go wrong as long as their defenses weren't breached. Still—she'd just check on the children. Seeing that they were safe would make her feel better. Probably one of them had made the sound.

"The wolf spider," said the television set as she walked toward the playroom, "does not build a web. He builds a prominence near his burrow, and from this vantage point, leaps upon unsuspecting prey."

Samantha looked at the shocking face of the wolf spider on the screen. It had eight eyes, a hairy face, and mandibles or mouth parts that appeared to drip poison. She glanced down at the sofa. The children were not there.

"Ricky? Tad?" They didn't answer, and she walked over and turned off the sound on the television set, the face of the spider still so frightening that she hated to go near the image.

"Ricky? Tad?"

The television had been playing to an empty room. How long might it have been talking to itself?

The sliding door was still closed, its snap lock in place, the broom handle still wedged in the track.

Well, they might have gone into the living room looking for her and, not finding her, gone on to the kitchen for a snack while she came in here. She turned around to go back to the kitchen, but as soon as she stepped into the breakfast room, she could see that the kitchen was empty. There were no crumbs, no splashes of milk either, to suggest they had been there. She ran to the stairs.

"Tad! Ricky! Are you upstairs?"

No answer. What if someone upstairs was holding them hostage, not letting them answer her? She raced upstairs, not thinking of a weapon, into Ricky's room, where some camp clothes lay on the bed, but no children. Tad's room. His closet. Her room, the guest room. The upstairs was exactly as she had left it two hours before.

But the front and back doors were locked. No one had left. No one had come in.

The basement! Could a man have come in through the basement windows?

She ran down the stairs. She thought she'd go through the

kitchen, get a knife, then turn on all the basement lights from the head of the basement stairs. She ran through the end of the living room, through the darkened dining room and pantry, and had just entered the kitchen when she heard a sound behind her.

From the stairs? The living room? She had just come from there.

"Ricky? Tad?"

The sound came again, a metallic click. She thought it came from the dark dining room, but the echoes in this house were so deceptive. . . . There was no one in the kitchen with her, and she could see nothing move in the shadowy pantry. She backed away from the dark.

No, this was ridiculous. If someone had her children, she had to find out *now,* before he hurt them. If he had not hurt them already. And if he had, she would kill him.

She took a step toward the darkened pantry. Then another. She drew nearer to the pantry. Beyond it were the dark dining room and the shadows of chairs. She stepped into the pantry.

And heard a sound behind her, in the kitchen.

She spun around. There was a figure against the light. He raised his hand, and in his hand was a knife.

Ricky! The light reflected off the knife. As he advanced into the pantry, she could see that his eyes were blank.

She backed through the pantry door into the dining room.

"Ricky!" Samantha screamed. "For God's *sake,* Ricky!"

There was no light of understanding in his face. Instead, she saw an abstract distaste. He looked like a person might look who was about to kill a chicken for dinner—faintly repelled, but determined.

"Ricky, please!"

Samantha backed up, as Ricky raised his arm and stepped forward. Behind her, in the dining room, she heard a footfall. She turned and screamed.

It was Tad.

Ricky studied the woman. His mind was narrowed to a single object, to kill the thing that had stolen his mother. He did not think of tomorrow, or the night outside, or even the walls of the room in which he stood. His mind was focused on one thing, the woman in front of him. And yet he was unusually alert. He had the clear, single-minded focus of the deep trance.

He saw the woman put a look of horror on her face. She was very good at it, he thought.

In his mind, he heard a voice. *She will look exactly like your mother. Shape-changers are terribly good at that. They should be called shape-stealers, you see. You understand, don't you, Rick? She has taken your mother's form. And the only way to get your mother back is to kill the imposter. Drive her out. Kill her.*

Ricky moved forward. He gripped the knife hard in his hand.

The woman turned, and both she and Ricky saw Tad standing behind her. Tad pulled a kitchen knife from his pocket.

The woman hesitated; she made a gesture toward Tad and then toward him as if she could not make up her mind. It was amazing how much like his mother's gestures these false ones were.

Quite suddenly, she made a jump to Tad's left and ran around him. She was into the living room, running to the study and the telephone. Tad glanced at Ricky and they walked, slowly, after her.

The woman was leaning over the desk, dialing a number.

Tad walked over and cut the telephone wire.

"Ricky! Please, Ricky! Please, Tad! I don't understand why you're doing this!"

She sounded so much like his mother.

"Tad! Ricky! What's the *matter* with you?" Her voice broke into a scream. "Stop this! I'm your *mother!* Don't look at me that way!"

Tad and Ricky stood side by side, staring implacably at the shape-changer. Tad brought up his knife. The woman ran out of the study, into the playroom. They followed.

After a very long time frozen in his crouching position, Dan noticed that the shrieking pain was gone. His back was numb. He wondered vaguely what that meant. Possibly his brain wouldn't receive any more pain signals. Carefully, he opened his eyes.

The sky was dark. Except for a red glow in the far west, it was black night. Some stars were already shining above him, and in the south the red skyline of the city of Chicago mimicked the sunset.

Ira lay dead in front of him on the ground. The small black dots that covered him must be dead bees. Dan tried to sense whether there were still bees crawling on his own skin. He could not tell. He had forced his mind to ignore his skin for so long that he was now confused.

It was too dark to be certain, but he could not see any bees in the air. He could not feel any creeping on his face.

Maybe they were gone.

Dan moved. Very, very slowly he straightened up. Instantly all the muscles in his back and legs responded with agony.

Gasping, then whimpering under his breath, Dan sank down on the grass. Nothing moved, on him or under him. He was not stung.

He sat, limp with the torture of his muscles and joints and the aftermath of terror, urging himself to move. Telephone Samantha. Warn her. Send the police to her house. Run.

Now he wished he had brought his car. He started to get up. Muscles twitched spasmodically. His knees gave way and he fell on his face, too dulled even to break his fall. He struggled to rise.

Samantha clung to the den door. In the distance the kitchen phone began to ring. She turned back toward it, and a knife slashed at her, slicing the back of her upper arm. She ducked and ran.

I'm imagining this! I can't think! I'm imagining this!

Samantha ran through the playroom, into the breakfast room, and into the kitchen. She started for the kitchen telephone, but there was no time. The children—*My God! the children!*—were right behind her, and they'd cut the wire before she could dial. Their footsteps were behind her, and she ran into the pantry. The phone stopped ringing.

She ran into the dining room.

If she could get to the front door, she might get out. But it was triple-locked, and they were too fast for her. She glanced back and saw them striding together, as if subliminally joined, across the living room toward her.

She ran into the dark study again, where the cut wire trailed on the floor, and then into the playroom. On the soundless television set a mud-colored spider with hairy legs was wrapping a fly in strands of webbing. She could see the bundle move as the fly struggled helplessly to break out of the web.

She could run upstairs. No, she'd be trapped up there. She ran through the kitchen into the pantry and dining room, thinking that if she got far enough ahead she might get a knife in the kitchen when she next passed through.

Get a knife and what? Stab her own children?

As she ran through the living room, she could see the boys come out of the dining room twenty feet behind her. They were closer now. They had all the energy, and all the time, and she was tiring. The combination of disbelief and terror had exhausted her.

She staggered into the study. She couldn't think, couldn't understand how this could happen, and yet she had to think. She ran through the playroom again, and in the breakfast room looked back. They were closer still, maybe fifteen feet.

Oh, God!

Around the house one more time, she ran full out. Breakfast room, kitchen, pantry, dining room, with footsteps jogging easily behind as she struggled to stay on her feet. Across the living room, the feet sounded closer and closer. Into the study she ran, and into the playroom.

She saw the sky outside the glass door, and ran to it, like a bird flying into a window thinking it was sky. But she knew it was glass, hoped it would break and either kill her or fall into pieces and let her out.

She crashed into it, shoulder and cheek hitting glass. It did not break. Half stunned, she sank to her knees for a moment. She saw the broom handle she had wedged in the sliding track and seized it as she stood up.

Ricky was coming at her across the playroom. The knife was in his right hand. His left hand was held edgewise in the tae kwon do stance he had learned, and he faced her broomstick with no fear.

She raised it, faced him, as he strode toward her. Then she felt a draft on her neck and turned.

Tad was behind her! He had gone back around the house, was standing behind her with a knife. Even as she turned, he sliced forward.

Samantha brought the broomstick around like a baseball bat at Tad's head. It caught him above the eyebrow. The knife flew out of his hand and a cut opened over his eyebrow. The broomstick was spattered with blood.

Tad sank to his knees.

Calmly, Ricky advanced on her, his knife at the ready.

"Oh, my God," Samantha said. "Tad! Get up! I didn't mean it!"

Samantha turned to Ricky.

"Ricky! Listen, Ricky! I don't know why this is happening, but if you have to kill me—listen, you'll be *caught.* Please don't—I can't let that—"

He came closer, raising the knife. Tad struggled to his feet.

"Ricky, your fingerprints will be on that knife. Here—oh, my God, no! You're all I have in the world! Let me stab *myself,* then. Give it to me!"

Tad picked up his knife, which had fallen to the floor. Blood ran down his cheek. Ricky came closer.

"No, I see. You won't give me the knife. You think I'll stab you. Wait!"

She turned and ran into the kitchen. She slammed open a cabinet, grabbed out a bottle of aspirin, opened the top, and scattered them all over the counter.

"Look at this! It's enough to kill me. They'll think it's suicide."

Ricky and Tad had followed her, patient, unhurried, and implacable. She crammed two aspirins in her mouth and nearly gagged. She seized a glass and filled it with water, then washed the aspirin down. She took up another and swallowed it. Then another.

She looked up. She had their attention. Their blank, unsympathetic eyes were staring at her.

"When I was in college," she gabbled, "a girl down the hall killed herself. She only took thirteen aspirin—"

Samantha drank another one down. "We were all surprised it took so few."

Samantha took another aspirin. How many was that? Half a dozen at least.

"Put away the knives," she said. "I don't want you to be seen with them." She was feeling sick. There was a sharp pain in her stomach. She took another aspirin. Then she noticed the deep gash on her arm. She had utterly forgotten it. "Wait. Leave that knife on the counter. You can tell them I cut myself with it."

She took another aspirin, watching their eyes.

She took another aspirin.

She picked up four at a time, stuffed them into her mouth, chewed, then washed them down with water.

More than a dozen.

Several were lying loose on the counter. She swept them together with both hands, six or eight of them, and jammed them, two-handed, into her mouth. She grimaced at the bitterness. The water tasted sweet when she drank it, by comparison.

She reached for more aspirin.

Tad's eyes began to fill with tears!

She took another aspirin. The tears ran over and down his cheeks, mixing with the blood. She took another aspirin and looked at Ricky. He had put his knife on the counter, and his mouth was open. He was breathing noisily.

She took another aspirin.

Tad said, "Don't."

Ricky said, "Mom."

Thirty-Six

They opened the door to the pounding noise. It was Dan.

"What's happened?" he yelled, after one glance at their faces.

"I took about a dozen aspirin," Samantha said, "or more." She was weaving, dizzy from terror and relief.

"Get to the bathroom!" Dan picked her up and ran with her. "Do you have ipecac?"

The police Dan had called arrived a minute later. Samantha was still being sick in the bathroom. Dan met them at the door, realizing immediately he had to make a decision.

"You called nine-one-one?" a stocky cop asked him.

Behind the cop was the village ambulance.

Dan had a split second to decide. Tell about the boys or not? Tell about everything—?

"I'm sorry," he said. "I gave you the wrong address."

"I don't get it," the cop said. "You gave us this address and you're here."

"Look. The accident took place at another house. I was coming here to tell these people about it and my mind screwed up. I gave you this address. I'll take you to the scene of the accident. I'll ride with you."

"He tried to kill me with those shears," Dan said.

The body of Ira Schultz, bloated blue-red and littered with dead bees, lay on the grass, ugly in the police lights.

"Then?" said Charles Elfenbein.

"Then the bees got him."

"Why'd he want to kill you?"

"Because I'd found out he was a killer."

"Why didn't you call us?"

"I'd just found out. I didn't really know until I faced him."

"Mmm."

"He's the man Henry Ax suspected."

Dan went back to Samantha's. He wanted to sit up with her to watch her.

"I telephoned as soon as I could move," he said.

"I heard the phone. I couldn't get to it."

He put his hand over hers. "It's over now."

"Will I be able to forget the boys attacking me?"

"Yes, you will."

"Yes," she said. "It wasn't really them."

"They don't remember it at all."

"Did you tell the police about the boys?" she asked.

"No."

"Oh."

"Should I have?"

She hesitated. "No. I'm glad."

"I told them he'd killed those people himself."

"Will they find the boys' names in his house?"

"I don't know. All we can do is hope not."

It took three days of searching through the house and a page-by-page search of all Schultz's papers, but finally Elfenbein found Schultz's records, hidden among his dental-supply receipts, written on the same invoice sheets as all his other accounts. They were labeled EXTRACTION EQUIPMENT.

The records contained only the names of the victims in code, the dates, and the amounts Schultz had collected, with two zeros dropped off. There were no notations about the boys.

They kept searching another week, hoping to find records telling where the money he had collected had gone. But there was no clue.

Epilogue

Tad and Ricky never remembered the evening. A psychiatrist took on the job of explaining in a general way to them and to Tony what had happened, but he never succeeded in breaking through the amnesia Schultz had imposed. He contented himself with convincing them that they had not been responsible, just in case those memories ever came back. Among the boys themselves, the fact that there were three of them made them all feel less isolated.

Garvey was a different case. He did not work well with the therapist. At times he pretended to remember more than he really did, and he appeared to take some pleasure in the telling of it.

The Village Board wanted to condemn the beehive as a hazard. Dan argued that the bees had saved his life. If they had not been so reliable, so dependable, so *predictable*, he would surely have died, and Schultz would still be in business. In a vote of five to four, the Board decided to let Camelli keep it. Swan came to town and helped move the hive to Camelli's own backyard.

They covered the hive with light-proof and bee-proof black plastic during the night while the bees were inside and picked it up first thing in the morning to move to its new site.

When Dan saw the little square of cement blocks Ira Schultz had laid down as a foundation for the bees, he had an idea. He pulled them up and there, underneath, was a flat plastic package.

Inside the plastic was an envelope. Inside the envelope were four file cards, with a nine-digit number on each. Dan called Elfenbein. Elfenbein said, "Piece of cake. We'll get into the banking system and they'll find those accounts for us. If any of the deposits were by check, we can find out who paid Schultz to kill."

Ira Schultz's mother-in-law told Ira's wife that she had always known he wasn't right for her. Ira's wife and their boys moved to Albuquerque, explaining to her friends they were moving so that the boys could play tennis all year.

Dan tried to find out what boy Schultz had used before Garvey, but he never succeeded. Garvey himself seemed to be doing well enough, but he was destined, in his junior year in high school, to run his mother's car into a bridge abutment at Green Bay Road while showing some boys in another car that he was not chicken. He would die several hours later of a neck injury.

Peter Winterthur recovered faster than Dan had hoped. One morning over a bowl of oatmeal, he decided to talk back to his father. His father yelled, but Peter yelled back. From then on, Peter was a changed young man. Peter's therapist could not explain why it had happened when it did, except to say, "You never know with folks," which was not a scientific description.

When Meyers Campbell did not come home at the end of July from his fishing trip, the couple who lived with him called the owner of the motel where he had left his car, who dispatched the guide to hike to the cabin and take a look. The guide brought back Campbell's body on a litter made of tree branches. Campbell had died of a stroke. Nobody inspected his medication.

At the end of August the scouts had a barbecue. Swan said the hive could get through the winter with the honey it had made, less nine pounds. Not bad for the first year.

The troop strained the honey from the combs. Kiri Obisawa made the wax into candles.

Samantha, Naomi Grey, and Mrs. Pyakoski made barbecued beef, the barbecue sauce sweetened with honey. The boys squeezed lemons for lemonade, which they sweetened with honey. Naomi Grey made honey-sweetened corn muffins and a salad with vinaigrette dressing, which was sweetened with honey. Mrs. Pyakoski made seven dozen brownies with honey. Samantha made pecan pies, sweetened with honey.

Frederick Lawton offered Samantha the house.

She didn't want it. She and the boys moved into a house in the less expensive southern end of Rivercrest. It was a plain, square house with a room on each corner. Nothing fancy. It pleased her a great deal. It just happened to be only half a block from Dan Camelli.

Steak Tartare

Steak Tartare

If you drive north from Chicago along Lake Michigan, you will pass through several increasingly wealthy suburbs. The first and oldest is Evanston. Then Wilmette, Kenilworth, and Winnetka. Winnetka is one of the richest municipalities in the United States. It may be that the average income in Kenilworth, nestled next to it, is higher than Winnetka, but Kenilworth is so small that it hardly counts. Basil Stone had therefore been thrilled to be hired as resident director of the North Shore Playhouse, located in Winnetka. It wasn't Broadway, of course, but it was a very, very prestigious rep house. And you rubbed shoulders with nothing but the best people. Like tonight.

He spun his little red Lexus around the curves of Sheridan Road, which ran right along Lake Michigan and therefore was the Place des Vosges of Illinois, *rue de la crème de la crème*, the street that accessed the highest-priced real estate in an already high-priced area. And the Falklands' mansion was on the lake side of Sheridan, the east, which meant beach frontage, of course, and was far tonier than living across the road.

These things mattered to Basil.

Pamela had given him the street number and told him to watch for two brick columns supporting a wrought-iron arch and elaborate iron gates. And there they were. He swung in, spoke his name into the post speaker, and the gates majestically opened.

God, the place was a castle. The drive wound in a lazy S up to a wide-pillared veranda. Pamela stood on the lip of the veranda like a Midwestern Scarlett O'Hara, framed among acres of flesh pink azaleas that swept away on both sides of the fieldstone steps.

"Welcome, Basil," she said, giving him a quick kiss on the cheek. He pulled back fast, not wanting her husband to see. Although everybody hugged and kissed when they met, didn't they? It didn't necessarily mean anything. She drew him in the front door.

Basil stopped just inside, trying not to goggle at the immense foyer. A tessellated marble floor flowed into a great entry hall, stretching far back to a double staircase, which curved out, up, and in, the two halves joining at the second floor. The ceiling was thirty feet overhead. The chandelier that dimly lit the hall hung from a heavy chain and was as big as a Chevy Suburban turned on its end.

Basil looked around, found that they were alone, and whispered, "Pamela, I *don't* think this was such a good idea."

"Oh, please!" she said. "Don't be so timid."

Timid! He didn't want her to think he was timid. He was bold, romantic. Still . . . "But what if he guesses?"

"He won't." She patted his cheek, leaving her hand lingering on the side of his face. Just then, Basil heard footsteps coming from somewhere beyond the great hall, and he backed sharply away from her.

Pamela laughed. She touched him with a light gaze, then spun to face the man who had just entered. "Darling," she said, "this is Basil. Basil, my husband, Charles Falkland."

Gesturing with his drink, Charles Falkland said, "I know she'll make a wonderful Kate."

"I'm very grateful that she wanted to do the show. With

her background in New York. Of course, Pamela is a brilliant actor. And as Kate, she has just the right combination of bite and vulnerability."

"Absolutely," Falkland said, placing his hand on the back of Pamela's neck possessively. "She is extremely accomplished."

Basil studied the room, taking time to answer. Must be cautious here. "Of course, you know we're an Equity house, so all the actors are professional. They'll support her beautifully."

"But why *The Taming of the Shrew*?"

"You'd rather we did a drama? Don't you feel that it's important for the general public to realize that Shakespeare can be light? Humorous? People are so deadly serious."

"Well . . ." Falkland said, drawing the word out, "some issues in life *are* serious, of course. Aren't they?"

"Of course, but—"

"But enough of this. Drink up and let me just mix us all a second drink."

Falkland busied himself with the bottled water, lime, and lemon wedges that the butler, Sloan, had brought in, and decanters of some splendid bourbon and Scotch, which the Falklands were too well bred to keep in labeled bottles, but which to Basil's taste in his first drink seemed like Knob Creek or possibly the top-of-the-line Maker's Mark. Not the kind you buy in stores, even specialty shops. You had to order it from the company.

"Here, darling," Falkland said, turning to Pamela. "Basil's and yours."

Pamela carried Basil's drink—in a fresh glass, he noted—to him, reaching out to put it in his hand. Her fingertips grazed his as he reached for the glass, and her thumb stroked the back of his hand. Basil's breath caught. How beautiful she was. He could scarcely believe his luck. Their affair had started the first day of rehearsals. Seeing her husband, and this mansion, knowing that she had been an actress of some considerable reputation, he could imagine that she might be bored in this big house, with a husband who looked fifteen years older.

Pamela left her hand next to his just half a second too long. Basil resisted pulling back. Surely that would only make it more obvious. But he thought Falkland had seen. Or maybe not. He'd been pouring his own drink, rather a stiff one. But he'd been casually looking toward the sofa, too, over the lip of the glass. Did he notice? After all, what would he see? A woman hands a man a drink. Just ordinary hospitality. Just what was expected.

Abruptly, Falkland said, "Pamela?"

"Yes, dear?"

"I just realized I've not chosen a dessert wine. I have a lovely Medoc for dinner. We're having a crown roast of lamb, and the dinner wine should be just right. But we need something to go with the zabayon and raspberries, don't we?"

"Yes, I imagine so, dear."

Basil noted that Sloan was waiting near the door that led from this great room to some unspecified back region. Briefly, he wondered why Sloan hadn't poured and passed the drinks.

"Well, go to the wine cellar with Sloan and find something special, would you?"

"Of course, darling." An expression of mild puzzlement passed over Pamela's face, not rising quite to the level of a wrinkle along her lovely brow.

"We need something beyond the ordinary for Basil, don't you think? Something that sings. A finale! A last act! After all, he is an artiste."

"Uh, yes, darling. It's just that you usually make the decisions about wine."

"Yes, but Basil is *your* friend."

"Of course."

"Help Mrs. Falkland, please, Sloan," Falkland said.

Pamela went out the door, and Sloan, after nodding to Falkland, followed her.

It was just a bit awkward with Pamela gone, Basil found. He rose, strolled about, stopping at the French windows facing the back, admiring the lake view, the private dock, and the yacht anchored there, sleek, long, and bright white even in the dying daylight. He tried a few questions about Falkland's line of work, but when the man answered at length, he realized that he didn't know what e-arbitrage was and couldn't intelligently carry on that line of conversation. Pamela was taking entirely too long with the dessert wine. She should have stayed here to protect him. After all, this damned dinner had been her idea. He wondered whether maybe she was a risk taker and liked to skate close to discovery. He'd had hints of that when he saw her drive out of the Playhouse parking lot at highway speed. Perhaps tonight she was teasing her husband. Well, Basil would have to be doubly careful, if so.

Then Falkland quoted, " 'And bonny Kate, and sometimes Kate the curst; but, Kate, the prettiest Kate in Christendom; Kate of Kate-Hall, my super-dainty Kate.' "

"You know the play."

"Oh, yes. I was quite a theater scholar once upon a time. In fact, I met Pamela through the theater."

"Oh?"

"I was a backer for one of her shows. She, of course, was the star."

"But she doesn't act outside of rep anymore."

"Oh, I need her all to myself. 'Thy husband is thy Lord, thy life, thy keeper, thy head, thy sovereign; one that cares for thee—' "

"Shakespeare has Kate present some good arguments against that point of view."

"Ah, but, 'Such duty as the subject owes the prince, even such a woman oweth to her husband.' "

Basil did not respond. How had he gotten drawn into this discussion anyhow? And where the hell was Pamela?

Sloan appeared in the arch between the great hall and the dining room. Basil was startled for a second to see him, and he realized how very soundproof the back regions were. One heard no sounds of cooking, or plates rattling, or glasses clinking.

"Dinner is ready, sir, whenever you are."

Basil had not studied Sloan before, since Basil had been fully occupied with other problems. But now he realized that the man was extremely sleek. His suit was as well made as Falkland's, or nearly so. His cheeks were pinkly smooth-shaven. His hair, thin on top and combed down flat with no attempt to cover the bald center, was rich brown and shiny. Therefore it was a bit of a surprise that, apparently unknown to Sloan, a small tuft, no bigger than the wing of a wren, was disarranged in back. Perhaps he had brushed against something while cooking, if indeed he was the person in the ménage who cooked.

Falkland murmured, " 'What say you to a piece of beef and mustard?' "

Basil winced. He was getting bloody damned tired of Shakespeare. "We should wait for Pamela, shouldn't we?"

"We'll just start on the appetizer, I think," Falkland said.

Basil sat across from Falkland, himself to the right and Falkland to the left of the head of the long table, a wide pond of shiny walnut between them. Candles were the only lights. The head of the table apparently had been left for Pamela, which made some sense, since it put her between them and she was the only woman present. Or absent, as was the case currently. Basil regarded the silver at his place setting with dismay. Why five forks? There were also three spoons, but he was sure he could figure those out. One was likely for coffee. Or dessert? There was a rounded soup spoon. A fellow director had once told him on a shoot, where they were doing a two-shot of the happy couple at dinner, that a small round soup spoon was for thick soup and a large oval soup spoon was for clear soup. But five forks, only one perhaps identifiable as a salad fork? Now that he thought about it, the setup was probably designed to intimidate him. Well, he wasn't going to let that happen.

He said, "Where is Pamela? We'll be done with the first course before she arrives if we're not careful."

"She might be—quite a while. Pamela has always had a difficult time making up her mind."

Basil had no idea what to say to that. He sat unhappily in his chair, wondering why Falkland kept the dining room so dark. It would make a wonderful set for—oh, hell. The kind of atmosphere Falkland had prepared would only be good for a show with a supernatural element. Or a murder. *Gaslight, Macbeth, Deathtrap.*

But, of course, it was just the natural dining behavior of the very rich. For the thousandth upon thousandth time Basil reflected that he should have been born rich. Candles at dinner were probably a nightly ritual at the Falklands'. He'd used them in his production of *An Inspector Calls.*

And of course *Macbeth.* Thank God he hadn't uttered the name of the Scottish play aloud. Very bad luck.

With the darkness crowding his shoulders, and the flicker

of the candle flames causing the shadows of his five forks to undulate as if slinking slowly toward his plate, Basil resolved to look upon the whole evening as a set of suggestions for his next noir production. Use it, don't fight it, he told himself.

Sloan entered. He carried two plates of something that surely must not be what it looked like. Surely it was just the low candlelight that made the lumps appear reddish and bloody and undercooked.

As the plate touched down in front of Basil with scarcely a sound, he saw it was indeed raw meat.

"Steak tartare," Falkland said. "A small portion makes a perfect appetizer. As a main dish it becomes a bit much, don't you think?"

"Uh, is he serving just us two? What about Pamela?"

"Oh, Pamela won't be long. As I was about to say, as an appetizer I have Sloan serve it without the raw egg. In these troubled times, people are uneasy about eating raw egg. Although if you can buy fresh new eggs from green-run chickens, there is really no danger. And of course with these new methods of preventing salmonella in chickens, something about the properly inoculated feed, you can be quite confident. Nevertheless, for the sake of my guests' equanimity, I forgo the egg and serve the steak tartare as an appetizer.

"Traditionally, of course, it is chopped fillet steak or sirloin, twice run through the grinder. Then mixed with chopped onions and garlic and capers and raw egg. Salt and pepper. And the patty is shaped with a depression in the center. Into that depression is dropped a perfect golden yolk. It is a beautiful presentation, really, the yolk a deep cadmium yellow, and the meat around it rich red. Well, like this, actually. So fresh it glistens. Do you see?"

"Uhhh, yes."

"Of course," Charles said, steepling his fingers as the manservant stepped back, "it can only be the very, very freshest meat."

"Uh, yes indeed."

"And never, never ground beef from the supermarket." He uttered the word "supermarket" the way another person might say "latrine." The man, Basil thought, should have been an actor himself. He certainly got all the juice out of a word.

"You're not eating. Now, these are the traditional accompaniments around it—capers, chopped onion, and minced parsley."

"Mmm-mm."

"Not used to steak tartare, Basil?"

"No."

"Some chefs mix in cognac as well, and garnish it with caviar. The Swiss even add anchovies. But it seems to me if you're going for the taste of fresh, raw meat, tarting it up with extraneous flavors is a waste. Don't you think so?"

"Uhhhh."

"Still, to revert to our earlier topic, I wonder why it had to be *The Taming of the Shrew*. There are more interesting Shakespeare pieces you could do."

"Uhhh. The trustees, actually."

"The trustees wanted it? Well, then I suppose you're stuck with it. They do hold the purse strings. But I wonder, as time goes on, if you could convince them to do Shakespeare's unappreciated masterpiece. I'm speaking of *Titus Andronicus*, of course."

"Mmm."

"It's reassuring to me, as a Shakespeare enthusiast, that the Julie Taymor film of it is coming out, at least. But there isn't any substitute for the immediacy of the stage."

"I agree, of course," Basil half whispered. "Real human beings near enough to touch. And *Titus Andronicus* is so Grand Guignol. It was Shakespeare's breakout play, you know. Made his name. Although at the time people claimed to be upset at all the violence."

"Media violence—"

"Fascinating to think that without it, without all that excess, we might never have known the name Shakespeare."

Basil picked up a heavy Francis the First fork. He touched the chopped meat. It was lumpy and bright red, with tiny flecks of gristle or fat. He wondered whether he could tell anything if he touched it with his finger. If it was warm—? Had it been in the refrigerator, or was it body temperature?

But he couldn't bear to touch it.

Falkland went on. "And what a story. The son of Ta-mora, Queen of the Goths, has been killed by Titus. For revenge, she has her other two sons rape Titus's daughter and cut out her tongue."

"I know," said Basil in a strangled voice.

"Then Titus, in an antic burst of exquisite revenge, invites Tamora to dinner and unknown to her, serves her a pasty— we'd call it a pot pie. I imagine—made from her two sons' heads."

"I'm familiar with *Titus Andronicus*, dammit!"

"Oh, of course you are, dear boy. You're a director. Terribly sorry."

"Uhhh."

"My word, Basil, you aren't eating."

"Auuhhh—"

"You haven't touched your steak tartare."

It could *not* be what he thought. It could not. How long had they been down in that cellar? And how would Falkland dispose of the—of the rest? But then he recalled the dock, the boathouse. This mansion backed directly onto Lake Michigan. Well, of course it did. It was on the high-rent side of Sheridan. But what about Sloan? Could Falkland possibly have Sloan so much in his pocket that he would do anything Falkland asked?

Inadvertently, Basil glanced up at Sloan, standing silent and lugubrious just left of the dining-room door.

Falkland caught his glance. "Sloan is such a gem," he said. "He's been with me for twenty-three years now."

"Oh, yes?"

"Since I agreed to accept him from the parole board. You see, they would only let him go if he had permanent, residential employment."

"Oh, yes. I see."

"In a home with no children."

Basil stared at his plate. If he so much as sipped a smidgen of water, he would be sick. Staring at his plate was worse. He averted his eyes. But it was too late. Perspiration started up on his forehead and he could feel sweat running into his hair. His face was hot and his abdomen was deeply cold.

Basil threw his napkin down next to the army of forks. He half rose. "I don't think I'm feeling very well—"

"Oh, please. We were so looking forward to this evening."

"I think I'd better go." He gagged out the words and could hardly understand what he himself had said. It sounded like "guh-guh-go."

The swinging door from the pantry opened. Pamela stood in the spill of kitchen light, holding a dusty glass bottle.

"It's a terrible cliché, I know," she said smiling apologetically, "but I picked out everything else and finally went back to the Chateau d'Yquem."

"Uh-uh-uh," Basil said, trying to stand upright, but bent by the pains knifing through his stomach.

401

"Basil! Are you ill?" she said.

Basil ran at a half crouch out of the dining room, through the long hall and the marble foyer, and pushed out the front door into the glorious cool night air.

"Oh, dear," Pamela said, still smiling.

Falkland said, "Fun, darling?"

"Fun. The best we've ever done."

STEAK TARTARE

Steak tartare is not everybody's cup of tea. However, like sushi, if perfect ingredients are chosen, I am told that it is safe. The classic form is . . .

FOR THE PURIST:

1 pound best sirloin or fillet trimmed of all fat and gristle.

Put it twice through a grinder, just before serving. Ground meat is an excellent medium for bacterial growth, so serve it at once. Do not buy ground beef from the store.

Mix in:

1 clove of garlic, minced

½ cup of chopped onion

1-2 teaspoons salt, depending on taste

1 teaspoon black pepper

1 egg yolk (you will need 5 eggs total for a main dish)

1 tablespoon capers

Shape into patties—four if you are using this for a main course, eight or more as an appetizer.

Generally, for a main course, make four flattish patties with a depression in the middle, and into each drop 1 egg yolk. Serve with parsley and more chopped onion and capers.

As an appetizer, shape into balls. You may roll the balls in minced parsley or finely chopped green onions. We are also told now not to eat raw eggs. It is possible to omit the egg yolk, but if you can get green-run chickens raised outdoors, many people believe them to be safe.

AND FOR THE FAINT OF HEART:

If all this is too much trouble or too scary, here's another recipe.

For deviled meatballs, mix the chopped beef as above. Form into tiny balls and sauté in a small amount of olive oil very lightly so as not to break up. Then add about ¾ cup of your favorite barbecue sauce. You can make it extra dynamite spicy if you like, since people will only have a small mouthful of each. Serve as an appetizer.

—BD

About the Author

Barbara D'Amato is the author of over twenty novels, including *Good Cop, Bad Cop*, which won the Carl Sandburg Award for Fiction. D'Amato has also won the Mary Higgins Clark Award, the Agatha twice, the Anthony twice, and the Macavity. A former president of Mystery Writers of America and Sisters in Crime, she has in the past worked as a surgical orderly, stage manager, researcher for attorneys in criminal cases, a carpenter for stage magic illusions, an assistant tiger handler, and occasionally has taught writing to Chicago police officers. Her research on the John Branion murder case formed the basis for an *Unsolved Mysteries* episode and she appeared on the program. Her musical comedies, written with husband Anthony D'Amato, have played in Toronto, Chicago, and London. Her most recent novel is *White Male Infant*.